Keith Baker is a forme
Affairs, BBC Northern
Down. He is the author of three previous acclaimed thrillers. *Inheritance, Reckoning* and *Engram.*

Praise for Keith Baker:

'Redolent of Patricia Highsmith, this is a taut, well-orchestrated piece' *The Times*

'Vivid and frightening . . . an intelligent thriller' *The Times Literary Supplement*

'Breathtaking . . . if you read no other thriller this year, buy this one' *Irish Times*

'So good it's hard to believe it's a first novel' Ted Allbeury

'A boisterous fast-paced adventure' *Financial Times*

'Move aside Jack Higgins, here comes Keith Baker' *Tribune Magazine*

Also by Keith Baker

Inheritance
Reckoning
Engram

Lunenburg

Keith Baker

HEADLINE
FEATURE

Thanks to the Society of Authors as the literary representatives of the Estate of John Masefield for permission to quote from 'Ships'.

First published in 2000
by HEADLINE BOOK PUBLISHING

First published in paperback in 2001
by HEADLINE BOOK PUBLISHING

10 9 8 7 6 5 4 3 2 1

ISBN 0 7472 6184 9

Typeset by CBS, Martlesham Heath, Ipswich, Suffolk

Printed and bound in Great Britain by
Mackays of Chatham plc, Chatham, Kent

HEADLINE BOOK PUBLISHING
A division of Hodder Headline
338 Euston Road
London NW1 3BH

www.headline.co.uk
www.hodderheadline.com

Lunenburg

Prologue

Heckman's Island, Nova Scotia, 1970.

The boat was painted black, darker than the night, which helped the boy conceal himself.

It was not much of a vessel, a squat flat-bottomed dinghy about six feet in length, but anything bigger would have been too difficult for him to handle. He was twelve years old and puny compared to most of his contemporaries, especially those who were becoming strong in the arm that could pitch or hit a baseball. His size made him feel left out. He loved sports but he knew he was condemned forever to be a watcher on the sidelines, not a player.

In conversation, his mother, not the warmest of souls, tried to avoid the subject of children but when it came up and she found herself forced to talk about her son, she would choose to describe him as slightly built. At school in Halifax they were less sensitive. They called him The Stick. In summer, when agile young limbs became brown in the sun, they made fun of his thin arms and legs, which was why, even now, in July, he kept himself covered up and wore clothing that was more in keeping with cooler days.

Tonight it was the usual blue jeans and docksiders, plus a grey cotton shirt with long sleeves. The clothing helped him blend with the shadows but it also covered his body and restricted the target area for the mosquitoes he could hear whining in the heavy, humid air. On his head there was a Toronto Blue Jays baseball cap, while on a strap round his neck hung a pair of binoculars which his father had bought for him last year. The night the men walked on the moon, he had gone outside in a mood of ridiculous optimism and peered up through the big Zeiss lenses until his neck hurt. He had seen nothing, of course, but he had seen a lot more since then. He smiled to himself at the thought.

Tonight the moon was huge and silver in the sky and distant stars glittered. Heavenly bodies. That phrase had a different meaning for him now.

A dog barked somewhere in the emptiness ahead and another answered it, almost like an echo. He drifted past a house built in a gap in the trees. Darkness cloaked it but he could see a picnic table and benches standing beside a barbecue that had gone cold. A rowboat, bigger than his, was tethered to a post at the end of the dock.

Heckman's Island lay in one of the myriad nooks and crannies along the tattered shoreline just beyond the town of Lunenburg. It was joined to the mainland by a small bridge and if it wasn't for the name you wouldn't know it was an island at all. But the people who had their homes here liked the sound of it, the suggestion of remoteness. Many of them, like his parents, kept their houses as vacation residences, summer places. Others lived here in virtual seclusion all year round. From the thin grey ribbon of a road, worn and rutted, little was visible. Mailboxes at the end of tracks leading through the trees were the only signs of where the properties lay. But here, on the stream that curled and twisted and eventually made it to the ocean, you could see everything.

He dipped the short oars into the water as gently as he could so that they made no sound. He had been on this brief, clandestine journey before and he knew to let the current do most of the work. He turned to see where he had got to. There was a faint glimmer ahead. He let the boat drift again and as he rounded a slight bend, he saw light spilling out from the windows of a house.

This was where he was going. To the place where the woman lived.

Often there was music. She liked to play her hi-fi loud. There was Dylan, whom he did not care for, and the Beatles, whom he did. Sometimes there were records by that folk singer, Joni Mitchell, and occasionally there was weird, kind of Indian stuff.

It was the music that had first drawn him here, when he'd been out in the boat one day and had heard it in the breeze. There was none tonight that he could hear but that didn't matter. That wasn't what brought him now, not any more.

Not now that he had seen her naked.

She never pulled the curtains. There was no need. Outside her window there was only the water and the trees. Or so she thought.

He felt his body stirring. Anticipation rippled over him, then guilt. For a second he looked back in the direction from which he had come but he reassured himself that his mother and father were dead to the world and wouldn't know that he wasn't asleep in his room.

They had barbecued, the three of them. His parents had had a few drinks with their steaks and when they thought it was getting late for him they had sent him to bed. Afterwards they had come up the stairs, stumbling a little, laughing. He had heard them giggling in their room, the bed creaking. Much later he had listened outside their door to his father's deep snores. It was then that he had dressed, opened his bedroom window, to slide softly down onto the porch roof, then to the deck.

He counted. He had made this trip six times. Always, he

feared what would happen if he was caught but he knew that in part it was the risk that excited him. That and the prospect of what he might see.

Before this, the only naked women he had seen were in magazine pictures: smiling blondes, carefully posed, like in the *Playboy* one of the boys at school had sneaked out of his father's drawer. But this was different. This was real. In his mind he tried to conjure her up. The white skin. The breasts with the dark nipples. The triangle of hair down below.

But her nakedness was just a start. He had seen stuff that the guys would never believe, that he would never be able to tell them about. Nor did he want to. This was his secret.

Because he had seen her with men. He had seen the men hard and erect. He had seen the things the woman liked to do. Just thinking about it was a delicious agony. He felt the increased beat of his heart and the pressure in his groin that he would have to relieve soon.

There were two men and they came to her at different times. Sometimes he wondered if each knew about the other but instinct told him they didn't. One of them wasn't a man at all, really, more a boy, although he was tall and well built. He was maybe eighteen, nineteen, younger than the woman, a whole lot younger than the other man. He wasn't good at guessing ages but he figured the second guy was old, about thirty, something like that.

He wondered which one of them was here tonight. Maybe she was on her own. He had no way of knowing. All he could do was take these opportunities whenever he could and then wait and watch.

Using one oar, he manoeuvred the boat closer to the far side where he would be unseen in shadows and darkness. A gnarled tree root, a familiar landmark, protruded from the wall of the river bank. He grabbed it and pulled himself and the dinghy in tight, then he took the bow rope and tied it to the root, tugging it to check that it was holding firm before he stepped out.

Suddenly he heard her laugh. Her voice soared from the window and startled him, making him think for a second that the laughter was directed at him, but that was impossible. He looked around. He was alone, undiscovered. No one could see him.

She laughed again. The sound was loud and mocking, as if she found something ridiculous, and he felt sure now that there must be someone with her.

There was a better position than this and he headed towards it. He walked swiftly but gently, bent over, staying among the trees, the binoculars swinging and bumping against his chest. Underfoot, the ground was soft with moss and lichens but there were loose rocks that could trip you up and dried twigs that would snap with a sound like a firecracker if you stepped hard on them.

There was a tree he had climbed before, one that afforded a safe, unseen vantage point. He found it and began to pull himself upwards. This side of the stream was slightly more elevated and gave him a downward angle on the house, so he did not have to go too high. He settled on a familiar branch, nestling in with his legs around the trunk, and then raised the binoculars.

Without them he would have had a clear enough view but with them it was even better. He scanned the scene. At the side of the house, abandoned more than parked, was the '67 station wagon in which he had often seen her driving around Lunenburg. Behind it was another car he recognised, a Chevy sedan he had seen here before. That meant it was the older guy tonight.

As usual, the place was all lit up. An old-fashioned kerosene lamp hung over the back door and cast a warm glow across the wooden deck. Inside, the kitchen lights were on and he could see right through the open inside door to the hall and the stairs. But it was the big bedroom directly above that interested him most.

The laughter had stopped. Instead, there were raised voices, hers and the man's. He brought the lenses into focus.

She was standing with her back to the window, wearing a long white dress. Her hair was dark brown, shoulder-length, all full and fluffed out as if it had recently been washed. The man was facing her. He was in shirt and trousers, his tie loosened. There was a glass in his hand and he looked angry. The boy had not seen him like this before.

Only part of the conversation drifted his way. The windows were closed to keep the bugs at bay but a top vent was open. The words came in snatches.

'. . . from her, do you hear me?' the man said.

The woman moved deeper into the room and said something in reply.

'. . . fooling yourself,' the boy heard. '. . . like that, do you think?'

Whatever she'd said, it caused the man's expression to darken. He put the glass down and walked right up to her, then slapped her hard across the face. The boy winced with the shock of the blow, as if it were his own cheek that had been struck, but to his surprise the woman just tossed her head and laughed.

And then she slapped him back.

For a second after that they did nothing. They seemed rooted to the spot until the man grabbed her by the hair and pulled her to him. She squealed with the pain, then his face was close to hers and suddenly he kissed her.

It was not a tender kiss, the boy could tell. It was fierce, almost violent.

She pulled away and stepped back, then she grasped the thin fabric of her dress and drew it over her head.

She was wearing nothing underneath. She stood there naked, save for several thin strings of Indian beads round her slender neck. The boy stared, his heart pounding and his mouth dry. Through the binoculars his gaze roamed over her. Those breasts. He wanted to know what it was like to feel them. Were they soft to the touch?

The man stepped into his vision, pulling off his shirt. He reached for the woman again and then they were together, clutching at each other, their hands everywhere. The boy grabbed at the ache in his own body. It was becoming unbearable.

As he did, the direction of the binoculars slipped and suddenly he saw that there was a movement somewhere else.

It was at the side of the house, near where the cars sat. His eyes searched the darkness for a few moments but everything seemed still once more. There was nothing. Yet he had been almost certain.

And then a shadow shifted. There was something all right, moving around the outside of the building. An animal maybe. Possibly a deer.

There were noises from the house. He lifted the binoculars again and stared at the bedroom. They were both naked now. The woman was bent over the bed and the man was behind her, pounding hard. He could hear her crying out with each thrust.

As he adjusted the focus his gaze fell and he saw the shadow outside the house move again, except now he could see that it was not an animal.

A figure stepped up on to the deck, a man, dressed only in a singlet and shorts, and in the light from the lamp the boy could see clearly who it was.

He held his breath. The figure stood still, staring into the darkness, and for a scary moment the boy thought he was looking directly at him, but then he turned, opened the porch door slowly and stepped into the kitchen.

The boy's palms were moist. He wiped each hand on his shirt in turn, keeping the binoculars trained as steadily as he could, following the progress of the newcomer.

In the bedroom the sounds of passion were becoming louder. The intruder raised his eyes towards the kitchen ceiling, then he began to move around, as if looking for something. It seemed as if he were opening drawers.

He stopped. He stood and looked down and then he left the kitchen and moved along the hall towards the stairs.

As he did, the boy could see that now he was carrying something in his hand.

For an instant he thought he should cry out. But he did not. Instead he told himself he wasn't here, that he was invisible. He felt a coldness in his gut that made him weak and he hugged the tree tighter, trembling and afraid that he might fall.

They were almost finished. The woman was on her back on the bed, the man on top, raised off her, his thrusts faster, his groans louder as she urged him on. And then the boy saw the bedroom door open.

He watched, unable to turn his eyes away, as the horror began. In the bushes below him startled night creatures heard the awful sound of it and scurried away to safety.

It did not take long but in that short time there was rage, there was savagery. And there was blood, so much blood.

He heard the woman scream, over and over again, until it was done.

He couldn't breathe. His chest and his brain felt as if they were bursting.

In the moments that followed there was a silence that clung to the night like a shroud.

Until the porch door slammed.

The intruder stood under the lamplight outside the house

and the boy saw that he was naked, carrying his flimsy clothing bundled in one hand. His broad chest rose and fell with the heaviness of his breathing and blood glistened as if paint had been splashed over him.

He looked around him at the floor of the deck for a moment, then he stepped down on to the grass and walked towards the bank. He paused only briefly before he slipped into the water and began to swim downstream.

Within seconds, the boy could no longer see any trace of him. All that was left was an eerie stillness and the lapping of the water.

And then the woman's screams started again.

Startled, the boy looked towards the house, staring once more at the nightmare scene, realising that what he had heard was the sound echoing in his head.

It was not the last time he would hear it. On nights like this it would come to him again, over and over, for the rest of his life.

1

Bedford, Nova Scotia, 2000.

The single slice of wholewheat toast popped up like a jack-in-the-box.

The weatherman was plump and cheery, buttoned into a double-breasted brown suit, an unwise choice because it made him look even wider than he was. He stood in front of a computer-generated map showing the maritime provinces of eastern Canada.

'And so across Cape Breton, Prince Edward Island and into New Brunswick, there's a twenty per cent chance of precipitation as the day wears on. Looks like Nova Scotia's going to escape the snow, though, at least until tomorrow.'

Gradually the map changed and became a shot of a city skyline with tall buildings that congregated along a harbour front and threw their reflections out on to the water.

'Bright blue skies over Halifax, as you can see, plenty of sun – but it's a cold January morning, not due to rise above minus five today, dropping down to minus eight tonight. On top of that there's a brisk wind coming in from the Atlantic and that chill will knock the temperatures down another notch or two.'

He gave a mock shiver and hugged himself.

Annie Welles left the TV and went into the kitchen, empty

coffee mug in hand, before he told her to wrap up well and have a nice day.

She took the toast out and dropped it onto a plate, then set it on the breakfast bar beside her nine millimetre Sig Sauer, snug in its pale leather holster. She got low fat butter substitute from the fridge and was pouring more coffee when the phone rang.

'Annie – it's Terry.'

She was tense immediately. She knew her ex-husband's voice; he didn't have to say. But the faces of her twin ten-year-old sons flashed into her mind. He never called unless it was about the boys.

'What is it? What's wrong?'

'Nothing – nothing's wrong. I wanted to talk to you before you headed out to work.'

She waited.

'The boys and me – I'm thinking of taking them on a ski trip.'

She felt relieved. Then she said, 'When?'

'In a few weeks.'

'Hold on a minute. That'll mean taking them out of school.'

'I know. But this isn't such an important term.'

'Terry, they're all important. I shouldn't have to tell you that.'

'Sure, okay, but it's just this once. You know how much they enjoy it and I've got a good deal on the cost of the trip.'

Terry would always look for a good deal. He ran his own civil engineering firm which had several lucrative new contracts with the city of Halifax and the Waterfront Development Corporation. He had a fine house on the expensive piece of shoreline that overlooked the stretch of water known as the North West Arm. He had a new wife and he had custody of the boys. He had got a good deal there, too.

She and Terry had first taken them skiing a year or so ago, just before it all went bad. They had been a little too young in her opinion but he had insisted. She remembered them slipping and sliding on the nursery slopes.

'Where are you thinking, Vermont?'

'Italy. The Alps.'

'The Alps? Jesus, Terry. How long for?'

'Not long. Maybe ten days.'

'Ten days?' She paused, thinking she sounded like an idiot, repeating everything. 'That's . . . I don't know. I don't know that this is such a good idea.'

In the aftermath of the divorce, it was one of the things they had agreed. Decisions about the boys would be taken jointly.

'They're very keen,' Terry said. 'I don't want to disappoint them.'

'You've talked with them about it? Before discussing it with me?'

'I had to see if they were interested.'

'Dammit, Terry, you knew what the answer would be. They're going to jump at the idea of skipping school, never mind a ski trip.'

'Look, here's Peter. He wants to talk to you.'

The boy was older than his brother James by five minutes and considered himself to be the senior twin.

She tried to protest. 'Terry, I—' It was too late.

'Hi, Mom. Can we go? Please, *please*?' The child squeezed the words out, imploring.

Terry had manoeuvred her into a corner. She knew she should resist this, that in their long-term best interests she should stand her ground. But if she said no, what would that make her look like? Big bad Mom, compared to Mister

Popularity Dad. He had plotted this one well.

'Hi, sweetie,' she said. 'How are you?'

'Please, Mom? Please?'

'We'll see. Let me speak with your dad again.'

When Terry came back on the line, she said, 'Look, we better talk about this later.'

'I . . . well, we can't. I've got until this afternoon. After today, the prices go up.'

She looked at the clock on the kitchen wall. It was eight thirty. The boys were going to be late for school. She was being made to feel that she was holding everything back. 'Damn you, Terry,' she said. 'Why do you do this to me?'

He didn't answer.

She sighed, knowing she couldn't win. 'Okay, okay, take them – but make sure you look after—'

'She says it's all right,' Terry called out, away from the phone. She could hear two young voices cheering in the background.

'Let me have all the details,' she tried above the din. 'Flights, where you're staying. Everything.'

'Sure, sure. There's plenty of time for that. Look, I really appreciate this. Gotta go. Ciao, ciao.'

The phone went dead. 'Thanks. Thanks a lot,' she said into it before she hung up.

The toast was cold and hard. She dropped it into the pedal bin and put the tub of spread back in the fridge, then she stood at the window with her coffee.

Her apartment was on the sixth floor of a relatively new block on Hammond's Plains Road, just above where it joined the Bedford Highway. The immediate vista was of the Empire cinema and the Mill Cove shopping centre. Beyond that there was the train track and then came the real view, the vast expanse of water that was the Bedford Basin, two miles wide and four miles long and God knows how many feet down, which made this place one of the world's great deep water ports.

To her right she could see the two bridges, the McKay and the Macdonald, each about a mile in length, stretching across from Halifax to the twin city of Dartmouth. Halifax, Dartmouth and the town of Bedford ringed the basin and formed what had been officially designated since 1996 as the Halifax Regional Municipality.

Annie Welles was an officer in the Robbery and Violent Crimes Unit of the Halifax Regional Police. All of this was their territory.

Since the divorce last year she had allowed her work to absorb her more and more, even though it was the job itself that had cost her the boys. It had hurt her deeply when the judge had made his decision, awarding custody to Terry on the grounds that her irregular and often long hours were not conducive to a stable environment for them. His comments had been so remarkable that the newspapers had reported what he'd said and even the Chief of Police had gone into print, making sympathetic mutterings about injustice, but what was done was done.

A consolation, such as it was, was this pleasant, spacious, two-bedroom apartment which the settlement had helped to pay for and where the boys came to stay often. But often wasn't the same as always. Nothing could make up for the fact that they weren't around her permanently.

Annie was thirty-four and she was a little slimmer than she used to be. The stress of the divorce had taken off several pounds that she had not put back on again but she wasn't complaining about that.

She and Terry had married when she was twenty-two and she had been in the police service for most of that time. It had been fine for much of their life together, when they could organise their domestic routines relatively painlessly, but that was before her transfer three years ago from general investigations to the more unpredictable criminal investigative section. From that moment on, cracks began to appear in their marriage until it fell apart and crumbled away from them altogether. Then Terry came home one night and announced calmly that he had met someone else and wanted a divorce. Just like that. No emotion, nothing. As if he was telling her he had decided to buy a new car.

She threw the remains of her coffee into the sink and turned the TV off. She lifted the Sig in its holster and clipped it to her belt, then went to the hall closet for her coat and hat. She tucked her short dark hair behind her ears and pulled the hat, a little woollen thing, right down. Like the man said, it would be cold out there today.

As she closed the apartment door behind her and headed for the elevator, she knew that it wasn't just the way Terry had railroaded her into this that was upsetting. It was the fact that the boys would be so far away from her. It was another wrench, another separation. On top of that she didn't trust his ability to look after them properly and she had a mother's dread of something terrible happening.

Outside, she put on dark glasses to cope with the brightness. The freezing air enveloped her and she felt the skin on her face tighten in its grip. She hurried to her car, then drove out of the private parking lot, down Hammond's Plains Road, and at the intersection with the highway she turned right.

Until recently, all the CIS units had operated out of the police building in Dartmouth but after Christmas they had moved to Gottingen Street in downtown Halifax where the police headquarters was being extended and refurbished. The builders had been at it a long time, with mess and clutter, the constant sounds of hammering and drilling, and she wondered sometimes if the job would ever be finished.

She clicked the car radio to 'search' but it had a thing about Shania Twain today so she tuned it manually to 90.5 and Information Morning on CBC. She listened to the regional news. There was a row between the Nova Scotia government and a hotel company who were building a new casino at the Halifax waterfront. The construction work was behind schedule and the Finance Minister was threatening to sue at the rate of ten thousand dollars a day for late completion.

Next came a story about paramedics who were protesting about new legislation being put before the House of Assembly which would curtail their ability to strike every time they came to look for a pay rise. Annie could see that this would mean more placards being paraded up and down outside Province House. There was always somebody there, complaining about something.

She listened to another report in which several residents of north-end Dartmouth were interviewed about the growth of street crime and the proliferation of drugs and prostitution. A local seniors group had got a petition together and was planning to deliver it to the Chief of Police in person. 'No one else will do,' one of them said.

I wouldn't bet on your chances, Annie thought. The people at the top of the department liked photo-opportunities but only when things were going their way.

As if to rub salt in that particular wound, there was a second Dartmouth crime story, this time about a credit union office being robbed. A masked gunman had entered the manager's home during the night, then had forced him to drive to the office and open it up. There was no indication yet of how much money had been taken.

'And on a happier note,' the newsreader told her, down in Lunenburg they were looking ahead to a royal visit next month. Prince William was coming to perform the official launching ceremony of the *Bluenose III*, the second replacement for the original *Bluenose*, the famous Nova Scotia racing schooner which had its image on the Canadian dime. Some public representatives were getting excited and wanted the occasion to be declared a public holiday.

She hardly heard the rest of it because a thought had entered her mind.

She reached the edge of the city. On her left, along the shore side of the highway, huge flashing billboards advertised once-in-a-lifetime holidays, new cars, new homes, new savings plans. They were positioned to catch the attention of the slow-moving commuter traffic heading into Halifax but the people who lived around here, in the houses on the right of the road, could see them too, although they had probably long since ceased to notice what was on offer. These residences were not Halifax's finest and few of the people from this neighbourhood would ever reach for the dreams that beckoned, except maybe the weekly lottery jackpot.

She turned right into one of the steep little streets, driving slowly past houses that were shabby and small. Faded paint peeled from their wooden frames and patches of frozen snow lay in their front yards. Of the few cars parked in the street, several were just a journey or two away from the breaker's yard, which was why, as she pulled up, she noticed a dark blue Dodge, almost new. A man was getting into it but she saw him only briefly before he drove away. He was about sixty, grey-haired, and both he and the car were out of place here.

She made a puzzled face to herself, then got out and walked to the house she wanted. A Buick several years old, the colour of a California red wine, was parked alongside. She tried the doorbell but it made no sound that she could hear so she knocked with a gloved knuckle.

The door was opened by a heavy-set man in a blue-striped

towelling dressing gown which he pulled tight around him as soon as he felt the cold. His hair had once been fair but it was going grey. Childhood pock marks had become little craters on his colourless cheeks.

He looked at her but did not speak. The hostility in his eyes said it all.

Annie took her sunglasses off and smiled. 'Hello, Ray. Not inviting me in?'

She brushed past him without waiting for an answer and walked into the house.

Ray McPhee closed the door behind her as she gave the little living room a once-over. She knew there was a tiny kitchen just beyond it and that stairs led straight from this room up to two small bedrooms and a washroom with shower, no bath. She was aware of all this because she had been part of a team that had once searched the house for stolen property.

But today the place looked very different from how she remembered. It was neat and clean, not the mess of her previous visit, and it seemed to have been decorated recently, warm shades that made it feel homely and comfortable. In this neighbourhood, that was quite an achievement.

She turned to McPhee. 'All alone? Wife gone out?'

'Gone period,' he grunted and she heard no regret in his voice. 'Cleared out a couple of months back.'

'And the dog?'

The last time there had been a bloodthirsty rottweiler. The place didn't smell like it was here now.

'Darth? Gone, too. I let her take him. She preferred him to me anyway.'

Darth. When she was a kid, her grandfather, over in Kentville, had had a black labrador he called Peach for some reason no one could ever figure. Darth seemed to work, though.

She took another look around. There were pictures on walls which had previously been bare. Several prints of a seafaring nature, featuring great heroic schooners battling through high seas, had been hung in an orderly group. Beside the display was a framed photograph. She went closer and saw that it was McPhee himself standing, smiling, outside a small cabin, its front festooned with fishing nets.

'Listen,' he said, 'I was just about to turn in. So what is this? What do you want?'

She didn't give him an answer. 'Yeah? What, were you at an all-night party?'

'No, I was at work.'

She gave a guffaw. 'Work? What work's this, Ray?'

'At the hospital. The QEII. I'm a part-time orderly. I was on the night shift.'

She tried not to show her surprise. 'Since when?'

'Since eleven last night.'

'Not what I meant.'

There was a glint in his eye that told her he knew that.

'A while after I got out. I've been there about nine months.'

She didn't respond. Instead she walked into the kitchen. From the window she could see the tiny back yard and the lofty fenced enclosure that used to house the beast called Darth. She wondered where the wife was and how she was coping with her canine parting gift.

She returned to the other room. 'You came into my mind just now when I was driving along the highway. I did a quick calculation and figured you must be out, oh, how long – a year?'

'About that, yeah. Look, can we cut this shit? Tell me what you're doing here and then maybe I can get to bed.'

'A credit union was robbed in Dartmouth last night. The

manager was taken from his home and forced to open up. Sound familiar to you?'

She knew it would. McPhee had been sent to prison in Dorchester, New Brunswick, on a five-year stretch for a credit union armed robbery carried out in an identical manner. It was his speciality and it was what had drawn her to this house after hearing the item on the radio. Annie, then a uniformed officer, had caught him in the act that last time and had managed to disarm and handcuff him before back-up arrived at the scene. She had received a commendation for her actions but, more than that, it had got her noticed, and so it had been a relatively short journey from there to the job she had now.

He shook his head. 'No way. I don't do that stuff no more.'

He turned away. There was a coathook on the wall under the stairs. He grabbed something from it and handed it to her. 'There you go.'

She found herself holding a white hospital tunic with a badge pinned to the pocket. It said *R McPhee* alongside the QEII logo.

'A jacket's not an alibi,' she told him, although she had a growing feeling that in this case it might be.

He snatched it back from her. 'Ah, but a roster is. And so are all the people who can tell you where I was between the hours of eleven last night and seven this morning. How would that do?'

She paused and looked at him and suddenly wondered what she was doing here.

And then she admitted to herself that she had called, not because of the Dartmouth robbery at all, but because after talking to Terry she had needed to give somebody a hard time. McPhee was simply a convenient emotional punchbag.

Finally she said, 'Okay, but you know I'm going to check.'

'Oh sure. You'll call the hospital and even though they'll

be able to vouch for me, it'll start them wondering, you know, wondering if I'm really the sort of guy they want to have working there. I'll see it when I go on duty tonight. Oh yeah. I'll see it on their faces. The doubt. The suspicion. Planted there by you.' He shook his head. 'You people. Cops. You're all the same. You don't believe anybody can change.'

There was an armchair. She sat down in it and settled back, folding her arms. 'Okay, so tell me. I'm all ears. Tell me how you've changed, Ray.'

He stared at her for a few seconds and she could see the light of anger in his eyes dimming gradually. Then he sat on the edge of the chair opposite, elbows on his knees. He seemed to be thinking how to respond, deciding whether he wanted to say anything at all. She let him take his time.

He was calm when he spoke eventually. 'I'd been inside before – but you know that.'

She nodded. McPhee was what – forty-two? He'd spent nearly half of that in the correctional system, one way or another.

'This time it was different. Up in Dorchester I kind of got to re-thinking my life and I realised that if I kept on like this I was maybe going to kill somebody and end up in jail forever or else somebody was going to whack me and that would be that. I got some good encouragement, encouragement to think in other ways. Very positive. I got assigned to duties at the prison hospital and discovered that I liked it, really liked it, you know? So I began working to maybe get some basic qualifications, which I did – a big surprise, I can tell you. The prison supported me. I never sat an exam in my life before, never mind pass one, and a little while after I came out the probation people helped me get into the QEII. That's it. Now I'm studying to be a paramedic. There's the books if you don't believe me.'

He pointed towards a table in the corner. There were

textbooks on it. One of them was called Emergency Care. She could see the words printed on the spine.

Her eyes searched his face. If all this was true, it was an impressive example of rehabilitation. This was another Ray McPhee altogether. She found it hard to take in.

'Saint Ray on the road to Dorchester,' she said.

'What?'

'Just kidding.' She stood.

'Although you're going to check my alibi anyway, right?'

'What can I tell you? I'm a cop. But let me just say that if you're on the level, then I won't make any trouble for you.'

They looked at each other, positions understood. He gave a curt nod of appreciation.

She began to walk towards the door but on the way her attention was taken once more by the picture of him on the wall. She tapped the glass with a finger. 'Where's this?'

'That? Oh, it's a little bolt-hole of mine.' A thin smile said that was all the information she was getting.

'Didn't know you were interested in fishing.'

'A man's got to have a hobby.'

'Not many trout streams in Dorchester.'

'No. Give me the sea any time.'

2

She didn't go to Gottingen Street straight away but instead headed for the QEII. At main entrance reception she flashed her ID and said she'd like to speak to someone in personnel.

'What's this about?' the receptionist said, peering over the top of her glasses at Annie's badge with its symbol of a lighthouse against the outline of a maple leaf. In return Annie gave her a look that said it was none of her business. The woman picked up the phone and said, 'Wait over there.' She pointed to a row of chairs. 'I'll see who's available.'

After a couple of minutes another woman appeared. She was about Annie's age, but blonde, and she had the guilty look that honest people always have when they come into contact with the police.

'I . . . may I help you? I'm Glenda Paige. I'm a human resources officer.'

'Annie Welles. Pleased to meet you.' She held out a hand.

The woman took it. 'What on earth's this about?'

'I'm checking something that might relate to a member of the hospital staff.' She looked around. 'It's a little delicate. Is there somewhere we can talk?'

Glenda considered. 'My office, I suppose.'

She led the way down a corridor to the elevator and hit the button for five.

'I hope there isn't a problem.'

'I'm sure there isn't.'

The doors opened on to an administrative floor. They walked down a runway between work stations where several women tapped on computers. Annie could sense that they were trying not to let her see them watching as she passed. Either they'd made her as a cop, which few people did, not straight away, or else the word had spread with the call from the front desk.

Glenda opened a door into a small office. 'Here we are. Now perhaps you'd explain.'

There was no invitation to sit but Annie figured the woman wasn't being rude, just nervous. It often happened. People wanted you out of their lives as quickly as possible.

'We've picked up a guy – well, I'll not go into the circumstances, if you don't mind – but he's carrying ID which says he's an orderly here at the hospital, name of Peter James. We need to know whether you have anyone of that name employed here and whether he was working last night between the hours of, say, midnight and four a.m.'

'Peter James? It's not a name I know. But we do have casual staff who come and go.'

'We have a feeling this guy isn't really who he says he is. It could be a fake ID or maybe he stole it. We just need to check. Do you have rosters that will show who was on duty? In particular I'm thinking of which orderlies were on last night.'

'Yes, I can get that for you. Wait here.'

She left the room and while she was gone Annie took a quick glance around. It didn't take a genius to work out that this was the office of a woman under pressure. The desk was covered with paperwork. Three metal trays were full and on the floor there was a stack of bulky files with names written on the covers. To the right of the desk, a computer waited, a Windows pattern blowing gently across the screen.

Annie reached over and clicked the mouse and up came

a half-written page with the word *Objectives* at the top. There was a long list of what some employee would have to aim for during the year. Performance appraisal. It was the way of the world, even in the police department, she reminded herself.

She turned away just as the door opened again.

'Here we are.' Glenda had two printed sheets in her hand. 'No one called Peter James.'

'Do you mind if I look?'

One sheet was a staff list of orderlies. A swift glance showed Annie that Ray McPhee's name was indeed on it. The other sheet was the roster and his name was there, too, just as he'd said it would be. Eleven a.m. to seven a.m. Emergency Room.

'And these were the people who were actually on duty last night? No calls in sick or anything like that?'

'No, I've already checked that. There were no changes.'

'That's very helpful,' Annie said. 'But you know, I really ought to make absolutely certain. Is there any way you can check whether anyone called Peter James works here – in any capacity, never mind as an orderly?'

'Sure, that's simple,' Glenda said, beginning to sound more relaxed. 'I've got the staff lists on the system here. It's just a matter of scrolling down through.'

Annie stiffened as Glenda went behind the desk but to her relief she saw that the screensaver was back. Glenda began to click through her files. Annie really didn't need her to do any of this, it was just to ensure the cover. She had told McPhee that if he was telling the truth she wouldn't make trouble for him. She would keep her word.

Glenda sat back. 'No Peter James.'

'No,' Annie said. 'Somehow I didn't think so.'

By ten thirty she was sipping coffee on a bench in the wide

hallway of the Law Courts building right beside the Metro ferry terminal.

Through the window at the end of the hall she could see out onto rippling water that looked grey and cold. The ferry to Dartmouth was setting off and way beyond it, an impossibly long vessel was heading out to sea, rows of fifty-foot containers stacked on its deck. From this distance they were like matchboxes. The ship made the ferry look like a bath toy.

Across the hall, in a heavy blue wool overcoat, sat a man in his mid-thirties, dark hair going grey at the ears. He also had a white shirt and a silver silk tie and she could see that the trousers of his grey suit were immaculately pressed. Everything about him said that he was somebody important, somebody on the way up.

The width of the hall was not the only gulf between them. Gil Claussen was her former partner. He had always had a stiff manner and would never have won an award for colleague of the year but she respected the fact that he was a good cop and, while together, they had been a successful team. However, in the months following her marriage break-up and then the divorce he had begun to behave differently around her. There had been remarks, little asides laced with sexual innuendo, glances that made her uncomfortable, but for a while nothing more overt. Then, when a bunch of them were having Christmas drinks in a downtown hotel, he had cornered her in the corridor and suggested he book a room where the two of them could go and fuck their brains out. She recalled the words vividly.

Even though she had suspected for some time just what was on his mind, it had shaken her. He was drunk, of course, which had given him the courage, but he had spoken to her like she was nothing more than a whore and with the assumption that she was ready and willing and available.

She had declined his offer. In fact, adopting his chosen vocabulary, she had told him to go fuck himself, then turned on her heel and gone back to her drink, trying not to let the others guess that something had happened.

Apart from anything else he had a wife and three daughters. She could have reported him for sexual harassment, but she didn't. It might have ruined him but it wouldn't have done her any good either. You didn't rat on a fellow cop – that was the unspoken rule. Plus she was one of only three women in a unit of twenty officers so if you factored in the whole macho culture thing, she might as well have handed in her badge and gone home.

She had never mentioned the incident again but neither had Claussen. There had been no apology from him, no sign of remorse. Instead he had begun to freeze her out, as if it were she who were guilty of an offence.

It was difficult to work with a partner who hardly spoke to you and she had been wondering what to do about that when fate had intervened in the shape of Sergeant Mark Gamble, the officer in charge of the Robbery and Violent Crimes Unit. He had called them both into his office and announced that for operational reasons he was splitting them up. There was nothing wrong with them as a team, he insisted, they were both good officers, but there were other people in RVC who would benefit from working with them.

She could tell that Claussen didn't believe this was a coincidence. Nor did anyone else. Annie knew there were rumours. Yet she didn't think Gamble's decision was connected.

Claussen got Bill Crisp, a nice guy, easy to work with, fair-haired, a bit younger than Annie, and since last week she had been partnered with Walter Flagg, a big rumpled man approaching fifty and retirement and looking forward to it. Flagg had come to Halifax eight years ago from

Hamilton, Ontario, and appeared never to have heard the words 'politically' and 'correct' used together. But he made her laugh and he nurtured no sexual ambitions in which she might play a part. Of that she was certain.

Deedes, another of the guys in the unit, had already started referring to them as Mouldy and Scully. Deedes could always be relied on to come up with a gag. Like the matter which had brought her to court today. He'd christened it the Scotia Nostra case and now everyone else was calling it that, including the media.

It was a hangover from her partnership with Claussen and one which they had hit on by accident last year. They'd been on Robie Street, on their way back from St Mary's University after interviewing the latest victim of a freak who was attacking students at night, when they'd picked up a call telling them there was something happening on South Street, reports of two men trying to bundle a third person into a car.

When they arrived at the scene, they saw a man running along the sidewalk with two other men after him. But as soon as the pursuers spotted their car, they turned and started running the other way. Annie and Claussen had gone after them, first in the car, then on foot as the men tried to make their escape across fences and back yards. A shot in the air from Claussen had stopped them.

Retracing their steps, they found a .22, recognised in the trade as a hit man's special, which had been discarded in the chase. A search of the men's car revealed ropes, a set of handcuffs and a baseball bat.

When identified, the two turned out to be brothers of Italian extraction who ran a dry-cleaning business. Their escaped prisoner was the owner of a small electronics store in a big shopping mall out of town. Further enquiries were to uncover that he was one of several victims of a protection racket which the two Italians had been operating among small business owners at various malls. Hence the Scotia Nostra tag.

The brothers were about to go on trial now on a range of charges including extortion, illegal possession of a firearm and attempted abduction. The smart money was on a sentence of fifteen years apiece.

Annie looked at Claussen. He had his head in the *Herald-Chronicle*, pretending she wasn't there. She stood up and walked over to him.

'Gil, I think it's time we had a proper talk. This thing has gone far enough.'

He didn't look up. He said quietly, 'What thing would that be?'

'This . . . whatever it is . . . between us.'

He glanced at her at last. His eyes were cold. 'There's nothing between us.'

'Yes there is. Maybe you've forgotten but I haven't. I have a very distinct memory of what it is.'

Claussen turned his face from her and stared at the paper again.

She decided to be more conciliatory. 'Listen, one way or another, we've got to work together in the same department.' She spread her arms. 'Look at us, for heaven's sake. What is this like? Can't we just call it quits, put the whole thing to bed?'

Bad choice of word. She turned away from him and folded her arms. 'Damn it, why am I feeling guilty about this?'

'I'm not the one who started the whispers, the one who went looking for a new partner.'

'I didn't ask for that. Splitting us up was the boss's own idea, nothing to do with me. And as for whispers, I didn't say anything to anybody. If I had, you'd have known about it, Gil, believe me.'

Claussen folded the paper and stood. They were about the same height. 'I don't like people talking about me behind my back.'

'Then maybe you shouldn't have given them any reason to.'

They were staring at each other like prizefighters psyching each other up when the courtroom door opened.

The Crown prosecutor in the Scotia Nostra case was a fussy looking man with a permanent frown. He wore a black gown which hung off one shoulder and there was a white ribboned bow tie at his neck. He could have been an English barrister in a court at the Old Bailey. He looked at Annie and Claussen but he didn't seem to register the tension hanging in the air between them.

'Look, I won't need to call both of you.' His glance settled on Claussen and he seemed to approve of the way he was dressed. 'You, Officer Claussen, I think. Anyway, you might not even be needed at all. They've entered a plea of not guilty, unwisely in my view, but I suspect they may change that once we begin our case.'

He opened the door. 'Right, let's get on.' He put an arm round Claussen to usher him in, then turned back to Annie. 'No need for you to hang around, Officer Welles. You won't be required.'

Claussen gave her a smug look. Slowly, the heavy door eased itself closed behind them. It made just the softest of whispers but she felt as if it had been slammed in her face.

3

When they wrote about him, which was seldom these days, the papers referred to Andrew Giles as 'the distinguished former BBC foreign correspondent'. 'Former' he certainly was, but not as 'distinguished' as he considered himself to be, although he dressed and carried himself in a manner that declared him a person of importance.

He certainly felt that way tonight. He was the master of ceremonies for the London Press Awards and here he was, on the stage of the Grand Ballroom in the Park Lane Hilton, dressed in black tie and a dinner jacket that still fitted him as perfectly as when he had bought it in Hong Kong some years ago.

Giles had been a correspondent of the old school, covering what was known in his day as the Far East, but doing so in the manner of a gentleman. That is, he felt it to be very poor form to actually go to the office every day. He filed reports only when he felt like doing so and on events which he, rather than the BBC, judged to be significant.

The Corporation tolerated this for a while because Giles was a familiar face, a personality of sorts, and when he was on song he could turn in a decent job of work. But it was a different BBC now, an organisation in a hurry, and it didn't have time for all this nonsense.

The last straw came after a hurricane in the Philippines, death and destruction on a huge scale, when Giles had decided that having lunch with the American Ambassador in Manila was more important than going to the stricken jungle villages to see for himself what had happened. After all, that was what these news agencies were for, wasn't it?

As a consequence the BBC had brought him home abruptly and given him a role as a roving UK correspondent, which required him to produce occasional reports of a quirky nature from up and down the country. This did not suit him at all. He was not used to a daily work routine, nor had he lived in Britain for a long time. It had become an unfamiliar place to him, almost a foreign country, and some of his pieces were so racist in tone that they could not be broadcast.

After a time he had resigned. At least, that's how he described his departure although the truth of the matter was that his contract had not been renewed. Following that, it wasn't long before he went the time-honoured route of many disgruntled ex-employees, hurling public abuse at the BBC, complaining that it was being run by accountants and consultants who knew nothing about the great ethos of public service broadcasting.

He found work of sorts with one of the British-based satellite channels where they were trying to turn him into a sort of home-grown Larry King, complete with shirt-sleeves and braces, but the show wasn't working well, audiences had never taken to it and top level guests were disinclined to appear. The series ran once a week, off peak, and the rumour was that it was about to be chopped.

For the moment, however, he was still in the spotlight, ignoring the fact, if he was even aware of it, that he had not been the first choice, nor even the second, for tonight's role.

As was the case with his own programme, top level personalities were disinclined to get involved with this event. In the dog-eat-dog world of the London media, it was a particularly carnivorous occasion. Professional jealousy and huge quantities of alcohol were a dangerous mix and last year's bash had distinguished itself for the number of fist fights which had broken out among the participants. As a result, this year the papers had all sent photographers, hoping to get pictures, not of the award-winners, but of the action.

To John Taggart of the *Sunday Chronicle* the whole set-up seemed like a form of organised self-abuse. Smoking a small Punch Havana, he sat at a table towards the front with eight members of the paper's editorial staff including the editor, Ken Shaw, a short square man in his mid-forties. Taggart had had a few drinks. He peered around him with a kind of alcoholic detachment, although he was not so drunk that he wouldn't be able to make it to the stage and back again without mishap. His turn was coming up soon.

There had been a champagne reception, although most people had started elsewhere before that, then there had been dinner, with far too much wine, and now they were on the liqueurs, in his case a Remy Martin which he swirled in a glass as big as a vase.

Fortunately, he would not be required to speak. They had dropped all that after the barracking which had greeted last year's recipients. The absence of acceptance speeches would not silence the hecklers entirely but cutting the amount of time you were up there on the stage limited their window of opportunity.

He listened to Andrew Giles reading the citation for photographer of the year. Even as a child in Scotland he had admired that resonant, burnished voice. Giles was the perfect choice for this, an old ham actor so wrapped up in his own ego and performance that he was isolated from everything around him, immune to any disaster that might unfold.

Standing to Giles's side, smiling with a grim fortitude, was the Shadow Minister for Culture and the Arts whose task it was to hand over the awards: thin bronze creations designed to look like a billowing newspaper page. After that, he would make the keynote speech, which would be tough going with this crowd.

As with the host, he had not been first choice. Every Government Minister and even some minor Royals had turned the invitation down, on the grounds, of course, that they were otherwise committed this evening, but Members of Her Majesty's Opposition did not enjoy the luxury of declining the opportunity to appear at such high-profile events. They needed all the exposure they could get. Even this.

Giles called out the name of the winning photographer. Across the room, a young man stood and started to head for the stage. There was some applause but mostly there was the sound of monkey noises, denoting the esteem in which those masters of the written word, the reporters, held their intrepid camera colleagues.

Taggart began to tense because he knew he was next.

'Now we come to the award for columnist of the year,' Giles announced when the photographer had returned to his seat, with a fresh barrage of jungle effects to help him on his way. 'Born in Scotland—'

'Fucking jock,' someone called and there was laughter.

Taggart smiled and told himself not to get rattled. It was a pound to a penny that the heckler wouldn't be winning anything.

Giles went on as if he hadn't noticed. 'After university in Edinburgh, this young man began his career in Glasgow in the hard-knock school of journalism that the newspapers of that fine city represent.'

'He's a fucking haggis-humper,' the heckler shouted and the laughter began to spread.

Still smiling, Taggart glanced in the direction of the voice. He could see who it was now: Ronnie Boyd, a reporter from the *Post*, a man he'd had no dealings with, as far as he could recall, and so he couldn't figure out whether Boyd had something against him in particular or the Scottish nation in general.

Taggart took in the rest of Boyd's table and saw that they all seemed to be enjoying his contributions. There was one exception. A slim woman with long dark hair sat smoking a cigarette and seemed as if she would rather be elsewhere. As Taggart looked at her, she turned his way and their eyes met. She gave him a nod and a discreet smile.

Judith Sefton was news editor of the *Post*. When she was a reporter, not so long ago, that smile had got men to tell her things they might not have revealed to anyone else. She'd had other ways of getting a story, too, rumour had it.

Whatever the truth or otherwise, she was trouble. With a headline-writer's gift for the cliché, they called her the Black Widow. Fleet Street, as it used to be known, was littered with the husks of her discarded conquests. Taggart smiled back briefly, then turned away to hear what Giles was saying.

'He made a name for himself with a series of special investigations exposing the links between a Scottish crime syndicate and a number of apparently respectable businessmen, all of them heavily involved in drugs and prostitution, with the result that the police were able to bring prosecutions and a number of people were given heavy prison sentences.

'For our award-winner tonight, this spectacular success was followed by a very swift move to London to the pages of the *Sunday Chronicle*. After a spell as a feature-writer, he was soon given his own column where he has continued to cement his reputation as a journalist of stature by providing something which, rather than being just a hotchpotch of gossip, is a source of regular exclusive material about the rich and famous, about celebrities, about politicians – but, perhaps most of all, about members of the Royal Family, an area of news interest which he is gradually making his own.'

'Wanker,' Boyd shouted.

'He is a frequent guest on popular radio and television shows, although I have to say he has so far not managed to appear on mine.' Giles shot Taggart a look but then returned to the text. 'All this and he is still not much more than thirty. Ladies and gentlemen, the winner of the London Press Awards 2000, columnist of the year category, is John Taggart.'

Taggart pushed his chair back and buttoned his jacket.

'Good boy,' Ken Shaw said as he passed. 'Fucking marvellous.'

A fanfare came from the PA speakers. There was applause but there were boos and whistles as well, mostly from Boyd's table. Unflattering remarks which Taggart could not decipher were hurled into the midst of the din.

He reached the stage, said thanks to Giles, then shook the Shadow Minister's hand and took the award. The man said something which Taggart couldn't hear but he assumed it to be of a congratulatory nature so he thanked him for it. As the noise began fading, Boyd's voice came again.

'Couldn't write his own fucking name.'

The microphone was just there in front of him and for a moment Taggart was tempted to deliver a retort but he resisted the urge. He had good reason for wanting to appear aloof, to seem as if he were not really involved in any of this, so he gave a smile and a little nod of thanks to the assembled gathering and went back to his table with the trophy.

Bottles of chilled champagne were waiting and Shaw was pouring liberally. They all stood to toast their winner. Shaw handed Taggart a glass.

'You should have told that arsehole Boyd where to get off.'

Taggart dismissed the suggestion with a shrug. 'I thought it was better not to let him think he was getting to me. Which he wasn't.'

'I'll get to him. If I see the fucker, I'll get to him.'

Drink could send Shaw in one of two directions. Either he was the life and soul of the party, generous, gracious, a teller of humorous stories, or he could become angry and red-faced and dangerous. More and more frequently, he was both in one evening.

Taggart didn't like the way this was heading.

'He's not worth it, Ken. Let's just enjoy ourselves.' He tapped a champagne bottle with a teaspoon. 'I want you to raise your glasses, folks, and toast the man without whom none of this would be possible – Ken Shaw, a great editor.'

They stood. '. . . Shaw . . . editor,' they mumbled, then drank enthusiastically. Taggart shot Shaw a cautious glance and saw that the gesture seemed to have defused him.

When the handing-out of the awards finished, there was a comfort break before the Shadow Minister had to get up to speak. People were starting to table-hop but many were heading out of the room and towards the bar, from where they were unlikely to return.

Taggart felt a hand gripping his shoulder and turned to see Andrew Giles leaning over him. Up close he could see the lattice-work of broken veins on his face and the unnatural darkness of the sparse hair.

'Jolly well done, my boy. Now, as I was saying, when are you going to come on my programme? Let's explore some of these Royal stories you've been doing, try to get an insight into what makes the Monarchy tick these days. What do you say?'

'Sounds good. I'll have to think about it, see when would

suit both of us. You know how it is. Why don't I get back to you in a day or so?'

He waited for further persuasion to be exerted but instead Giles relaxed his grip. He raised his arm and waved to somebody and Taggart saw that it was the editor of a serious broadsheet for whom Giles wrote an occasional article about the BBC whenever it got itself into trouble.

Giles backed away. 'Excellent, excellent. Don't leave it too long.'

But that was exactly what Taggart was going to do. In fact, if he left it for just long enough there would be nothing to appear on at all, nothing to refuse, because the show would be gone. It seemed as if Giles was the only person who didn't realise this.

The truth was, he had no intention of going on any programme, but especially not Giles's, to talk about his stories. He had worked too hard on his connections to ruin them now. That was why he hadn't bothered to put Boyd down when he'd had the chance. It was a question of image, of reputation. He wanted to appear as if he were above that sort of thing.

Since he had begun his column, Taggart had made it his business to try to get an 'in' with the friends and advisors of the Prince of Wales but his real purpose was to win the confidence of his son, Prince William. He wanted the first interview with him, a world exclusive. Winning the approval of the father would help.

In fact, the signs were good. A former girlfriend from university, now working with a London PR firm, had married a member of the Prince of Wales's staff. Through these channels, Taggart had picked up several stories involving this side of the Royal Family, all of them pieces which did the image of the Prince of Wales no harm at all.

Things were on the move. Very soon Prince William

would be going on a short official visit to Canada, where they loved him. He had been several times before and they greeted him there more like a pop star than royalty. Taggart was going too. Quietly, the way these things were done, St James's Palace had made it known to the owner of the *Chronicle* that when the visit took place, it would be agreeable if he were the person the paper sent along to cover it.

It was a long game that might last years but Taggart was happy to play it, although timing was important. If he was still working for the *Chronicle* when he got the interview then the paper would be likely to make all the money out of it. But if he got the interview on his own terms, then he stood to make a fortune.

Particularly if it was for television.

The printed word was one thing but in this case pictures were better. You only had to think back to the famous interview with Princess Diana to see that. So Taggart had made plans. He had a friend who ran an independent production outfit making current affairs programmes and documentaries but together they had formed a separate company, which for the moment existed on paper only, for the express purpose of the William interview, if it ever happened. Time and watching his step would tell.

'And what the fuck do you want?' Ken Shaw asked.

Taggart turned to see who he was talking to.

'Nice to see you, too, Ken,' Judith Sefton said.

She wore a long black dress made of a fabric that seemed as if it would evaporate if you touched it. Red straps like threads held it up. She thrust her hair back from her face, which she probably did a thousand times a day. It was a confident, sexy gesture.

'I've just come over to say congratulations to John here.' She smiled at him. 'Very well deserved. And I wanted to let you know that at the *Post* we're not all like Ronnie Boyd.'

'I know what you're doing,' Shaw scoffed. 'Fucking Mata Hari. You couldn't afford this boy.'

'And neither can you,' she said without taking her eyes off Taggart, 'if one believes everything one reads about your circulation figures and your advertising revenue.'

Shaw reddened. Taggart knew that what she had said was true. The *Chronicle* was slipping and there were question marks over Shaw's editorship. Taggart had even begun wondering how long he should stick around, although the sight of his payslip every month usually put such thoughts out of his head. Apart from that, he liked Shaw and he knew that jumping ship would damage him badly.

'I appreciate the gesture,' he told her.

'Can I touch it?'

Their eyes locked. There was a moment, then he said, 'of course,' and handed her the award.

She caressed it with slim fingers. Her nails were a daring red and matched the straps of her dress.

'Heavy,' she said.

'Absolutely.' Of that there was no doubt.

The Shadow Minister didn't have such a bad experience after all, largely because by the time he got up to speak, the audience had thinned out. The only people who bothered to remain in their places were those who didn't drink, and there weren't many who fell into that category; those who couldn't be bothered to move; and a few who actually wanted to hear what he had to say.

Taggart and his party did not fit any of these camps. When the champagne was finished they headed for the noise and bustle of the bar. There they split up gradually and found new faces to talk to. Taggart sat with a couple of features people from *The Times*, his award on the table in front of him. He kept a careful eye on it. These things had a habit of vanishing if you weren't careful.

Every now and then he glanced round the throng, looking for Judith Sefton, asking himself if he was mad. His better judgement told him to forget about her but his better judgement was on the wane. He was a man, with all the weakness that entailed, he was half drunk and he was excited by the fact that she'd had the balls to come over to his table and declare an interest. And not one that was professional either. They'd all seen that.

All of a sudden he noticed Frank Hailes, who edited the *Chronicle*'s review section, pushing his way through the crowd, looking worried. When he spotted Taggart he hurried in his direction. He nodded to the people from *The Times*, then took Taggart to one side.

'John, I could do with a hand. There's a bit of bother.'

'What is it?'

'It's Ken.'

Hailes led the way out of the bar towards the men's cloakroom at the top of the main stairs. A lot of noise was coming from that direction, a crowd was starting to gather and Taggart could hazard a guess that they weren't all queuing up to answer the call of nature. With some difficulty, they pushed their way through. Once inside, what they saw stopped them in their tracks.

'Oh Christ,' Taggart said.

Ken Shaw and Ronnie Boyd were rolling around on the floor, punching and scratching and kicking at each other like a couple of drunken breakdancers. A group of men were standing around. Some cheered them on, others watched in fascination, while two actually stood side by side at the bank of urinals, pissing contentedly and carrying on a conversation as if none of this was remotely out of the ordinary.

A memory came to Taggart. A vision of the toilet block

at school in Stranraer. He saw himself and a ginger-headed lad called – what was his name? – Willie Tweed, that was it. He had said something to anger Taggart, a remark about his father. Taggart had hit him and then they had battled it out on the floor in much the same manner as this until a teacher had come in and dragged the pair of them away.

There was blood from somewhere. It was spattered over the tiles and on the clothes of the two combatants.

'Shit,' Hailes said. 'It was only a bit of verbal a moment ago.'

'Right, let's sort this.'

Taggart reached down, grabbed Ken Shaw by the shoulders and pulled him upright. Shaw tried to struggle free, his feet kicking wildly, but Taggart and Hailes had a solid grip on him. Getting the message, a couple of the spectators decided to lend a hand. They grabbed Boyd and began to haul him towards the door.

'Fucking moron,' Boyd shouted. 'You couldn't edit a fucking bus ticket.'

It was a common enough term of abuse in journalism but Taggart had never thought that it made much sense. No one could edit a bus ticket. A bus ticket was a bus ticket. There was no editing involved. But perhaps that was the point.

The blood was coming from Shaw's nose and it was all down the front of his shirt. He was very drunk and he might well be concussed but Taggart wasn't going to send for an ambulance. A taxi would do. He had to get him off the premises before this made a great front page picture for somebody else's paper. The *Post* probably.

'Bastard,' Shaw said, suddenly alert. 'Where . . . where is he? Where's the fucker gone?'

Taggart ignored the question. 'Let's get him out of here,' he said to Hailes.

They grabbed handfuls of paper towels from the dispenser

and stuck them under Shaw's nose as they manoeuvred him towards the door. They had trouble beating their way through the crowd outside but they made it. And then the first camera flashes started.

'What kept you?' Taggart muttered under his breath.

'I've got a cab. Come with me.'

He looked towards the voice and saw Judith Sefton standing to one side. She had her coat on and Taggart's award in her hand. Without waiting for their response, she turned and led the way down the stairs. They hurried after her.

The cab was at the side door. 'Look, I'll get him home,' Taggart said to Hailes. 'See if you can retrieve the coats. We'll get them at the office in the morning.' He pulled a cloakroom stub from his top pocket. 'Ken, where's yours?' But Shaw had lapsed into a state of angry muttering, like a dog growling in its sleep. At least the bleeding seemed to have stopped. A quick search of his pockets located the stub successfully, then Taggart gave both of them to Hailes.

'Here,' the driver asked, 'is this geezer going to bleed all over my cab?'

'Don't worry about it,' Taggart said. 'We won't let him.'

He shoved Shaw in, then he and Judith climbed in after him and the cab moved off. With a final 'fuck it' Shaw promptly fell asleep.

'What'd he do, fall or something?' the driver wondered, looking back at them from his mirror.

'Yeah, something like that,' Taggart told him.

'So where to?'

'Where does he live?' Judith asked. 'Hope it's not Oxford or somewhere.'

'Hampstead, I think,' Taggart said. He shook his editor. He was lying there like a pile of old clothes. 'Ken, where do you live?' The only answer was a couple of grunts.

'He's bound to have something on him,' Judith said.

Taggart searched Shaw's pockets and found his wallet. There were credit cards in it and cash but nothing else.

'Have you got a mobile?' he asked Judith. 'I didn't bring mine.'

She put her hand into her bag and took out a small Nokia. Taggart dialled the number of the *Chronicle* news desk. It was a Thursday and they always worked later towards the end of the week, coming up to deadline. Dermot Dillon, the news editor, answered.

'Dermot, look up Ken's address for me, would you?'

'What are you talking about? I thought you were out with him?' Dillon had a Dublin accent that was just as strong as when he moved to London from the *Irish Independent* twenty years before.

'I am. I'm trying to get him home.'

'Ah, I see. Trouble. Would drink be involved at all?'

'Big time.'

'Right you are. I take it all will be revealed?'

'In due course.'

Taggart got the address, gave it to the driver, then handed Judith her phone and sat back. 'I didn't say thanks. I should have done that.' He smiled at her. 'I don't know what the equivalent of a knight in shining armour is. A woman in a black dress, maybe?'

'No problem. I'd ordered the cab anyway, then I heard what was going on. And I thought you wouldn't want to lose this.' She handed him his award and their fingers touched.

He said, 'I don't understand why you're so keen to protect Ken Shaw. I'd have thought you couldn't stand him.'

'Don't be silly. You know it's not him I'm interested in.'

She put her hand on his thigh. He watched the London streets go past. This was a journey that would lead to trouble. He couldn't think of anything to say that wouldn't sound idiotic but when her fingers moved up to his crotch he realised that what she found there told her everything she needed to know.

They reached Shaw's house. He was a dead weight but they managed to haul him out of the cab and keep him standing upright. Judith asked the driver to wait. Taggart hunted for a key.

'Has he a wife?' she asked.

'Divorced. Lives here on his own, as far as I know.'

He found the key in Shaw's pockets and they let themselves in. Taggart lowered him down on to a settee. The nose bleed had definitely stopped but his clothes were a mess.

'What about you?' Judith said.

'What do you mean?'

'Is there a wife?'

She was a single-minded woman. It occurred to him that even if Shaw had been lying there dead it wouldn't have made any difference to her.

'No.'

'Lover?'

'Nothing current.' He hauled Shaw's jacket off and put it across him. 'There. I think he'll be all right. When he wakes up he can sort himself out.'

They left the key on a table in the hall and closed the door behind them.

'Where now?' the driver asked.

'I'm just along the road a bit,' Judith said. 'How about you?'

'Far side of the river.'

'Then it looks like it's me first.'

In a few minutes they were outside a house in a quiet street in Highgate. They both got out. There was no discussion about it. Taggart paid the taxi and told the driver to go on. He tried not to catch his eye.

Judith opened her front door and led the way into a living room where there was soft lighting on bright colours, greens and blues and Tuscan red. She threw her coat down on a settee and turned to face him, a look of triumph in her eyes.

He wanted this. It was a big mistake, no good would come of it, but he wanted this, here and now.

He pulled her to him. As they kissed he took his jacket off and threw it aside. Then he eased the thin red straps from her shoulders. She let herself fall back slowly until she was on the settee and he had slumped to his knees in front of her. He buried his face in her breasts and as his tongue circled a nipple she thrust her fingers into his thick dark hair.

He found her lips again. She reached forward to unzip him and plunged her hand inside. After a few moments she let go, then lay back, raising her hips and pulling the long dress up above her waist. He eased her panties down and threw them away. It didn't matter where. Her legs parted and she took him in her hand again to guide him in.

He groaned, partly because of the pleasure of it and partly because he'd just remembered that he'd left his award in the taxi.

4

Point Pleasant Park, at the southern tip of Halifax, was one hundred and eighty six acres of open woodland, winding trails and shore paths where people strolled and jogged and cycled in all weathers.

It retained several reminders of its past life as a military installation established to defend the city from a sea-borne invasion. There was the Martello tower, built in 1796 and now designated a national historic site, and there were the ruins of several fortifications, like Fort Ogilvie and the Cambridge Battery. In summer, these landmarks were transformed into stage sets by students performing Shakespeare in the balmy evening air. But it was not summer now. It was winter, in a city that felt it hard.

Cobb Landry was tired. He was always tired. He couldn't remember when he'd last felt any real energy. Wrapped in a heavy parka and a wool ski hat to keep the wind off his bald head, he walked slowly and wearily, feeling the cold roaming through the corridors of his thin body and wrapping itself round his bones.

Every now and then he lifted the compact binoculars which hung round his neck and searched the woodland around him. To the casual eye he looked like a birdwatcher and there was a time when he'd been a fairly enthusiastic one. Nova Scotia was right in the middle of the annual migratory flight path which made it a good place to be an ornithologist. In fact, not that far away, on McNab's Island, out in the harbour, there was even a fine colony of ospreys. But Landry wasn't watching birds today. He was watching a man.

The man was running. He did not run at any great speed but he moved at a steady, firm pace which Landry knew he would sustain for the next hour. He envied him his vigour. He did this three mornings a week, whatever the conditions and always at the same time, because he was someone, Landry knew, who needed a fixed, unshakeable routine in his life. That was what he was used to.

He wore a heavy jogging suit, wool gloves and a ski hat, not unlike Landry's own, pulled well down to cover his ears. Watching the way he moved, you could see that he was trim and agile, someone who looked after his physical well-being. But once you got close to him, it was a surprise to find that he was not a young man. He had turned sixty-three just a matter of weeks ago. Landry could have told you that.

From a discreet distance he studied the thin face, pinched and reddened by the pitiless cold. He saw determination in the expression. It was the face of a man who had survived, who had refused to allow himself to be destroyed by the things that had happened to him. Instead, it was Landry, almost twenty years his junior, who was being destroyed, being eaten away by the cancer which had returned to his body after the fool's paradise that the doctors called a period of remission.

Within a few months he would be dead. He did not want to die. There were those who said that when death was imminent it brought a feeling of resignation, a calm acceptance, a sense of self-knowledge, but Landry had not experienced any of that. Maybe if he'd believed in God, it would have made a difference. He envied people who were certain that there was another place. All he saw ahead was the fact that he would cease to exist, a concept that terrified him.

If he hadn't been so lonely, if there'd been someone else in his life, it might have helped. He found himself waking in the night, unable to breathe, knowing that what was to come was the end, the black empty nothingness of death. When these attacks happened he sat alone and trembling until the panic faded. There was no one to comfort him. There never had been.

He lowered the binoculars. The man was coming his way. In a few moments he would be heading up the hill and in among the trees where Landry would not be able to see.

He had watched the man a lot since finding out about him. He knew where he lived and what he did with his time, now that it was his own. His telephone number was not listed but Landry had it. He had memorised it, planning the moment when he would call.

He was very near now. Landry heard his feet on the frozen ground, saw his breath like smoke in the air and in the second that their paths crossed he thought he felt a wave of heat from his body. Locked into his run, absorbed by the physical challenge of it, the man paid no attention to him because he did not know who Landry was. But soon that would change, once Landry had summoned up what was left of his courage.

It was very late in the day, maybe too late to make any difference, but he knew that before he died he had to do what was right.

5

By the time Taggart's train was an hour out of Euston on its way up through England, he had scanned all the Monday morning papers and they lay in a discarded pile on the table.

A man on the other side of the carriage cast the occasional curious glance as he tapped away on a laptop, his jacket in a heap beside him. Taggart had a feeling the man had recognised him, either from his television appearances or from the picture that decorated the top of his page every Sunday, but was trying not to show it. That was the English way. Studied indifference.

It didn't trouble him. This morning he was the real John Taggart, the one who was always there inside, not the image he had created for public viewing.

He was going to see his mother.

He rested his head on his hand and looked out the window. Somewhere in the ghostly vision created by the passing countryside and his reflection in the grimy glass he saw his past.

He saw an only child, born in the tiny seaside town of Portpatrick, on the Scottish south west coast, where his mother had a corner shop that had been left to her by a maiden aunt. There was a cramped flat above it. That was his home, where his mother and he had lived, keeping themselves to themselves.

He had never known his father or even who he was.

Taggart was his mother's family name. All he knew was that as a teenager she had emigrated with her parents to Nova Scotia where they had died some years later in a car accident. There had been no other relatives, at least none that he had ever been made aware of.

He had asked about his father often enough.

'Is he still in Canada, Mum? Is that where he is?'

'Forget about him. Best that you don't know anything about that side of things.'

Her voice was an intriguing blend of two accents. Scotch with a dash of Canada Dry. That was how he described it to her once. She had managed a smile.

School had been in Stranraer, to where he took the bus in from Portpatrick each morning. One day when he was twelve, when they were at the tea-table, just finishing sausages, baked beans and chips, he said, 'Billy Moore's parents are getting divorced. He told me in English this morning. Is that what happened to you, Mum? Did you and—'

'Your father's dead. I think it's about time you knew that. There's no point asking about him.'

She cleared the plates away and busied herself at the sink while he sat in a shocked silence. Then he said, 'How did he die, Mum? Was it an accident?'

'He was sick. It happened a long time ago. Now don't ask me any more.'

He tried but it was no use. She had closed a door.

After that he found himself listening for clues. When she talked to customers in the shop, village acquaintances, she referred sometimes to Nova Scotia. He walked behind her conversations like a beachcomber but he picked up nothing of value.

It wasn't hard to work out that she must have already been pregnant when she moved back to Scotland. Since he was born six months after she took over the shop, it was reasonable to assume that he had been conceived in Canada. And now here he was, about to go to Nova Scotia himself for the first time, to cover Prince William's visit. Yet he would travel there and return and at the end of it all he would be none the wiser about his origins.

As a boy, the thought of Canada had always had an appeal. At primary school he had covered over the suspicious parental gap by making up a story that his father had been a fur-trapper and a lumberjack who'd been killed diving off Niagara Falls. In his child's mind, he created a heroic legend and although he knew it was a lie, it sustained him somehow, and prevented him dwelling on what he believed to be the truth.

He was his mother's guilty secret, unworthy and unwanted. He could see it in her relationship with him, how she could veer from moments of great affection to long periods of coldness when she would withdraw and have nothing to do with him. The past was why they lived where they did, hidden away in a town where no one knew anything of their history.

He had tried to make amends for the unsatisfactory nature of his existence, seeking her approbation for the things he was good at, like school football, but she had always been frugal with her praise. Yet he had never wanted for anything. When he got the A levels he needed for university, there was no question of his not going and she had paid for his four years in Edinburgh without a qualm.

It couldn't have been easy for her. He could never overlook that fact.

He wondered how he would find her today.

He turned back from the window, checked his watch, then took out his cellphone. He dialled his flat and followed it with the code number for his voicemail messages. There was only one but as soon as he heard it he wished he hadn't bothered. It was from Judith Sefton.

'Thought I might have caught you before you went wherever it is you've gone this morning. Obviously not. Or else you're not picking up. How many times do I have to call you? Or are there to be no more crumbs from the master's table?'

He had not seen her since that night a week ago. He had woken in her bed at six in the morning, got up and dressed quietly and then he and his hangover had crept away without disturbing her. She had tried to reach him several times subsequently but he had avoided her, thinking that if he was never available then she might take the hint. Unfortunately it looked as if that wasn't going to work.

He would have to face up to this and level with her, letting her know there was nothing for her to pursue here; that he wasn't interested. But she was a persistent woman and she would not take rejection well. That was becoming clear. Although trying to keep out of her way was only making matters worse. 'Hell hath no fury' and all that.

He'd been a fool to get involved. He didn't even like her. But there'd been no stopping him that night. He tried to think of the old saying, something to do with the things that you could never take back. He couldn't remember them all but the spoken word was one, the sped arrow another. You could add the male ejaculation to the list.

He would have to call her when he got back. Anyway, she had his damn award. The taxi driver had found it in the cab and brought it back to her house a couple of days later.

He settled back and dozed for a while but his sleep was interrupted once or twice by calls. One was from Ken Shaw's secretary, trying to arrange lunch at the Groucho. He wondered what that was about but if she knew she wasn't saying. Ken had been subdued since the night of the awards.

His picture on the front of the *Post* the morning after, bloody nose and all, hadn't done much to improve how the *Chronicle*'s management felt about him.

At around noon, the train reached Carlisle, at England's northern edge. His journey wasn't yet over but he would make the rest of it by road. He got off and went to the nearby Hertz office for a car he had already booked, then he drove out of town, stopping briefly at a service station for a sandwich and a bar of chocolate which he ate travelling along the A75, the road to Dumfries.

The moment he saw the sign that told him he was entering Scotland, a sense of anxiety grew in him. As if to emphasise the feeling, the brightness of the English morning had gone, replaced by sullen grey skies. By the time he got to Dumfries it was raining hard and he had his sidelights on.

Near the southern outskirts of the town stood an impressive house that had once been the home of a well-to-do Victorian family. Built of sandstone that was now dark and weathered, it sat in well-kept wooded grounds where rhododendrons waited to bloom. Rosebeds, pruned almost cruelly, lined the driveway.

The place had long since passed from private hands. For the past fifty years it had been owned by the local health authority and the elegant exterior and lovely gardens were a deception that concealed the pain within. This was a hospital for the mentally ill.

It was where they'd been keeping his mother since the night she tried to kill him.

Granger Newton was the new consultant, recently moved down from Dundee. Taggart had never met him before. It was one of the reasons he had come today.

Newton was a tall thin man with a slight stoop developed in childhood when his height had made him feel uncomfortable among his more diminutive peers. He was dark-suited and bony and might have looked sinister were it not for the genuine warmth of his smile and a vigorous handshake.

They talked in his office. Outside the rain had turned to hail that rattled on the latticed windows.

'Will you be in Scotland for long?'

'Back to London tomorrow. I'm driving over to Portpatrick after this to see the woman who's running the shop for my mother. I'll spend the night there.'

'In the flat?'

'No, I don't think so. It's been a while. There's a hotel. I'll stay there.'

'I understand,' Newton said, then clapped his hands as if summoning a servant. 'Well now, I should tell you that there's some better news. As I'm sure you know, your mother's been on a regime of anti-psychotic drugs since she's been here.'

'I was aware of that, yes.'

'Well, we've changed the medication slightly and I'm pleased to say that we're beginning to see some improved response.'

Taggart sat forward. 'That's fantastic. Great news. Does it mean . . . can I speak to her?'

Newton shook his head sadly. 'I'm afraid I can't take that risk just yet. Until we're on firmer ground, there's always the chance that she may still try to harm you – and quite possibly herself. Not to be ruled out. I hope you understand.'

Taggart nodded and sat back again. 'Yes, of course.'

'Since you and I haven't met until today and haven't had the opportunity to talk, I wouldn't mind spending a little time trying to explore a bit of the background.'

'Certainly. Whatever will help.'

'But, naturally, you can see your mother even if you can't talk to her.' He stood abruptly, as if the thought had just occurred to him. 'Under the usual conditions, needless to say. Would you like to do that first?'

His shoes creaked as he escorted Taggart down the hall and into an office with a smoked glass window through which they could watch without being seen. Silently, they looked in on a rest room. At a desk near the door, a nurse pored over paperwork while four people, two men and two women, sat in front of a television. It troubled Taggart to see that they were watching the Teletubbies.

'That's unlikely to return anyone to sanity, I would have thought.'

'Amazingly, some of our patients find it soothing,' Newton said.

The four people looked tired, worn out by whatever internal demons haunted them. Noreen Taggart was fifty-nine years old but she looked much more. She had once been auburn but now her hair was white and unkempt in what Taggart could only think of as a slightly mad way. She was thinner than the last time he'd seen her, Christmas Day, the first one he'd ever spent by himself. He had booked into the Turnberry Hotel for two nights and even though he'd been among a crowd of festive revellers he'd felt totally alone.

His mother sat on the edge of a chair, fidgeting with her fingers and staring at the television screen, but to him it appeared as if her eyes were fixed on something far beyond. He watched her until he felt guilty about doing so. Then he turned to Newton. 'Let's go back.'

In the office, tea had appeared and there were oatmeal biscuits on a plate. The two men sipped in silence for a while. Eventually Newton said, 'If you feel up to it, I'd like you to tell me about that night. Everything that happened.'

Taggart finished a morsel of biscuit. 'I'm sure it's well documented in the file.'

'But I haven't heard it from you.'

Taggart was silent for a while, then he said, 'I've been thinking a lot about it. It's more than just that night. To explain it, I would have to go back.'

Newton extended a welcoming palm. 'By all means. Whatever suits you.'

For the next ten minutes, Taggart found himself talking openly and easily about his early life, his childhood, and what it was like growing up with his mother in Portpatrick. Newton sat and listened without interruption. What Taggart told him was like a confession and it occurred to him that he was treating this man as if he were his own personal psychiatrist.

He came to more recent events. 'It was after I left home, first to go to university and then to work in Glasgow, that I began to see that she'd changed.'

'In what way?'

'She was becoming more introspective, more withdrawn. She always had the tendency to be like that from time to time but this was different somehow.'

'How did you respond?'

'I suppose I rationalised. I thought it was just the way she was. I didn't want to think of her behaviour as an illness. I realise I should have.'

Newton smiled. 'Twenty-twenty hindsight's a wonderful thing.'

'I just imagined that she saw me as something of an intrusion, now that she was living entirely on her own. So I sort of got used to it. But then, much more recently, there were further changes. She began to become hostile towards me. There was an anger I hadn't seen before. Either that, or she avoided me altogether. Do you know Portpatrick?'

'Been there once or twice. I know the Crown. The pub.'

'There's a cliff path at the end of the harbour. It starts at the steps by the old swimming pool and rambles along the edge of the golf course out towards a place called Dunskey, a big estate. She used to go for walks up there, in all weathers. It can get quite windy. Lonely. I worried about her safety.'

'So what did you do?'

'Spoke to her about it, of course, asked her what was wrong, but she more or less ignored me. Then I had a word with Molly Gray, who's worked in the shop alongside her for as long as I can remember. She's running it on her own now. It was hard getting Molly to talk at first, since she didn't want to be disloyal, which I understood, but eventually she admitted to being worried. It was the silences she said she couldn't understand. That and my mother's increasingly cool attitude to customers, especially those who'd been coming into the shop all their lives. People in the village were beginning to talk. Oh, they'd always talked about her, of course, but this was different. I tried the local GP, discreetly, asking his advice.'

'And how did he react?'

'I got the impression that he was suspicious of my motives. At any rate, he said there was nothing he could do unless my mother came to him herself. I didn't think there was much likelihood of being able to persuade her to do that. And then came that Saturday night.'

He paused for a second, preparing himself.

'Eight months ago. I hadn't been home for six weeks so to make up for that I insisted on taking her to dinner at Knockinaam Lodge along the coast. Do you know it?'

'Heard of it. Haven't been there.'

'We had a great meal which she ate and enjoyed and although it was one of those nights when I made most of the conversation she seemed fine, more relaxed than I'd seen her for a while. We came home to Portpatrick afterwards and then I left her in the flat – she was going to bed – and I walked along the seafront to the Crown to round the night off with a couple of whiskies. I stayed there about an hour and then went home.'

'What time was that?'

'Just after midnight. The flat was quiet and there was no sound from her room. I went to bed and then at about two a.m. I heard a floorboard creak. I woke up and there she was, standing with a kitchen knife in her hand. I didn't know what the hell was going on. I started to say something but she lunged at me with the damn thing. I moved out of the way pretty quickly, but not fast enough to escape entirely.'

He rubbed his left forearm. 'She caught me here. It needed a dozen stitches. But the sight of all the blood seemed to do something to her. She dropped the knife then and sort of collapsed. I wrapped my arm in a towel and called an ambulance, more because of her than the injury, to tell you the truth. As soon as they arrived and saw the set-up they rang the police.'

'But nothing ever came of it? I mean, no charges?'

'No. I managed to bluff my way. I said it had been a horrible accident, a misunderstanding. I said my mother was unwell, that she'd mistaken me for an intruder.'

'And they believed you?'

'Probably not but they didn't take the matter any further, not after I got the GP galvanised into action at last and he referred her for psychiatric examination.'

Newton tapped a finger on his chin. 'So then, why do you think she attacked you?'

Taggart looked at him. 'She said something. I didn't tell the police this. I haven't told anyone until now. She said . . . she said something like it was time to make me pay. Pay for what I'd done.'

'And what *had* you done?'

'No idea.'

'You can't think of anything that might have made her want to harm you?'

'Nothing at all. Apart from being born.'

The hail had stopped. Taggart could hear the trees groaning in the wind. He glanced at Newton. 'I'm sorry. I shouldn't have said that. It's unfair'

'No, it's not unfair if that's the way you feel. So you think that might be it?'

'God alone knows. But I always felt I was a burden she'd been left to carry. One that she didn't really want.'

Newton nodded his head for a few moments. 'How did she feel about your father?'

'She hated him.'

He spoke the words with such a certainty that he felt he had to explain.

'It's the way she tried to erase him so completely. I'm the only sign that he ever existed.'

Newton was giving him a look that said he was curious about something. 'Your mother would have been roughly your age when you were born?'

Taggart thought. 'Yes, that's about right.'

'You know, when we met today I wouldn't have recognised you. I mean in the sense that there isn't a great facial resemblance between you and her. You're darker.'

'Yes. I always assumed that I must look like my father.'

'You've never seen a photograph?'

'Never.'

Newton stared at him as if he were searching his face. 'You know, maybe you do look like him. Maybe you look very like him indeed – or at least the way she remembers him.'

6

The Late Watch was on a windy corner of Cornwallis Street, up the hill from police headquarters. It was a watering hole for cops, run by an ex-cop, and around its walls there were photographs of cops, both in and out of uniform. Behind the bar, bowling trophies stood on a mirrored shelf and there was a display of souvenir pennants left by teams from visiting police departments.

Casey Plante hobbled around, cleaning glasses, refilling others. He was a former member of the Halifax force but a bullet fired by a bank robber trying unsuccessfully to make a getaway had left him with a hip injury that restricted movement in one leg and had put paid to his career. He had gone into part-ownership of the Late Watch ten years ago, courtesy of the compensation he had received from the city. Not long after the place had opened, someone had drawn a caricature of him. In pride of place behind the bar, it showed him in a waiter's apron and a police cap. In one hand he held a tray with two giant glasses of beer and in the other he had a gun. Written above was the pledge – To Serve And Protect.

Cop's joke.

Not all of the people who frequented the Late Watch were in the police department. The bar drew a mixed crowd, including some patrons on the fringes of respectability, who got off on hanging out where the cops did and occasionally had bits and pieces of information to pass on. There were lawyers sometimes, too. The cops reckoned they looked shiftier than the snitches.

It was early evening, not yet seven.

'And again, Casey, please,' Walter Flagg said. He was sitting on a tall stool at one of the high-top tables along with a couple of off-duty technical unit guys. They were hooked into a game of Trivia. Electronic keypads sat in front of them and their eyes were fixed on a monitor above the bar.

Casey came out from behind the counter and refilled their glasses. Like a lot of men in Nova Scotia, Flagg and his friends were rum drinkers.

'Well, if you're going to ignore me, I'm going home,' Annie said. 'You're the one who twisted my arm to come in here, remember.'

'And whatever my friend's having.'

Casey looked at her and at the half glass of Moosehead she was holding but she shook her head and he moved off.

She was at a table in the corner. Flagg had thrown his overcoat beside her. It smelled cold and musty and she wondered when it had last been dry-cleaned, if ever. Sitting up there on the stool, he looked like a giant from a fairytale. He was six foot two and she could see that about twenty years ago he would have been handsome in a haphazard kind of way but his looks had soured and sagged with time. So had his build. Everything had gone south.

She looked at the screen where the game was being played. Each competitor had his own 'tag'. Flagg had logged on as Anvil. Claussen had asked him about it once, in here one night, and he had explained that his grandfather had been a blacksmith. It was a nickname they'd given him in the army, before he became a cop.

The mention of a blacksmith had sparked a conversation about other skills that were little-needed these days. Lamplighter was one, so was washboard manufacturer and Annie had wondered whatever happened to the typewriter repairmen who used to come into the office with their little briefcases full of oils and sprays in the days before computers.

'Need a bit of help here,' Flagg said.

His opponents didn't bother to protest. He wasn't scoring well tonight and Annie's assistance wasn't going to make any difference.

'Hit me.'

'Who won the best actress Oscar for her role in *Fargo*?'

The questions were multiple choice. You pressed A, B, C or D on the keypad to give your answer.

'C,' Annie said. 'Frances McDormand.'

'Who?'

'She played the part of a cop freezing her ass off in North Dakota. I kind of know how she felt.'

Flagg registered his answer. The game finished. Getting Frances McDormand didn't prevent him having the lowest score. Casey switched the monitor back to TV. One of the tech guys was smiling and had his palm open. Muttering, Flagg handed him a ten dollar bill, then he levered himself off the stool and took his drink over to Annie.

'Gambling's not allowed in here,' she told him.

'I know. A cop might come in and catch us.' He thought for a second. 'Yeah, I saw that movie, come to think of it. Guy got shoved in the wood-chipper, right?'

'That's the one.'

'I remember. You know, we should take in a movie some night, the two of us.'

'You asking me on a date?'

'Oh, sure. In my dreams.'

She laughed. As she watched, his words dawned on him and his face reddened. 'Jeez, no, I didn't mean . . .' He rubbed his hand through his hair. 'Christ, Annie, I—'

'Take it easy, Walter. It's okay.' She was still laughing. 'So what would we see? Are you an Eastwood man?'

He took some of his drink. 'Not any more. You seen some of his stuff lately? The way he casts himself with those younger women? *True Crime* – you see that one?'

She shook her head.

'Disgusting sight. Christ, I've got a better body than he has.' He pulled his stomach in and patted it.

She raised a doubting eyebrow. 'You think so? Put it this way – you should have. You're about twenty years younger than he is. Anyway, I bet if you were a big star his age, you'd do the same.'

'Yeah.' He smiled a faraway smile. 'Rene Russo.'

Casey called to them. 'Hey, look who's on TV.'

They turned and stared at a face they both knew. Claussen was standing outside the Law Courts with microphones being thrust at him. Casey turned the sound up.

'Crime like this can't be tolerated and we're very pleased with the outcome. But of course investigations are always a team effort. No one person can take the credit.'

'But you're going to try anyway, you asshole,' Flagg said.

The Scotia Nostra case had come to an end. As the prosecutor had guessed, the accused men had changed their plea to guilty once the jury had begun to hear the evidence. The verdicts were in now and the judge had just handed out the expected sentences, fifteen years apiece.

After being rejected as a witness, Annie hadn't gone near the courthouse again. She always felt detached from a file once she'd completed her work and it had become a matter for the Crown but she did not feel detached now, watching Claussen.

As the camera position changed, she spotted a tall, striking black woman standing in the background. Nina Henry was the department's director of public affairs but in the office they reckoned she was more than that. People called her the real deputy chief. Henry liked to get their people on TV when there was a positive story to tell. Claussen made a good interviewee. He looked smart, he sounded professional. He had ambitions, too, and this would do them no harm.

'Shit,' Flagg said. 'That was your case as much as his. Why aren't they interviewing you?'

'Because I wasn't there, Walter, was I?'

She was starting to sound bitter but she couldn't help it. The item ended with a reporter stand-up and then the bulletin moved on to something else. Annie finished her beer and gestured towards Flagg's glass.

'Another?'

'Only if you're having one.'

She shook her head. 'No, I'm tired. I'm going home.'

'Then it's okay. I'll sit here for a while, nurse this one.'

She stood and started putting her coat on.

He looked at her. 'You know, maybe I should have a quiet word with Claussen one of these days. Just him and me. Man to man. See if I can change his attitude about a couple of things.'

'And what would be the point of that?'

He shrugged. 'I dunno. I might enjoy it.'

'Look, Walter, I'd leave it if I were you. Claussen – I can handle him. Do me a favour and keep out of it.'

'Just an idea, that's all.'

'Yeah, well, not the best one you ever had.'

They said good night. Outside, she pulled her hat well

down and buttoned up her coat against the chill. Snow was falling lightly. By Nova Scotia standards it had been a relatively mild winter so far but people who lived in the Maritimes never let themselves be deceived. Just when you thought it was over, it could return with a vengeance. Blizzards in April were not unknown and this was only the beginning of February. She wondered how much snow there would be for Terry and the boys when they got to the Italian Alps. She had their flight and hotel details now, all written out and secured under a magnet on the door of her fridge.

She did not take the highway home but rumbled across the McKay bridge because she always enjoyed the night-time view. Below her spread a pattern of light: the curving Bedford shoreline like a discarded necklace, Halifax and Dartmouth gleaming proudly at each other across the harbour. At the far side of the bridge, she threw her seventy five cents into the tollbooth basket, then made the sweep away from Dartmouth, along Burnside and down towards Bedford.

The Sunnyside mall was open late so she stopped there. Pete's Frootique sold fruit and vegetables of every conceivable kind and colour but she avoided the more exotic varieties tonight and restricted her choice to onions and vine tomatoes, broccoli and oranges and a bulb of garlic. Then she headed for Sobey's at Mill Cove and filled a small trolley with basics, including milk and bread and pasta. To round off, she went into the Liquor Commission next door and bought a couple of bottles of Australian chardonnay and a six-pack of Keith's.

Once home, she put tagliatelle on to boil, chopped up the tomatoes, onion and garlic and heated them slowly in some olive oil.

When she'd been married, cooking had always been her

thinking time. Now that she was alone, all of her time was. More and more she found herself not just thinking but brooding. Claussen's face was in her mind now. He had looked so assured on the news, a man going places, while she was now partnered with Walter, who was going nowhere at all. Maybe she was going there with him. Maybe agreeing to be teamed with him had been a mistake. She hoped he wouldn't do something stupid. She didn't need a protector.

In the living room she turned the CD player on. Diana Krall began to sing, her voice like Scotch and cigarette smoke. She poured herself a glass of wine.

A phrase on the piano reminded her of her father. It was like the sort of thing he would have played. She sat with her drink and thought about him. He had died seven years ago. For most of his life he had worked in a lowly management position at the old Port Authority but in his spare time he had been a well-respected musician, leading a piano trio that was popular in some of the local night spots. He had even made an LP for a record company in Toronto but he'd had no ambition to take things any further than that.

Her thoughts turned to her husband. Ex-husband. Terry didn't like jazz. In fact, he didn't have much time for music of any kind. That was another thing they didn't have in common. It seemed as if every day she found more and more evidence of their incompatibility.

Yet it hadn't always been that way.

There was a picture of Peter and James on the wall. She had taken it herself, last summer up in Cape Breton, and was so pleased with the way it had turned out that she'd had it enlarged and framed. She had given Terry a copy, too, but she didn't know what he had done with it.

In the almost identical faces of the two boys she could

see the shadows of Terry and herself, the man and the woman who had created them. There had been happiness once. She refilled her glass and went to the kitchen to check the food, thinking that there was damn little of it now.

'The vultures are circling over me,' Ken Shaw muttered.

He was in one of his 'black dog' moods. They alternated with the days when he was all fired up, full of energy and ideas. He and Taggart were in the bar of the Groucho. Taggart still didn't know what he wanted. Maybe he just needed someone to talk to.

'Surely not,' he said, although he knew Shaw was right. The rumours were getting stronger.

Shaw sipped his gin and tonic. Taggart had a glass of champagne. The Groucho was its usual untidy self, chairs and tables all over the place, newspapers strewn around, most of them open at the review sections. A well-known television personality came in. Taggart saw him inspecting himself in the big mirror behind the bar but no one else paid any attention.

A waiter came and told them their table was ready. He put their drinks on a tray and they followed him upstairs. The dining room had interesting paintings and a glass-domed roof on which the rain was thudding silently. Their table was by the wall. At the one next to it four men were worrying about funding for a television drama they wanted to make.

Menus appeared and Shaw ordered wine.

'I'm making a few changes, having a go at some new things,' he said, keeping his voice low. The acoustics of the room carried everything. 'We're boring. Fucking boring. Don't you think?'

Taggart buttered a slice of onion-flavoured bread. 'There's always room for improvement, yes.'

'Too right. We're getting stale.'

Taggart thought that Shaw must be the last person to notice. It occurred to him again that it might be time to move on.

A waiter came and took their order. They both chose roast duckling with puy lentils. When he'd gone they talked for a bit about things the paper might try. Out of the blue Shaw said, 'I want you to go to New York for a while.'

'New York?' So that was it.

'For a few weeks. Before you go on this Canadian thing. Write some stuff about all the famous Brits living there. For a start, there's two London plays running on Broadway at the moment. Big hits. We'll use lots of pictures.'

Taggart sipped his drink and made a face as if it tasted bitter. 'I don't know, Ken. The thought of New York's attractive naturally but it's a bit showbizzy this, isn't it? All a bit *Hello*. Hardly cutting edge journalism, wouldn't you say?'

Shaw shot him a look. 'What? And you think the stuff you do now is?'

The waiter came with their meals and warned that the plates were hot. Across the room a blonde woman with a sleeveless dress that showed off her unseasonably brown arms was telling a sheepish young man that he should not have turned down an offer to appear in an ice-cream commercial without consulting her.

'Thanks, Ken,' Taggart grunted, picking up his fork. 'Thanks for the compliment.'

Shaw laughed, as if he were enjoying his star columnist's discomfort. It seemed to help his mood.

'Come on, John, you know this stuff you write is shit. It's popular shit but it's still shit, wouldn't you say? But that's fine, that's what people want so let's give them some more of the old Taggart magic, only this time in New York. Now drink up and don't be so fucking touchy.' He grabbed the wine bottle and poured them both a generous glass.

Taggart felt hurt. He couldn't help it. He said, 'If it's shit, then it's shit that wins awards.'

Shaw laughed again. 'Jesus, John, you're not starting to believe your own publicity now, are you?' He leaned forward. 'Look, son, don't take offence, it's not just you, it's all crap, the whole fucking thing. Journalism in this country died thirty years ago when Murdoch came on the scene. We don't produce newspapers now – they're all fucking comics. But there's no point in complaining about it. That's the way it is and we've just got to get on with it. What fucking choice do we have?'

After they'd eaten, they went back to the bar for coffee, Taggart subdued and still bruised by his editor's home truths. Shaw ordered a brandy but Taggart declined. He excused himself and headed for the cloakrooms which were situated near the club entrance, at the bottom of a set of narrow stairs.

As he was coming back up, he met a woman on her way down.

'Well, look who it is. The elusive Mr Taggart.'

Judith Sefton was soaked. She had been caught in the rain without a coat and she was not in a good mood. Taggart knew that seeing him would not improve it.

There was no escape. Just at that moment he wished more than anything that he had phoned her.

'Judith, look – I should have called. I meant to talk to you—'

'Forget it.' She pushed past him. 'Oh and by the way, if you're looking for your crappy award, you might try the Camden council refuse collection service. I threw it in the bin.'

'You what?'

'You heard. I don't like being fucked around. Maybe you'll remember that in future.'

She gave him a last poisonous look, then opened the door of the ladies' room and went inside.

He stood staring at the closed door for a moment before he turned and went back upstairs. He felt furious, partly with her, but mostly he was angry with himself for being foolish enough to make such a bad enemy.

He thought of New York. Maybe getting out of town for a while wasn't such a crazy idea.

7

On a sub-zero Thursday morning two weeks after that, Cobb Landry shuffled along the sheltered cloister on Lower Water Street, past Leo the hairdresser and the factory clothing store, towards Perks, the coffee shop.

It was almost time.

He bought a *Globe and Mail* at the news-stand and went in the side door. Perks was on a corner, with views in two directions, and Landry found a window table where he could see everything. He got a mug of regular coffee and ignored the sticky chocolate confections and the blueberry muffins. Not that they were going to do him any harm, not now; it was just that his appetite was poor these days.

When he sat down and took his hat off there were one or two glances but he was used to that. The chemo had erased the hair from his head as if it had never been there. On the phone he had told the man that was how he would recognise him.

He opened the paper and folded it at the world news page but his mind was not on any of the stories it contained. Yesterday he had finally found the courage to call. He had dialled the man's number and without giving his name told him he had information which would be useful. Figuring the guy might hang up, thinking Landry was just some sort of crank if that was all he said, he had added something to catch his interest.

It had worked. Now they were about to meet.

Landry looked around. Three girls sat at one table, two men at another. The men had briefcases, the girls little rucksacks, the handbag for the modern woman. He could see into the kitchen where a fat man with a T-shirt like a second skin was rolling pizza dough. Perks was open twenty four hours a day. People dropped in while waiting for a ferry or a bus but the place gave the illusion of catering for world travellers. Five big clocks told the time in Vancouver, New York, London, Vienna and here in Halifax where it was almost eleven a.m.

Landry waited.

From inside a shop opposite, a man in a short padded coat and a trapper's cap watched him while appearing to study the crystal glassware displayed next to the window. He picked up a chunky vase and checked that no one was looking before he peeled the price tag off the bottom.

'Can I help you with anything?' The assistant was a young woman with hair like wheat stubble and a silver ring hooked into the top of her right ear.

He held out the vase. 'Is there a price for this?'

'There ought to be.' She took it from him and turned it upside down. 'No. Let me go check.'

'Thanks.'

When she had gone, his glance returned to the coffee shop. He tried to take the measure of the man who was waiting for him.

The girl came back. 'Eighty-five dollars.'

'Mmm. I'm not sure. I'll think about it. Maybe I can just look around for a while?'

'Sure. Go ahead.'

He gave the place another couple of minutes, just a reasonable length of time to spend browsing without making her suspicious, then he thanked her and left. The shop bell dinged as he went out.

He crossed the road and headed left along Lower Water Street until he found a doorway where he stood, hugging himself against the cold, watching. He was further away from the coffee shop but he could still see the bald head and the way the man looked up whenever anyone walked in.

He waited.

At eleven forty, declining a second refill, Cobb Landry got up from his table, put his hat on and buttoned his coat. He had hung around long enough. The guy wasn't coming.

He felt odd about that, a mixture of disappointment and relief, and he wasn't sure what to do next. Should he call him again?

Outside, he stood and looked around for a moment but among the passers-by he did not see the person he had come to meet. He walked along the street towards the parking lot where he had left his car, a red Mitsubishi compact. On the way home he would think about his next move. Or whether there would be one.

An hour after Landry's departure from Perks, George Poyner stood at his office window with a piece of paper in his hand, watching the man who had just given it to him cross the road and walk down the street past Sam The Record Man's shop.

Poyner was a private detective with the build and suspicious eyes of an ex-cop, which he was, and the complexion of an enthusiastic drinker, which he also was. His was not one of Halifax's better-known investigative agencies. His premises were modest, just enough room for him and his secretary and their filing cabinets and computers, but he had a good downtown address, on the second floor of a building on Barrington Street, not far from the junction with Spring Garden Road, and he wasn't complaining.

Most of his activity was corporate stuff on behalf of insurance companies and law firms but every now and then he took a little bit of domestic business, often involving tracing people who did not want to be found; errant husbands or wives. It was this kind of investigation most of all that reminded him of his days on the force.

The work was steady. He had more money now than he had ever had and there was the police retirement pension in the bank every month, come rain or come shine. Plus the woman he lived with had her own professional interests, a couple of hairdressing salons located in two of the big shopping malls. And as if that wasn't plenty to be going on with, there was the other money, most of it invested, but part of which had helped him buy the nice house by the water in Bedford. He sometimes smiled with satisfaction when he thought of how he had come by his good fortune.

The man was gone from view now and Poyner's attention returned to the piece of paper. A licence plate number was written on it. What he had been asked to do was easy, a run-of-the-mill job for him, but what was behind it was intriguing. He thought about the things the man had just told him then he picked up the phone and began to punch in a familiar number. This was a client he needed to know more about.

A fifteen-year-old boy had been stabbed over at Sullivan's Ponds in Dartmouth. He had just recovered consciousness in hospital after an operation to save his life and Annie and Flagg wanted to try to talk to him. They had their coats on and had just told Birgit, the office assistant, where they were going.

Birgit's parents came from Sweden and she had fine blonde hair that was almost silver. Deedes was crazy about the girl. Annie saw it in his face every time he looked at her, although Birgit didn't seem to notice.

Mark Gamble came out of his office. He was in his early forties with big square glasses that were like windows. He looked worried although no more than usual.

'Where are you headed?'

They told him their plans.

'Can you take this on your own?' he asked Flagg.

'Sure. What's up?'

'Head of Operations is giving some people a briefing.' He nodded to Annie. 'You're one of them.'

'A briefing? What about?' Annie asked.

'I think we'll leave that to him.'

'So when's this happening?'

'Right now. Better get yourself downstairs.'

She knew that meant the watch room. It was a windowless place on the ground floor where the shift teams did a hand-over and brought each other up to date but it was also used for other operational meetings and occasional briefings.

'Why don't I just wait here for you?' Flagg said. 'There's no rush with this thing.'

Annie went downstairs. As she walked in, she glanced at the marker board that listed current incidents and the officers working on them. The Dartmouth stabbing had the initials WF and AW alongside. Rows of desks made the place look like a classroom. Two other officers from her unit were already there, plus three from general investigations, all waiting in a sullen silence, none of them wanting to admit they didn't know what any of this was about. Annie took a desk in the second row. She was still in her overcoat and she felt like she was being kept in after school.

The door opened and Oliver Gryce, the Head of Operations, entered. He was about forty, ranked a Superintendent, and he was just three heartbeats away from the office of Chief. Four, if you counted Nina Henry.

Although he ran Operations, Gryce was not a sleeves-rolled-up kind of cop, not normally. He was one of the new breed, a manager, and more at home in the bar of the Royal Nova Scotia Yacht Squadron than up the street in the Late Watch. He had been in the old Dartmouth force originally, working in administrative support, before being selected for a management training scheme which had fast-tracked him to his current position of eminence in the new structure. His skills were in business planning, controlling budgets, achieving savings targets. Annie had never actually known him to become involved in an operational matter yet in the past two weeks he had been more in evidence around the office on account of the absence of Staff Sergeant Dean Wilson, who headed CIS.

Gryce ran Wilson, while Wilson ran Gamble and the heads of the other CIS units. That was the way it worked. Now Wilson was ill and while he was out, Gryce was doing the job himself, probably trying to prove something, Annie thought.

With him now was a dark-haired man about her own age with darting eyes that searched the room. He was from the RCMP and his name was Larry Steyn. She had worked on an investigation with him once and they had not exactly hit it off. He had been promoted a couple of times since then. He was now a staff sergeant involved in special operations.

Gryce introduced him. Steyn gave the room a curt nod and a once-over. He spotted Annie. She nodded back and gave him a smile she didn't mean.

'Thank you all for coming,' Gryce said, as if they'd had a choice. 'The reason for this rather impromptu gathering is that I want to inform you of the fact that we're about to embark on a significant joint forces operation with our friends in the RCMP. It's something for which you have been individually selected.'

JFOs were a regular feature of Canadian law enforcement, where you had federal and local police involved in the same territory. To avoid getting in each other's way, they often worked together. Sometimes that made a difference, sometimes it didn't. It depended on the case and who was running the show. She looked at Steyn's expressionless face. The signs were not good.

'At this stage,' Gryce continued, 'I'm afraid I can tell you very little other than that. But I want you to be prepared to start work on this thing at a moment's notice. Please make sure your desks are cleared and that you don't get tied up with anything that can't wait or that your senior officer can't pass on to someone else. The RCMP will have primacy in this matter and the operation will be under Staff Sergeant Steyn's command. We've been asked, and have agreed, to provide our expertise and assistance, which is where you come in.'

Annie groaned inwardly. What he meant was that they would be doing the donkey work on this, whatever it was, the shit the Mounties didn't want.

Gryce turned to Steyn. 'Would you like to add anything?'

'At this time, no, other than to emphasise how extremely crucial it is that we preserve confidentiality here.'

No sweat, since you haven't actually told us anything, Annie thought, yet the fact that Gryce himself had come down here to give them this peculiar little pep talk spoke volumes. Something big was in the air.

Gryce smiled at them. 'I'm sorry I can't ask you if you have any questions because right now we can't give you any answers. Once again I apologise if this is a bit of a mystery but I need you to be alert and ready when the time comes.'

They broke up shortly after that, filing out of the room and exchanging shrugs and puzzled glances. Gryce and Steyn were talking in the corridor. Steyn was buttoning up his coat and putting on his gloves. When he saw her he turned his back.

'Excuse me,' she said as she brushed past them.

Upstairs in the office Flagg was at his desk with a mug of coffee.

'That didn't take long. So what was it all about?'

'Search me. Your guess is as good as mine. But I have a feeling it's going to mean trouble.'

8

That evening, while his wife Edith got things ready in the kitchen, Harry Orbach sat in the living room of his home in Dartmouth watching basketball on TV. It was yesterday's game, the one he'd forgotten about and thought he had missed until Cobb across the street had come to the door this morning with a video cassette.

'I saw you going out last night,' he had said, 'so I taped this for you just in case.'

That was Cobb Landry for you: always reliable, a good friend.

For example, look at the way he'd helped with the deck. Harry was fifty-seven, a sales representative for a timber company, but his experience of selling wood did not extend to being any good at working with it. The new deck he had started in the summer sat half-finished and abandoned at the back of the house under a layer of frozen snow. Most of it had been constructed by Cobb who had come over to lend a hand one day and had more or less taken over the project. But gradually the more strenuous parts of the job had got to be too much for him and when winter arrived the thing had gone on hold.

Harry frowned. He wondered if Cobb would be around in the spring to help finish up, whether he would be with them when they had their first barbecue out there. He shook his head to clear the thought away and looked at his watch.

Cobb was coming for dinner, as he often did. He lived alone and Edith liked to make sure he ate properly.

Seven-thirty. He should have been here half an hour ago.

Harry looked out the front window into the quiet residential avenue. He and Edith had moved to this house two years ago because it was smaller and more manageable than their previous one. Now that the last of their three children had flown the nest they did not need so much space.

There were lights in Cobb's house and his car was there, parked in the driveway. Harry took his glasses off and paused the VCR, then went into the kitchen. Edith had the oven door open, checking the roast chicken. The skin was brown and crispy, the way he liked it, even though his doctor had told him it was something to avoid.

His wife stood up, her cheeks and neck flushed.

'He didn't say he'd be late?' Harry asked.

She shook her head. 'No.'

'Maybe I'll give him a call.'

They looked at each other.

'Just to check,' he said and lifted the phone. The number rang half a dozen times and then the machine kicked in. He hung up without leaving a message.

'No answer?' Edith said.

He shook his head. They stood in silence, each wondering privately if this might be the moment they had always worried about but never spoken of.

'I'll pop over there,' Harry said. 'Make sure he's okay.'

'Good idea. Take a coat.'

He didn't have to be told. He took a cap as well, and his gloves, and went out into the bitingly cold night, hurrying down his driveway because he didn't want to be out here any longer than he needed to. He went across the road and round the side of the house to the kitchen door. He gave a sharp rap on the glass before he walked in.

'Hey, Cobb,' he called. 'What's happening, buddy? Your dinner's going to be cold.'

There was no one in the kitchen but from the sitting room at the front he could hear the TV on loud.

He went along the hall and pushed the door open. 'Hey, Cobb, what's—'

Landry was on his back on the floor, his neck twisted awkwardly and his smooth head shining in the light from the TV where an episode of Seinfeld was in progress.

A man was crouching beside him.

He had his back to the door but when Harry opened it he turned with a look that Orbach would describe later as wild-eyed. The man was thin-featured, a few years older than Harry was. They stared at each other, frozen in place for a second until Harry gasped, 'Oh my God, what have you done?'

His words were like a signal. The man straightened up and lunged forward. Harry lurched back in fright and fell over a chair. But it was the door the man was going for, not him, and he was through it and away in a flash. Harry struggled to his feet, looked quickly at Cobb Landry's dead eyes, then ran after the intruder.

He was getting into a dark car parked a few doors down. It looked like a Dodge.

'Hey,' Harry called to the night, 'Stop that guy! He's killed Cobb!'

His voice echoed in the empty street, then the car screeched away without lights and without Harry getting its number. He would have needed his glasses for that and they were beside the VCR where he had set them. He ran back into the house and from the phone in the kitchen he dialled 911 and asked for police and an ambulance but when he returned to the front room, he knew that medical help wouldn't be necessary. Cobb hadn't moved. His eyes were open and staring.

Seinfeld was trying to persuade George to call some woman. Harry leaned across the body and turned the TV off.

Shore Drive curved along the edge of Bedford Bay, which was a secluded and pretty corner of the Bedford Basin. The houses were big and expensive, sheltered among their own trees, with views right across the water towards the lights of Halifax. It was an enviable place in which to live and it took money to do so.

American film crews sometimes came here to shoot movies, pretending it was Long Island or New England. At around ten that night Dick Vogel was trying to remember the name of the one John Hurt had been in not so long ago. It would come to him eventually.

Vogel was an architect who had designed his own much-admired house near where Shore Drive ended in a little peninsula. Right now he was out walking his red setter, striding down the steep hill from his home. The night was quiet with only the distant hum of the traffic on the highway and the sound of his feet on the gravel.

There was a sharp crack.

It halted him in his tracks because it sounded a bit like a gunshot or, at least, what he imagined a gunshot must sound like. He waited, trying to work out where it had come from, but he heard nothing else. The dog looked at him, questioning why they had stopped.

He walked on. A car appeared round a bend, coming towards him. He could see it slowing at each mailbox the way people did when they were looking for a number, then it turned into a driveway and disappeared among the trees. Moments later he heard its doors slamming. He knew the house it had gone to, a big old place on the edge of the water.

He had gone about a hundred yards when he heard more shots, several of them in quick succession. He was certain now that that's what they were. As he looked into the darkness, there was the unmistakable sound of glass breaking. A lot of it. Like it was someone's window being smashed. The dog began barking.

Vogel took his cellphone from his pocket. He thought for a second, then assured himself that he was right about this. He hit 911.

A car started. It rumbled out of the driveway into which he'd seen it disappear, then it came racing along the road in his direction. For a second he thought it was going to hit him or the dog, then it was past and away, leaving black spots in his eyes from its blinding headlights.

Now there was the sound of another car. He grabbed the dog and got off the road but the car disappeared in a different direction, down one of the avenues which joined Shore Drive like little tributaries.

For a few moments, silence returned to the darkness. Then doors began opening and people with torches emerged from their homes. The dog started barking again and on the phone, a woman was asking him what kind of help he wanted.

Deedes and his partner Neidermayer got the call.

Inside the house, they found a man's body with two gunshot wounds to the chest. Furniture was overturned and there was blood everywhere. The glass from what used to be a big living-room window, installed many years ago before these things were reinforced, glinted in the snow covering the front lawn.

ID in a wallet told them the dead man's name was George Poyner, that he was a private investigator in Halifax and that this was his house.

'Business must be good,' Neidermayer remarked, admiring the surroundings.

'Not any more,' Deedes said, looking at the body sprawled on the floor.

The bullets which had killed Poyner weren't the only ones that had been fired. The crime scene technicians, padding around in their sterile white overalls, found several more embedded in the walls and scattered around the floor they found the shell casings from two separate weapons. It all matched with what the passer-by, Mr Vogel, said he'd heard.

'Christ, this is the fucking OK Corral here,' Deedes said.

Within an hour of the shooting, Shore Drive looked like it had been turned into a film set again, with lights and screens and TV vans and police vehicles. Deedes and Neidermayer knew it was going to be a long night. But in the morning the murder of George Poyner and the killing of Cobb Landry a few hours before it would be small time stuff compared to what was happening somewhere else.

Sixty miles south, near the town of Lunenburg, a massive stone-built house stood on a hill, hidden from the road by pine trees and by the huge wall that protected its seventeen acres of grounds. But if the house could not be seen from the road, it could be seen clearly from the sea, poised at the head of an open slope that ran to the ocean's edge where a private dock jutted out into the water.

Three cars and a big black command wagon sat waiting in darkness near the huge electronically controlled gates and just out of range of the security cameras mounted on them. Meanwhile, on the water, two boats, long and sleek and using no lights, had cut their engines and were drifting slowly towards the shore.

When the boats reached the jetty, armed men in combat clothing with the letters RCMP on their backs stepped hurriedly ashore, then fanned out silently and began to run up the hillside. There were infra-red security beams, they knew that, but the direction of them was altered every day and they had no way of shutting them off. So they were relying on speed and surprise and superior manpower.

But they hit the first beam sooner than they'd anticipated. The moment they did, alarms began, a shrieking banshee chorus that echoed across the water. Lights flooded the grounds, turning the night into dazzling day, and men armed with Steyr sub-machine pistols came running out of the house.

One of the raiders had a loudhailer. He called to them, 'This is the RCMP! Drop your weapons and stand where you are!'

With the noise of the alarms it was hard to hear. There was a second of uncertainty and then the men from the house started firing.

As the Steyrs began crackling, the RCMP team took cover and returned fire with assault rifles. Two of the guards went down, one of them with half his head blown off, the other with a kneecap shattered. When they saw this, the rest of them dropped their weapons and raised their hands. The shooting stopped. It had lasted ten seconds.

An RCMP medic ran forward to assist the injured man. Where his companion lay, blood, brain and bone were spattered on the brickwork of the elegant terrace.

They herded the other guards inside. Someone hit the switch for the gates and the waiting cars swept up the drive. Men in overcoats but with body armour underneath leaped out and ran into the house.

In the hallway, with its priceless paintings and precious antiques, they saw the man they had come for. And they saw that he was not alone. There was another man there and it was his presence that stopped them short.

One of the officers spoke into a handset.

'There's a problem,' he said. 'You won't believe who's with him.'

Mahone Bay was just ten minutes from Lunenburg, an hour away from Halifax. It was a tiny town, postcard-perfect, with beautiful sunrises and three lovely old churches that stood side by side to take the early morning light.

At eight o'clock the next morning, the town's only pharmacist unlocked the front door of his premises and immediately knew that something wasn't right. He went in quickly and saw that the back door was open. It had been smashed in, probably with a kick, and the wires to the burglar alarm had been cut.

He hurried to the cash register. The money was still there from last night. He counted it. It had not been touched.

He stood in the centre of the room, scratching his head. It all seemed just the way he had left it.

9

The sound of the phone shocked Taggart from sleep.

He sat up in his hotel bed, leaden-limbed. He had been in New York for all of one day and the jet lag felt like a virus. He looked at the clock. *Six a.m.?* Jesus.

He grunted a hello.

'John? You awake?'

It was Ken Shaw in London.

'Not yet.'

Down the phone came the sound of people laughing.

'I've got you on the speaker. We're in the middle of the editorial conference here. Have you heard the news this morning?'

'Give me a break, Ken. Do you know what time it is?'

'Indeed I do. Time to get moving, my boy. Now listen. We've got a story for you. You wanted hard edge? Now here's your chance. Remember the American embassy in Karachi?'

Of course he remembered. Everybody did. A year ago, thirty-eight people had died, most of them US personnel, when shells containing poison gas were fired into the embassy compound.

'What about it?'

'All right,' Shaw continued. 'Now if you remember, the State Department offered a five million dollar reward for information. Well, it seems that as a result of that, they've now got hard evidence that the chemicals used to make the gas were specially provided by one of the many companies owned by a guy called A.J. Carne. Ever heard of him?'

'Can't say I have.'

'It's not his original name. He probably anglicised it from Khan. His father was from Pakistan but his mother was white. Canadian. He's a mega-millionaire but not the showy type. Very private guy, paranoid about security, keeps a lot of bodyguards. He owns several homes around the world, all the usual rich people's places, plus a property near Lunenburg in Nova Scotia.'

'Lunenburg?'

'Thought that would interest you. Yes, Lunenburg – which Prince William is due to visit and which is where Carne was last night. Now get a load of this. At about ten o'clock special squads of the RCMP, acting on behalf of the FBI and the American State Department, raided the place. The idea was to arrest him and hold him for extradition to the United States. The Americans are trying to rustle up a murder charge against him for supplying the chemicals. Anyway, the whole thing turned into a bloody mess. Carne's men opened fire and the Mounties fired back and killed one of them. And then when they get into the house, they find that Carne has been entertaining a friend of his called Fergus Morton.'

He paused.

'Should that mean something to me?' Taggart asked.

'Fergus Morton has just been sworn in as the new Lieutenant Governor of Nova Scotia. The Queen's representative, no less, the man who'll be welcoming Prince William in a few weeks' time. And now here he is associating with a wanted terrorist suspect.'

Taggart got out of bed. He turned the TV on and found a channel showing news. Heavily muffled against the cold, a reporter was doing a stand-up in the dark with the aid of a camera light. The indent on the screen said: *LIVE –*

Lunenburg, NS. There were cut-away shots of police vehicles and men with the letters 'RCMP' on the backs of their parkas.

'It gets worse,' Shaw said, 'or better, which is how I look at it. Carne is a Canadian citizen and although there's an extradition treaty between the US and Canada it can fall down in murder cases when there's a risk of someone being shipped off to a state which has the death penalty. In this instance, attempts are being made to have the case tried in Colorado, which is where some of the victims came from.'

'And where they execute people?'

'Correct,' Shaw said. 'It's a hell of a political minefield. All sorts of international ramifications. Great story, though. At the moment, Carne's being held under house arrest while his lawyers go to war with the Nova Scotia Attorney General. Plus he's got doctors popping out of the woodwork. Seems he's got a history of heart problems. On top of that, politicians all over the country are weighing in, civil rights groups of various kinds, too, all shouting about the Mounties being the FBI's lackeys, erosion of Canadian sovereignty, that kind of thing. And this is the calm, placid atmosphere into which Prince William is going to sail innocently. So what do you think?'

'Well, for a start, I think I'd better get dressed.'

At six thirty a.m., Annie and her hand-picked colleagues were each called at home and summoned to another meeting with Larry Steyn, this time at the RCMP headquarters. By seven fifteen she was pulling into the parking lot in front of the big red-brick building on Oxford Street. Inside, the lobby was as immaculate as ever – polished marble and wood, flags standing like sentries at the door, the two officers behind the front desk in crisp, starched shirts. But there wasn't the air of calm superiority she usually felt when she walked in. There were a lot of people around for this time of the morning, people in a hurry, with things on their mind.

She did not wonder why. She had seen the news. What had happened at Lunenburg last night was reverberating around the world.

A couple of her colleagues arrived. As they went up in the elevator with visitor badges clipped to their coats she wondered what was in store. There was no doubt in her mind that the Lunenburg events and this JFO were connected. Nevertheless, right at that moment she would much rather have been downtown at police headquarters. Halifax was not a city known for an excessive murder rate but overnight there had been two: a bank official with a broken neck at his home in Dartmouth and a private detective shot dead at his house in Bedford. She knew Shore Drive. She jogged there sometimes.

Unfortunately, neither of these cases was going to involve her. Instead she had Steyn to look forward to.

She was tired. She had said goodbye to her boys last night because they and their father were on a six a.m. flight to Milan. She had woken several times in the dark hours, thinking the unthinkable; plane crashes, avalanches, but she had eventually drifted into a heavy slumber and she'd been dead to the world when the call from Steyn's people woke her.

They got out of the elevator on the third floor, walked along the corridor and into the meeting room. Unlike the watch room at Gottingen Street, it had windows, although the view wasn't much, just the wall of the building next door that housed the forensics department. Steyn was already there. So was a roomful of RCMP guys who looked at them as if they were late. They sat where they could. No one offered to make space for them.

Steyn stood up, his face taut. The pressure was obviously on.

'Okay,' he said, 'first, let me tell you we have two visitors this morning.'

Annie followed his eyes towards two men who were sitting at the end of the front row. They did not move or look round and made no attempt to acknowledge what Steyn had said.

'As you know, Prince William is visiting Nova Scotia soon. These gentlemen are colleagues from British security and I've asked them to sit in on our meeting this morning.'

Which probably meant they had insisted, Annie thought. The two men said nothing. Annie couldn't even see their faces and Steyn didn't give their names. He said, 'Last night the RCMP were engaged in a significant arrest operation in relation to a major international terrorist incident. As you've probably seen, the operation has had some unforeseen political consequences which may delay the actual extradition it was intended to assist.'

He paused and his eyes searched the room, not for his own people, but seeking out the team from Gottingen Street, as if to warn them not to make any smart remarks. Annie met his gaze and held it for a moment, which she figured was comment enough.

'Your role is the second phase of the operation,' he said, looking away from her. 'We had already anticipated that the arrest would cause considerable interest among protest groups and dissident factions. It's likely that all sorts of people will want to turn up, both from here in Canada or from the States, maybe even further afield, either to mount pickets at the court building when the hearing eventually takes place, or at Lunenburg where the suspect, Carne, is being held. Of course, we don't want to prevent legitimate protest, free speech, that kind of thing, but we have an obligation to ensure that order is upheld. And we don't want a Seattle all over again.'

Amen to that, Annie thought. Protest groups had disrupted the world trade conference there last year. There had been serious rioting, the centre of the city had been wrecked and eventually the chief of police had resigned.

Steyn gave a weak smile. 'Of course, we're hoping all of this will be history by the time the Prince gets here.'

He nodded towards a young RCMP officer who lifted a handful of folders from a desk and started distributing them.

'These are some of the people we don't want to see around here,' Steyn said. 'Seattle did provide us with one thing – a very clear look at the kind of anarchist groups and individuals who might want to become involved with this. They try to find a situation they can adapt for their own ends, where they can cause maximum mayhem. They use the Internet to send each other messages, to plan their tactics. The people you'll see in these dossiers are well-known troublemakers, hardline political activists of various kinds, many of them with a violent record. Most, I am happy to say, are not Canadian citizens and in the circumstances it should not be too difficult to keep them at a distance or place them under arrest if we have good reason to.'

Annie's folder arrived.

'Also in these packs are details of the duties to which you have been assigned, plus contact numbers here of the people to report to in my office. I want you to study all this for a few minutes, ask any questions you need to, and then I want you to get out there and get on with the job. Time is important. We mustn't waste it.'

Annie opened the file. She ignored the wad of mug-shots and hunted for the duty sheet first to see what she had been given.

She found her name. She had been assigned to the airport. The shifts would be six hours at a stretch, helping Customs and Immigration watch out for undesirables. It was warm and dry at least but it was the most boring job she could think of.

'Questions?' Steyn wondered, looking round the room.

'Yes,' Annie said. 'How long's this going to take?'

'As long as it needs to.' He gave her a sour smile. 'Don't worry. The moment you're no longer wanted, you'll be the first to know.'

By the time she got back downtown, the office was buzzing with the Poyner and Landry murder cases. She found Gamble.

'Boss,' she said, 'could I have a word? It's about the JFO.'

He ushered her into his office. It was not much more than a cubicle with frosted glass panelling which provided a notional privacy.

'What's the problem?'

'I hate to ask this, but is there any way you can get me out of this thing?' She told him about the airport watch. 'I could be of much more assistance here instead of sitting out there like some eastern European secret policeman. I just think—'

'No.' His jaw twitched with irritation. 'Head of Operations asked me to pick people for this job. I picked you. So you get out there and do it and you do it right. And don't let this department down. After last night's fiasco, the RCMP will be looking to dump some shit on somebody and I don't want it to be us. Have you got that?'

His phone rang and he snatched at it. She backed away, hands raised in surrender.

'Fine, fine. Just thought I'd ask.'

She went out into the main room, feeling her face reddening, wondering what the hell was eating him. She liked Gamble. He was a fair man, a good boss, but he was getting harder to talk to these days.

Her own phone rang.

'Annie, it's Jeff.'

'Jeff? I don't know anyone called Jeff.'

Jeff Cameron ran the school of journalism at the University of King's College. Sometimes Annie gave the occasional talk to students about how the police department worked. Cameron and his wife had been friends of hers for a couple of years and they had been supportive shoulders to cry on when her marriage was breaking up.

'Sorry, I know. I haven't called for a while. But tell me you're not doing anything for dinner tonight. Or are you up to your ears in blood with these murders?'

'Not exactly.'

'This Lunenburg debacle hasn't anything to do with you, has it?'

'Only in a very round-about way.'

'Jesus, what a thing to happen. It could bring the whole Nova Scotia government down, you know.'

'Not my problem. What's this about dinner?'

'How are you fixed?'

'Fine, I guess. Is there a reason?'

'I've got a friend who's flying in from New York this afternoon.'

'If I allow him.'

'What?'

'Nothing. Never mind.'

'I'd like you to meet him. His name's John Taggart. He's a journalist from the UK, writes a column for the *Sunday Chronicle*.'

'Never heard of it.'

'He's quite well known over there, as a matter of fact. He was due to come here in a couple of weeks to cover Prince William's visit but he rang me this morning to say he's arriving a bit earlier than planned. You can guess why.'

'The Lunenburg landings?'

'Yeah. This place will be swarming with journalists by the end of the day.'

Annie thought of how busy the airport would be. She looked at her watch. She was due there in twenty minutes.

'Listen, Jeff, I've got to go.'

'So can you make it? I just thought you might be a good person to help him, give him some general background, you know?'

'You can do that yourself. You don't need me.'

'Yes, but you can do the law and order bit better than I can. Seven thirty at the Hotel Halifax. What do you say?'

The thought of dinner in a nice restaurant at the end of what looked like being a dreary day was appealing.

'Okay. Sounds good.'

'And don't worry. We won't ask you to give away any state secrets.'

In her first few hours at the airport she kept an eye on the influx of news people. Jeff had been right about that. There were camera crews from everywhere but she tried not to make herself too conspicuous as she watched them. She didn't want them to think they'd arrived in a police state, even though at this moment she felt she was making a small contribution towards turning it into one.

After a London flight had passed through, she told the immigration desk she was taking a break. There was a coffee bar in the departures area that did a good *latte*. She bought one, then began to stroll through the concourse, past long queues of people waiting for flights.

'Mom!'

The voice cut through the commotion and she looked around to see her son Peter hurtling towards her. Beyond him she saw James standing with Terry. And with them was Barbara, the new wife.

She scooped Peter into one arm, holding the coffee away from her in case it spilled. 'What are you doing here? I thought you guys had gone.'

'No, we've been waiting here all day.'

She took his hand and they walked to where the others stood.

'The flight was delayed,' Terry said.

Barbara smiled and gave a timid 'hi'. She was a thin, dark-haired woman in her mid-twenties. Terry was thirty-nine. Annie nodded a perfunctory hello.

Terry sounded a bit ratty. 'There was a problem with the incoming plane.'

'Problem? What kind of a problem?'

He tried to wave away her anxiety with the sheaf of boarding passes in his hand. 'Nothing to worry about. Some air-traffic-control thing at Milan held it up.'

'So when are you leaving?'

'Any time now.' He glanced briefly at a departures monitor and then frowned at her. 'So what brings you here?'

'I had to drive out on a bit of business.'

'Oh?' Terry looked around for signs of any other police activity but saw none. 'This Lunenburg thing have any implications for you?'

She sipped her coffee. 'Kind of. Around the edges.'

'Mom, I'm tired,' James said.

He was pale. God knows what time they'd had to get up. They must have been hanging around here for hours. So much for Terry and his good deal with the flights.

She stooped to kiss the boy. 'I bet you are, darling, but you can sleep on the plane. It won't be long now.'

'My insurance will take care of this delay,' Terry said. 'It really means we lose the whole of the first day.' He looked at Barbara. 'You know where those documents are? You'll make that call?'

'I said I would. Don't worry about it. But you know, I think you're wasting your time. It really isn't the airline's fault if there's an air-traffic-control problem.'

Annie sensed a note of irritation. An awkward silence gathered.

'I should go,' Annie said. 'I have work to do.'

'No, wait, don't go yet, Mom,' Peter pleaded.

'Hold on. Here we are,' Terry said, his eyes on the departures monitor again. 'Boarding gate 18. That's us.' He kissed Barbara swiftly then smiled at the boys. 'Okay, guys – Italy here we come.'

The children revived instantly. They threw themselves on their mother with hugs and kisses that brought a lump to her throat.

'Now you two have a good time, you hear? And be careful.'

'We will,' they chorused.

'And don't be doing anything stupid.'

'We won't.'

'Now off you go.'

They turned away from her. James went over to Barbara. She bent towards him and he kissed her on the cheek. Peter followed suit. Annie felt a stab of jealous anger, as if they had betrayed her. She wanted to pull them back, to say: *she isn't anything to do with you.* But it wasn't true. This was the woman they lived with, the woman who had taken her place in their father's life, who took care of them every day.

And then they were off, heading towards the gate beyond which only passengers were allowed. The boys turned a couple of times and waved but Terry kept on going.

In a moment they were out of sight and the two women found themselves alone.

Barbara shuffled nervously, pushing her hair behind her ears. 'That was a nice surprise for them, your turning up like that.'

Annie shrugged. 'Just the way it worked out. I didn't know they were still going to be here.'

There was a pause.

Barbara said, 'Listen, you might like to know that I wasn't in favour of this trip either, taking them out of school and everything.'

Annie said nothing.

'But you know Terry.'

'I used to,' Annie said. 'Or at least I thought I did.'

Barbara looked shyly at her. 'You know, maybe we should talk some time.'

'Now why would we want to do that?'

She threw her empty coffee cup into a trash can and walked off.

10

Carrying his Toshiba in its slim case, Taggart drifted along with the stream of passengers off the flight from New York. On the walls of the airport corridor there were photographs showing off the natural attractions of the Maritimes, picturesque areas like the Lighthouse Route, the Annapolis Valley, Cape Breton. They were all very pleasant to look at but if there was any Canadian blood in him he did not feel it being stirred by what he saw.

At immigration he queued up. Over in a corner, a dark-haired woman with a businesslike air was having a word with two back-packers and studying their passports. At the desk, a man in uniform gave him a practised appraisal, then asked him the purpose of his visit and how long he was planning to stay.

'I'm a journalist. I'm going to be here until after Prince William's been and gone.'

'Who do you work for?'

Taggart told him and showed his *Chronicle* ID to back it up.

'Lot of you guys coming through here today. Always when there's trouble.' The man handed him his passport and said, 'Welcome to Nova Scotia.' It didn't sound like he meant it.

One frosty greeting was followed by another. New York had been bad but Halifax was worse. He felt the difference when he stepped outside the terminal after collecting his bag. The cold stung his ears and made his eyes water.

An Avis minivan took him to the parking lot where he picked up his hire car, a mid-range Chrysler, which was all they'd had. There was a run on rentals today and he had not been first off the mark.

The route to Halifax was well signposted and the highway in front of him was clear of any serious traffic. It was not the M25.

After about half an hour, the signs told him he had a choice. He could go left to Halifax over a bridge or he could drive straight on, reaching the city via the town of Bedford. He chose the latter.

Bedford, when he got there, did not seem like a town at all, not in the way he understood. It was a collection of shops and banks, malls and restaurants and supermarkets, all lining the highway. He stopped at a red light. A seafood place maintained that its lobster was the best value in town. On his right there was a big wood-framed episcopalian church and beside it a community hall. A sign outside announced a talk on UFO sightings in the Maritimes. Taggart looked around him, thinking that he was something of an alien himself.

As the town began to thin out he saw at last the enormous expanse of the Bedford Basin and the two mighty bridges. He passed the railway tracks and the container depots where cargo cranes stood like iron giraffes. He looked down across the naval yard and saw steel grey vessels riding at anchor and then he was in Halifax itself, heading towards where the silver waterfront office towers, shaped like huge cartons, were sparkling in the sun.

The Hotel Halifax, on Barrington Street, one of the main routes towards downtown, was not hard to find. He pulled into a parking bay for guests, got his bag and checked in.

His room was on one of the higher floors and he stood at the window for a moment taking in the view, the traffic on the McKay bridge, the blue waters of the harbour, the vast ships heading in and out of the port.

When he turned again he noticed that the voicemail light on his telephone was flashing.

It was Jeff Cameron. 'Hope you had a good flight, John. Listen, I've asked someone to join us for dinner tonight. I know you won't mind. It's a woman by the name of Annie Welles. Good friend of mine. She's with the Halifax police. Works in their robbery and violent crimes unit. I thought she might be able to give you a bit of a briefing. She'd be a useful contact for you and, well . . .' he gave a chuckle '. . . she's not unpleasant to look at. Thirty-four. Divorced. Give me a ring if this is a problem.' He laughed again and rang off.

Taggart smiled. He had called Cameron from New York this morning to say that he was on his way. The two men had been friends for a long time, ever since Taggart's days in Glasgow. Cameron had been on the staff of a Toronto paper then, one that was owned by the same parent company, and he had come to Glasgow on a year's exchange. He and Taggart had shared a flat. It seemed like a lifetime ago. Now he wondered what Cameron was playing at and what 'not unpleasant to look at' meant, exactly.

He connected his laptop and found a stack of e-mails from the paper telling him the kind of story they were looking for. Basically, they wanted something no one else had. But then what else was new.

It was early afternoon but almost seven p.m. in London. He called the office and talked for a while to Dermot Dillon, the night news editor. Since Taggart had his own page he didn't normally work through Dillon or deal with straight news. This was a novel situation for both of them but Dillon was a friend, which helped. When they'd finished their discussion he asked to be transferred to Ken Shaw.

'No point. He's not there. We've been looking for him ourselves. Since lunchtime. Seems to have gone AWOL.'

Taggart frowned. Shaw was always in the office at this time on a Friday night. It sounded as if he was off somewhere, hitting the booze.

When he'd unpacked, he went downstairs to reception and searched through the maps in a stand at the desk until he found one that showed him how to get to Lunenburg. In preparation for Prince William's visit, he had accumulated a lot of background material on the town and now he wanted to see how it matched up with the place itself.

He saw from the maps that he could get to Lunenburg by taking the Lighthouse Route that wound around the coast but if he went that way, the daylight would be fading by the time he got there. Instead, after a brief conversation about directions with the receptionist, he got into the car and headed for the main highway, route 103.

Soon he was away from the city and marvelling at what he saw around him. He had expected to see plenty of trees, since this was Canada after all, but he had not been prepared for anything like this. The road stretched through endless forests of pine and fir, here and there dappled with thickets of bare grey birch that from a distance looked like smoke. In places the forest was interrupted by frozen rivers and there were lakes edged by reed beds that would soften and turn into swamp when the warm weather came. In the water, broken branches had been caught as they drifted. They reached out of the ice like the arms of drowning men.

Inside an hour he was travelling through the countryside on the outskirts of Lunenburg. Here it was less wooded, and colourful farm houses were sprinkled around hilly fields partly coated with snow. Where the snow had disappeared, it left uncovered grass that was a sickly yellow, drained of life by lack of light.

He reached an intersection. Beside a sign welcoming him to Lunenburg, a white car was parked. It had red, yellow and blue flashes on the side and the letters RCMP. He drove up to it and stopped. There were two officers in the car. One of them was drinking a coffee. Taggart took out his driving licence and ID.

'I'm trying to find—'

'The Carne place,' the one with the coffee said. He made a face as if he had just tasted something bad.

'That's right.' Taggart smiled. 'I guess everyone is.'

'You and half the world.'

They were on Dufferin Street, a wide residential avenue with big houses. They said that what he needed first was to get to a place called Mason's Beach Road and they told him how to do so. After that he should just keep going; he'd know the Carne house when he saw it.

He drove on until he was on Tannery Road which, according to their directions, was leading him the right way. Then all of a sudden he was at the edge of a broad natural harbour and the old town of Lunenburg revealed itself. It sat across from him on the opposite shore: timber buildings in rich reds and blues and ochres spread along the dockside. It was a town from another age. Mirrored perfectly in the stillness of the water, it looked like a mirage.

He parked at a picnic site and got out to look. There wasn't a sound or a movement. He felt as if he had been transported suddenly to a different world, a different time. He could almost see the redcoats disembarking from tall-masted ships, hear the whinnying of horses, the thump of cannon.

He gazed on the beauty of it for a few minutes, then told himself he had better move on.

Soon Lunenburg had disappeared behind him and he was

driving round twisting waterside roads. He passed a forest in miniature that turned out to be a Christmas tree farm, then an old wooden church with peeling paint. Outside scattered houses NASA-sized satellite dishes were secured. He thought of the sign he had seen in Bedford. With receivers like these, you could attract UFOs like moths.

A few miles further on he came to a second RCMP vehicle check, two patrol cars this time, where they told him that they were not letting any more visitors along this road, only residents or people passing on through. None of that applied to him so he would have to go the rest of the way on foot.

He parked the car up on the verge, locked it and started to walk. The afternoon temperature was dropping. He was wearing a warm coat and gloves, and chinos which would have been adequate for a UK winter but after a couple of minutes his legs felt as if they were not covered by anything at all.

When he rounded a bend he knew he had reached the Carne place.

Not that he could see it.

An invading army had taken over. Where there should have been empty pasture there was now a huge media encampment, the fields by the side of the road packed with satellite vans and other communications trucks, all lined up in rows. There had to be a hundred people here, from what he could see, most of them talking into their cellphones.

He wandered among the throng. The majority were American or Canadian but there were Europeans as well. He met a couple of people he knew – ITN's New York man and two blokes from Reuters. There was a big iron gateway that he assumed led to the Carne house but men in RCMP parkas kept the pack well away from it. At the edge of the quarantine area, cameramen waited, lined up like a firing squad.

He was introduced to an RCMP press officer who had nothing much to tell him.

'You guys could be in for a long wait. Me too, I guess.'

He was right. This was a siege that could drag on. Taggart could see that the participants were frustrated already and getting very cold. They stamped their feet and drank coffee and tried to keep warm.

He stayed for half an hour until he knew he was wasting his time. He would get no story hanging around here but at least he had seen what was going on. He hurried back up the road to where he had left the car.

In a few minutes, heater blasting, he had reached Lunenburg again and this time he decided to go right into the old town itself.

Close up, it was just as beautiful as it had been from a distance. The town dated from 1753 but the architecture was mostly Victorian with variations, each building an individual masterpiece, some of them pompous and proud, others smaller, looking as if they'd been made out of gingerbread.

He drove slowly up and down and in and out of the grid of streets that sloped steeply to the dockside, where he parked and got out. A single trawler stood at anchor and several small yachts were tied up, covered with tarpaulins on which snow lay like a crust. The harbour had that universal smell, the oily, fishy, seaweed tang that he knew so well from growing up in Portpatrick.

He left the harbour and walked up to Montague Street where there were shops and restaurants. Only some of them were open. It struck him how quiet the town was, like a museum. There was almost no one about except himself. He tried to imagine what it had been like in the old days, when Lunenburg was at its prosperous peak, sending fishermen to sea and building the great sailing ships that had trawled the Grand Banks of the Atlantic.

When he had got to the end of the street and cut down towards the seafront again he saw that there was some activity at one of the boatyards. A sign said that the place did ship repairs. The doors of a big shed were open and there was light and noise inside. Curious, he stepped over a chain barrier in order to take a look.

'That's far enough, sir.'

A security guard in a peaked cap was standing in the doorway of a hut. He looked bulky in a heavy coat and Taggart had the uncomfortable feeling that he might be armed.

'I just want to take a look around. Is that okay?'

'Sorry. Only authorised personnel allowed.'

Taggart stepped back beyond the chain. 'All a bit mysterious, isn't it? What's the big secret?'

'No secret. Just security.' The man looked at him. 'You're not from around here.'

'No, I'm from the UK.'

'I can tell from the accent. If you were local you wouldn't need to ask.' He nodded towards the shed. 'Ever hear of the *Bluenose*?'

Taggart stared at him and then at the shed. Of course. The *Bluenose*. He hadn't been thinking. It was why Prince William was coming. Lunenburg had been the birthplace of the original *Bluenose*, the fabled racing schooner. It had been built here in the Twenties, at the Smith and Rhuland yard along this dock. After the vessel foundered in 1946, there had been *Bluenose II*, its replacement, run by the Nova Scotia Government as a tourist attraction, a floating ambassador visiting other North American ports and available for private sailings and charters out of Halifax in the summer months. It had been built for a quarter of a million dollars in 1963 but over the next thirty five years at least another half a million had been spent on repairs and rebuilding.

And now that *Bluenose* had gone too. In its place, there would be *Bluenose III*, the new millennium version, funded by a wealthy businessman to the tune of four million dollars, it was said – although no one knew the exact figure – and about to be donated to the people of Nova Scotia. It was being launched soon so that it would be on the water and have trials completed before the summer season. The launching ceremony would be performed by the Prince, accompanied by the Premier of Nova Scotia and the new Lieutenant Governor, whose acquaintance, Mr Carne, was a prisoner in his home just a few miles away.

An open-backed Toyota truck came rumbling up and without offering any challenge the security guard let the chain fall so that it could pass. The vehicle slowed and the driver took a good look at Taggart. In turn, Taggart saw a man with a broad face the colour of weathered wood.

'Who have we here, Len?' The voice sounded as if it was coming from the bottom of a barrel.

'An English journalist, Mr Mansell. I told him he couldn't come in here without proper authority.'

The man put the handbrake on and got out. He was about six feet five and made Taggart feel like a dwarf. He wore a heavy lumberjack coat in a bright red and green check. Thick trousers were tucked into heavy boots.

'English. Is that so?'

'Scottish, as a matter of fact. With a bit of Canadian blood, I'm told.'

'Better still.' The man smiled and held out his hand. He had fingers as thick as bananas. 'Deke Mansell. I'm the skipper of the new *Bluenose*. Do I take it you're interested in seeing her?'

Taggart had expected a crushing handshake but was relieved to find that Mansell's grip was restrained.

'John Taggart. Yes, very much.'

'Well, I have to admit that having a journalist taking an interest in what we're doing here makes a pleasant change from all the goings-on over there.' He waved a huge arm in the vague direction of where the Carne house would be. 'Lot of goddamn nonsense. You're not part of that pack of hounds, then?'

'No,' Taggart said, not quite telling the truth. 'I'm actually here to cover Prince William's visit. I kind of specialise in royal reporting.'

'Is that a fact? What paper you work for?'

Taggart told him and saw that it didn't mean a lot.

'Have you ever met the Prince?' Mansell asked.

'Yes, a couple of times. His father, too.'

Mansell seemed impressed. 'Well now, there's a thing. Canada's not quite tied to the old country the way it used to be but I have to say you'll find a lot of people here in Nova Scotia who still have a great deal of respect for the Crown. I happen to be one of them.'

'Nothing wrong with that,' Taggart suggested. 'You can go forward as a country and still respect your traditions at the same time.'

Mansell beamed. 'Which is just what I say.' He put his arm round Taggart's shoulders. 'Listen, why don't I bring you in and show you our baby and you can tell me what you think of her.' He looked at the security guard. 'It's okay, Len, I'll take care of this from here.'

They left the Toyota where it was and walked into the shed. Taggart gaped when he saw what was inside.

The vessel stood on the slipway, towering over them, kept in place by chains and powerful wooden beams. Half a dozen men were at work. Taggart could smell paint and tar, hear the sound of hammering and of wood being sawn, but all he had eyes for was the *Bluenose*, the sheer strength and majesty of her.

Mansell said, 'She's a hundred and forty three feet long, twenty seven feet at her maximum beam and she has a main mast that's a hundred and twenty five feet ten inches. You can walk under her bilges the length of the keel without bending over.' He smiled at Taggart. 'Well, most people can.'

The long, sleek hull gleamed with fresh black paint – not blue, Taggart noticed – and the delicate decorative scrollwork shone golden.

'Douglas fir for the masts and the booms, mahogany for the deck hatches and the skylights. The hull's made from red oak, spruce and pine.'

Taggart stared up at the beautiful craft. 'She's magnificent.'

'That she is. "They are grander things than all the art of towns. Their tests are tempests and the sea that drowns."'

Taggart didn't know the quotation.

'Masefield,' Mansell said. '"They are my country's line, her great art done by strong brains labouring on the thought unwon. They mark our passage as a race of men. Earth will not see such ships as those again."' He laughed. 'Except perhaps this one, eh?'

They walked down the slipway and around the vessel while Mansell continued with his litany of facts and figures, how the mainsail would be four thousand one hundred square feet, that the lifeboats were fishing dories, the fact that the combined weight of the fastenings, nails, bolts and screws came to almost three tons. He showed Taggart the twin propellers and the copper ground plate for lightning protection, he pointed out the long, sweeping underbody, almost straight.

'This is called a run, which is what makes a fast schooner fast. The water doesn't hold on, you see. It leaves her cleanly and doesn't create any eddies that might hold her back.'

'She's beautiful,' Taggart said. 'You must be very proud.

And the man who's paid for all this – I've forgotten his name – that's quite an act of generosity.'

'Cary Eisener. He stood on this very spot yesterday, as a matter of fact, but he went to Europe this morning, won't be back until the launch. Yes, he's a fine man. Born and bred in Lun'burg. Made a fortune in the electronics business. All this is the result.'

'Was she built here?'

'No. We don't have yards like that here any more. She was built in St John, Newfoundland. The boys here are just giving her the finishing touches. It didn't seem right for the town not to have any part in her construction so here we are.'

They went into a little office where Mansell opened a drawer and produced a bottle of Captain Morgan. Half an hour later, with the rum warming his veins and a bellyful of seafaring anecdotes to digest, Taggart said goodbye and wandered back towards his car, ruminating on Nova Scotia hospitality and how he would have to work something about the *Bluenose* into his story for Sunday.

Along the way he came across something he hadn't seen the first time.

It appeared to be a monument of some kind, built on the side of the quay. He wondered how he'd missed it and then realised it was because he had gone up to Montague Street earlier and had not walked the whole length of the harbour.

As he got closer, he saw that it was more than a monument. It was a memorial, consisting of four pointed black marble slabs in the shape of a compass with an obelisk in the centre. On it was engraved: *Dedicated to the memory of those who have gone down to the sea in ships and who have never returned. And as a tribute to those who continue to occupy their business in great waters.*

He thought of Mansell and Masefield and the *Bluenose*

and the men and women and ships that had been the soul of this place.

Down the side of each slice of marble there were the names of vessels which had been lost and those who had died on them. The list was long. He moved around, reading the name of each person, pronouncing the unfamiliar names aloud.

Selig, Zeller, Tibbo, Gaunt, Whynacht.

Among the ships were vessels called Cathleen Spindler, Penny Fair, Excellence, Reliance. He read every one. Then he stood back and realised that it was almost dark and he was alone.

It was cold. He should go.

But there was something about this place. Something that made him reluctant to leave it.

[illegible]
the [illegible]

[illegible] the side of each [illegible] the
[illegible] of [illegible] which has been [illegible] and those who had
[illegible]
the [illegible] of each [illegible]
[illegible]

[illegible]

[illegible]

[illegible] said. [illegible]

[illegible]

[illegible]

114

11

Annie stood in bra and pants, looking into the open wardrobe, trying to remember the last time she had pondered over what to wear for dinner. All she ever had to think about these days was clothes for work.

But what was she doing? This *was* work, she reminded herself. Dinner with Jeff and his journalist friend was not entirely a social occasion. Did she want to meet them looking like a cocktail waitress? She reached in and lifted out a dark grey trouser suit and in a drawer she located the black merino wool polo neck she liked to wear with it.

When she had dressed, she debated whether she would take the car or not, and then decided she would. She would have only one glass of wine, maybe two at the most. The department came down like a ton of bricks on any of its own who were caught driving while impaired and if she couldn't drive, she couldn't do her job. The best she could expect was to be back in uniform, pushing paper somewhere in the administrative division. She shuddered at the thought. *One* glass of wine.

She reached the hotel in about twenty minutes. Jeff hadn't said precisely where they would meet but she presumed it would be the bar. She saw him immediately. He hadn't dressed up, or maybe he had, in his own way. He was standing with a glass in his hand – rum, no doubt – wearing a brightly patterned chunky sweater that she wondered if he kept for special occasions. Gina, his wife, the mother of their three children, was on a stool next to him in slacks and a jumper that was a little more subdued. She was a lecturer in politics at Dalhousie. Annie hadn't known she would be coming.

They were both listening to a man in a shiny dark suit who had his back to her. Jeff spotted Annie and interrupted. The man turned and Annie saw that he was slim-faced and pleasant-looking, thirty or so, with short dark hair. He smiled a greeting and shook her hand when Jeff introduced them.

'Annie Welles – John Taggart.'

'Pleased to meet you,' Taggart said. 'I'm glad you could come along.'

'Happy to be here.'

He had an English accent with a slight Scottish inflection that made her think for a fleeting second of Sean Connery, although he didn't look remotely like him. Too young. Not rugged enough. But quite nice, all the same. She kissed Gina and Jeff on the cheek and then Jeff asked her what she was having to drink.

'No wait, it's my shout, I'm in the chair,' Taggart said. 'What would you like?'

'Just a Perrier, please. I'm driving.'

'Me, too,' Gina said, holding up a glass with tomato juice in it. 'I drew the short straw.' She paused. 'Poor you. You never have an option.'

Annie shrugged. 'It's not a problem. I could have got a cab if I'd wanted.'

'Annie's divorced,' Gina explained to Taggart.

'Yes, eh . . . Jeff said something.'

Annie glared at Jeff. He looked uneasy. 'I just mentioned it in passing, that's all.'

Taggart handed her her drink. He seemed to be staring

and she wondered what else had Jeff told him.

She said, 'Jeff tells me you work for the Sunday something.'

'*Chronicle*. I write a weekly column. I was supposed to be in New York for a few weeks to do some stuff, then I was due to come here for Prince William's visit. But when this raid happened at Lunenburg, I turned out to be the nearest person to hand so they told me to get up here as quickly as possible.'

'Do I get the feeling then that hard news isn't exactly your beat?'

'Now hold on a moment,' Jeff said. 'Let me tell you a few things about John here.'

He spent the next sixty seconds giving her a brief but glowing account of Taggart's journalistic exploits in Glasgow. Taggart didn't seem to be listening to any of it. He was staring at Annie again. He said, 'Look, this is stupid, but have we met before?'

Everyone laughed at him. He shook his head. 'I'm sorry. That sounded crass. But I thought—' He clicked his fingers suddenly. 'The airport. You were at the airport today. I saw you when I was coming through Immigration. You were talking to two people, looking at their passports or something.'

Annie gave a little nod of congratulation. 'Very observant of you, which is more than I can say about myself, since I didn't notice *you*.' She smiled. 'And I'm the one who's supposed to be looking out for suspicious characters.'

'Oh?' Jeff said. 'Tell me more.'

A waiter was coming towards them.

'Over dinner,' Taggart suggested. 'What do you say? I think they're ready for us.'

They went into the dining room. Their table was at the

window. Outside, the tall waterfront buildings were glowing and the McKay bridge was a slender finger of light stretching across the velvet blackness of the harbour. They sat down and Annie realised that they looked like two couples out for the evening, an impression underlined by their appearance: Jeff and Gina in their jumpers, she and Taggart in suits. They ordered and Taggart chose the wine, a bottle of red and a bottle of white, both top-end Australian. Annie watched him study the list like a man who knew what he was doing.

When the wine waiter had gone, he looked towards the view. 'It's beautiful here. I had thought it might be—'

'Dull,' Gina said. 'Yes, well, Nova Scotia can be pretty enough at times but dull is the word you're looking for. God, I'm starved for a decent play, a bit of opera. The most cultural event we have is the annual Halifax Tattoo. Which is great if you like bagpipes.'

Taggart smiled. 'When I was a student I got a summer job once working at the Edinburgh version. I think I've heard enough bagpipes to last me the rest of my life, thank you very much.'

Annie flashed Gina a look. 'You make Halifax sound like a real dump. There's a lot going on here if you know where to find it.'

Jeff gave a condescending smile. 'Annie's an unreconstructed Haligonian.'

'If you mean I like living here and don't absolutely *yearn, dahling*, to be in Toronto or Montreal, then yes.'

Taggart chuckled. 'So what would I find if I looked?'

She pondered on that. 'If you like rock music, there's a good scene. Interesting bands. Like Sloan.'

'Who live in Toronto now,' Gina said. 'Which kind of proves my point.

'I thought you preferred jazz,' Jeff asked.

'I do. It doesn't mean I don't know what's going on.'

Taggart frowned. 'Sloan. I think I've heard of them. I thought they were American.'

The others groaned.

'What? What did I say?'

'Just the usual assumption,' Jeff explained. 'Not every talented North American person is from the United States, you know. The Americans always claim them once they become famous but you'd be surprised at the number of celebrities who are closet Canadians.'

'Like who?'

Jeff thought. 'Donald Sutherland.'

'Yeah, well, I knew that. Hardly a big revelation there.'

'As a matter of interest, he's from St John, New Brunswick,' Gina said. 'What we'd call local.'

'Jim Carrey,' Annie said.

'Really?'

'Yep. And let's see: Matthew Perry out of *Friends*. Mike Myers, the Austin Powers guy.'

'Michael J. Fox,' Jeff said.

'Come on, do me a favour,' Taggart protested.

'No, really,' Jeff told him. 'He's from Edmonton, Alberta.'

'Pamela Anderson,' Annie said. 'I think she comes from somewhere in British Columbia.'

'Although maybe not all of her,' Taggart suggested and they laughed.

Their first course arrived. They clinked glasses and wished each other *bon appetit*, then began to eat, making appreciative murmurings about the quality of the food.

'So what were you doing out at the airport?' Taggart said eventually.

It occurred to Annie as he said it that he was probably quite a good journalist. He was curious but he had taken his time, allowing her to relax first, maybe let her guard down. And she *was* becoming relaxed, enjoying the food and the company and the wine. She looked at the glasses. They were big. She had drunk nearly half of hers already. She would have to be careful.

'Maybe a couple of ground rules first,' she said. 'Jeff asked me to give you a bit of a background briefing, which I'm happy to do, but anything we discuss here is off the record, okay? Nothing attributable.'

'Not a problem. If there's any question you feel you can't answer, that's fine by me.'

She sipped her wine. 'We have these things from time to time called JFOs, Joint Forces Operations, where the local police and the RCMP team together. I'm involved in one at the moment. The business at Lunenburg has stirred a lot of things up. It's likely we'll get people heading here to make a protest of some kind, either out at Lunenburg or at the Law Courts when our friend Carne makes an appearance there. Naturally, after what happened in Seattle last year, there are some concerns. What we're doing is keeping an eye open for known troublemakers, the kind who have a record of political violence and who'd be inclined to turn a peaceful demonstration into a full-blown riot.'

'That's ridiculous,' Gina said. She had said yes to half a glass of red wine and her neck was flushed. 'What is this – China? This is a democracy, a free country.'

'Gina, hold it a minute,' Jeff told her.

'No, it's okay,' Annie said. 'I can't say I'm entirely comfortable with the situation myself but we do have an obligation to do everything we can to maintain order. That's what the law-abiding citizens of Halifax will expect from us.'

She was beginning to sound like Larry Steyn.

'Interesting,' Taggart said. 'I went to Lunenburg today.'

'Another dull place,' Gina said. 'Nothing ever happens there. It's like a nice box of chocolates except that when you open it you find it's empty.'

'I got a private viewing of the new *Bluenose*. It's a wonderful vessel. Do you think any of this, this extradition business, could have an effect on Prince William's visit?'

'You mean, would it be cancelled?' Jeff asked.

Annie shook her head. 'I doubt it. If Halifax was in flames or something, then, sure, yeah. But that's not going to happen. We're too well prepared. Anyway, we've got a couple of people from British security sitting in with us at the moment, monitoring the situation.'

Taggart raised his eyebrows and Annie wondered if she'd been wise letting that slip.

'As a matter of interest,' Gina asked, 'what would happen if there *was* major trouble – like riots and lootings?'

Jeff scoffed. 'This is Halifax, honey.'

'No, seriously, it wouldn't be the first time. There were riots after the war, you know. VE Day. People were celebrating on the streets and they ended up raiding the stores.'

Annie considered the question. 'It would depend on how bad it was, whether it was something we and the Girks could handle or whether it needed something more than that.'

'Girks?' Taggart asked.

'Sorry. Local cop slang. In French the RCMP are known as the Gendarmerie Royale du Canada. GRC. We call them Girks.' She turned to Gina. 'We had the G7 summit here a few years ago, don't forget. You don't get a bigger potential security headache than that but it passed off perfectly. Anyway Shearwater's just across the harbour.' She looked at Taggart. 'That's the military forces base. They'd be put on some kind of standby.'

Taggart nodded. 'So tell me about the new Lieutenant Governor?'

'As straight as they come. Quite a popular figure. Carne's an old friend of his. I guess he knew nothing about any of this.' She put her knife and fork down and sat back. 'Listen, folks, maybe we shouldn't exaggerate my role here. I just happen to be part of this JFO at the moment – not a very big part either. My normal job is robbery and violent crime. And the sooner I can return to that, the better.'

'Back to a peaceful life, eh?' Taggart said.

'We have our moments. Two murders last night.'

As she said it she knew she sounded defensive, a country bumpkin trying to impress a city slicker with this astounding statistic. Two murders. Big deal.

'So how does your police department operate?'

For the next few minutes, she gave him a cut-down version of the talk she sometimes gave to Jeff's students. After that Jeff and Gina steered the conversation back towards politics, a subject on which they were intense, a passionate double act. Annie listened to them finishing each other's sentences, finding the right words for one another. She and Taggart chipped in every now and then but for the most part they were bystanders.

Gina said, 'Did you hear our great Premier being interviewed today, talking about how Canada can't duck its responsibilities as a member of the international community, that we have to do our bit in the war against terrorism, even here in Nova Scotia?'

'Which appears to mean letting the RCMP run amok, shooting people,' Jeff added. 'Just to keep the Yanks happy. I notice that Ottawa hasn't said much. Jesus, who sanctioned this operation – John Wayne? What sort of top-level consultation was there? I tell you, the opposition parties won't rest until they force an election over this.'

'And maybe no bad thing either,' Gina agreed.

They had reached the coffee stage. Annie finished her second cup and looked at her watch. It was after eleven.

'I don't want to break up the party but—'

'No, you're right,' Jeff said. 'And I've got to take the babysitter home.'

Annie remembered Terry doing that. A million years ago.

Jeff lowered his voice. 'Now, John, about this bill—'

Taggart waved the idea away. 'Don't be absurd. The paper's taking care of this.'

Jeff looked relieved. 'You're sure?'

'Listen to what the man says,' Gina told him. 'He's sure, he's sure. You knew perfectly well that this would be on John's expenses. Quite legitimately too. Didn't you bring Annie along so that he could pump her for information?'

They laughed and went to get their coats. Taggart said he'd walk them to their cars. Outside, it was snowing a little and they had to clear it from the windscreens. When the Camerons had left, he shook Annie's hand and thanked her for coming.

'You've been a lot of help,' he said. 'I appreciate it.'

Flakes of white were settling on his hair.

'No, I enjoyed myself. Thank you for dinner and a very nice evening.'

As she drove away she saw him in her rear-view mirror, watching her go.

When she got home, she didn't feel like going straight to bed. That was the coffee. Too much of it, too late. She took a Bill Evans CD from the rack and poured a glass of red wine as a nightcap, then threw her shoes off and sprawled on the settee.

She had to admit she found Taggart, well . . . interesting. He had not come on to her in any way, he had not pressed her to have more wine when she had said no. He had listened attentively when she spoke, asking pertinent questions, and at the end of the evening he had shaken her hand in what was almost a formal farewell.

But what did she expect? It was business. She'd said so herself. All she was was a contact giving a visiting journalist some background information. Did she seriously think he might have looked on her in any other way? She felt herself blushing and wondered – God – had *she* come on to *him*?

She sat up straight, trying to rewind the evening in her head. Bill Evans began playing *Some Day My Prince Will Come*. No, she had been fine. They had not delved into personal matters, which was good. Taggart would have seen her as a calm, professional woman in control of herself, absorbed in an important job, yet alive to the wider world around her.

Who was she kidding? He would not have seen that at all. She got to her feet and went to the window. Beyond Mill Cove the moonlight shimmered on the water. Coloured lights moved slowly in the darkness as a vessel headed out to sea. He would have seen her as an anal retainer, clutching her thoughts and her emotions close to her, the way she always did, refusing to give anything away. That's what he would have seen and it would not have interested him one bit.

She felt a sudden surge of guilt. Good God, she was thinking about a man. When was the last time she'd done that? It seemed – not wrong exactly, but not quite right.

It was Terry, damn him, still holding her back. That was the problem. Him and her own sense of loyalty. Although she felt no emotional bond, she had not yet shaken off the ghost of her commitment. It was as if beneath it all she still thought of herself as his wife, existing in some kind of suspended animation.

It was time she pulled herself out of this.

She came away from the window. She reached for the phone book and looked up the number of the Hotel Halifax, then dialled and asked for Mr Taggart's room. The phone rang half a dozen times – where was he? – and then it was answered by the voicemail. She paused for a second, then took the plunge.

'Hi, it's Annie Welles here. Listen, I just want to thank you once again for a great evening and the thought occurred to me that if you're free in the morning maybe you'd like to take a look round Halifax. I'd be happy to be a tour guide. So why don't you give me a call tomorrow if you're interested?'

She left her number, then hung up.

There were certain things in life which you couldn't undo. Murder was one. Leaving your voice message on someone's machine was another.

Taggart was not in his room because when Annie had left he had gone back to the bar. It had sounded noisy and interesting so he had popped in for a look and found it busy with the loud conversation and laughter of visiting journalists spending their employers' money. A couple of people looked his way and he gave them a nod. Even though he did not know *who* they were, he knew *what* they were. He could tell. They all could. They were always able to sniff each other out.

He ordered a brandy and thought about what the hell he was going to write for Sunday. The new Lieutenant Governor and his connection with A.J. Carne was the direction to go but an investigation like that would take weeks, months. He had a couple of hours.

Mostly, though, he found his thoughts turning to Annie Welles. Jeff hadn't been wrong. She was more than 'not unpleasant to look at', she was an attractive woman, yet he had a feeling she didn't think of herself that way. The divorce had damaged her confidence and self-esteem, perhaps, made her wary. Or maybe that was the policewoman part of her. Whatever it was, she had been reserved and cautious and he wondered what she was like when she was more relaxed.

By the time he got back to his room he had made up his mind to call Jeff in the morning and get her phone number. He'd just have to put up with the mockery that would ensue when he asked.

The voicemail light was flashing. He thought of his mother, as he always did when the phone rang at night.

There were two messages. The first one was from Dermot Dillon at the news desk.

'John, where the hell are you? Call me as soon as you can. It's urgent.'

Taggart wondered why he hadn't phoned the mobile. He felt his pockets for it but it wasn't there. Then he saw it on the bedside table. Its display screen told him he had missed three calls. He looked at his watch. It would be five a.m. in London. Dillon would have gone home by now. But he had said it was urgent.

He powered up his laptop and went into his file of home numbers, then dialled Dillon's.

'Dermot, it's John in Halifax. Sorry to wake you at this hour.'

'Christ, I've been trying to get you.'

'What's all the fuss?'

'Ken's gone.'

'Excuse me? Say that again.'

'Ken's gone. He's been fired. The management have issued a statement, saying he's decided to step down. I've sent you the text by e-mail.'

'Decided? What are you talking about?'

'Health reasons, they say. You know how these things work.'

'Jesus. Where is he?'

'Nobody knows. Off getting drunk somewhere probably.'

That was why he hadn't been around earlier. Taggart had a vision of him lying in an alleyway somewhere. He would have to try and reach him somehow. 'So what happens now? Is somebody standing in?'

'No. They've appointed a new editor.'

'Who?'

'Eric Mayne.'

Taggart's heart sank. Eric Mayne was the editor of the *Post*, where Judith Sefton worked.

'He just turned up in the office tonight with the proprietor. They said Ken had resigned and Mayne was now in charge.'

'The king is dead,' Taggart muttered.

'And there's more.' Dillon named three other editorial executives – all gone. 'I'm surprised they haven't got rid of me, too.'

'Nah, they won't sack you. You're good at your job.'

'Since when did that have anything to do with it? Mayne will be bringing his own people in. He's started already. Are you ready for this one? There's a new assistant editor in charge of news.'

Taggart knew what was coming.

'Judith Sefton,' Dillon said.

In Taggart's mind there was a sudden image of an angry woman on the stairs of the Groucho.

When he finished talking to Dillon, he thought of trying Shaw's home but it was an ungodly hour so he decided to leave it. Instead, he went into his computer mailbox and read the press release that Dillon had sent. It was full of stuff about re-focussing the paper, building on its strengths, developing innovative journalism.

It was a load of crap. But that wasn't the real issue. Judith Sefton had him where she wanted him, right in her sights. He might be the *Chronicle*'s star columnist but that wouldn't matter. They wouldn't fire him – there was no way the management would agree to that – but there wasn't a future for him at the paper. She would make sure of it. Life would become intolerable and one way or another he would have to go.

It was his own damn fault but there was no point in dwelling on that now. The thing to do was find a friendly harbour somewhere. Lots of people had made it clear that they'd love to have him, except it was impossible to knock on doors in London when you were sitting in a hotel room in Halifax, Nova Scotia.

His phone light was still flashing and then he remembered he hadn't listened to the second message.

It was Annie Welles, which surprised him. He wondered what had made her call but found himself feeling flattered that she had. At the same time, though, a guided tour was not exactly his number one priority right now.

At four a.m. Judith Sefton's call woke him but didn't surprise him. He had been expecting her to ring.

'Congratulations,' he said.

'Fuck you. You can count yourself lucky that you were already in Nova Scotia before this happened. I wanted to bring you back but Eric talked me out of it, said there wasn't enough time and it would be too costly.'

'Delighted you think so highly of me.'

'You imagine you're fireproof, don't you?'

'No, but you know as well as I do that something with my name at the top is one of the few things in the *Chronicle* that people can be bothered to read.'

'At the moment. Things can change. Let me just tell you

that your days are numbered, with or without your precious royal seal of approval. Have you got that?'

'Nice talking to you, too, Judith,' Taggart said and hung up.

He had tried to sound cool but his heart was thumping nevertheless. He lay back on the bed in the dark. War had been declared and he had a feeling he wasn't going to be on the winning side.

12

It was Saturday morning. Annie's boys rang her at eight to say that they had arrived in Italy safely and were having a good time. Terry came on the line briefly, telling her there wasn't a lot of snow and that he wasn't sure just how much ski-ing they would actually get. The news didn't exactly break her heart.

She had coffee and some fruit and pottered around the apartment. Taggart didn't ring. The moment she woke she had regretted leaving that stupid message. By ten, the regret had turned to a feeling of humiliation. He wasn't going to call. She had made a fool of herself.

He called her at eleven.

He said, 'I'm sorry I didn't ring you earlier. I had to finish my piece for tomorrow's paper. It took longer than I thought.'

'No, that's fine. Don't worry about it.' She hoped she sounded calm, that he wouldn't hear the tingle of excitement she felt.

'So what time does the tour start?'

She arranged to meet him at the old Alexander Keith's brewery, which was now a weekend market. It was only a short walk from his hotel. When she arrived forty minutes later, he was standing at the entrance to the scrubbed stone building, drinking a carton of coffee. He looked different from last night. The smooth dark suit had gone and he had fallen in step with the climate. He wore a warm fleecy jacket and a DKNY baseball cap, as well as jeans and sturdy footwear, but the ensemble, however subdued, looked expensive. She felt dowdy in her little hat and long wool coat.

His smile helped. 'Your call last night was a lovely surprise.'

She felt embarrassed. 'It was just an idea, something that occurred to me when I got home.'

'Believe me, it was just what I needed to take my mind off a few things.'

'Such as?'

He waved a hand. 'Trouble at work. You don't want to know. Now then, where shall we go?'

'In here for a start.'

She headed down the steps into the building. There was the smell of fresh coffee, fried chicken, noodles sizzling in a wok, but the place was not as crowded or as colourful as in the summer when the arts and crafts stalls were in full bloom. She led the way into a long room of cold stone, scented with the earthiness of fresh vegetables, then she handed Taggart a plastic basket.

'What are we looking for?' he asked.

'Whatever's good.'

After a couple of minutes, the basket held aubergines, cucumber and organic potatoes.

Taggart pointed. 'Those courgettes look past their best.'

'Zucchini. We call them zucchini here.'

'You say zucchini, I say courgettes.'

She winced. 'Gershwin was wise to ditch that line, don't you think?'

'So you do know something about music?'

'A little, I guess. My father used to play the piano.'

'Used to?'

'He died some years ago.'

'I'm sorry.'

'It's okay. You get over these things. What about you? Parents still around?'

'My mother's alive.'

She glanced at him, hearing something in his voice. There was a shadow in his expression. She turned and took a last look round the stalls. 'Okay, that's it. Let's pay for this and go. Time to see the sights.'

Once outside again, they headed up to Spring Garden Road, past St Mary's Basilica. Hot greasy smells came from a sidewalk kebab stand. In front of the public library, a statue of Winston Churchill, grey and obese, glowered with apparent disapproval.

They wandered in and out of different streets while she showed him places of interest. On Barrington Street she pointed out the Lieutenant Governor's official residence. Some photographers were hanging around, being watched by a couple of uniforms sitting in a Halifax regional patrol car. She waved in at them as they passed and they waved back.

They walked up George Street, at the top of which was a big white clock tower. He asked her about it.

'It's the old town clock. Probably our most distinctive landmark. Queen Victoria's father had it built, you know. The duke of something – I can't remember. He was the commander of the British forces here at the end of the eighteenth century.'

The tower stood at the edge of the Citadel, a huge grassy open space crowned by a star-shaped fort where sentries had once watched the approaches to Halifax from every angle. Here, at the highest point of the city, the wind was sharp and icy cold but the view was magnificent. She talked about the bridges and she directed his gaze towards Bedford and Dartmouth, to McNab's Island in the mouth of the harbour, to the open expanse of the commons and the public gardens on the inland side.

As they walked around part of the perimeter, she pointed down Gottingen Street towards a long brick building with plastic sheeting hanging over its main entrance.

'That's where I work. You know, I look out on this every day and never really see it.'

'A shame. It's quite a place. The whole town's very distinctive. Reminds me a little of Edinburgh.'

She smiled at him. 'We're kind of proud of our city, us Haligonians. So, as a reward for saying all the right things, why don't I buy you lunch?'

'You don't have to do that.'

'Are you hungry?'

'As a matter of fact I am.'

'Then don't give me an argument.'

She took him down Duke Street, all the way to the harbour-front where the Historic Properties were sited, tall wooden buildings that housed craft shops, galleries and restaurants.

'These were the old warehouses. They were rotting away until the city decided to restore them. All this – all along here – used to be the centre of Halifax's sea trade. Two hundred and fifty years ago, you'd have had smugglers and pirates landing their cargoes here, privateers unloading ships that they'd captured, press gangs wandering around kidnapping people to join the navy.'

'Treasure Island stuff, eh?' He peered into the window of a shop that sold porcelain. 'Life looks a bit more delicate now.'

'Maybe. Not entirely. We still get a bit of trouble every now and then from sailors on shore leave. Some mornings our drunk tank sounds like the United Nations.'

They went into Salty's, a restaurant right at the harbour's

edge. She recommended the chowder. It was hot and steaming and delicious and they each had a glass of draught Keith's to wash it down.

As they ate she told him more about Nova Scotia and her city; about the great Halifax explosion of 1917, when two ships, one loaded with TNT, collided in the harbour and 2,000 people were killed; about the rum-running years of Prohibition; and about the city's role during the war as a key port for the Atlantic convoys.

'My father used to tell stories about how each night the entire Bedford Basin was crammed full of ships, that you could walk right across them from one side to the other. And then when you woke up in the morning they were gone. It was as if they had never been there.'

'You've always lived here?'

'Born and reared.'

'Why the police? Was it in the family?'

'No. I was at university when the department started a graduate recruitment scheme. It sounded attractive. I applied and got in.'

'And you like it?'

'Most of the time.'

She ran a finger down the condensation on the side of her glass and thought for a moment about the failure of her marriage, how the job had contributed to that. But she didn't want to get into anything personal here, anything to do with her private life. So far she had kept this superficial.

She said, 'Work and marriage . . . sometimes the balance . . .'

'I understand. Or at least I think I do. Though I've never been married myself.'

'No ties?'

'Not in that way, no.'

She glanced at him. It was in his voice again, the same

slight wariness she had heard back at the market. There was something there, something he didn't want to talk about. But that was fine. He was entitled to his privacy. So was she.

She changed the subject. 'So you've written your story?'

'Yes.' He made a face. 'Not exactly a masterpiece. I went on the what-does-all-this-mean-for-the-royal-visit angle. That's what people at home are interested in.'

'And what *does* it mean?'

'Short answer – nothing at all.'

'How do you know?'

He smiled. 'Jeff might not have mentioned it but I kind of specialise in royal stories. To do that, you need good sources. Mine tell me there's no question of the visit not going ahead so that's what I wrote. Plus I incorporated some of the background security stuff we talked about last night and various bits and pieces I managed to glean this morning from the local papers and TV.'

'So what happens now?'

'I don't know. I'm kind of playing things by ear. There's . . . well, there's a bit of a crisis at the paper.'

'What kind of crisis?'

'A few personnel changes at the top.'

'Does it involve you?'

'Not yet, but I think it will before very long. I should really be back in London trying to sort a few things out but at the same time I'm supposed to be here for the royal visit. I'll have to see how it goes.' He pondered for a second, then looked at her with a question in his eyes. 'If I'm going to be here for a while, do you think we could see each other again?'

It took her by surprise. 'I . . . well, I don't know. I can't really – it depends on how this JFO goes. It's hard to—'

He gave a soft laugh. 'Don't panic. It's just a thought. I

have your phone number, so may I call you at least?'

'I . . . I guess so.'

She drove back home a short time later, furious that she had behaved like such a blithering idiot. Damn it, why hadn't she just said yes to him? It would have been a date, dinner again, maybe, that was all.

She wasn't used to any of this, that was the thing. Apart from Claussen's obscene overtures at Christmas, this was the first man who'd expressed any interest since the divorce. Taggart wasn't asking much, just some indication that she wasn't totally unavailable, but she didn't know how to respond. She had been married when she was twenty-two and she was thirty-four now and when you added it all up she didn't have much experience of being single.

It was easy when you weren't interested – you just said no. But this was different. She didn't want to say no – she just didn't want to risk saying yes.

Taggart found a cigar shop on Granville Street and decided to treat himself to a packet of Montecristo number fours. He was in a good mood after his morning with Annie. In spite of her caution about seeing him again, there was something there all right.

His cellphone rang and interrupted his thoughts. It was Dermot Dillon from the office.

He said, 'Dermot, look I'm sorry. I know it's not fantastic but at least the royal reassurance bit is something no one else will get. Should keep Miss Sefton and co happy at least. Where's it going to run, do you know?'

'John, it's not that. I'm not calling about your copy.'

'Oh, then what?'

'It's . . . there's more bad news, I'm afraid.'

'God, not more departures. Who's gone now – not you?'

'No, it's not me. It's Ken.'

'What do you mean, Ken?'

'I'm afraid he's dead.'

'Don't be ridiculous.'

'Bank tube station. Right in front of the train. Nobody could have stopped him.'

13

The evening at the airport was dull and uneventful, with the exception of one passenger, an Indonesian who came off a flight from Amsterdam with a fake passport.

Whether he had anything to do with the Carne business was anyone's guess but he was being held for a while to see if his real identity could be established. After that he'd be sent back to Holland and he would be the Dutch authorities' problem from then on. He certainly wasn't Annie's. This was the sort of thing the immigration people could handle on their own; it didn't require her assistance. She felt over-qualified and under-valued and Steyn and Gamble and everyone else involved in this dumb scheme weren't high on her popularity list.

But on Sunday she was off duty. In the morning she thought of ringing Taggart, just to say hello, but she resisted the temptation and tried to put him out of her head. A diversion was required so, since the day was bright and clear, she put on running clothes and went jogging, heading along the highway to Bedford, then down over the railway crossing and on to Shore Drive.

Her route took her past the house where the murder of the private detective had taken place. It wasn't hard to identify. Although it was on a little wooded promontory and not immediately visible from the road, crime scene tape sealed the area off and a patrol car sat in the driveway. She slowed her pace as she went by. She was curious about what had happened there but she knew that that was partly because it wasn't her case. Other people's investigations always seemed more interesting.

In the evening she walked down to the cinema at Mill Cove where the best thing on offer was a weepie with Susan Sarandon. As she watched it she thought of how she had spent her day, how depressing it was that she had all this freedom, yet nothing much to do.

She checked her messages when she got back. Taggart hadn't called.

In fact, her telephone didn't ring at all until six the following morning. When it did, it jarred her from sleep. She thought at once that it must be a call from the boys in Italy but to her surprise it was Mark Gamble. In spite of the earliness of the hour, he was ringing her from headquarters.

'I want you here for a meeting at seven,' he said.

'What's going on? Has something happened?'

'You'll find out.'

'I've got to be at the airport again by eight.'

'No you haven't. That's been changed.'

'But why?'

'We'll talk about it when you get here.'

And so at ten minutes to seven she found herself walking into the office, accompanied by a feeling of dread. Gamble was never the most communicative of people but there had been ice in his voice on the phone.

Through the frosted glass in his little cubicle she could see his shape at the desk. She knocked the door and went in. He was talking to someone on the phone. When he saw her he said, 'She's here now,' then rang off.

She thought he looked sad somehow, disappointed.

She said, 'Yes, here I am. What's all this about, Boss?'

He stared at her for a second, then muttered, 'You're a fool, do you know that?'

The words shocked her. 'I . . . I don't understand.'

He came out from behind the desk. 'Gryce wants to see you. Come with me.'

He walked out of the office and she followed. Gryce? What was this? They went along the corridor and up the stairs to the next floor where the top brass lived. With every step, the sense that there was something very bad in store increased. They passed the Chief's office, then the Deputy Chief's. Gamble stopped at the door marked Head of Operations and knocked before they walked in.

The office was spacious. It had bright windows and a good view of the Citadel hillside but her eyes were immediately on the table at the end of the room and the people sitting behind it. Oliver Gryce sat in the middle and on either side of him were Larry Steyn and Nina Henry, who was shuffling papers that looked like photocopies of newspaper cuttings. Gamble went forward and took a seat beside Steyn. Annie stood where she was, uncertain what to do, puzzled and anxious.

Gryce gestured to a chair in front of the table. Nobody spoke to her, not even to suggest that she take off her coat. She sat down and looked at Gryce. 'I'm sorry, sir, but can anyone tell me what—'

'Do you know a man called John Taggart?' he asked abruptly.

The question startled her. She paused to collect herself, then said, 'Well, yes, I do, as a matter of fact. He's a British journalist. I met him the other day.' She looked at each of their faces. 'Nothing's happened to him, has it?'

Nina Henry pushed a sheet of paper across the table. It was a faxed photocopy of part of a tabloid newspaper page.

'This appeared in the London *Sunday Chronicle* yesterday.'

Annie picked it up. A three-deck headline in heavy type read:

ROYAL
VISIT
SCRAPPED

The byline said:

From John Taggart, Halifax, Nova Scotia, Saturday.

Her stomach began churning. She felt sick. She swallowed hard and then while the others watched she started to read:

'Prince William's visit to Nova Scotia in two weeks' time was dramatically called off last night.

'A source close to St James's Palace said that in the light of the current security crisis in this historic Maritime province there was no question of allowing it to go ahead.

'Concern for the Prince's safety has been building since a raid by the Royal Canadian Mounted Police on the home at Lunenburg, Nova Scotia, of A. J. Carne, a businessman suspected of being involved in organising the poison gas attack on the American embassy in Karachi last year in which 38 people died.

'The raid itself led to a shoot-out in which one man was killed and another seriously injured. It was carried out at the request of the FBI and the US State Department who want Carne to be extradited to America to face murder charges that could lead to his execution.

'Currently he is being held under house arrest while his lawyers go to war with the Nova Scotia Attorney General. Although there is an extradition agreement between Canada and the US, it does not automatically include extradition to states where there is the death

penalty, in this case Colorado, the home of several of the Karachi victims.

'In the meantime, tension has been mounting in Nova Scotia and the affair has caused a major political storm, not only because of the extradition row, but because when arrested at his home Carne was entertaining the man who has just been sworn in as the Province's new Lieutenant Governor.

'As the legal battle goes on, various right-wing, civil rights and ethnic political groups are expected to travel here to protest and fears are growing that they may clash with each other and the police in a re-run of the kind of violent scenes which took place in Seattle last year during the world trade conference.

'Security has been stepped up around Lunenburg, a United Nations Heritage Site, which the Prince was due to visit to launch Bluenose III, *a replica of a famous racing schooner. The RCMP and Halifax regional police have set up a joint team to look for known militant political activists.*

'One of its key officers, Halifax detective Annie Welles, told me last night: "We're worried that things might get out of hand. There's a military forces base at Shearwater, near here, and they're on standby in case of a major outbreak of trouble. There are British security people here, too, and they're watching things on a day-to-day basis. But it would be my guess that to be on the safe side they'll call the visit off."

'Last night it was confirmed that the Prince's trip would not now go ahead. An official statement is expected tomorrow.'

Annie glanced down the rest of it, her heart thumping, then she looked up. Gamble was staring at his hands.

Gryce and Steyn were looking at her with a kind of emptiness in their eyes. It was not anger or distaste; it was as if she had ceased to exist. But Nina Henry regarded her with curiosity.

Annie addressed herself to her. 'I . . . I never said any of this.'

'You talked to this man Taggart?' Gryce asked.

She looked at him. 'Yes.'

'Did you tell him about the JFO?'

'I gave him some background information. Off the record. He didn't say he was going to write anything like this. In fact he said he was writing about the visit still going ahead. I didn't say anything about calling it off or about things getting out of hand. That's nonsense.'

'Did you mention the fact that there were British security people here?'

'Well . . . I may have.'

'Did you or did you not?'

'Yes. But it was all meant to be unattributable.'

She felt as if there was a noose around her neck and that it was tightening with every answer.

'And Shearwater?'

'I explained what it was, that's all.'

She swallowed. A moment ago she'd been worried about Taggart. But what had he done to her?

Nina Henry spoke. 'It took a little while for this to detonate but it's all over the news this morning. I'm surprised you weren't aware of it.'

'When I got the call I came straight here. I didn't turn the TV or the radio on.'

'We didn't know anything about it until some of the agencies picked the story up and started quoting it. Then people put in requests to the Premier for a statement. Late last night he issued one, expressing dismay and disappointment that the royal visit was being abandoned without the courtesy of any consultation. However, three hours ago, St James's Palace issued its first official comment, denying that any such decision has been taken, and condemning this as an irresponsible piece of journalism. They say they'll be reporting the matter to the British Press Complaints Commission.'

Gryce said, 'And your name in the middle of this has caused a great deal of embarrassment to this department. You're not authorised to talk to the press about anything but especially not about ongoing operations. Your actions have been reckless.'

She found courage from somewhere. 'With respect, sir—'

Gamble glared a warning but she kept going.

'All I did was give Mr Taggart some very general background information. He has let me down very badly, betrayed a confidence.'

'And so have you,' Steyn said, speaking for the first time. 'You've jeopardised an entire operation. I think—'

Gamble interrupted. He told her, 'There's no question of your remaining on the JFO team. For the moment, you'll return to work here on office watch duties while a disciplinary hearing is set up. Do you understand?'

Office watch was the pits, the worst duty, dealing with all the walk-in stuff, filling in forms. It was a job for young officers learning the ropes on their way in or for has-beens on their way out.

She said, 'Yes, I understand.'

But a disciplinary. What would come out of that?

She looked at Gryce. 'Sir, I just want to say how sorry I am that this has happened and to assure you that it wasn't my fault. I didn't mean—'

'Save it for the disciplinary,' Gryce said. 'I'll reserve any further comment until then. Sergeant Gamble will talk to you when we've finished here.'

He looked at something in the papers in front of him, then turned away to talk to Nina Henry. The meeting was over. She had been dismissed.

Somehow she managed to stand on lifeless legs and make her way to the door. When she got outside she had to lean against the wall for support. Tension throbbed in her head like a drum.

She couldn't believe any of it. What had just happened to her? She felt shock and fear and suddenly there was anger, rising in her as if from a spring.

She hurried along the corridor, down the stairs and out of the building. Gamble would be looking for her soon but she didn't care just at the moment. It couldn't make matters any worse and there was something she had to do.

She got into her car.

At the desk of the Hotel Halifax she flashed her badge and asked for John Taggart's room number. Half a minute later she was knocking on his door.

When he opened it she was taken aback by his appearance. He was unshaven and dishevelled and there was a heavy darkness under his eyes as if he hadn't slept.

'Annie.' He seemed relieved to see her. 'I've just been trying to call you at home. I wanted to explain.'

She walked in and slammed the door. His room smelled stale. On the unmade bed she could see a fax of the cutting she had read a short time ago.

'Do you know the shit you've dumped me into?'

'What do you mean?'

She told him what had happened.

He put his head in his hands and sat down on the edge of the bed. 'Oh, Jesus, I'm sorry.' Then he looked up at her. 'If it's any consolation, I've just been fired.'

'No,' she said, 'it's no consolation at all but I can't say I'm heartbroken to hear it.'

As she stared at him she could feel her anger changing to disappointment. She thought she had seen something in him but he had let her down, betrayed her. Why did men do that?

'This is such a terrible mess,' he said. He picked up the cutting. 'Look – that wasn't the story I wrote. Please believe me. There's a woman called Judith Sefton. She must have taken my copy and rewritten it, made all that stuff up.'

'And just why would she do that?'

'We . . . I got kind of involved with her briefly. Then I made the mistake of ignoring her afterwards. She's been threatening to get back at me ever since. Yesterday – when I told you about a crisis at the paper – I didn't tell you the details. They brought in a new editor and he hired Judith as the executive in charge of news. They fired Ken Shaw, the existing editor, and then he went and threw himself under a train.' He shook his head. 'Christ, I still can't believe it.'

Annie was unmoved. 'You lied to me. You said you wouldn't use my name, yet you invented all this and quoted me as saying it.'

'I'm sorry. I admit I did use your name in my original copy, just to give it a bit more authenticity. I didn't think it would matter. I thought the story would appear in the UK and you'd never see it. But the quotes I used – they weren't harmful or sensational, not like those that appeared. Judith has taken your name and made up this other stuff.'

'Which she wouldn't have been able to do if you hadn't mentioned me in the first place.'

'I'm sorry. I really am. I didn't mean you any harm. Is there anything you'd like me to do, anyone you'd like me to speak to? Would that help?'

She gave a laugh. 'What do you think?'

He nodded. 'I spent last night being *hounded by the press*

– I think that's the expression. A strange experience to find yourself on the other side. Then the new editor called and fired me. He said I'd caused the newspaper great embarrassment by writing what was a total fabrication. They're sending someone to replace me. I'm going to try to sort a few things out today on the phone, then I'm going to fly back and see my lawyer. I've still got the original story filed in my computer, although that doesn't necessarily prove anything, and I've got to see if my usual sources will stick up for me. I suspect they won't, though. I think they'll run for cover.' He paused. 'And then there'll be Ken's funeral.'

It was too bad that somebody had died but that wasn't her concern.

It had been a mistake coming here. She'd thought that confronting him would achieve something but it hadn't.

His phone rang and he stood to answer it. When his back was turned, she went to the door and without another word she walked out. As she hurried down the corridor she could hear him calling her name.

14

At Gottingen Street, she saw that word had got around. It had travelled fast, in the time-honoured tradition of bad news, and it was on the faces of the people she passed as she walked in. Upstairs, the unit room was no longer quiet and the day had swung into action. Claussen was there. So was Flagg, sitting at his desk in the corner behind paperwork that was growing like a compost heap. As soon as he saw her, he put up his fists and punched the air.

'Keep fighting, kid.'

Claussen threw her a hostile look.

Gamble poked his head out of his office and waved her in. He closed the door and sat down behind his desk. 'Where the hell were you?'

'I had to get some air.'

He let it go, then gave her a mournful look.

'Jesus, Annie, what happened here?'

He sounded weary.

'Boss, believe me, I didn't do anything. We all talk to people off the record. You know that. They just never screw us like this.'

She told him about her dinner date with Taggart and the Camerons, then she told him about Taggart's explanation of how the story had come to be written.

'When did he tell you this?'

'Just a little while ago.'

'Which is where you went to get the air, I take it?'

She nodded.

He swivelled sideways in his chair to look at the foggy glass and turned a pencil over and over in his fingers, tapping it on the desk.

He said, 'Gryce shouldn't have let Steyn sit in on the discussion, Nina Henry either. She's a civilian, for God's sake. But he's into openness, transparency – that's the current word. And who am I to argue?'

Annie wasn't sure she should be hearing this. He seemed to be speaking more to himself.

He looked round at her again. 'The move to office watch was my solution. Gryce went along with it when I talked to him on the phone before the meeting. But Steyn and I had words after you left. He said you should have been suspended right away. I told him it was none of his fucking business, then Gryce asked me to apologise. Great, huh?'

As she listened, it began to dawn on her that she wasn't the only one in trouble. Gamble had to be feeling some of the reverberations as well. It was he who had nominated her for the JFO and therefore he would have to bear some of the responsibility for her actions.

'Boss, I'm sorry if I've given you a problem – I really am.'

He shrugged. 'It's just the circumstances. Steyn's loving it. Anything that deflects attention away from them and makes somebody else look bad. But Gryce wants us to bounce back from this pretty damn quick.'

'Is there anything I can do to help?'

He gave her a pained look. 'Don't even think about it. Just keep your head down. Now get out of here. I've got to talk to Claussen.'

When she left the office, he called her former partner in. Claussen walked past her as if she wasn't there.

She wandered over towards Flagg's desk. 'Hi, Walter. How's it going?'

He had taken his jacket off and she could see that even though this was Monday morning his shirt wasn't a fresh one. He sat in an aura of aftershave applied with abandon but as always she could detect an undercurrent of last night's booze. Sometimes she wondered if it might be more recent than that.

She wasn't entirely sure about Flagg's domestic circumstances but she was certain they were nothing to write home about. He lived way out in Sackville, in a ramshackle place by a lake, but she had never been invited there and she suspected no one else had either. There was no Mrs Flagg. That much she did know.

'Christ, how's it going with you, more's the point? Word has it they're busting your ass over this newspaper thing. That's a tough break.'

'What can I say? Excrement occurs.'

He laughed. 'That's the spirit. Don't let the bastards grind you down.'

She didn't want to talk about this any more. She perched herself on the edge of his desk and said, 'So what's happening in the real world? How're you guys getting to grips with these murders?'

'Well, now, two interesting cases, that's for sure. This guy Cobb Landry, killed over in Dartmouth? I'm working on that file with our friend Claussen.'

'Nice for you.'

'Oh, we're getting along fine except every now and then I have to remind him I'm not some sort of fucking rookie just learning the game.'

She smiled. 'Which you would do in your usual tactful manner. So this Landry, what's the story?'

'Yeah, well, we don't have an answer to that yet. Guy

was a bank official. Somebody snapped his neck for him.'

He sat forward suddenly and made a violent wringing motion with his hands.

'Thanks. I get the picture.'

'Very neat. No sign of a struggle, no sign of a break-in but we have a witness who saw the killer before he ran out of the house.'

'That's something. Description any good?'

'Yep. Our guys have worked up a computer picture based on what he told us. It's been in the papers and on TV this morning but I guess you've been a bit too busy to see any of that.'

'Just a tad.'

'I've got one here.' He startled to rustle among the papers on his desk but the search didn't produce anything. 'Well, there was one. Shit.'

'Don't worry about it.'

He gave up. 'Like I said, an interesting case. Turns out the victim was dying of liver cancer, as a matter of fact.'

'Really? Did he know that?'

'Oh sure. He was bald as a coot from the chemo. The doctors had already told him he didn't have long. Couple of months.'

'What are the domestic circumstances?'

'Not much. Never married. Lived alone. He worked at the Scotiabank headquarters downtown, part-time for the past while at his own request. Seems he wanted to keep his life as normal as possible for as long as he could.'

'Poor guy.'

Flagg nodded thoughtfully. 'Yeah. When I go, I want to go quick. None of that lingering death shit.'

'So why was he killed? If there was no struggle, no break-in, it kind of indicates that it must have been someone he knew.'

'Isn't that always the way?'

'What about the witness?'

'A neighbour. Name of Harry Orbach. Landry was due at his house for dinner. He came over to see what was keeping him and found the killer leaning over the body.'

'Did he recognise him?'

'Says he never saw him before.'

Annie gave him a look.

'And yes, I know what you're thinking. Did Orbach really see a perp or did he do the business himself?'

She shrugged. 'You never know.'

'You never do. Except we've looked at Orbach's story and it seems to check out. There was a car parked outside Landry's place and neighbours heard it speeding off when Orbach came out of the house shouting.'

'Licence plate?'

He shook his head. 'Just a description. Dark sedan. Black, maybe. No make.'

'Not a lot of help. What about the other killing – Shore Drive? Who's working that?'

He nodded towards the far side of the room where Deedes and Neidermayer were sitting. 'They caught it.'

'I went running on Shore Drive yesterday. Passed the house. Nice quiet place.'

Flagg winced. 'Running? Jesus, you don't want to do that, give yourself a heart attack.'

'Thanks, I'll bear that in mind.'

'To tell you the truth I don't know much about this one but from talking to the guys there I don't get the impression that it's moving too fast. The victim was a man name of George Poyner. Ex-Toronto homicide cop, operating in Halifax since getting his PI licence about ten years ago. Ever come across him?'

She shook her head. 'Don't think so.'

'Yeah, well, maybe not. The work he did was mostly civil stuff. The guys in Fraud say they rubbed shoulders with him once or twice, all above board, apparently.'

'Wife? Family?'

'He shared the Shore Drive place with a woman who owns a hairdressing business. No kids. There was a wife once in Toronto, long gone. Anyway, the current squeeze is out of the picture. She was away for the night, down in Boston. Solid alibi.'

Annie gave him another look.

He laughed and waved a finger at her. 'Boy, you've got a suspicious mind. And so have Deedes and Neidermayer. They're checking whether she stands to benefit in any way from her boyfriend's untimely departure. That's all I know.'

'What kind of a gun?'

He called out. 'Hey, Deedes, what kind of gun in the Poyner shooting?'

'Why do you want to know?' Clem Deedes called from his desk without looking up.

'It's just me being curious,' Annie said, 'wondering what you guys are up to, that's all.'

Deedes raised his head and smiled at her, then he got out of his chair and walked across.

'Hi, Annie. Feeling a bit left out of the action?'

She gave a rueful smile.

He nodded in sympathy. 'I heard. Some tough shit. What can I say?'

'Not a whole lot.'

'Anyway, Poyner. You were asking about the gun. The question is, which gun?'

'What does that mean?'

'Poyner took two nine-millimetre slugs in the chest. We found more bullets in the walls and casings on the floor, but they weren't all from the same weapon. The only gun we found was Poyner's own, a .38 Smith and Wesson that was locked in his desk drawer. It hadn't been fired. Wasn't even loaded.'

'So we're talking two unidentified guns?'

'Two guns and two cars driving away from the scene in different directions. One of them almost knocked a witness down but didn't, fortunately, otherwise we wouldn't even have this much.'

'Robbery? Anything taken from the house?'

'Not that we can ascertain but the place was a mess when we got there. And then there's the front window. One of those old plate glass affairs. Somebody went through it. There was a lot of blood. We lifted some of it from the fragments.'

'Okay, everybody, can I have your attention please?'

They turned. It was Gamble. He was standing at his office door with a folder in his hand which meant he was on his way to a meeting. He always was. Claussen stood beside him with a thin smile.

'Fuck, what's this?' Flagg said. He hauled himself out of his chair and he and Deedes walked over. So did the rest of the room. Annie stayed put. Whatever this was, she knew it did not concern her.

Gamble said, 'I want to let you know that we're putting together a special task force to work on the Landry and Poyner killings. I know they're two separate cases but in the circumstances, with all the public heat out there for once reason or another, SMT are keen that we get results as quickly as possible. I've asked Claussen here to head up the team, to be lead investigator as from this moment, reporting directly to me on a twice-daily basis. Whatever he needs, I've assured him we'll be able to get it. I've already asked for extra support staff for case-mapping and typing reports so that you people aren't unduly tied up with paperwork.

The bottom line is – I want these cases put to bed by the end of the week.'

There was muttering. Gamble glared.

'And anyone who doesn't want to be part of this can ship the hell out.'

The muttering stopped.

He looked at Claussen. 'All yours.' Then he tucked his folder under his arm and left the room. Immediately he'd gone, Claussen called Deedes, Niedermayer and Flagg into the little office and sat down behind the desk as if it was his own.

The SMT Gamble had referred to was the senior management team on the floor above. What it really meant in this instance, Annie guessed, was Oliver Gryce. He had thrown Gamble a curve ball that was going to be difficult, if not impossible, to hit. End of the week was a tall order but cracking these cases quickly and making a song and dance about it when it happened would help the department recover from the mess she had dropped them in.

Claussen was the lead officer. She detected the hand of Nina Henry there. Henry saw him as the coming man. Of that there was no doubt. Gryce would not have been hard to persuade and Gamble would have had to go along with it. But he would not be happy with the thought of the ambitious Claussen breathing down his neck. She looked at the men talking in the little office.

The phone on her desk was ringing. She went over and picked it up and found Jeff Cameron at the other end.

'Annie, I called John at the hotel to tell him what an unprincipled asshole he was and when I'd got that off my chest he told me what happened. Christ, I'm sorry. In my wildest dreams I never thought you would get into any kind of trouble.'

'Don't worry about it, Jeff. It's not your fault.'

'I know John's really cut up about this.'

'And so he should be.'

'Why don't you try and sort this out with him?'

'I don't think so.'

'Talk to him. A cup of coffee or something.'

'Goodbye, Jeff.' She hung up.

'Officer Welles?'

A young woman was standing at her elbow. Annie recognised her as a clerk from one of the other units.

'Yes, that's me.'

'I'm really sorry, but I've been told I can take this desk.'

15

Downstairs, someone showed her where to sit, but for the most part people ignored her or gave her wary sideways glances. She felt as if she were a stranger from another world who did not have long to spend in this one.

Her desk was at the back of the room on the main public floor. There was a big counter at the front, like a bank, and manned for the most part by civilian clerks who handed out forms and took details of lost property or drivers' licences and car insurance certificates which people had been asked to produce. Occasionally, someone turned up to report a crime: a break-in or a stolen vehicle or a street mugging, which is where office watch came in.

Having an experienced officer on tap from one of the investigative units was something of an unaccustomed luxury for the Watch Commander, Staff Sergeant Jean Bonnard, a big-chested man with a white moustache, and rather than treating her like a pariah he tried to make her feel at home. She did her best to appreciate the effort but it was difficult. She felt conspicuous and uncomfortable, plus the big room was draughty and dusty and full of noise with all the work being done to rebuild the front entrance. It was like sitting in a train station.

But she took advantage of Bonnard's hospitality and asked him if someone could bring her PC down. Then she spent twenty minutes or so trying to get her desk into shape.

It had become a dumping-ground for unwanted paper. After a brief attempt to read some of the stuff, trying to work out if there was anything that was important, she gave up and deposited the whole lot in a black bin bag, out of the way. Someone else could sort it out after she had gone. Whenever that would be.

The morning settled into the uneventful monotony of routine daily trivia until at about eleven a.m. it was broken by a commotion at the front counter. A small elderly woman came in with a long brown paper parcel that the cop at the door didn't like the look of. When he asked her what it contained, she opened it up and took out a rifle. After a moment's minor panic, with everyone moving back out of the way and a couple of people actually ducking behind the counter, he took it delicately from her hands and someone went and got Annie.

The 'rifle' was actually a pellet gun which the woman had found in her back garden. Annie took the weapon and dispatched it to the technical unit, then she wrote up the woman's details and after a brief conversation sent her on her way.

The next caller to need her attention was a middle-aged man who came in to report a robbery. He had a black eye and a heavily bruised nose which he claimed had been given to him by two young women who had relieved him of his wallet as well as some jewellery which had belonged to his late wife. Annie brought him into the interview room so that they could discuss this in private.

His name was Bryant Kimbrough. 'They were guests in my home,' he said with indignation and a sense of insult, making it sound like a sophisticated social occasion that had gone dreadfully wrong. But from his address, in a shabby corner of West Halifax, Annie guessed that the story was likely to be different. This was not the Great Gatsby she was dealing with here.

'Can you tell me the names of these women?'

He looked uncomfortable. 'I'm not really . . . one was called Charlene, I think. I'm not sure of the other one.'

'So you don't really know them all that well?'

'No, we met last night for the first time.'

'And where was that?'

He gave her the name of a bar which she recognised straight away. It was in the south of the city, down near the container terminal.

'Then I take it that these two women are hookers, Mr Kimbrough?'

'I, well . . .' he shifted nervously and wiped his palms '. . . I wasn't aware of that at the time, of course.'

'No, of course you weren't.' She gave him a wintry smile. 'Have you been to that bar before?'

'Once or twice, yes.'

'But you'd never met these women?'

'I'd seen them. Last night was the first time we spoke.'

He told her what had been stolen and she wrote it down. The item of jewellery which concerned him most was a silver locket on a chain. It had his late wife's initials on it – 'R.K.' for Ruth Kimbrough.

'And how did they manage to get hold of that?'

'I keep it on top of the dresser in my bedroom.'

Annie raised an eyebrow. 'Where they saw it?'

'They must have, yes.'

She asked him to describe the two women and he did. She wrote that down too but they could have been hookers anywhere, in any port in the world.

'I'm going to have to refer this to my colleagues in Vice. They may know who this Charlene is, and her partner in crime. We'll get a few people in for an identification parade and see if you recognise any of them.'

'What will happen then? Will I get my things?'

'They may still have your property although I doubt it. They'll try to sell the jewellery pretty quickly, probably for only a fraction of whatever value it has. These girls need cash to feed their drug habits, pimps, whatever. If they don't have the stuff, then when we charge them it will be mostly on your word.'

'Will I have to appear in court?'

'If they plead guilty, no. If they plead not guilty, definitely.'

'I don't want that. I don't want all this fuss – court – everything. I just want my belongings.' He pushed his chair back abruptly and stood. 'Look, maybe I made a mistake here.'

'A mistake?'

'Maybe I'm jumping to conclusions. Maybe I put the locket somewhere and forgot.'

'I see. And the bruises on your face. Are they a mistake, too?'

He put his hand to his nose and gave a weak smile. 'Yeah, well, accidents happen.' He pointed to Annie's notes. 'I . . . I want to withdraw my complaint. I think I may have been a bit hasty.'

Annie sat back. 'It's up to you, Mr Kimbrough, but I hope you haven't been wasting my time with this.'

'No, I don't want to do that but you can't do anything without a complaint, can you? Or without my co-operation?'

'In this instance, not a lot, no.'

'Then I'm sorry if I've troubled you.' He began to button his overcoat.

Annie told him, 'Look, I don't know what's going on in that head of yours but I'm passing all this to Vice anyhow. If they find any girls with this stuff, then you're back in here, pronto, to talk about it. Do you understand what I'm saying?'

Kimbrough nodded. He seemed agitated, anxious to get away.

'I'm sorry, Officer. I didn't mean to be a nuisance.'

Annie showed him the door. 'And take my advice and keep away from that bar.'

When he'd gone, she checked with Records to see if there was anything on him but the search drew a blank. Then she went up to Vice with the story and spoke to an officer called Janice King to whom it was just another john being rolled. Annie gave her Kimbrough's name and address.

'The thought of appearing in court threw him.'

'As it would.'

'He said one of them was called Charlene. I guess that doesn't mean anything.'

'Charlene, Darlene, Arlene – one name today and another one tomorrow.'

Annie nodded. 'You know, I've a feeling he might go back to that bar and try to find the stuff himself.'

'I hope not. Somebody could get hurt that way. Most likely him,' Janice said, and told her they'd keep an eye open.

Annie went back to her desk. She put her notes on Kimbrough in a drawer, just in case, then she wrote his name and address on a piece of paper and stuck it in her pocket.

Just after noon, one of the civilian assistants turned to her. 'There's a call on line eight. Somebody from the Parole Service. Think maybe you should talk to him.'

She picked up the phone and introduced herself.

A voice said, 'This is Eric Benjamin. I'm a parole supervisor.'

She had met him before. She pictured a short man, about fifty, with a squat nose and baby-pink skin.

'Yes, Eric, what can I do for you?'

He seemed to be having difficulty telling her. 'It's . . . well, I don't know. I'm having a bit of a problem. It's one of my *clients*, as I like to call them. He was due with me at nine this morning but he hasn't turned up.'

'So, what – are you reporting a parole violation?'

'Maybe, I'm not sure. It's not like him. And this wasn't just a routine meeting either. Well, it was, that was part of it, but . . . jeez, I don't know. I just hope something hasn't happened to him. I've tried his home number several times but he's not there. I left it for a while to see if he would appear but he hasn't.'

Annie frowned. This wasn't making a great deal of sense.

'Just hold on a second, Eric. Can you tell me who this person is?'

'It's Aaron. Aaron Gaunt.'

He said the name as if it was that of a friend, not a client. She wrote it down.

'And he's on parole?'

'Statutory release.'

'So he's served a full sentence?'

'Yes.'

'How long was he inside.'

'Thirty years.'

She whistled. 'I assume we're talking murder here. What did he do?'

'He stabbed a woman twenty-one times.'

A couple of minutes later, when she'd finished the call, she told Staff Sergeant Bonnard about it. Since it was time for a lunch break, a privilege, she had to concede, that she didn't always enjoy upstairs, she suggested that maybe she should go down to Benjamin's office to continue the conversation there. Bonnard agreed and said he would get a patrol car to stop by Aaron Gaunt's home and have a look.

Benjamin had given her the address, a house in a street off the top of Spring Garden Road.

Benjamin worked out of a government building on Hollis Street. She called him back and told him she would be with him in a couple of minutes. It was just a short walk but it was a cold one. As she set off down Duke Street, the wind was as sharp as a knife. It seemed to sweep up from the harbour, swirl around the Citadel and then blow back down again. There was no escape from it. She pulled her collar up and hurried along.

When she got to Benjamin's office, she found that he had been thoughtful enough to send out for coffee and sandwiches. He took her coat and she asked him to tell her about Aaron Gaunt.

'He's been out of prison for three months and this has never happened before. Look, we both know parole violation goes on all the time and we have to go chasing after people, then send them back to jail again, more often than not. But they're petty criminals, the persistent offenders, the guys who are screwed up on drugs, for instance, or else go on the run after committing another crime. Aaron Gaunt's not like that. He's not one of that kind.'

'He's a killer. That would worry me.'

Benjamin nodded. 'He *was* a killer. Once. I've got his file here. Why don't you have a look at it? And eat while you're doing that. Please. The file has everything you need to know about him, including my own reports. You'll see what I mean. It's the best way of explaining it to you.'

She nibbled on a chicken salad sandwich and digested the information in the file at the same time. It did not take her long to agree that he was probably right. The missing man was sixty-three years old and from what she could see he was unlikely to be a run-of-the-mill parole jumper.

But even though there was a lot of stuff about Gaunt now

there wasn't enough about Gaunt then. She looked at a photograph, with the date stamped on the back, taken not long before his release. He was a thin-faced man with eyes that told her nothing. She wanted to read more about the crime for which he had been sentenced. Instead there was just a simple statement of the facts, that he had been convicted in 1970 of the first degree murder of a woman named Cassandra Breaux at a place called Heckman's Island, near Lunenburg. He had been jailed for life, which meant thirty years.

God, that was a long time.

On the other hand, there was a great deal of information from the Correctional Service about Gaunt's time in Dorchester prison, including the remarkable fact that he had gone in a murderer but had come out with a degree in sociology and a doctorate in behavioural psychology. On top of that, since leaving prison, he had embarked on a research study, sponsored by the Correctional Service, into how lifers and other long-term offenders were handled in prison and how successfully or otherwise they were prepared for re-integration into the community.

She read Benjamin's reports on the progress he had been making.

'This is quite a mind here.'

'Brilliant. He's done some fantastic work, both in prison and since he came out.'

'You seem to know him well.'

'Well enough. Enough to know that something's wrong.'

'How did he get his doctorate?'

'He started to study after he'd been inside fifteen years or so. Dalhousie took him on. He studied by mail for the most part, as an external student. Later he received individual tutorials in prison. It took him a long time but then he had plenty of that. He read all the time. He must have accumulated hundreds of books of one kind or another over the years. The prison even stored them for him in a room next to the library. He wrote some terrific papers on rehabilitation, got through all the exams.'

'How did he sit them?'

'Sat them in Dorchester in a room on his own. He got the sociology degree first. His thesis for his doctorate was based on his prison experiences. This morning we were going to look at a draft of his current study before sending it off to some people in Ottawa.' He shook his head. 'He's not the sort of person who would just not turn up. Something must have happened to him.'

Annie asked if she could use his phone. She called Bonnard's extension. He wasn't there but eventually she discovered that a patrol car had called by Gaunt's house as requested. She tracked one of the officers down in the canteen.

'Did you find anything?'

'No, the house is intact, all locked up, and it doesn't look like there's anybody there. We spoke to a neighbour who hasn't seen the guy since Thursday.'

'Is it possible he's inside, maybe ill or something?'

'Possible, I guess. But his car's gone.'

'Make?'

'Dodge. Blue, the neighbour thinks.'

'Licence number?'

'Haven't got it.'

She turned away and asked Benjamin if he knew but he shook his head. She would get the answer from vehicle licensing.

She said into the phone, 'Listen, I think you better get back over there straight away. I'm afraid you're going to have to force an entry somehow.'

'What? You sure about this?'

'We need to make sure there's no one there. And don't worry about the watch commander. I'll clear it with him.'

She rang off, wondering what Bonnard would say when she told him. She put the file back on the desk and said to Benjamin, 'There's not that much in this about the actual murder, just that he killed this woman out near Lunenburg. I'd have expected more detail.'

'That's not what the file's about. We try to concentrate on the man, not the crime, unless there's some long-term recurring problem in relation to it. What's in there is an assessment of Aaron Gaunt's development in prison and his state of mind since release. The past is the past. But, you know, it was a big story at the time.'

She gave him a pained look. 'Do me a favour, Eric. I was four.'

He smiled. 'Of course. Sorry.'

'You remember it, though.'

'Yes. Unfortunately I wasn't four. I must have been twenty or so. The story was simple. Aaron killed this woman Cassandra Breaux. He'd been having an affair with her and they had a fight in her house. Neighbours heard screaming and called the police and they found him naked with a knife in his hand, standing over her body. All kind of straightforward. His defence was that he didn't do it, someone else had come into the room and knocked him out, then killed her.'

'Anything to support that?'

'Not a thing. He had a knock on the head, sure enough, but the police reckoned that was as a result of the fight with the woman. There was furniture scattered around and blood everywhere but no evidence of a third party.'

'So he got sent up for thirty years, first degree.'

Benjamin nodded. 'Apart from the savagery of the attack itself, there was evidence of premeditation. Seems he'd threatened to kill Cassandra Breaux because she'd said something about telling his wife what they were up to.'

'Where's the wife now?'

'They divorced years ago, not long after he went up to Dorchester.'

'Kids?'

He shook his head. 'No relatives at all, as far as I know. The thing is, Aaron's drawn a line in the sand when it comes to his past life. And from my point of view, that's fine. He's had a long time in prison to deal with what he did and now he wants to move on in a positive way.'

'So how does he live? This house of his, is it rented?'

'No, he owns it.'

'How come he has that kind of money?'

'He was in the electronics business years ago, before all this. The company got sold and he invested his share. It grew pretty steadily all the time he was inside. Towards the end of his sentence he was allowed temporary leave, ETAs first, then UTAs.'

'Which is what?'

'Escorted temporary absence and unescorted temporary absence. ETAs can be applied for at any time during a sentence. Lifers are allowed to apply for UTAs three years before their full parole eligibility date. Over a period of time, this allowed Aaron to acclimatise himself to the outside world and to start making plans for when he would get out. He found the house last summer. Thanks to his healthy financial situation he was able to pay cash.'

Annie thought. 'I'm puzzled about one thing. How come he did the full stretch? Why didn't he get out five years ago? He'd have been entitled to parole after twenty-five years, wouldn't he?'

Benjamin looked as if she had found out something he

didn't want her to know. 'That's in the file, too. Maybe you hadn't come to it. He did apply for parole when he was coming up to the twenty-five year mark but something happened. There was a tip-off to the prison authorities that he was using drugs. When they searched his cell, they found crack cocaine hidden in his bed frame. There was no way he was going to get parole after that. He never applied again, just did his time and that was that.'

'And was he – is he – a user?'

'Nah, not Aaron. He's healthy and fit as a fiddle. Looks after himself like an athlete. No, somebody just wanted to screw up his chances. Who knows what enemies he made in prison in thirty years.'

Annie stood and got her coat. 'Eric, I hear everything you're saying. You know this guy better than I do and you've obviously got faith in him but I don't like the idea of a convicted murderer—'

He started to protest but she didn't let him.

'I know, however long ago it was. I don't like the idea of him being unaccounted for. Does he have friends?'

'If he does, I don't know about them. Aaron's the kind of guy who communicates what he wants to communicate but nothing more. I guess I've always thought of him as a bit of a loner. I don't know much about what he does with his time, outside of the things he's been writing, but as long as he's not in any kind of trouble that's okay with me. After thirty years in jail, I can understand anyone wanting to have a bit of privacy, can't you?'

He looked a bit uncomfortable. It occurred to Annie that he was beginning to realise he knew rather less about Gaunt than he should.

She said, 'If he's not in the house, then what I think we should do is check the hospitals and issue details of his car once we have them. If we're still drawing a blank after that, then we'll put out a description on the basis that this is a possible parole violation.'

Benjamin looked disappointed but he nodded in agreement.

'It's all I can do,' she said. She pointed to the file. 'There are some details in here that I need. Can I take copies?'

When she got back to Gottingen Street Bonnard had also returned and she filled him in, adding an apology for sending the patrol cops back to the house without prior reference to him.

'I thought it was important not to waste any time,' she told him and waited for a rebuke.

But he smiled and said. 'I can see now why you get into trouble.'

The patrol guys returned. They'd got in by taking a ladder to an upstairs window where a fanlight was open. There was no sign of Gaunt in the house.

Annie told Bonnard she should get a proper warrant and take a look around the place but there were other things to do first. She called vehicle licensing and got a number for Gaunt's Dodge, then she got it into the system as a car to look out for. Next she set about calling the hospitals, including some of those out of the city, like Bridgewater in Lunenburg County, to see if Aaron Gaunt had been admitted or if they had anyone of his age and description for whom they didn't have a name. Two hours later she was still getting nowhere and decided to call a halt to this line of enquiry.

Her computer hadn't appeared yet but maybe Bonnard had forgotten. She didn't want to push her luck and go to him again, like some spoilt hotel guest complaining about room service, so she decided to go upstairs and get it herself.

She felt nervous going into the familiar room, as if she had been banished and had no right to be back in this forbidden territory, but people were busy and didn't seem to notice her. Flagg wasn't around and she was relieved to find that Claussen wasn't there either. She looked at Gamble's office but the frosted glass didn't indicate anyone inside.

She walked towards her desk. The young woman who had taken it over had set the computer on the floor. She looked up nervously.

'I've come for my PC,' Annie said.

'I'm sorry. I had to move it because of this.'

She gestured to the surface of the desk. It was covered with boxes and lever arch files and soft folders.

'Where did all this come from?'

'The murder victim's office. Mr Poyner. Officer Claussen wants me to log everything.'

Annie nodded. 'I'm trying to remember your name. It's Claire, right?'

'Yes. Claire Stacey.' She smiled, pleased that Annie knew.

Annie bent towards the computer. Claire had set a book on top of the monitor. It was an A4-size diary.

'This part of it, too?'

'Oh, sorry,' Claire said. 'There's not enough room.'

'Do you mind if I have a look?' Annie asked, already leafing through it.

'No, help yourself. I'm sure that's all right.' But she didn't sound entirely certain.

Annie smiled. 'I'm just a nosy parker.'

She saw that Poyner, if this was his writing, had been in the habit of jotting down notes next to where appointments and times were written in. She wished she was on a case like this instead of dealing with something that might turn out to be nothing. She turned to Thursday. Poyner had been murdered that night. What had he done that day? It was a question she knew Claussen would already have asked but she couldn't resist looking for herself.

There were some appointments in the morning but none in the afternoon and in the blank space a name was written.

At first she thought she was seeing things.

Then she must have gone pale or something because Claire said, 'Are you all right? What . . . what is it?'

She didn't answer. Instead she kept looking at the page where the name 'Gaunt', with an exclamation mark in the margin, seemed to stare back at her.

16

All sorts of possibilities clamoured for attention in her brain as she flicked backward and forward through the pages of the diary to see if the name appeared anywhere else. It didn't. Just on that one day.

She was so gripped that she didn't even notice that Claussen had come back into the room.

'What the hell are you doing with that?'

He had a cup of coffee in his hand. He put it down on the edge of the overflowing desk and snatched the diary from her.

'Hold on a minute, Gil. I came up here to get my computer and I discovered—'

He turned his irritation on Claire. 'Did you give her this?'

'She didn't give me anything, Gil. Leave her alone. I just picked the thing up out of curiosity. I found a name in there.'

'Look, keep out of it. You're not part of this investigation. Right now you're not even part of this unit. So why don't you go back downstairs where you belong?'

'Jesus, Gil, if you'd listen to me I might be of help here.'

The door opened and Walter Flagg came in, making puffing noises and taking his overcoat off.

'Damn stairs,' he said.

He saw Annie and Claussen glaring at each other and Claire sitting wide-eyed in what looked like a line of fire.

He walked over. 'What's with you two?'

Claussen didn't look at him but held an arm out as if to keep him at bay.

'I can handle this, thank you.'

'Listen,' Annie said, still focussed on what she had seen. 'There's a name in there that might mean something. The name "Gaunt". It's written in on the day Poyner was killed.'

'So what?' Claussen said but she could hear a hint of curiosity entering his voice. He couldn't stand her being anywhere near these cases but he wasn't stupid either. He couldn't afford not to hear what she had to say.

She told him, 'I've been checking up on a possible parole violation this morning. A man called Aaron Gaunt. Aged sixty three. Released from Dorchester a few months ago after serving a full thirty-year life sentence for murder. Nobody's seen him since Thursday, the day Poyner was killed. If you look at Thursday in that diary, you'll find the name Gaunt in it. What if it's the same person?'

'And what if it's not?' Claussen said but he turned to the page nevertheless. He studied it for a second or two and she could almost see his mind making a judgement.

He said, 'All right, maybe it's worth a look. Let us have whatever details you've got and we'll take it from there. And then I'd be obliged if you kept away from this room, like you're supposed to, and didn't interfere any further.'

'Wait a second,' Flagg told him. 'You don't own the fucking place. You can't talk to Annie like that. It sounds to me like she's doing you a favour. Or maybe you hadn't noticed.'

'Walter, don't bother,' Annie said. 'I can take care of myself.'

Claussen looked pained. 'Why don't you just get on with your work, Flagg, and get out of my face?'

Flagg pushed him in the chest. It wasn't a hard push but Flagg was a strong man and Claussen wasn't expecting it.

He lurched back, off balance, and hit the styrofoam cup he had set down. It toppled over and a stream of steaming black coffee flooded across the desk. Claire leapt to her feet and began to snatch papers from its path.

'Jesus, Flagg, you're an asshole,' Claussen said. 'A stupid fucking asshole.'

'And you're an arrogant prick. One of these days I'm going to teach you some fucking manners.'

'What the hell's all this?'

Gamble was coming into the room, back from yet another meeting. The folder in his hand said 'budgets' on the cover.

They turned to look at him, all except Claire who kept on cleaning up. She had grabbed a newspaper. It was soaking up the mess successfully but it was leaving inky smears all over her hands. Nobody spoke until Annie said, 'It's just an accident, Boss. Some coffee got spilled.'

'I thought you were supposed to be working downstairs.'

'I am. I had to—'

'She's come up with something that might be a lead in the Poyner murder,' Flagg said.

'Oh?' Gamble raised an eyebrow and looked at Claussen who nodded reluctantly.

'It's a possibility, yes. But it also might be nothing.'

'So tell me,' Gamble said and then listened as she explained.

While she was doing so, Claire went off to wash her hands and somebody told Flagg there was a call for him. He picked up the phone on Annie's desk. A drip of coffee ran down the mouthpiece and fell on to his jacket but if he noticed he did nothing about it. The call had his full attention.

'What? You're sure about that? She's not getting confused? She definitely means the Landry thing?' He listened. 'Yeah . . . right . . . thanks. I'll get on it.'

He hung up. The others waited, intrigued by his tone.

'That was Deedes. He and Neidermayer are at Poyner's office going over some stuff with the secretary. Get this. She's been talking to them about some guy who came in to see Poyner on Thursday. She says she saw the paper and the TV this morning and she reckons that the computer fit of the guy we're looking for in the Landry murder is a match for him.'

'What?' Gamble said. 'Wait a minute, wait a minute. The Landry murder? Surely there's no connection? That has to be a mistake.'

'You heard me ask. But that's what she says.'

'Did she mention the name of this man who called? Was it Gaunt?' Annie asked.

'Deedes didn't say. I should have asked.'

Claussen stepped away and walked over to his own desk. When he came back he was carrying a photocopied computer picture. Annie guessed it was what Flagg hadn't been able to find earlier in the day. She took it from him and looked at it. These things, however scientific, could go badly wrong and sometimes bore little or no resemblance to the person they were meant to represent. A half-remembered face, usually seen for a few seconds in difficult circumstances, then the memory translated by computer graphics – there was plenty of room for error. But in the picture now in her hand she thought she could detect certain echoes of the photograph of Aaron Gaunt that she had seen in Eric Benjamin's file.

'Have you got a shot of this Gaunt guy?' Gamble asked her.

'A photocopy. On the desk downstairs. I'll go get it.'

Gamble looked at Flagg. 'Get Deedes and Neidermayer to bring the secretary in and you'd better get hold of your Landry witness – what's his name?'

'Orbach.'

'Yeah, Orbach. Let's get him in too and show them both the picture.'

He turned towards his office as his phone began ringing. Annie raced downstairs for the material she had brought back from her visit to the parole supervisor.

When she returned, Flagg examined the picture. 'Yep. I suppose it could be my guy.'

Gamble had disappeared somewhere. Claussen was using the phone in his office, something he seemed to do at every available opportunity.

Flagg followed her gaze. 'Look at him in there, staking his claim to the territory.'

'So where'd the boss go?'

He pointed a finger towards the ceiling. 'Upstairs, more than likely. You know what it's been like since Wilson went off sick. He's up and down to Gryce's office like a squirrel on a tree.' He reached to take the folder from her. 'I guess I should relieve you of all this.'

She looked at his outstretched hand. It was a reminder that however interested she was, she was not working these cases. She said, 'Sure. Take it.'

He moved off with the file, reading. Claire returned to the desk, smelling of soap and perfume, and got back to the task of making out her inventory. Annie stood in awkward isolation for a moment, feeling separated from it all once again. She didn't want to leave but there was nothing to keep her here. She bent down and started unplugging the computer.

'Better get what I came for.'

She lifted the monitor and told Claire she'd be back for the rest. She was on her third and final journey, carrying her printer and all the leads, when she met Gamble coming back in. His eyes were bright and he seemed excited about something.

'Put that thing down. We need to have a word.' He beckoned to her to follow him.

She set the printer down beside a puzzled Claire and said, 'Don't ask.'

Gamble glared in at Claussen. 'Do you think I could have my office back?' He said it loudly enough for everyone to hear. Claussen wrapped up his telephone conversation with awkward haste.

'We have to talk. The three of us,' Gamble said and closed the door. He took his seat behind the desk. Annie sat down. Claussen looked confused, then did the same.

'What's going on?' he asked.

'Well now, an interesting thing has happened,' Gamble said. He picked a pencil up and began his usual routine of twirling it between finger and thumb. 'I got a call to go up and see Head of Operations and when I was there I took the opportunity of telling him about this new possibility, this guy Aaron Gaunt. He had some news for me, too. It seems that someone has been talking to the *Herald-Chronicle*, dropping the hint that Annie has been reprimanded over this business with the British newspaper, that she's been taken off regular duties and is going to have to face some kind of disciplinary hearing. Now how do you think they might have got hold of that, Gil?'

Claussen blinked a couple of times.

'Wait a minute – are you accusing me of this?'

'I'm not accusing anybody. I'm just asking a question.'

Annie glanced from one to the other. Gamble sat cool and calm but Claussen was getting hot under the collar.

'How the hell do I know how they got hold of it? Anybody could have told them. You know how this place leaks. The whole damned building knows about it.'

'Pierce Bryson's been calling Nina Henry for a comment.'

Annie smiled inwardly. Pierce Bryson was Claussen's

contact at the *Herald-Chronicle*. Everybody knew that. Claussen often dropped him titbits that were to their mutual professional advantage. Bryson had written a feature on the Scotia Nostra case with Claussen's name prominent throughout. But for him to call like this about a tip-off was none too subtle. It was tantamount to saying: this way to the source.

'And what's that supposed to mean?' Claussen asked. He shifted uncomfortably in his seat. 'Okay, so Pierce Bryson's a friend. But I haven't talked to him about any of this.'

'What it means is that Nina isn't pleased and neither's Gryce. Bryson wants to know if any action being taken against Annie is at the specific request of the RCMP. Gryce doesn't like that. But, more important, the Chief himself didn't like it when Nina told him what was going on.'

He stared at Claussen and waited for a reaction.

'I hope she hasn't been suggesting that this had anything to do with me,' Claussen said. 'Because I give you my word that it hasn't.'

Gamble didn't provide him with a straight answer, nor did he acknowledge the assurance. 'The Chief doesn't exactly warm to the idea of a perception out there that when the Mounties say "jump", we say "how high".'

'Of course not,' Claussen said, trying to recover himself and to make it sound as if they were all on the same side.

Annie looked at the two of them and knew that this wasn't anything to do with her or Nina Henry or Oliver Gryce or the *Herald-Chronicle* at all. It was the latest skirmish in a turf war, with Claussen being reminded whose territory this was and who was in charge.

Gamble turned to her. 'The Chief didn't know you'd been moved to office watch. He has *reviewed* that decision and suggested to Head of Operations that perhaps it would be best, for the moment anyway, if you continued with your normal work.'

'What?' Claussen said.

'Do you have a problem with that, Gil?'

'You mean I'm back on the team?' Annie asked.

Gamble nodded. 'Yes. The Chief's also pleased that we might be getting somewhere so, since you've stumbled on this thing, you'd better stick with it.'

'It was luck – that was all,' Claussen muttered, unable to contain his resentment.

Gamble gave him a thin smile. 'Maybe so. But it was more luck than you'd had so far. Am I right?'

Claussen didn't answer. High on his cheeks there were red patches like burn marks. Annie could feel anger radiating from him.

Gamble said, 'Right now, Nina is telling our friend – *your* friend – Bryson, that he has somehow been given the wrong end of the stick. She will tell him that, yes, there has been some discussion about the British newspaper article but Annie Welles is a valuable member of the unit working these murder cases and anything else is an internal matter. Gryce is also talking to Steyn at the RCMP to put him in the picture.'

'He won't like it,' Annie said. 'He might decide to sing a different song.'

'I don't think so, otherwise it's his ass. The chief himself would make sure of that with a call to the head of the division.' He gave her a look. 'But none of this means you're out of the woods. The disciplinary will still go ahead, understand?'

She nodded.

'As far as everything else is concerned, nothing has changed. Gil's the lead investigator. You go where he points. You report to him, he reports to me. Got that?'

'Staff Sergeant Bonnard. I'd better—'

'Don't worry about Bonnard. I'll break the news to him.' He looked at Claussen. 'Any questions, Gil?'

Claussen shook his head.

Gamble stood to indicate that the meeting was over. 'Good. So let's get to it.'

They found another desk for Claire, and Annie got hers back, complete with re-installed computer.

She sat and thought about what was happening. Somehow she was making waves all over the place. Even the Chief was getting involved now. She felt elated, her delight heightened by Claussen's displeasure and the fact that he couldn't do anything about it. Talking to a journalist had backfired on him. The irony of that wasn't lost on her. Taggart's worried face flitted through her mind momentarily.

Calling Bryson had been a stupid move, one that Claussen should have known would lead to suspicion being thrown on him. He was a much smarter man than that, surely? Unless he was telling the truth and he hadn't tipped Bryson off. If that was the case, then who had?

She looked at Gamble busying himself in his office. Claussen had his eyes on that chair; he made that plain enough. She wondered how far Gamble would go to keep him out of it.

Poyner's secretary arrived. Her name was Chloe and she was a small blonde in her early twenties. Annie and Flagg took her into an interview room, the one where she'd talked to Bryant Kimbrough earlier in the day about the hookers and the missing jewellery. They showed her the photograph of Gaunt but she seemed uncertain. Annie had the feeling that she didn't want to get too deeply involved.

'It might be him. I'm just not sure.'

'His name's Aaron Gaunt,' Annie told her. 'Mean anything?'

'Oh yes. That's the name of the man who called on Thursday.'

'Did he have an appointment?'

'No, he was a walk-in. We get those from time to time.'

'And what did he say he wanted?'

'He said he needed to talk to George – Mr Poyner – about finding somebody.'

'And Mr Poyner was willing to see him?'

'Yes. He never turns anyone away.'

'Do you think he knew him?'

'How do you mean?'

'Do you think he and Mr Poyner knew each other? Had he been there before?'

'I don't believe so. I went into Mr Poyner's office and told him there was a man called Gaunt who wanted to see him. He didn't react as if it was somebody he knew.'

'How long have you worked there?'

'Since November, that's all.'

That fact seemed to remind her that she was out of a job now because her employer was dead. Tears came to her eyes. She took a handkerchief out of her bag and blew her nose. Annie waited.

'So who did he want Mr Poyner to find?'

'Search me. He wasn't in there very long.'

'And Mr Poyner didn't enlighten you?'

'Look, I just take care of the paperwork, what there is of it. Sometimes George – Mr Poyner – has cases he keeps to himself.'

'You mean they don't go through the books?'

'So what? It's none of my business. Anyway, I left shortly before lunch on Thursday. I had the rest of the day off because

I had a dental appointment. I didn't see Mr Poyner after that.'

Flagg had a photograph of Cobb Landry which he had obtained from Scotiabank. It was his official ID shot but it had been taken before he went bald. He showed it to Chloe anyway.

'What about this man? Ever seen him before? He might not have had much hair lately.'

She shook her head.

'Ever hear the name Cobb Landry?'

'Only when I read the paper.'

'You never heard Mr Poyner mention him?'

'No, I don't think so.'

They let her leave shortly after that.

They knew now beyond doubt that the man in the diary was the same Gaunt who hadn't turned up today for the meeting with his parole supervisor. Annie passed the news to Claussen. He didn't say anything, not 'good' or 'thanks' or 'well done', but that was all right with her. She didn't want any of that from him.

The next person to look at the photograph of Gaunt was Harry Orbach, Cobb Landry's neighbour. At first he was certain but then not quite so sure.

'I don't know. It might be, it might be. It was all so quick, you know.'

Annie hadn't met Orbach before. He looked pale, a bit fidgety.

She asked him, 'How have you been, Mr Orbach, since this happened?'

'I'm not sleeping very well, I must admit.'

'That's perfectly normal. You've had a dreadful shock and it will take a little time to get over it.'

'I guess that's so.' He smiled at her. 'I'm grateful for your concern.'

Before he left he looked at the picture again. 'You know, I think maybe it is him, yes.'

But Annie had a feeling he was saying that because he thought it was what she wanted to hear.

When he had gone, they got into a huddle with Claussen and Gamble, discussing what they had now established: Aaron Gaunt had called on George Poyner on Thursday to ask him to find someone.

'Landry?' Gamble wondered.

Annie nodded. 'Could be. Question is – how do we find out?'

'Better pass this on to the others,' Claussen said.

He called a team meeting. He seemed to have recovered some of his confidence and composure. Annie had to give him credit for the way he could bounce back. He told the group where they had got to and then he started assigning tasks. As he did so, Annie sensed the feeling that always came when a case began to open up. It was as if they were finding a way out of a room that until now had appeared to have no exit.

It was all moving very quickly in one direction, a direction in which she had pointed them, yet, strangely, doubt was beginning to niggle at her. She thought of Eric Benjamin and how he had spoken of Aaron Gaunt.

In her mind, she began to review the situation.

What exactly did they have? First, two murders. Second, a missing man, a convicted killer, who might – just might – be connected in some way to both victims. Had Gaunt visited George Poyner, the private detective, asking him to trace Cobb Landry for whatever reason? Then, had he called on Landry, a terminally-ill bank official, and broken his neck? And afterwards, what had happened at Shore Drive? Was Gaunt mixed up with that, too? It was difficult not to think that there had to be some link.

They circulated a description of Gaunt and his car and passed it on to the RCMP. For the moment, it was agreed not to release any details to the media since there was a better chance of finding someone if he didn't think you were looking for him. Gaunt had no passport, at least not a legitimate one, which was forbidden for the time being under the terms of his release, but Canada was a big country to get lost in and if it really was him they wanted, then he had had a head start since Thursday night.

Four days. That wasn't helpful.

She got herself a coffee and sat down at her desk, then she picked up the phone and called Eric Benjamin.

'I can't believe it,' he said when she told him what was going on. 'I can't believe he would do anything like this.'

'None of these names mean anything to you. Cobb Landry? George Poyner?'

'No, not a thing. Look, you know your job, I'm not telling you how to do it, but there has to be some other explanation.'

'You may be right but in order to establish that, we've got to find him first. If he contacts you, you'll let us know?'

'Of course. But, believe me, I know Aaron Gaunt. This isn't him.'

'Or so you hope.'

She rang off.

Flagg glanced at her. 'So far so good.'

She sipped her coffee. 'Yeah, maybe.'

He noted the tone. 'What's the matter?'

'It's just . . . well, Walter, I don't know. I'm the one who started the ball rolling and for some reason I don't feel very sure about it all of a sudden.' She looked at him. 'How do you see it?'

Flagg pulled his chair over and sat down facing her. 'How do I see it? Okay. We've got Gaunt visiting Poyner and now he's disappeared. Orbach's almost positive Gaunt's the guy he saw kneeling over Landry's body. Gaunt could have hired Poyner to find Landry so that he could kill him.'

'But getting Poyner involved – that doesn't make sense. Once Poyner heard of Landry's murder he'd be bound to come forward and tell the police.'

'So maybe then he kills Poyner to try to cover his tracks. What's wrong with that?'

She smiled at him as if he were an endearing idiot. 'A lot, as a matter of fact. How the hell would killing Poyner cover his tracks?'

'If Harry Orbach hadn't seen him, he could have killed Landry and killed Poyner and nobody would have been any the wiser. But once Orbach had got a look at him and maybe a description was in circulation, then he definitely couldn't risk Poyner coming in here to us and saying: excuse me, I think I know the guy you're looking for.'

'His name's in the diary – Gaunt. He told the secretary who he was. If he was going to do all this, why the hell did he use his own name? From what Chloe suggests, this would have been a cash transaction, right? Not through the books. He could have said he was Bill Clinton.'

'Clinton wouldn't have got as far as Poyner's office. He'd have stayed with Chloe.'

She shook her head. 'I'm sorry, Walter, but there are all sorts of holes here. What about the two guns used at Shore Drive? What about the two cars? What the hell was that all about?' She finished her coffee and threw the empty container into the bin. 'You know, the more I talk about it, the less happy I am.'

'Wait a minute. Let's cut to the chase here. Are you telling me you think we're barking up the wrong tree?'

'No, not necessarily. I think we've got to find Gaunt okay but there's a whole lot more to this than we're seeing.'

'You don't think he killed Landry? For Christ sake, Orbach caught him in the act.'

'You haven't talked with Eric Benjamin, the parole guy. He knows Gaunt better than anyone and I find him very convincing. He strikes me as a man who knows people, who isn't hoodwinked easily. There's no way he believes Gaunt would start killing, then turn himself into a fugitive, not with everything he's been through.'

'Why not? He did thirty years for murder. He killed once, he could do it again.'

'Maybe. But what could possibly have started all this?'

Claussen's voice came from behind her. 'That's what I want you to find out.'

She turned round to him.

'I want you to start on his background, dig out everything you can, all the old files you can get hold of, as well as his most recent history, bank statements, phone bills – you know the drill. I'll put Bill Crisp to work on it with you.'

She knew this was Claussen thinking of something that would keep her quiet and out of the way for a while. In an investigation, following the paper trail was probably the most tedious and time-consuming part, yet she acknowledged that it was important and that it was where things could be missed if you didn't concentrate.

And it was time she saw inside Gaunt's house.

She wrote up an application for a search warrant, then Crisp, ever eager, said he would take it down to the Law Courts where a judge would have to authorise it. While she waited for him to come back, she decided to call the police at Lunenburg. She needed to see the Gaunt case file and the book of evidence, if they still existed after all this time. Lunenburg was the place to start.

'Lunenburg – Mahone Bay police,' a woman said. Her voice was light and youthful.

Annie told her who she was and asked her who was in charge.

'Right now, I am. My name's Debbie Randall. I take care of the office here. What can I do for you?'

'Is your chief around? Can I talk to him?'

'No, I'm afraid the chief won't be returning today and all our other officers are out. Can I help in any way?'

'I'm not sure. I'm trying to dig out some stuff on a murder case in Lunenburg thirty years ago. You're probably too young to remember it. It happened at a place called Heckman's Island. A woman was killed.'

'Cassandra Breaux.'

Annie was surprised. 'Yes, that's right. That's her. You remember?'

'I'm fifty-two years old, Officer Welles. Of course I remember. We haven't had a case like it before or since. Why the interest now?'

'It's just something that's cropped up during an investigation. I need to try to get hold of the original case file and the book of evidence.'

Debbie sounded doubtful. 'Hmm, I don't know. If that stuff is anywhere it will be over in Bridgewater where the trial took place. Trouble is, it might not have been kept at all. Things get moved, departments change buildings. As I recall, it was a straightforward case, no appeal, no retrial or anything, no fresh evidence coming out of the woodwork. And if that's so, then it may simply have been ditched. Things like that don't get kept for more than fifteen, twenty years unless there's a good reason. But if you want, I'll try some people I know at the Bridgewater courthouse.'

'That would be terrific.'

'Not today, mind. I don't think they'd exactly welcome a call right now.'

Annie looked at her watch. It was four thirty. The day was disappearing fast.

'No, I guess not.'

They agreed to talk again tomorrow, then Annie said thanks and rang off.

Crisp arrived back with the warrant and told her he was lucky to have found a judge still there. They got themselves ready. By the time they drove away from Gottingen Street they had both checked their weapons and were wearing lightweight body armour under their shirts. Since the patrol cops had already been in the house and no one appeared to be there, it didn't seem as if any of this would be necessary but you never took chances. Not in this game.

Crisp took the wheel. Ten minutes later they pulled up outside a small townhouse with blue woodwork that seemed freshly painted. A patrol car sat by the kerb.

Crisp went over to the driver. 'Nothing?'

'*Rien*. Nobody's come by and nobody's in there.'

Annie stood and gazed around her in the deepening cold and the gathering dusk. This was a peaceful street, in spite of its proximity to the bustle of Spring Garden Road, which was even busier now that the rush hour was well under way. All the houses looked like this one, well-kept and quietly dignified, with steps up to the porch and tiny front yards bordered by picket fences.

They went in the front door, which the previous police visitors had opened on their way out and left unlocked. In the hallway they listened to silence then Annie took a pair of thin rubber gloves from her pocket and put them on. Crisp did the same.

They decided not to separate but took each room together. In keeping with the neat exterior, the inside seemed freshly decorated, painted in plain creams or soft yellows. The furniture was new but plain. As they moved around, Annie saw that the house was unlikely to tell them much about the person who lived here. It was tidy and clean and utterly anonymous. There were no family photographs sitting around, no ornaments or memorabilia of any kind, and the walls themselves bore no paintings or prints.

But what the house did have was Aaron Gaunt's books. There were shelves of them in almost every room.

'This guy likes to read,' Crisp said.

Dickens, Hemingway and Shakespeare sat with Proust and the poems of Eliot and Auden. Ulysses rubbed shoulders with *Mein Kampf*, while modern crime thrillers by Cornwell and Patterson were lined up with novels by Gore Vidal and P. G. Wodehouse. There were geographical guidebooks and studies of American history, as well as British political memoirs and biographies of everybody from Freud to Balzac.

Annie took some of the books out at random and leafed through the pages.

'You think he's read all these?' Crisp said.

'Every one, I'd say.'

At the back of the house they found a small room which had a desk and a computer and another bookcase, this one holding textbooks, heavy duty stuff on psychology, psychiatry, social science, plus big manuals on electronics and computer technology.

'Bingo,' Crisp said.

He switched on the PC but it told him he didn't have the password to get in. Nor did they have the time right now to sit and try to guess what it might be.

One shelf of the bookcase held box files. Annie started to go through them. She found bank statements and Gaunt's household accounts, like his phone and utility company bills. She would take all these with her.

In another file she found other financial records. She gave a soft whistle.

'Get a load of this.'

Crisp looked over her shoulder. 'Jeez, this is serious money here.'

Aaron Gaunt's assets in high yield accounts, in stocks and bonds and other investments, ran well into seven figures. He was a rich man.

When she'd finished with the file she put it with the rest and then turned her attention to the desk where a thick sheaf of pages was held by a bulldog clip. A cover sheet said 'End Of The Sentence'. She opened the document and started to read some of it:

> 'Unintentionally, within institutions there is competition for limited resources. As a result those who are most likely to be released in the short term receive immediate priority, while the needs of those who have little likelihood of imminent release are left unresolved. For long-term offenders, this means that the possibility of programme participation does not emerge until release is almost upon them, by which time much potential for development may have been lost. A way should be found in which lifers and long-term prisoners can participate in correctional careers. This would be a much more desirable alternative to allowing offenders to drift within the system for many years before attention is eventually focussed on them.'

She flicked through to the end and found that it was incomplete. There was a final half page of text and then a list of handwritten notes, things like: *Here take in Palmer study. Reference to Flanagan 1996.*

There was a notebook, too, an A4 legal-style pad, pages

and pages of writing in a careful italic hand, the raw material, she had no doubt, for Gaunt's study. She put it and the draft document with the rest of the things she was planning to take away.

The only other item on the desk was a small memo pad with a cover in black leather. On the first page it said:

To do:
Fri–Sat: Finish draft.
Sun: Point Pleasant a.m. PM – Prepare notes for Eric discussion Mon.

At the bottom there was a word that had been written in capitals: PRESCRIPTION.

A phone number was with it. She showed the notes to Crisp. 'What do you make of this?'

He read, then said, 'Not exactly the thoughts of a man who was planning to kill somebody and go on the lam.'

'So what the hell happened?'

But she did not get an answer from him. Nor did she get one from the drawers in the desk, which yielded nothing when she looked through them. There were no address books or Filofaxes, no other notes of any kind. Nothing here told them anything about what had brought Aaron Gaunt to George Poyner's office last Thursday.

They were walking towards the kitchen when they heard a noise.

They both heard it at the same time. They looked at each other and drew their weapons.

Crisp went through the door first, the Sig in his hand covering the room in an arc.

A big mackerel grey cat stood in the middle of the kitchen floor. It gave them a haughty look, miaowed, then walked over to Annie and curled itself round her legs.

Crisp pointed to the back door. 'Cat flap. That's what we heard.'

On the floor was a water dish and a food bowl, both empty. The animal miaowed again. Annie searched through the cupboards until she found a bag of food. She poured some into the bowl and the cat began to eat eagerly. She filled the water dish and set it down again.

Crisp smiled at her. 'Don't expect any thanks from this guy. He'll be out of here again once he's eaten his fill.'

'You got a cat yourself?'

'No. You?'

'Not since I was a kid. I like them though.' She bent to stroke the animal's head and it purred loudly in response.

'You're welcome,' she said.

They examined the rest of the kitchen. Every surface was bare and shining. A drainer stood empty beside the spotless sink. In cupboards they found tinned food, bread and cereals. In the fridge there were vegetables and some chicken fillets, fruit juice, milk and mineral water. Not much else. There was a washing machine but no dishwasher.

Annie thought of her own home. She lived alone, too, but if anyone came into her kitchen they would see more signs of habitation than this. They would find newspapers and mail on the breakfast bar near the phone, gift coupons from Sobeys, notes and forgotten reminders under magnets on the fridge, and usually a cup or a plate in the sink, waiting for her to wash them.

But then she hadn't been in jail for thirty years. She pictured Aaron Gaunt here each morning, cleaning everything, like he was back in his cell and getting it ready for inspection, feeding his companion, the cat.

She had thought that the house wouldn't tell her anything. Instead, in its own quiet way, it was telling her a lot.

They went upstairs. There were two small bedrooms and

one large one which was bare and uncarpeted.

'The mystery of the empty room,' Crisp said, standing in the centre of it.

'Too big, I guess. He must be using one of the smaller ones. More the kind of space he's used to.'

Both of the other rooms had freshly made-up beds with tightly-tucked blankets instead of duvets. Gaunt's room, they figured, had to be the one with the clothes in the closet and the small, well-stocked bookcase. The bedside table had a phone and a lamp. There was no alarm clock. His life would no longer be governed by institutional ritual but Annie would have bet money on his being a creature of routine who rose early and was still ruled by his own internal timing, the legacy of a lifetime.

In the closet there were a couple of pairs of pants and two suits that looked new. The same was true of the shirts and sweaters and underwear they found in the drawers. It was all winter clothing, nothing for summer, but then there was no way of knowing what else had been here and might now be missing.

There were two pairs of shoes: a smart black pair and a pair of well-used Nike trainers. Hanging up they found a jogging suit and sweat pants. Annie remembered Eric Benjamin's remarks that Gaunt was a man who behaved like an athlete.

The bathroom was the same as the kitchen – immaculate: soap set neatly in a dish, one solitary toothbrush and single tube of toothpaste in a glass, towels folded on a rail. Above the wash basin was a cupboard in which she found shaving equipment, deodorant, a bottle of aspirin and a hairbrush. The hairs trapped in it were a silvery grey.

On the floor stood a little bin. Annie stepped on the pedal and looked inside. The lining held an empty toothpaste box and something else, something that she didn't recognise.

She took an evidence bag from her pocket and reached in.

'Found something?' Crisp asked.

'Not sure.'

She lifted out a short plastic object that was pointed at the end like a disposable pen. It was hollow and empty.

'That's an insulin pen,' Crisp said.

'A what?'

'An insulin pen. For diabetics. They don't use syringes and all that stuff now, you know. They get pens like this. This would do one dose at a time.'

'How do you know?'

'My sister's diabetic. She uses them.'

Annie thought for a second, then she took out her mobile phone and rang the office. She asked for Flagg but Birgit told her he wasn't there. She went through to Claire instead.

'Listen, do you have that stuff I brought up this afternoon, the stuff about Aaron Gaunt?'

'Yes. Officer Claussen asked me to open a Gaunt file. I've got it in front of me.'

'Good. Would you have a look through it and tell me if there's anything in there about Gaunt being a diabetic?'

'Sure. Give me a second.'

Annie waited, listening to the subdued hubbub of the unit room in the background.

'Yes,' Claire said in a few moments. 'Here it is. Insulin-dependent diabetic.'

'Great. Thanks.' She rang off.

She put the insulin pen in the bag and waved it in front of Crisp.

'Okay,' he said, 'so he's diabetic. Where does that take us?'

'This does one shot, you said.'

'Yes.'

'So I don't suppose your sister goes running back to the pharmacist every day, does she? How many of these things does she get at a time?'

'A whole box, enough to last weeks, maybe months.'

'Right. So where's the rest of Gaunt's supply?'

Crisp looked at her and then clicked his fingers. 'The prescription. The note downstairs.'

17

She stayed in the office until about eight, going over the Gaunt material, becoming more and more convinced that they had to find him but less and less comfortable with the idea that he was a killer. At least a killer for a second time.

She was heading out the door when Deedes and Neidermayer, who'd been sitting over at the night desk corner, sprang into action and began putting their coats on.

'What's the excitement, guys?'

'We got a C-113 call. Woman's body down at Hooker Alley.'

A C-113 was murder. Hooker Alley was what the cops called a grimy part of town at the south end. It was where the bar was, the one where Bryant Kimbrough had met his two lady friends.

She thought about that and then said, 'Mind if I tag along?'

'Why the interest?' Neidermayer asked but didn't object. On the way through the cold, dark streets with the roof light on their Chevy Lumina flashing and the siren whooping, she told them of Kimbrough's visit that morning. As she talked about it a feeling began to develop in her gut. It clenched itself into a knot when they got to the scene and she saw that they were only two blocks from the bar.

The woman's body lay in an entry-way beside a building

that had once been a Turkish restaurant but had been closed down because of hygiene problems and had never re-opened. It was boarded up and dismal, the once-illuminated sign above the door smashed into jagged fragments. In the entry, several bulging bags of trash were piled. The sub-zero temperatures meant that there was no smell from them but the neighbourhood rats had been curious nevertheless. Several of the bags were ripped open and their entrails, empty takeaway cartons, used diapers and God knows what else, had been strewn around.

All this was visible with the aid of a couple of powerful lights which had been set up by the crime scene boys who had arrived and were getting into their white overalls. Two patrol cars blocked the entrance to the alley and four uniformed officers were trying to round up people who might have seen or heard anything. In this area, that was going to be difficult, like trying to herd a flock of cats.

Annie, Deedes and Neidermayer walked up to where the woman lay flat on her back, arms and legs spread like an eager sunbather. She wore white knee-length boots and a short black skirt that had ridden up her thighs where it met a big belt with a heart-shaped buckle and a thin t-shirt with a deep cleavage. Her only concession to the weather was a short coat made of fake fur. It would not have offered much protection on the street but at this time of the year the girls tried to operate from bars like the one Annie could see just a few yards away, a Moosehead sign glowing outside it.

The medical examiner hadn't arrived yet but his opinion as to the cause of death would hardly be necessary. Nor would a search for the murder weapon. Beside the body lay a slab of wood, heavily blood-stained, which Annie figured had been wrenched from the windows of the abandoned restaurant.

'Christ, who did this?' Deedes muttered.

The victim's head had been cracked open and was surrounded by a huge halo of black blood in which Annie thought she could detect fragments of skull. She had no idea what the woman might have looked like in life. Her face had been destroyed by repeated blows.

'Anybody know who she is?' Deedes asked one of the uniformed cops.

'Yeah, I do,' said a female voice with a reluctant grunt.

Annie saw a heavy-set woman dressed in a similar hooker's uniform to the one worn by the body on the ground. She wore a red-haired wig that made it look as if her head was on fire.

Deedes asked, 'You got a name for her?'

'Charlene. Her name's Charlene. I don't know no last name.'

Annie grabbed Neidermayer and dragged him aside. 'That was it.'

'What?'

'The guy who came in this morning. Kimbrough. He said one of the women who rolled him was called Charlene.' She fumbled in her pocket and took out a piece of paper. 'I've got an address.'

They left Deedes where he was and took the Chevy, wailing up through the city towards west Halifax. When they got near Kimbrough's street, a dim row of worn-out wooden bungalows, they cut the siren and the speed. The house was number fifty seven. Two doors away from it they stopped and got out. The lights were on and there was a car at the kerb, an old Nissan. They could hear the engine clicking as it cooled. Annie felt the bonnet. It was warm.

They drew their Sigs and walked towards the house. They didn't have a warrant, just Annie's hunch, and they couldn't storm in on the strength of that. They would have to try the front door. If that didn't work, then Neidermayer would go round the back. But as Annie raised her hand to ring the bell, the door opened. She and Neidermayer stepped aside, guns raised in front of them.

Bryant Kimbrough stood in the doorway in a shirt and jeans that were covered with blood. There was blood on his arms, and his hands looked as if they had been soaked in it.

'Okay, Mr Kimbrough,' Annie said, keeping the Sig levelled at him, 'stay right where you are.'

Kimbrough smiled. He had something clutched in his fist. He held out his hand and opened it up. In the palm was a locket. Even through the smears of blood on the silver, Annie could see the initials: 'RK'.

'See,' Kimbrough said. 'I managed to get it back.'

In the end, she didn't get home until three a.m.

They arrested Kimbrough and brought him down to the station where Neidermayer read him his rights and his cautions and asked if he understood it all. Kimbrough said he did and then Neidermayer asked if he wanted a lawyer, which he refused. Instead, he wanted to make a statement.

From it, they learned that he was a former schoolteacher who had taken to the bottle after his wife had died. Then he'd got fired and had fallen on hard times. On occasions, he had to admit, he resorted to cheap hookers for company.

Some time after leaving Gottingen Street he had driven down to the bar and hung around outside for the rest of the day, watching for either of the girls to appear. At about six, Charlene had emerged with a man and had taken him up the street to the alley. Kimbrough said he'd watched her giving him head. When the man had gone, she started walking towards the bar again but Kimbrough had got out of the car and grabbed her. It was then that he saw she was wearing the locket. Enraged, he had torn a piece of wood from the window and beaten her to death with it.

'I drove home to wait,' he said. 'And then you came for me.'

'All this because he didn't want to appear in court,' Annie said to Deedes when they read it over later and watched the videotape of the interview. 'Well, he's going to appear in court now. That's for sure.'

She didn't sleep well when she got home.

She stared at the ceiling, telling herself that she could have stopped that woman's death. She had not stood in Kimbrough's way when he'd said he had made a mistake, that he wanted to drop the complaint. Because of that, Charlene had ended up in an alley with her face turned to mush.

She felt as if she had failed. It made her more determined to get this Gaunt business right.

Deedes and Neidermayer were still in the office, up to their eyes in paperwork, when she got back in at eight. They would be in court this morning. They had prepared a Crown sheet with the charge, then an information sheet giving details of the crime. Kimbrough would be remanded in custody and a trial date would be set. At the moment he was downstairs in the lock-up. Annie had come in that way and had been angered to see him on a cot in one of the cells, sleeping peacefully, which was more than she'd been able to do.

Crisp had already arrived and had heard about her night. 'Trouble seems to follow you around,' he said.

They got down to work. The phone number on Gaunt's

memo pad was that of his physician. His name was Dr Wendell Kapp. Crisp had already got hold of him. Once he had hacked his way through the resistance of the patient-confidentiality undergrowth by telling the doctor that Gaunt might be in need of medical help, Kapp had provided him with the information they needed.

The missing man was indeed due a new prescription for insulin and he would probably have only enough left to last a few days. Without a re-supply, Gaunt was going to get very sick but short of checking with every pharmacy, every medical centre, every hospital in the Province, or maybe even further afield if he had managed to leave Nova Scotia altogether, there was very little progress they could make that way.

Annie and Crisp looked at each other, each of them waiting for the other one to make the first move. Then, with a sigh of resignation, Crisp volunteered to make a start.

Later Debbie Randall called from Lunenburg to say that there was no trace of a case file or book of evidence anywhere in the county. That almost certainly meant that it didn't exist any longer. Annie thanked her anyway for going to the trouble of checking.

Debbie said, 'I saw the bulletin come in on this parole jumper, Gaunt. That's the same guy, isn't it, the one who killed her?'

'Yes.'

'Gee, who'd have thought he'd have survived? Since you're asking about the case, you think his disappearance has something to do with the Breaux murder? After all this time?'

'No,' Annie said, 'it's just me being curious and trying to find out as much about him as I can.'

If she couldn't see the actual file, then she could do the

next best thing. She got her coat and headed downtown to the offices of the *Herald-Chronicle*, first informing Claussen where she was going. She hated having to clear everything with him, knowing how much he was enjoying this master-servant arrangement, but those were the ground rules Gamble had set and this was the only way she could stay involved.

The *Herald-Chronicle* was at the end of Argyle Street, in a big corner building. Its archive was all on disk, which meant that her search was a lot quicker and cleaner than in the days of heavy, dusty files containing every edition for every day of every year. An hour later, with the assistance of a clerk called Archie who had helped her check things once or twice before – he liked the idea of being involved in police work and he was an occasional drinker at the Late Watch – she reckoned she had everything she was going to get.

There were a couple of coffee shops nearby, neither of which she had ever been in, but Archie directed her to what he considered to be the better of the two. Carrying an envelope thick with print-out copies of stories from the files, she crossed the street to it. It was mid-morning and people were taking a break from whatever it was that occupied their time but she managed to lay claim to an out-of-the-way table where she could sit undisturbed, something she knew she wouldn't be able to do in Gottingen Street.

She ordered a coffee and a Danish and started to go through what she had. In the first cutting, there was a picture of Gaunt as he had been thirty years ago: slightly fuller in the face than in the more recent photograph, his hair darker and thicker, but time and adversity had not totally erased the man he had once been.

She sipped her coffee. When it had come up on the screen in the *Herald-Chronicle* office, something about the photograph had struck a chord with her. But the chord was incomplete, as if some of its notes were missing. The feeling was there again now as she held the picture in her hand.

She put it to one side and then picked up the next cutting, a lengthy article which had been written by a feature reporter. It was what was known in the trade as a backgrounder and it would have involved several weeks of research, its eventual publication timed to coincide with the conclusion of the case and Gaunt's sentencing, when the matter would no longer be *sub judice* and there was no risk of influencing a jury.

The headline said: SEX AND SLAUGHTER ON HECKMAN'S ISLAND.

Following that there was the reporter's by-line and then the story began:

> Aaron Gaunt had it all.
>
> A lovely young wife, a successful business, a brilliant future. But it wasn't enough for him.
>
> He had to have Cassandra Breaux, the hippy divorcee of Heckman's Island, as well.
>
> His desire for her led to her murder and his downfall. Now he has nothing – just the prospect of 30 years behind the high walls of the penitentiary at Dorchester, NB, to look forward to.

So far, so lurid. Nevertheless there were facts beneath the foliage of purple prose. As Annie read on, she learned that Gaunt had been an inventive electronics engineer and with a partner, Chuck Eisner, he had set up a small factory near Bridgewater, where they had begun making miniaturised hi-fi components, a development which had soon attracted the interest of major manufacturers, especially those in Japan.

Both men were young and talented. Gaunt had the technical brain, Eisner a flair for business.

But Gaunt also had an eye for beautiful women, a weakness that not even marriage to his pretty wife Noreen would satisfy. And when he was introduced at a party to the exotic Mrs Breaux, the seeds of his destruction – and her murder – were sown.

Six months before her brutal slaying, Cassandra Breaux moved from Montreal to Lunenburg. She called herself a writer but that seemed to consist of half-finished manuscripts, rambling notebooks and some scraps of poetry. Recently divorced, she appears to have told people that the house by the water at Heckman's Island would provide her with the kind of solitude she needed to work in.

There's not a lot of indication that it did. No evidence has come to light of much in the way of literary output. Instead the house became a secret love nest for her and Aaron Gaunt.

A neighbour, who did not want to be named, said: 'We used to wonder what she did there. Sometimes there was music playing. You could hear it at night. But this is the kind of place where you can keep yourself to yourself.

'Now and then she was a guest at drinks parties but that kind of dropped off after a while. The men seemed to flock to her whenever she was there. The women didn't like that.'

Cassandra Breaux was a fascinating figure to the strait-laced residents of Lunenburg, driving around in her Ford station wagon, dressed in colourful hippie clothes and beads, asking for brown rice at the grocery store, finding a shop that sold joss sticks.

That started people wondering about drugs. The night of the murder, their suspicions were confirmed. In the wrecked bedroom, amid the blood and the broken furniture, police found a small ivory box that contained a quantity of marijuana.

There was a photograph of Cassandra Breaux.

Annie had expected some variant of the hard-eyed femme fatale. Instead, she was presented with the image of a flower child, dressed in flowing cheesecloth, a fresh-faced young woman, almost a girl, with a wide smile and a mane of curls spilling to her shoulders from an Indian headband.

She read on:

Aaron Gaunt's world was one where you had to make something of yourself, like his father and grandfather had, two men who had been born into the great Lunenburg boatbuilding tradition. Gaunt went a different way, seeing that the future lay elsewhere, but his ambition and drive were just the same.

He and Cassandra Breaux were like chalk and cheese but in spite of their differences something sparked between them.

Until it was extinguished in such a bloody manner that hot July night.

At his trial he said he didn't do it, that someone else was in the house that night, that he was knocked unconscious and when he came to she was dead.

But that claim was never going to go very far. Not when you're caught with the murder weapon, a bloody kitchen knife, in your hand and your business partner gives evidence that you've been threatening to kill the woman whose body is lying on the floor and whose blood is all over you and the room.

Indeed.

She skipped down through the rest, tiring of the heavy-handed dramatics, and then she put it away and turned to the daily reports.

The trial hadn't lasted long since the evidence was straightforward, an open-and-shut case, as the previous writer would undoubtedly have put it, but the *Herald-Chronicle* had gone to town on it every day.

What she read supported everything that Eric Benjamin had already told her, that the Crown had opted for first-degree murder partly because of the brutality of the deed but also on the grounds that it had been premeditated. They had based that largely on statements from Gaunt's partner, to the effect that he had been trying to end the affair but that Cassandra had threatened to tell his wife everything. Under examination in court, Chuck Eisner had also brought up the matter of Gaunt's violent streak, describing how he had been known to settle a business problem with his fists, and he had given evidence that on the day of the murder Gaunt had said he was going to Heckman's Island to sort things out once and for all.

The final report concerned the last day of the case. The headline read: GAUNT GETS THIRTY YEARS and, *Outburst from dock as sentence is passed.*

There were details of what the judge had had to say, calling the killing 'a crime of the utmost savagery', but what interested Annie more was the description of Gaunt standing up to launch an angry tirade in Eisner's direction.

The words he used were printed in italic: *'Look what you have done. Don't think you'll escape what you've done to me. I'll see that you don't.'*

The paper described this as a chilling threat. After uttering it, Gaunt appeared to have been led away and that was that. For the next thirty years.

A waitress came with a top-up. Annie put all her stuff back in the envelope and sat back to ponder on what she had read. She had started wondering about Chuck Eisner when she was interrupted.

'Great, you're still here.'

She looked up. It was Archie the clerk, muffled in a long scarf and a thick coat like an inflated lifejacket. He sat down and began to undo it, then he reached into his pocket and took something out. It was another cutting, which he had slipped into a flimsy transparent cover. He handed it over to her.

'I found this after you left. I was going to fax it to you but then I thought I'd come in here, just in case.'

The waitress came back and he ordered a cappuccino. Annie looked at what he had brought. It was a short item, just a couple of paragraphs, and it was dated a year after the trial.

KILLER'S WIFE GETS DIVORCE

The wife of convicted murderer Aaron Gaunt was granted a divorce today.

Gaunt, who is serving a thirty-year maximum life sentence for the murder of his lover, Cassandra Breaux, at Heckman's Island, Lunenburg, would not be contesting the petition, the lawyer for Mrs Noreen Gaunt, Angus McMurray, told the court at Bridgewater.

Mrs Gaunt was not in court. Mr McMurray told reporters later that she had left the family home in Lunenburg since the conviction of her husband but he would not reveal where she was currently domiciled.

Mrs Gaunt never once attended the trial of her husband in Bridgewater last year.

Annie stared at the cutting and then read it once more.

New doors were opening. Where had Gaunt's wife gone? Where was she now? She checked the lawyer's name again. Angus McMurray.

'Any use to you?' Archie asked eagerly.

'I can't tell for certain yet.'

He gave a conspiratorial glance over his shoulder, then he leaned forward, speaking low. 'I wish I knew why you wanted all this stuff. You can tell me, you know.'

'Can't do that, Archie. But I promise you – it's really not very exciting.'

She thanked him for his assistance, then gathered her things to leave. His face showed his disappointment that she wasn't letting him in on her secrets and he didn't argue when she insisted on paying for his coffee.

On the way back to Gottingen Street she stopped off at Eric Benjamin's office. She had a couple of questions for him.

'When he was in prison, did Gaunt ever try to make any contact with his wife?'

'Not that I'm aware of. After the murder she cut herself off from him. But it's something we've discussed since he came out.'

'You have?'

'You remember I told you he had drawn a line in the sand. What was past was past. But I know, even though he hasn't said as much, that he feels tremendous guilt over what he put her through. If he could, I think he'd want to make amends. I don't think he ever really did anything about it, but he talked sometimes about trying to find her, maybe using a private detective.'

She almost ran back to the office.

When she got there she told Claussen she wanted to try to trace Gaunt's wife.

'What if it wasn't Landry he wanted to find? What if it was her? Or maybe it *was* Landry he was looking for. I don't know – maybe Landry was mixed up with the wife in some way. Is that possible?'

She was confused and she knew she sounded it. Claussen looked at her and said nothing.

She said, 'I just feel that I have to talk to this lawyer who represented her at the divorce hearing. I think there's something more here.'

'Don't tell me – a hunch?'

She ignored the sarcasm. 'What's there to lose?'

He thought, then nodded. 'Okay, fine, go ahead. Just don't take too long about it.'

She found the law firm in the Halifax phone book and noted that its offices were on Granville Street, not that far away. She rang and a woman answered.

'Angus McMurray Associates. My name is Jessica. How may I help you?'

She had a hard-edged Maritimes twang. Annie guessed that she might be from Cape Breton.

'My name is Welles. I'm with the Halifax Regional Police. I'd like to speak with Mr McMurray, please.'

Jessica seemed untroubled by this announcement. 'Just a moment. I'll put you through to his secretary.'

Another woman came on. She had a softer voice, as if she were speaking in confidence and did not wish to be overheard.

'Mr McMurray's office. This is his secretary, Miss Bloom.'

Annie didn't like people who gave themselves titles. She explained who she was. Miss Bloom was as unimpressed as Jessica had been.

'I'm afraid Mr McMurray's in a meeting right now. May I ask what it's in connection with?'

'It's in connection with a murder case I'm working on.'

'I see. Well, I don't think I can interrupt him but perhaps I can take your number and he might wish to call you.'

'Sorry, there's no *might* about it. Here's my direct line. If he hasn't called me in ten minutes, I'll be there in person in fifteen. And mention the word murder to him. It's spelt M-U-R-D-E-R. Got that?'

She hung up and regretted instantly that she had allowed the attitude of some snooty secretary to get under her skin. She was tired, tense. Behaving like this wouldn't get her anywhere. McMurray wasn't obliged to tell her anything and if he didn't want to there was nothing she could do about it.

But her phone rang again within five minutes. A man's voice said, 'My name's McMurray. I gather you've been trying to get hold of me.'

'Thank you for calling back. I appreciate it.'

'My secretary seemed to think it was somewhat urgent. A murder case, is that right?'

'Two of them, as a matter of fact.'

'Two? And how are we involved, may I ask?'

'Not at all, directly.'

'Then why are we having this conversation?'

'Thirty years ago, you represented a Mrs Noreen Gaunt in a divorce petition against her husband, Aaron Gaunt. We're interested in tracing Mrs Gaunt's whereabouts.'

'When was this? Thirty years ago, did you say?'

'Give or take.'

He gave a little laugh. 'Then it's not me you want to talk to. Thirty years ago I was a student.'

She paused, confused. 'But I read something. It said Angus McMurray was the lawyer who—'

'My name is Tom McMurray. Angus McMurray is my father. He retired nine years ago.' He laughed again. 'I must say, Officer, I'm not that impressed with your attention to detail. You've simply got the wrong man. You keep this kind of thing up, you might have one or two false arrest suits on your hands, don't you think?'

She was glad he couldn't see the redness of her face and neck.

'I'm sorry,' she said. 'I saw the name in the phone book. I asked for Mr McMurray. I just assumed—'

'Never assume. My father used to have a sign in his office that said just that. Perhaps I might recommend it to you as a motto.'

'Thanks, I'll remember.'

She knew he could hear her discomfort; it was impossible to hide. But when he spoke again there was a slight change in his tone, as if he had had his fun and enough was enough.

'Why don't you go ahead and talk to my father?'

'That . . . that would be useful.'

'He's still in the land of the living, thank God, and still firing on all cylinders too. He lives at St Margaret's Bay. He's not in the book but I'll give you the number although I have to advise you that there's no guarantee he'll want to talk to you.'

'If I get into difficulties I'll mention the fact that we've spoken. That might help.'

'What makes you think that?'

'Because you're obviously fond of him and I have the suspicion that the feeling might be mutual.'

He laughed. 'In this case, Officer Welles, you have assumed correctly.'

He gave her the number and she rang it straight away.

Angus McMurray answered in a loud voice. Behind him she could hear a big band, heavy on the brass, trumpets at the upper edge of their range.

She told him who she was.

'What can I do for you?' he bellowed.

'You think you could tell Stan Kenton to take five so we can talk?'

She had to shout it. Birgit and Claire were looking at her. Crisp was on another phone and frowned. She smiled an apology.

McMurray didn't answer but suddenly the music stopped and she realised he must have gone to switch it off.

'Stan Kenton, eh,' he said when he came back. 'You knew that?'

'"Intermission Riff", unless I'm mistaken.'

'Well now, I have to say I'm impressed.'

'What is it about jazz fans? They always think no one else could possibly know what they know or like the music they like.'

He chuckled. 'In my case, maybe it's just age. As you get older you get to become a kind of a stranger in your own life. Younger people take over the world. They've never heard of the things that filled you full of joy when you were where they are. That's why it's so satisfying to meet a fellow traveller once in a while. You ever hear Kenton in person?'

'Unfortunately, no. I was too young. My father did, though. He used to tell me about him playing here some time in the fifties.'

'Nineteen fifty-five. I was there. There was a US marine band in town that day. They were all in the audience. It was fantastic. What did you say your name was?'

'Annie Welles. But my father's name was Dave Corbin.'

'Dave Corbin? The piano player?'

'Yes.'

'Good God, I used to go and see him perform. He's your father?'

'Was. He died a few years ago.'

'I'm very sorry to hear that. He was a fine musician. You know I think I actually have an album of his somewhere. My goodness, this is amazing. Dave Corbin's daughter. Well, well.'

She left him musing on the thought for a while, then she told him why she was calling. He hadn't asked how she got his number so she didn't enlighten him or invoke the name of his son. She didn't have to. Their shared musical interests had got her over the first hurdle.

'We're trying to find a man called Aaron Gaunt. We understand that you acted for his wife in her divorce petition thirty years ago.'

A different note crept into his voice. It wasn't hostility but there was an alertness.

'Aaron Gaunt – you mean he's out of jail?'

'Yes.'

'When?'

'Several months ago.'

'And how come you don't know where he is?'

She told him about the murders of George Poyner and Cobb Landry and how Gaunt seemed to be linked.

'I see. So where do I fit in to your thinking?'

'In order to try to track him down, I need to know everything I can about him. His parole supervisor said he'd talked about searching for his wife, hiring a private detective to do it. I need to know if it's at all possible that he could have done so, whether he might have managed to make some kind of contact with her.'

'Unlikely, I would have thought.'

It suddenly struck her that she had assumed Noreen Gaunt was still living. *Never assume.*

She asked him. 'Is she still alive?'

He paused. 'Noreen Gaunt was my client. Even though I'm retired, there's still absolute confidentiality in that relationship. The law recognises that.'

'I know and I respect that. But you haven't answered my question.'

He paused again. 'To tell you the truth, I don't know.'

'Is there any way you can find out?'

He said nothing.

She told him, 'If her ex-husband's out there looking for her and we don't tell her – what then? What if something were to happen?'

Once more there was silence. Then he said, 'You'd better come and see me.'

An hour later she was sitting at his kitchen table with a bowl of home-made chowder steaming in front of her.

'You won't have had lunch,' he said as soon as he opened the door. She had insisted that that wasn't necessary but he had ignored her protest, ushering her into a house that was as cosy and comfortable as a favourite old armchair.

McMurray lived at Indian Harbour, in a nook of St Margaret's Bay. The house had big windows overlooking a grassy half acre that led to a rocky shore where choppy waters broke under a steely sky heavy with sea mist. There was piano music playing. He had obviously found her father's album and she could see him glancing at her to see if she recognised it.

She said, 'I play that one at home now and then myself. It's not bad, is it?'

He smiled. 'Nope. Not bad at all. He had the touch.'

He sat opposite her, tucking into his own bowl with gusto. In her mind's eye, on the way in the car, she had envisaged him as a distinguished figure in a suit, a corporate type, as he may well have been once, not this ruddy-faced man of about seventy with a grizzled beard and a fisherman's sweater.

The chowder was fantastic and she told him so.

'Made it myself.'

'You live here alone?'

'Since my wife died a few years back.'

'I'm sorry.'

He smiled. 'I get to play my music louder, now that there's nobody to complain about it. Only, I wish there was.'

They sat silent with thoughts of mutual loss and listened to the piano.

He said, 'You don't look like your father.'

'Considering he had a moustache and not much hair, I'm relieved.'

He laughed. 'You must take after your mother then. Is she—'

'She lives out in Winnipeg. My brother and his family are there. She moved to be near them not long after Dad died.'

'What about you?'

She saw him glance at her left hand.

'I'm divorced. I have two sons.'

'Sorry to hear it. The divorce, I mean, not the sons. I have a son myself.'

'Yes, I know. I spoke to him earlier.'

'I know you did. He rang me a little while ago.'

'Ah.' It was time to get down to it. 'So what can you tell me?'

He wiped his mouth with a napkin and got up. 'You want a beer?'

She had a glass of water. 'No, this is fine, thanks.'

He went to the fridge and took out a bottle of Labatts. He sat again and took a swig from it, then he looked at her, as if weighing her up. She finished her chowder and pushed the bowl aside.

'Aaron Gaunt,' he said. 'I never thought I'd hear that

name again. I guess everyone thought he'd die in prison.'

'He didn't. He made it through. The full thirty years.'

She told him about Gaunt's academic achievements, his doctorate and the work he had embarked on.

He listened to it all and then he said, 'Noreen Gaunt went back to Scotland.'

She frowned. 'I don't understand. Back to Scotland? What do you mean?'

'As soon as the case was over, that's where she went. As far as I'm aware, she's been there ever since.'

'But why Scotland?'

'She wasn't born here, you see. She didn't come from Nova Scotia originally. She emigrated to Canada with her parents when she was about ten. They died in a road accident shortly before she got married. I don't know where she is now or if she's still alive but I know that's where she went when she left here. I dealt with her affairs through a firm of lawyers over there. She had a bit of money from the divorce. The family home at Lunenburg was sold and Gaunt agreed to let her have the proceeds but she didn't want him – or anyone else – to know where she'd gone.'

Annie felt disappointed. Gaunt's wife was a lost cause. She could be anywhere in the world, never mind Scotland. This was going nowhere. She had led herself up a blind alley. Claussen would be happy about that.

McMurray got to his feet and collected their bowls and spoons. He put them into the sink and began washing them.

'So, it's hardly likely he'd ever find her now,' Annie said.

'She even reverted to her maiden name to wipe all traces of him away. Except—'

He paused. He placed the bowls in a drainer and dried his hands on a towel.

'Except what?'

He sat down and took another pull on his beer and looked at her again, as if making up his mind what to say. He sighed. 'I might as well give you the whole story. There was something she couldn't wipe away, or at least didn't want to. Something he didn't know about, something she didn't want him to know.'

She waited, feeling a tingle of expectation.

'When Aaron Gaunt murdered that woman, Noreen Gaunt was pregnant.'

The piano stopped at that moment and its last notes seemed to be suspended in the sudden silence.

McMurray said, 'By the time I handled her divorce a year later she had had the baby.'

Annie found her voice. 'A child . . . there was a child. And . . . and he doesn't know?'

'I guess not.'

'A boy or a girl?'

'I never found out.' He gave a wry smile. 'Gaunt lost out on a lot of things. For a start he doesn't know about the kid and on top of that he could have become a very rich man.'

'He didn't do too badly. I've seen his financial records.'

'Oh sure, when he got bought out of the company he would have got some money but nothing compared to the fortune that was made when it got sold to the Japanese about fifteen years ago. He's bound to know that, too. He'd be worth twenty or thirty million now if he hadn't killed that woman. Sort of thing that would make a man feel kind of sour, don't you think?'

'Do you know the name of the law firm that you dealt with in Scotland?'

He shook his head. 'Can't remember. It'll be in a file somewhere in storage in the office, I guess.'

Her pager went off.

Its urgent beeping startled both of them. She took it out of her pocket. The display told her that Flagg wanted her to call him.

'I'm sorry about this. Can I use your phone?'

'You mean you don't have one of those damn cellphones too?'

'I'm afraid I do. But it's in the car.'

'You can call from in here.'

He brought her into his living room. A telescope on a stand was mounted at the window next to an armchair of worn green leather. Outside, wading birds were parading along the shore with long, bobbing strides.

'My crow's nest,' he said. 'I see all I want to see of the world from here.'

The phone was on a side table beside a photograph of a younger Angus McMurray and a thin-faced woman with auburn hair. He left Annie to her call and went back to the kitchen.

'I thought I'd better let you know that your wild goose is barking up the wrong red herring,' Flagg said when she reached him.

'I've just discovered that myself.'

Flagg said, 'Anyway, Gaunt didn't go to Poyner to find his wife. It was definitely Landry he was looking for.'

'How do you know?'

'Because we've just had a visitor, a friend of Poyner's who works in the vehicle licensing office. Says he was troubled by what happened and had to talk to somebody. He says Poyner called him on Thursday to ask him a favour. He gave him a licence number and said he was trying to find the owner of a car.'

'Which turns out to be Landry's.'

'That's the one.'

'He took his time letting us know.'

'We've already had words about that. I threatened him with withholding evidence. So what about you? Did you learn anything?'

'Yeah, Gaunt has a kid he doesn't know about. I'll fill you in later.'

When she'd finished she went into the kitchen again.

'I've got to get back,' she told McMurray. 'Another development. Thanks for your time and for the chowder.'

'I hope I was some help to you.'

'Well, it was certainly unexpected to learn about Gaunt's child but I don't know that any of this has brought me any nearer to finding him.'

But as he showed her to the door, something occurred to her.

'By the way, you said Noreen Gaunt reverted to her maiden name. Can you remember what it was?'

'Wait a minute.' He rubbed his forehead like a genie with a lamp. 'Begins with a "T". Oh yes, I remember now. Taggart. It was Taggart.'

Annie stared at him.

Then she turned and ran to the car. The envelope of cuttings was on the seat. She rummaged through the contents until she found the picture of Aaron Gaunt thirty years ago, the picture that had intrigued her for some reason which she had not been able to figure.

Except she could figure it out now. Now that it was staring her in the face.

McMurray walked towards her.

'What's going on?'

'I've just realised something. Something I should have seen before. I might never have spotted it if I hadn't spoken to you.'

'But what is it?'

'I'm sorry. I haven't time to explain.'

She got into the car and reversed fast out of the driveway, leaving him standing there in confusion. As she hit the road for Halifax, she punched the speed-dial number on the phone and got the unit room. Birgit answered and fetched Flagg for her.

'Walter, I want you to do something quick.'

'Where are you?'

'Heading back. I need your help.'

'Shoot.'

'I want you to call the Hotel Halifax and see if John Taggart is still there.'

'Taggart? The reporter who wrote that stuff?'

'Yes, yes. Forget all that for a minute. If he's still around, can you go over and hold on to him until I get there?'

'Well, sure, yeah, but what's this about? And what do I tell him?'

'Just tell him I need to talk to him urgently. And call me back when you've got him.'

He did so less than two minutes later. 'He's checked out.'

'Shit. Then try the airport. He was due to fly to London today.'

'England or Ontario?'

'Oh for Christ's sake, Walter, what do you think?'

'Okay okay. Keep your hair on.'

'Find out what flight he's on.'

She changed direction, heading away from Halifax and north towards the airport. After a couple of miles her phone rang again.

'Okay, do you want the good news or the bad news?' Flagg said.

She hadn't time for this nonsense but she said, 'Better give me the bad news.'

'Okay. He's on a flight to Toronto leaving at thirteen forty-five.'

She looked at her watch. It was two fifteen.

'Well then, that's it. I've missed him.'

'Not necessarily. I take it you want the good news now?'

'Jesus, Walter—'

'The good news is that there's very heavy snow in Toronto. They're down to one runway and all flights in and out are delayed. The flight from Halifax has been put back an hour.'

She thumped the steering wheel. 'Damn it, why couldn't you have said that in the first place?'

'Because this way was more fun. Now do you think you might want to tell me what's going on?'

'At the airport. Meet me at the airport. I'll tell you then.'

She put her foot down. So many thoughts. So many possibilities.

She reached the airport in record time, although with everything in her mind she almost forgot to take the off-ramp that led from Highway 102.

She pulled up outside the terminal door and ran into the building, flashing her badge at the security guards. She produced it again at the entry to departures where they didn't seem surprised to see her.

'The other guy's already gone through.'

They let her in a side door so that she didn't have to go via the security arch which would have gone into hysterics when it detected her gun. She ran the rest of the way.

The departure lounge was full of people who looked like they had been there a long time. At this time of year, Toronto wouldn't be the only place snowed in. Rumpled shapes were stretched out on the seats, asleep, and at the bar it was standing room only. Children ran around, disowned by mothers weary of trying to entertain them.

She couldn't see Taggart anywhere. Then she spotted

Flagg at a gate at the far end with a couple of airport officials carrying walkie-talkies.

'By the time I arrived, they were all on board, belted in,' he explained when she reached him. 'But I've asked the guys here to hold the plane for a few minutes.'

'If it doesn't get away now,' one of the men said, 'then we'll have to take them all off and there'll be a delay of at least another two hours. That'll be a disaster.'

'We won't take long,' Annie assured him.

First she took Flagg to one side to tell him what she had learned, then all four of them headed down the covered ramp towards the aircraft door where the cabin staff stood peering out, wondering what was going on.

Annie glanced inside quickly. It was one of the smaller commuter planes, a Fokker, with two rows of seats on each side.

'Passenger Taggart?' she asked a stewardess who had OD'd on duty-free Chanel.

The woman checked her clipboard. 'Fourteen B.'

'We need to talk to him. Can you get him out of there? Tell him there's a telephone message, whatever. Don't say it's the police in case any of the other passengers pick up on it. We don't want them to think it's a security threat or something.'

'Sure. I understand.'

The woman walked down through the plane with curious eyes following her. Annie watched, too. She couldn't see Taggart at first but then she did. He had taken his jacket off and was in an open-neck shirt. His dark head was bent over a magazine.

To her surprise, she found that she was pleased to see him. Something touched her inside and threw her off track for a moment.

The stewardess spoke to him. He looked up, then peered

towards the front of the plane. Annie saw the concern on his face as he spotted her. They made eye contact. She felt a knot of doubt tighten inside as she considered what she was about to do.

She had to know for certain. But if it was true, then all of this would change his life forever. What right had she to do that?

She couldn't back out now.

He was walking towards her. The stewardess came behind him and when they reached the front she pulled a little curtain across to protect their privacy. Taggart's eyes shifted from Annie to Flagg whom he was seeing for the first time, lurking round the corner in the galley.

'What is it? What's happened?'

'It's okay,' Annie told him, 'at least . . . look, we need you to get off the plane so that you can come back downtown with us.'

'You what? What are you talking about?'

'A case – cases – we're working on. You might be of help. But I can't explain here. It's best if we talk downtown.'

'Hold on – what is this? Have I done something?'

'No. We just need to talk in private.'

'Well, I'm sorry, Annie, I can't do that. I've got to get back to London and it's touch and go whether I'll make my connection now. I've lost my job, remember. Can't we talk about this on the phone tomorrow or something?'

'That wouldn't work.'

'Well, it's going to have to. Unless you're going to arrest me, I'm staying right where I am.'

Flagg started to move towards him but Annie gestured that he should keep back. She was going to have to tell Taggart. Here and now.

'Your mother,' she said.

Taggart's eyes widened. 'What about my mother?'

'Is her name Noreen?'

He stared. 'How . . . how do you know that?'

She took a deep breath before she spoke again. 'Because I think I may have found your father.'

18

Annie stood with Gamble and Flagg, invisible to Taggart on the other side of the glass through which they could observe the interview room. She wondered where Claussen was. He didn't yet know of her discovery.

Someone had brought Taggart a cup of coffee but he hadn't touched it. Beneath the fluorescent strip with its sickly light he sat pale, reading and re-reading the cuttings which were the story and the truth of who his father was.

On the way in from the airport and since arriving at Gottingen Street, she had asked him things about himself. He had answered without complaint, responding to her enquiries without any apparent reservation, as if he were only too willing to help. She had seen this sort of thing before. The bereaved, relatives of murder victims or those killed in traffic accidents, often reacted this way in the early stages of shock, busying themselves with an emotionless focus, until the reality sank in and the grief and the anger took over.

In this case a bereavement wasn't involved. On the contrary, he had discovered that someone was alive. But it would bring him pain and confusion nevertheless.

What he told her left her in no doubt. It all tallied. His own birth date, his mother's Nova Scotia background and the blank spaces in her past. He was Aaron Gaunt's son.

'But I'm still not entirely clear where this takes us,' Gamble said.

'Me neither,' Flagg agreed.

'I know, I know. I'm not sure myself,' Annie told them. 'But you can see why I couldn't let him disappear. Not just like that. It's too close a connection to waste. There has to be some way he can be of assistance.'

'How?' Flagg asked her. 'He doesn't know anything about Gaunt and Gaunt doesn't know he exists.'

'We can't force him to help us,' Gamble said. 'We can't hold him here. If he wants to go home, we can't stop him.'

She was aware of that. 'But he won't want to go right now. I'm sure he won't. Not while he's trying to come to terms with all this. And there may be something – I don't know – something he can tell us.'

She didn't sound convincing. Bringing Taggart back had been a knee-jerk reaction, pure and simple, and, besides, she had questions at the back of her mind about what her real motives might have been. But she had to remain professional about this.

They went back to Gamble's office. Claussen still wasn't to be found.

'Boss, can I book him into a hotel?'

'What?'

'A hotel. A couple of nights maybe. He's got to stay somewhere and it isn't fair to ask him to pay for it himself.'

'Fair? What's with this fair? If memory serves me right, you told me he hadn't exactly been *fair* to you.'

She didn't respond. She couldn't tell him that the anger had faded and that her emotions were confused.

He sighed. 'Okay, go ahead.' He waved a finger at her. 'But something modest, mind.'

She rang the Royal Citadel, a new hotel on Granville Street. It would never have fitted Gamble's definition of modest, but one of the assistant managers was an old friend and gave her a cheap rate that Annie knew he wouldn't argue about. As well as that, the hotel was quite near to hand, which had to be of some advantage.

A few minutes later she drove Taggart there. In the car he sat silent and staring and she wondered once again what she had done by dumping the reality of his life on him.

At the hotel, she got his bag from the back and carried it in. He walked alongside her, not really seeing anything, as if his gaze and his thoughts were far off in some mysterious place. He signed the registration card absently and then they took the lift up to his room.

It was small, front-facing, and decorated like a country inn, with a pine floor, an antique-looking table and scattered rugs. An armoire stood against the wall and a couple of wicker chairs sat on either side of a window which looked out onto the street. Annie dumped the case on the bed and for the first time Taggart seemed to realise that she had been carrying it.

'Oh, I'm sorry. I should have done that. That was very ill-mannered of me.' His voice was quiet.

'It's fine,' she said. 'Don't worry about it.'

She smiled at him. He looked frightened and alone and very different from the person she had met just a few days ago. A few days. Was that all it was? A lifetime had passed since then.

He turned from her and walked to the window. For a few moments they stood in silence with just the faint sounds of the city drifting up from the street below.

'It wasn't me. It was him.'

He muttered it and she couldn't quite hear.

'I'm sorry?'

He swung round. 'It was him she was trying to kill. In her poor tortured mind she imagined that's who I was.'

She didn't understand. Then he told her.

For the next half hour he talked about his life, about his mother's illness, her attack on him and his recent conversation with the doctor in the hospital at Dumfries.

'She said she was going to make me pay for what I had done. But it wasn't me she was talking to. You saw the resemblance between us eventually. My mother must have seen it every time she looked at me. How could she have expected to hang on to her sanity, living like that?'

He looked towards the window again.

'She kept it from me all those years.'

He put his hand on the edge of one of the wicker chairs and slumped down into it as if his energy had abandoned him. She took the seat opposite.

'She lied. All my life I wanted to know more about him. She told me he was dead.'

'Hiding the reality like that, she must have been trying to protect you.'

'She had no right to do that. She let me live a lie.'

Annie paused, then said, 'And maybe I had no right to tell you the truth.'

He looked at her. 'You did what you had to. I don't blame you for that. It's not your fault that my father's a murderer. But it's his fault that my mother's in . . . in a lunatic asylum. For God's sake, he destroyed her thirty years ago and he's still doing it. And where does that leave me?' He frowned. 'But come to think of it, yeah, maybe you shouldn't have told me. It's a terrific fucking thing to find out, isn't it – that you're the son of a killer. What if I'm just like him? What if I've got a homicidal streak, too?'

He rubbed a hand through his hair, then sat forward with his head in his hands. For a second she almost reached out and touched him.

He groaned. 'Oh, God, I don't know what I think. All of

a sudden I have a father. Part of me wants to meet him, maybe just once, to tell him what he's done to me and my mother. But another part of me wants to run away from all this, go back home to London, close the door and forget about it.'

'Except you know you can't do that.'

He looked up again. 'No,' he sighed. 'No, I can't.' He sat back. 'So what happens now?' He held his arms out as if passing something over to her. 'You're in charge.'

She nodded. 'I have to be straight with you: I don't exactly know. But I just feel that having you here has to be of some benefit.'

He looked at her and she knew he was wondering if there was anything hidden in what she'd said. She moved on quickly. She had already told him the basic facts about the murders of Cobb Landry and George Poyner. Now she told him more, recounting her discussions with Eric Benjamin and telling him about the work Gaunt had been doing.'

'Your father – there's no doubt that he's connected to these killings somehow. But I'm not at all certain he's the murderer. At least not in both cases.'

'Why not?'

'Because it doesn't feel right.'

'Doesn't feel right? That's not going to stand up to much cross-examination. I thought you went on evidence.'

'Which is pretty damned thin on the ground, not to mention no indication at all of possible motive. Look, I've been to his house. I can't reconcile the feeling that place gave me and the way Eric Benjamin talks about him with the notion of a man who'll break somebody's neck and then shoot some private detective he apparently never met until that day. That would be like . . . like a wild animal on the rampage.'

'What about what happened at Lunenburg thirty years

ago? He was an animal then, the way he killed that woman, wasn't he? We know he's a man with a temper and that he's prone to violence.'

'Maybe so, but that was passion, rage.'

'Then what if this was, too? You said it yourself. An animal running wild.'

'He got his freedom back after thirty years in jail. Why would he risk that?'

'Maybe it doesn't matter to him. Maybe he doesn't care any more.'

She didn't believe that and she told him so. 'Apart from that there are guns involved this time. How would he know about such things? Two cars were heard at the Poyner shooting as well. How do you explain that?'

'He's an ex-con. He must know other ex-cons. In thirty years in prison you can learn a lot of stuff.'

She listened to the bitterness in his voice. This was his father he was talking about, a father he had never met, who didn't know he existed, a father whose own hitherto unknown existence had had such a profound and probably damaging effect on his life but, more particularly, on that of his mother. Feeling hate and resentment and perhaps even thinking of revenge, Taggart would knock down anything that remotely suggested Gaunt might not be guilty. At this stage of his shock, that was the only way his mind would allow him to respond.

She said, 'I've booked you in here for a couple of days, just until we see how this pans out. But don't worry, the department's paying.' She smiled. 'Except that doesn't mean you go crazy with the minibar or the *à la carte* menu. That article you wrote—'

'I told you I didn't—'

'—with my name in it, I'm still not out of the woods as far as that's concerned. If you don't mind, I don't want extravagant and wilful spending of department funds added to my list of black marks.'

He gave her a little-boy smile. 'I'll be as good as gold.'

She nodded gently. 'I'm sorry if this makes things difficult for you – I mean your job and everything.'

'Yeah, well, all of a sudden it doesn't seem so urgent any more. But thank you for the thought. As I recall, the last time we spoke in a hotel room, you couldn't have cared less.'

'I was very angry. I felt let down, disappointed. I felt you'd abused me.'

'And now?'

'I'm getting over it.'

'I'm sorry. I was wrong to use you. But whatever happens now, at least it means we've had a chance to talk again. It distressed me, the thought that we had parted company like that. I want to make it up to you, Annie.'

They were sitting forward, their knees almost touching. Her hands were folded in her lap. When he reached his own hand out and placed it over them, she felt her warmth responding to his. She knew she should draw back. This was not professional. He was – what was he? Not a witness – you couldn't call him that. She didn't know what he was but at this moment, with her heart beating hard in her chest, she was a woman, not a badge.

He was looking at her eyes, at her mouth. In a second he would lean forward and try to kiss her and she didn't know what she would do if he did, although she didn't think she would want to do anything to stop him.

And then her cellphone rang.

She blinked, he sat back and the moment passed as suddenly as it had arrived.

It was Flagg calling. 'Trouble,' he said. He was keeping his voice down.

'What's going on?'

'Something's happened. You might want to get back here.'

19

When she pulled into the headquarters parking lot she saw three cars at the rear entrance. They didn't belong to the department. Although they were unmarked and to all intents and purposes anonymous, she knew who had arrived in them.

The sliding metal shutter at the side of the building was at half mast so she ducked in under it and hurried up the steps towards the lock-up. At a glass-panelled inside door she pressed a buzzer and almost at once the lock gave an answering click.

The smell was always the first thing that registered, an odour of heavy-duty industrial disinfectant that never quite managed to mask the underlying presence of old urine. Sometimes it was not so old. Like right now.

Someone was making a lot of noise in a foreign language. She walked along a short corridor which had bare stone walls and lights that were on permanently, encased in metal cages to prevent damage. Broken glass could be used for troublesome purposes.

She passed a row of single cells with iron bars in need of fresh paint. The cells were empty. This was not a place of long-term occupancy but a staging-post for miscreants in transit. If there had been a guest book and the guests had known how to write their name and place of origin, which might not always be the case, then it would have shown that visitors from half the countries in the world, and certainly those which had some connection with the sea, had passed this way.

Bryant Kimbrough had been here briefly but now he was gone. After his court appearance he had been taken to the Correctional Centre at Sackville and there he would remain until his trial.

The noise and the smell were coming from the drunk tank, a single big cell fitted with sluices running out to a couple of drains in the centre of the floor. Two men were having an argument while a third slept in a corner. The men were dark-haired and dark-bearded with skin that suggested a Mediterranean origin. Hearing them up close, Annie thought they might be Greek. As she passed they spotted her and forgot their dispute. They began to shout and whistle, stretching their arms out through the bars, grabbing the air in her direction. She ignored them, turned a corner and came to where a uniformed constable sat behind a desk, as if in the role of receptionist, except that he wouldn't be asking his guests for an imprint of their credit card or which newspaper they would like in the morning.

This was Bart, a middle-aged and overweight veteran with the grey skin of a bad diet. He had a can of Diet Coke beside him and he was munching a doughnut from a Tim Horton's box. A paperback sat open on his knee. On the wall a bank of monitors gave him a view of his domain, including the door through which he had allowed Annie to enter.

She had never been able to figure out Bart's watch system. Day or night, he always seemed to be the one on duty. He was also the person you came to if you wanted to find out anything. Somehow, down here in his dungeon, he heard it all.

The voices of the Greeks, or maybe they were Turks, echoed from the other side of the wall. On one of the screens Annie could see them, still calling out and gesticulating.

Bart paid them no attention. He gave Annie a brief nod and then resumed his reading.

It was a kind of a ritual that when you came this way you made some sort of hotel-type remark.

'I think they're complaining about room service,' Annie said.

Bart didn't look up. 'No, they want a suite. And a better view.'

She had almost passed him when he said over his shoulder, 'I suppose you know you have visitors from Oxford Street.'

'Thanks. I noticed.'

She hurried up the stairs. Bart had confirmed what she already knew. Those were RCMP cars outside. And Flagg wouldn't have called her unless their presence had a bearing on the Gaunt case.

When she got to the door of the office she knew straight away that something significant had happened. Four men in suits and overcoats were bundling material into boxes and plastic evidence bags. As she watched, she realised they were taking away everything that had been gathered in the two murder files.

Crisp, Flagg, Deedes and Neidermayer stood looking on in a glum silence, as if the bailiffs had just moved into their home. Birgit sat firmly behind her desk, apparently determined that they weren't going to take that.

Flagg saw her. 'What's going on?' she asked him.

'I don't know.' He pointed at the RCMP men moving around quietly and methodically, ignoring everyone except Claire. One of them was talking to her, going over everything she had logged in her inventory. 'They're like aliens, for Christ sake. The invasion of the body snatchers. They turned up just before I called you. That guy Steyn was with them. Claussen and the boss were in a huddle before that, then Gryce came down.'

'Where's the boss now?'

'They all went upstairs to Gryce's office.'

She stepped in front of one of the RCMP men.

'Why are you taking this stuff? This is our property.'

'Not any more. We've been told to remove it.'

'But these are Halifax regional police matters, nothing to do with you.'

'Sorry. I can't help you. You need to talk to Staff Sergeant Steyn and your own senior people about that.'

'Yeah, right. Don't tell me. You're just obeying orders.'

He didn't respond. She glared at him for a second, then turned and headed out of the room.

'Where are you going?' Flagg said.

'Upstairs.'

'Annie, hold on a minute. Don't do anything stupid.'

She wasn't listening. She took the stairs two at a time and when she got to the next floor she marched determinedly down the corridor towards Gryce's office although she wasn't at all certain what she was going to do when she got there. But she had to know what was going on.

She had just reached the door when it opened and she found herself face to face with Larry Steyn, coming out. He had a book in his hand. It was Poyner's diary.

She looked at it and then at him. 'What the hell is all this?'

Behind Steyn came Claussen and Gamble. Claussen gave her a strange smile. Gamble looked pale and drawn and his mouth tightened when he saw her.

'You shouldn't have come up here,' he said. 'We'll talk about this downstairs.'

He shut the door. They stood in the corridor, Claussen, Steyn and Gamble in a semi-circle, with Annie facing them.

She said, 'The Girks are downstairs taking our stuff away. Can anybody tell me why?'

'We're taking this over,' Claussen announced.

'We? What do you mean – we? Since when did you join the RCMP?'

'There's been a change in plan,' Gamble said in a dull voice. 'These two cases will be handled by the RCMP from here on in. Claussen's been seconded to the investigation, to represent our interests.' He scanned the empty corridor. 'We shouldn't talk about this here.'

Annie stood her ground. 'I don't understand. What have they got to do with this? This is Halifax regional police business.'

'Not any longer, it isn't,' Gamble said. 'The decision was taken to call the RCMP in and hand it over to them once we came into possession of some new information. There was no other choice.'

'What new information?'

'When you were checking Gaunt's background you missed something,' Claussen said.

'I didn't miss anything. In fact, I found something. I found his son.'

'So you did. His son. Who turns out to be your friend Taggart the reporter.'

He smiled and she knew he was trying to goad her. He couldn't resist an insinuation. The way he spoke made it sound as if there was some sort of a plot here, with her in the middle.

'Discovering who he is is bound to help somehow.' But she said it with hope, rather than any real belief.

Claussen made a face. 'He's a novelty item. Not of any practical value.'

'Get on with it,' Gamble said.

Annie looked at the two of them and sensed that the

slender cord that held their relationship was fraying, being worn away by the strength of Claussen's ego and the sharp edge of Gamble's stress. Steyn was watching with a contemptuous detachment.

'All right, I will,' Claussen said. 'What was the name of Gaunt's business partner?'

She frowned. What game was this? She thought and then remembered. 'His name was Eisner. Chuck Eisner.'

'And where is he now?'

'I don't know.' She had a bad feeling. 'I haven't had a chance to check.'

The truth was she hadn't bothered, not after Archie the clerk had come into the coffee shop with a cutting which had given her a better idea.

'Don't worry,' Claussen said. 'I've already done it.'

Steyn came off the sidelines. 'Does the name Cary Eisener mean anything to you?'

Oh shit.

She felt as if the ground were falling away from under her feet.

She nodded. 'The *Bluenose* guy.'

'The *Bluenose* guy,' Steyn agreed.

'Full name Cary Charles Eisner,' Claussen said. 'Known to everyone as Chuck, except he dropped the name round about the time he became rich. Then he added an "e" to his surname, maybe to place a bit of distance between himself and his previous persona, for whatever reason, but probably not unconnected with friend Gaunt. Now he's Cary Eisener, millionaire businessman and philanthropist. Has been for the past fifteen years.'

Annie felt weak. It hadn't registered at all.

Eisner, Eisener, Eisenhower, Eisenau, Eisenauer. With its myriad variations, it was a common name all along the eastern seaboard, both here in Nova Scotia and down into

New England. It had never dawned on her who he was.

'Cary Eisener,' Steyn said.

She knew now why the RCMP were taking over; he didn't have to tell her. But he was going to. He would want to rub it in.

'Eisener – who has put up all that money for the *Bluenose III*. The same Eisener who was threatened in court by Gaunt, the same Eisener whose evidence went a long way to ensuring that Gaunt would be convicted of first degree murder.'

She glanced at Gamble. He looked deflated and embarrassed by the scene that was being played out around him and which he could do nothing to stop. Steyn and Claussen were glorying in her discomfort like two bullies in a school playground. That made her mad. But mostly she felt angry with herself. She had missed something that was under her nose. That was sheer, bloody incompetence. Claussen, for all his faults, was no slouch. He had established the connection while she'd been off chasing after Taggart.

Taggart. It meant she would lose responsibility for him now. Where would he fit into all this?

Steyn said, 'I don't know what the score is with these two victims, Poyner and Landry, or how Gaunt's involved in their deaths, but if there's anyone he might really want to get to, it's Eisener. And he's on record as having threatened him.'

'Thirty years ago,' Annie said.

He seemed surprised that she was daring to speak. He glowered. 'It's still a threat. And we don't know where Gaunt is. He's broken his parole and disappeared. That's not good. Thirty years in jail can give a man time to think, to plan, to brood about how to get your own back.'

'It can also give you time to change your mind, to become a different person.'

He gave a dismissive laugh. 'Well, that's very charitable of you. But fine, you can be a believer in the rehabilitative powers of the correction service if you want to. Me, I'm going to concentrate on the notion that it's not a good idea to have a situation where Aaron Gaunt might try to get into close proximity with the man who helped put him in jail.'

'But if you find Gaunt, that doesn't automatically mean you've found the man who killed Landry and Poyner. Where's the motive? And there's no hard evidence that he was anywhere near Poyner's place that night.'

'The results of the blood on the glass fragments came back,' Claussen said. 'It's a match with Gaunt's blood type.'

She didn't waste her breath pointing out that that didn't exactly prove anything.

'Frankly,' Steyn said, 'I don't give a shit whether he killed them or not. Finding this guy – that's all I'm interested in.'

'Where's Eisener now?' Annie asked.

'He was in Halifax all last week but now he's in the UK,' Claussen said, 'not due back in this country for another couple of days. When he arrives he'll go straight to Lunenburg to make sure everything's in order for the launch.'

Steyn said, 'We have four days to clear this mess up and we've got to do it quietly. Those are my instructions. No public alarm. Prince William's visit to Canada is only a matter of days away. He'll arrive in Lunenburg to launch the new *Bluenose* and he'll sail out in it in the company of Eisener and the Premier. If this man Gaunt hasn't been found by then, the Lunenburg part of the visit will be called off. It would be too risky. Eisener, his Royal Highness, the Premier – all of them together for substantial periods, out in the open while a potential threat remains unaccounted for? No way. We can't have that.'

Claussen added, 'Of course, if the Lunenburg part of the visit is cancelled, the real reason can't be given. At least, not publicly. The Premier will have to know, naturally. No one wants him making unhelpful statements alleging that Nova Scotia's being snubbed again and we don't want people to get the idea that there's a person out there who might be a danger to the Prince. You can imagine how that would play in the media.'

'Between them, our Government and the Brits would have to come up with something,' Steyn said, 'some plausible reason for the visit not happening. God alone knows what that might be. Although it's ironic, don't you think, that it might make your friend Taggart's load of bullshit look authentic after all.'

'Taggart,' Claussen said. 'We'd better talk to him. Where is he?'

Annie told them.

'What does he know?' Steyn asked her.

'Nothing. I broke the news to him that he's Aaron Gaunt's son. He's still trying to get a handle on that.'

Steyn's pager beeped. He checked it, then said, 'Everything's loaded. Let's get out of here.'

The discussion was over. He and Claussen set off down the corridor, the urgent stamp of their shoes on the hard floor announcing that they were men who had serious business to attend to. Annie and Gamble watched them go. When they'd gone she turned to him.

'Sorry, Boss. Bad mistake. My attention was diverted. I should have spotted who Eisener was.'

Gamble shrugged as if to indicate that it didn't matter. But she knew it did. Claussen would make a meal of this.

The fact was if she had seen the link herself, the result would have been just the same. They would have had to call in the RCMP.

But she could imagine how the meeting in Gryce's office had gone. Steyn would have been only too happy to point out that valuable time had been lost, that they should have become involved sooner, probably making the point that if it hadn't been for Claussen, they might not have become involved at all.

He and Claussen seemed to be getting on well in their new double act. She hoped they'd be very happy together.

She looked at her watch.

'What time is it?' Gamble asked.

'Seven.'

'Seven? Already?'

'Yeah. If we're through here, Boss, I think I'd like to go home.'

He nodded, then he said, 'It's a long time since I bought you a drink.'

She thought at first that he must be joking. She told him, 'As a matter of fact, I don't think you've ever bought me one.'

'Well in that case maybe this is a good time to start.'

20

It wasn't as if a hush fell on the Late Watch when they walked in. That would not have been possible, not with the sports channel on the TV barking out a boxing commentary and Rita McNeil on the music loop that played all day and which Casey never bothered to change, having long since ceased to even notice it. He switched it on in the morning when he came in and switched it off early the following morning when he left. In the intervening hours, Rita and other east coast stalwarts sang on tirelessly.

If there wasn't a hush then there was a definite stillness. It settled over those who knew who Gamble was, who knew that he never came in here and knew that the fact that he had done so tonight was an event of a sort.

Flagg was one who recognised this, although he pretended not to, leaning on the bar with his shoulders hunched and a glass of rum locked in his fist. Deedes and Neidermayer were two more, sitting at a corner table and trying to blend into the gloom. Even though they were off-duty at last and there was nothing wrong with their being there, they reacted as if they had been exposed in the perpetration of some misdemeanour.

Annie gave them all an awkward smile, an apology for being the cause of their discomfort, and at the same time she hoped they got the message that this wasn't her doing.

No one spoke until Casey did. 'Well, look who it is.'

Gamble walked up to the bar. He seemed to have recovered from the embarrassment of the corridor confrontation and the situation into which he had been dropped. He nodded to Flagg, then said, 'Hello, Casey, how's it going?'

'Going just fine, Mark. To what do we owe?'

'Just thought I'd buy my colleague here a drink. We've had an eventful day.'

Flagg grunted at that. Gamble looked at him.

'And you, too, Walter. What will you have?'

Flagg was thrown by the offer. 'Well, eh, I guess I could manage another one in there.' He thrust the glass towards Casey. 'Thanks, Boss.'

Gamble turned round. 'Annie?'

'A beer's fine, thanks.'

'And I'll take a rum and coke myself. Oh, and, you'd better see what those other two are having as well.' He gestured towards the barely discernible reflection of Deedes and Neidermayer in the big mirror behind the bar.

They took their drinks to a table. Gamble sat with his back against the wall. Annie didn't want to sit beside him because that would look too intimate so she took a small stool and sat in front of him.

'Your good health,' Gamble said and took a deep taste.

'Yeah, cheers.' She sipped. 'You and Casey go back, then?'

'Long time. I was there the afternoon he got shot. He was a good cop in his day.' He sat back with his arms stretched along the edge of the upholstery. 'So how are your boys, the twins?'

Annie was caught unawares by the question. She had anticipated that he might want to launch into some kind of post-mortem on the events of the last hour. But not this.

'They're . . . they're fine. They're on a ski trip with their father. The Alps.'

'The Alps? Like, you mean Europe?'

'Yes.'

'Nice break. Are they having a good time?'

'I think so. As far as I can tell.'

She was expecting a call from them tonight. She wanted to be home when it came, not sitting here. But she couldn't exactly get up and leave, not until she had found out what Gamble wanted, because she was certain there was something else, not just this amiable small talk and a sudden need to unwind in her company.

She glanced around carefully as she drank some more of her beer. Flagg was watching them out of the corner of his eye, as if he was on a surveillance detail. Meanwhile two fresh bottles of Moosehead had appeared in front of Deedes and Neidermayer.

'Does he come in here a lot?' Gamble asked. He didn't look at anyone but she knew who he meant.

'Who?'

'Flagg.'

'I couldn't say.'

He gave a slight smile. 'No, of course you couldn't. Very diplomatic.' He paused and sipped his drink. 'The disciplinary will be next week, maybe Thursday.'

The change in direction took her by surprise again.

'Oh. I see.'

'Best to get it over with.'

'Sure.' She toyed with her beer glass.

'Don't worry about it. It's no big deal. It'll probably end up as a reprimand, although they might suggest a note in your personal file. If I can avoid that, I will.'

'Who's *they*?'

'Gryce. Cole from Professional Standards. And me. A note in the file can get in the way of promotion. You wouldn't want that.'

'Well, no, I wouldn't but promotion's the last thing on my mind right now. With everything else that's been happening, I'd have thought I'd be lucky to hang on to my job.'

Maybe he could give her some reassurance. But maybe he couldn't. Maybe he had brought her here to tell her she was finished in the unit. But if that was the reason, then he was going about it in a peculiar way.

He said, 'Don't let people like Steyn and Claussen get to you.'

She looked at him and thought of suggesting that he should take his own advice.

He told her, 'Finding out who Taggart was was a good bit of detective work, no matter what they say.'

'Yeah, well, there you go. I don't see that it's going to be much use. He's – what did Claussen call him? – a novelty item.'

'What is it with you and Claussen anyhow? Where did this tension between you come from?'

'It's nothing.'

'Nothing? When he takes every opportunity he can to undermine you? That's nothing?'

'We just . . . well, we're just different, that's all.'

'I don't think so. I don't think that's all. You guys were okay when you were partners, as far as I remember. At least I don't recall any personal problems. So what happened?'

'Nothing happened. Everything's fine.'

She should shut up. That would be best. The more she insisted, the less convincing she sounded. But why was she protecting Claussen? Why didn't she just tell Gamble the facts: that Claussen had come on to her and that he believed she had been spreading the word about it?

She said, 'Sometimes people who work together start to get on each other's nerves. It was a good idea of yours to split us. Crisp and Claussen work well together now and I like working with Walter. He's been around. There's a lot I can learn from him.'

Gamble leaned forward and lowered his voice. 'There's *nothing* you can learn from Walter Flagg. That's why I teamed you with him – to smarten up his act. The guy's on his way out, should have been retired a long time ago. He's a dinosaur. But we took him on from Hamilton when we were expanding the investigative division and we needed experienced officers, wherever we could find them. He wouldn't get a job here now. We've got good people of our own, home-grown, like you.'

She found herself unable to warm to the flattery, tied in as it was with a hatchet job on Flagg. She was uncomfortable. Gamble was normally a bit more circumspect than this. It wasn't like him to be openly critical of other members of staff but in the past few days she had already seen the management mask slip a couple of times.

He sat back. 'How can I put this? If there was ever – *any* – suggestion of some kind of inappropriate behaviour towards you, you'd tell me about it, wouldn't you?'

'From Walter?' She laughed.

'No, I'm not talking about him.' His gaze hardened. 'You know that.'

She gave a cautious nod. 'I'll bear that in mind.'

'Because I won't have anything like that in the unit. Nor

will Gryce. Or the Chief. It's right up there on top of the list.'

She had seen the leaflets about sexual harassment and harassment at work which the human resources office distributed from time to time.

He studied her. 'On the other hand, you know, an interested observer watching you and Claussen might be tempted to jump to the conclusion that there had been . . . well . . . *a thing* between you once upon a time and that maybe that was why you were scratching each other's eyes out.'

She felt her cheeks redden. 'Believe me, there was never anything like that. That's just ridiculous.'

'I don't know that it's so ridiculous. Men and women working closely together in a team. It happens.'

'Huh. Not with me, it doesn't.'

She said it just a bit too decisively, as if it was based on something other than simple principle. Their eyes met and she saw that she might as well have told him the truth.

He smiled in quiet triumph. 'Let me just say that if there's ever a problem you feel you can't talk to me about, you can go to someone from EAP. You know that, don't you?'

'Yes. But that won't be necessary.'

She held his gaze as if to say that the subject was closed.

EAP was the department's Employee Assistance Programme. It occurred to her now that she also had the right to talk to someone from EAP while getting ready for her disciplinary interview. On top of that, the regulations allowed a statutory day off in order to do so. If you didn't take it, you couldn't claim you hadn't had time to prepare.

She said yes to another drink and Gamble went to the bar to get them. While he was gone, she thought about what he was doing. It was obvious that he was trying to find a way to get at Claussen. But tempting though it was, she was not going to help him, at least not by providing a weapon in the shape of a sexual harassment allegation. She had been through all this in her own mind after the Christmas fiasco and she felt no different about it now.

On the other hand, there might be different opportunities here if she played her cards right. She felt frustrated about being dumped unceremoniously from the Poyner and Landry cases and from the pursuit of Aaron Gaunt. And Gamble certainly felt humiliated that the rug had been pulled from under him and his unit.

When he came back with the drinks, she said, 'This Gaunt business—'

'I just want to forget about it for the rest of the night, if you don't mind.'

'Me too. The trouble is I can't. The whole thing disturbs me.'

'Then you should pass your concerns on to your *good friend* Mr Claussen.'

'I have. You heard how that went.' She paused. 'How would it be if you let me think about it for a day or two, maybe make a couple of enquiries? Just to tidy up?'

'Drop it. It's not our case any more.'

'Sure. I know that. But if I did manage to come up with something, that would be pretty good, wouldn't it?'

He looked at her and waited so long before replying that she thought he wasn't going to.

He said, 'It would depend on what it was and how it was obtained. If something landed in your lap and didn't look like it was the result of some unauthorised investigation, that would be useful to all of us.'

She nodded. She understood. He was willing to go along with something that might upstage Claussen, particularly if there was some way he could take the credit for it. The down side was that if she was caught messing around with this she was on her own. He would wash his hands of her. And that would be that.

As if to underline the freelance status of her proposal, he said, 'You know, you're owed some personal time and you've got the disciplinary to think about. Why don't you take a couple of days off duty?' He looked towards Flagg. 'I'll put him and Crisp together in the meantime, while Claussen is down in Oxford Street playing with the boys in red serge. What do you say?'

'Fine.'

They had a deal. Of sorts.

By the time she got home, she had missed the call from her sons. Instead, the voicemail had received it.

'Hi, Mom,' Peter said. He sounded miffed by her absence. 'Why aren't you there? We told you we'd call.'

She could hear him and his brother fighting over possession of the phone while Terry's voice grumbled in the background.

James was next. 'Love you, Mom. We're having a great time here. We'll try and talk to you tomorrow.'

There were fumbling noises and she heard him ask, off-stage, 'Do you want to say anything?' There was no answer, just a click and then dead air. Terry apparently had nothing to say to her, at least nothing he wanted to commit to a voicemail message.

She hung up and thought about phoning them back but then decided against it. It was too late where they were. They would have made the call before going to bed and they'd be asleep by now. At least she hoped so.

But almost immediately the phone rang.

'Where have you been?' Taggart asked. 'I've had a couple of goons from the RCMP here, asking questions. They say they're taking this business over. And not only that, they've confiscated my passport. What the hell is this?'

She was about to explain but then she stopped herself.

It had been a long time since Angus McMurray's chowder.

'Have you eaten?' she asked him.

21

She made two phone calls, one to a cab firm, the other to a restaurant, then she showered quickly and changed into something more off-duty, a silk blouse under a blazer, her good Calvin Klein jeans and a pair of lightweight Timberlands. Loafers would have been better but it was too cold.

She poured a glass of white wine and as she sat at her dressing table and did her face, she ran through all the reasons why what she was doing was not a good idea. But then again, there was no professional compromise, she convinced herself. Not any more. The Gaunt affair was no longer her concern, at least not officially, so she could see Taggart if she wanted to. Nevertheless, Steyn might not view it that way, which was why she had arranged that they should meet at China Town, a restaurant off the Bedford Highway, where they were less likely to be seen.

She felt a stirring of excitement, as if she were on the brink of an adventure. It was caused in part by the sense of freedom that had come from Gamble's nod-and-a-wink approval of her proposal that she should try to tie up a few loose ends in the Poyner and Landry cases, although, for the life of her, she had no idea what that meant or where she was going to start. But it was brought on mostly by the secretive and almost forbidden nature of her dinner with Taggart in – she looked at her watch – fifteen minutes time.

She downed the remains of the wine, grabbed her coat and hurried to the door. Her taxi would be waiting.

She had decided not to drive because that was three drinks now and she knew she would have more. She wanted to have more. The wine, consumed so rapidly, gave her a distinct buzz. She wanted to laugh and get drunk and do stupid things but as she settled into the back of the cab, she told herself to calm down. Taggart would not feel like celebrating anything, not after the day he had just endured.

What was happening to her? Where was her normal good sense? What had she to be so happy about?

His undisguised and candid interest in her had made the difference. She had begun to think she was unattractive except to people like Claussen who saw her as an easy and readily available lay. She had begun to think she was boring, too, maybe sexually inadequate as well, which might have been why Terry had left her for someone younger and no doubt more imaginative. Who knew what his reasons were. He had certainly never tried to explain it all to her.

She had been wary of Taggart initially and reticent about responding to him in anything other than a superficial way, however amicable that was. Then had come the *Sunday Chronicle* debacle and her anger had allowed her to close the door on him altogether.

But it hadn't ended there. His remorse at the trouble he had caused her was genuine. So was his pleasure at the fact that their paths had crossed again and that a parting on bad terms was not the end of the story. It even seemed to make up for the hard truth of what she had revealed to him about his father. She thought of that moment on the plane. It was suddenly vivid in her mind, retrieved with absolute clarity. At the very sight of him, her instincts had responded and caught her unawares. That was the truth of it.

Still, she had to ask herself: was she simply getting carried away? Was she behaving like a silly, lonely woman, flattered by the attentions of a handsome young man? *Younger* man, as a matter of fact. That was worse.

China Town was located down off the highway and stood in isolation near the shore. She saw that she had been lucky to get a reservation. A waiter in a white tuxedo showed her across the big crowded room to a table for two over by the window. There were fake carnations in a vase and a scented candle flickering in a burner. She took a menu but declined a drink. She would wait. She sat facing the door and watched for Taggart. Outside, the night was cold and crisp and the lights of the shoreline fluttered on the clear surface of the water.

She saw him before he saw her. In that instant, as he stood at the doorway, she could see him as he was, bewildered and anxious, a man lost. A waiter approached him, then gestured to where she sat. He smiled and looked relieved, then headed towards her.

He was in a jacket and an open-necked shirt, the same clothes from earlier in the day. He didn't say hello. He sat and frowned slightly and straight away said, 'So can they do that – take my passport?'

She experienced a fleeting moment of disappointment that he hadn't told her she looked nice. She felt nice and she had detected one or two appreciative glances when she walked in.

She told him, 'If they think you can be of help in these cases and there's a risk you might leave the country, then yes, now that there are big security issues involved.'

'What big security issues?'

She explained about Eisner or Eisener or whatever his name was and what it meant, the connection with the royal visit and how the RCMP had taken over the case.

'Jeez,' Taggart said. 'That's a hell of a story.'

'Yeah. And one you can't write.'

'Not for the *Chronicle*, maybe. But I'm a freelance now, remember. In my business that's what we call it when we're out of a job. So it doesn't stop me writing for someone else.'

'And getting me into more trouble? Thanks a bunch. You know, it wouldn't take a genius to work out where the story had come from.'

He thought for a second, then smiled apologetically. 'You're right. I didn't think. I get carried away with things like this. I'm sorry.'

A slim girl in a high-necked silk dress interrupted politely to ask them in a Sino-Scotian accent if they had chosen. Taggart hadn't even looked at the menu. To make life easy for everyone, Annie suggested the special for two. They opted for beer instead of wine.

She asked him who had been to see him. He couldn't remember their names but he described her two adversaries perfectly.

'Steyn and Claussen,' she said. 'Steyn's RCMP but Claussen works with us. He would have been the better dressed of the two – the one with the grey suit and the grey silk tie?'

He nodded in acknowledgement. 'So if the RCMP are in charge of this, what's he doing working with them? Is it – what did you call it – a JFO?'

'Not exactly. Claussen's been seconded, to represent our interests, as it's being described. He and Steyn seem to get along. Frankly, they're welcome to each other.'

'I take it you're not a fan of either of them.'

'I had a run-in with Steyn once, a long time ago. And Claussen's just an asshole.'

'I see. Do I detect some history here?'

She frowned at him. 'If you're suggesting what I think you're suggesting, the answer's no.'

'I'm not suggesting anything.'

She considered. 'But it's true that he did try to hit on me once.'

'And don't tell me – he's happily married, couple of kids, pillar of the community.'

'Something like that, yes.'

She had never spoken about it openly before and it gave her a sense of relief to have done so. Their beer arrived in tall thin glasses. They clinked them in a toast.

'You look terrific,' he said. 'Is it okay to say that?'

'Yes. You can say that if you want.'

'You won't think I'm hitting on you, too?'

She gave a little smile. 'I might.'

He said, 'You don't look like a policewoman tonight.'

'And what does a policewoman look like?'

'I dunno. Not like you, anyhow.'

'Did I look like a policewoman before?'

'A bit. It's in the eyes usually. That wary look. You don't have it tonight.'

They held each other's gaze as they sipped their drinks. Then Taggart's face darkened slowly as his thoughts drifted away into another place.

'I can't get him out of my head. I have to meet him, to confront him.'

'Looks as if there's a growing list of people who would like to do that.'

'Just once, you know? And then maybe that's it. Then maybe I can forget about him and get on with my life.'

She nodded, thinking that his was a life which had changed beyond recognition in the short time he had been in Nova Scotia.

Their food arrived and they spent a bit of time dipping into the selection of dishes. They both declined chopsticks. 'Life's too short,' Annie said.

'I think there's a way to find him. I think I could do it.'

She looked at him, a forkful of king prawn and bean sprout poised in her hand.

He said, 'I've been talking to Jeff. He was surprised to find that I hadn't gone back to London. Then I told him.'

She put the fork down. 'Told him what? About Gaunt? You shouldn't have done that.'

'Well, I kind of had a reason for telling him since I need his help.'

'To do what?'

'You know this Internet newspaper that he runs as part of the course at the university?'

She nodded. First there had been NovaNewsNet, a ground-breaking website which had made a significant name for itself. Then Jeff Cameron had joined the faculty and recreated it as JournaLink. Very different from the old-style student newspaper of the hot metal era, it was more than just a training exercise for his budding news hounds. He and they had succeeded in making it a journal of considerable expertise, turning out occasional investigative pieces which the professional, full-time media often found themselves following up, although at first they had been embarrassed to do so and reluctant to give credit. But the stories produced by JournaLink were impossible to ignore and now its pages were scanned eagerly

'I had this idea that one of his students might write something – maybe an interview with me – at any rate a piece saying that John Taggart, the British journalist who was at the centre of the row over the royal visit, is the son of Aaron Gaunt, a Lunenburg businessman who was sentenced to life for murder thirty years ago. If a story like that ran, then it would be almost inevitable that some of the local press would pick it up and carry it themselves.'

'You're not serious.'

He sat forward towards her, his voice lowered. 'It wouldn't say anything at all about the two murders, you see. It wouldn't mention his connection to them. Then, what if he – Gaunt – saw the story? What if he saw it and then tried to contact the son he didn't know he had? He's bound to be as curious about me as I am about him. I'd make sure there was enough detail in the article to convince him that I'm the real deal. He doesn't know my mother kept it all a secret. I could say it's something I've known all along.'

'So in that case why wouldn't you have made contact before now, written to him in prison or something?'

He thought. 'Mm. Good point. Okay, so maybe I say I've just discovered he's my father.'

'And how have you managed to do that?'

'By . . . by doing some research on Lunenburg in preparation for Prince William's visit which, after all, is what was meant to bring me here in the first place. I could have been digging through some old files, read about the murder case and put two and two together – more or less the way you did.'

'And what then? What if he does contact you?'

'Then maybe we arrange to meet. But before that I tip off the RCMP and they nab him.'

She groaned. 'Oh, great. This is just great.'

'You don't like it.' It wasn't a question.

'No . . .' she didn't say *you idiot* but it was in there, in her tone. 'I don't like it.'

She looked around for eavesdroppers, of which there appeared to be none, and when she spoke again it was with a quiet insistence.

'For a start, you're planning to place yourself in a lot of danger. What if Gaunt *is* a killer? What if he *is* responsible for all this stuff? He might have a weapon. And we're not dealing with your London bobbies here, you know. The

RCMP will be armed to the teeth. Have you forgotten what happened at Lunenburg, what got you up to Nova Scotia in such a hurry?'

'But if I—'

She held up a hand. 'I haven't finished. Once the papers pick up the JournaLink story, they'll do their own archive check and before you can blink they'll have made the Eisener connection, and a hell of a damn sight quicker than I did. Then they'll start trying to find out where Gaunt is. After that, all the pieces will begin falling into place. I can think of at least four or five people in our department who wouldn't mind telling them what they want to know, off the record, anything to fuck up the activities of the RCMP and their dear colleague Mr Claussen.'

They had both stopped eating. A waiter came by and asked anxiously if everything was all right with their meal. Annie told him it was and ordered two more beers.

When he'd gone, she said, 'And once that's out in the open, your role in this little tale will fade into insignificance. Instead, the story becomes an epic about the hunt for Aaron Gaunt, blood-crazed would-be assassin, who for the past thirty years has lived for the moment when he can exact his revenge on the man who put him in jail. It goes world-wide at that point, how he's a threat to Prince William and everything, the royal visit gets called off . . .' She paused. 'You get the picture.'

'But the laws of libel. You can't just say whatever you like.'

'There are ways. Anyhow, the American media aren't bound by the same restraints. Come on, you're the journalist. You know how it's done.'

She was feeling very sensible again. The glow was fading. It was a shame but this wasn't the time.

She sipped her fresh beer. 'Let's face it – if Gaunt ever *is* found, there's a strong possibility he doesn't come out the other end alive. Strange things sometimes happen *in the interests of security*. At any rate, I wouldn't lay odds on the chances of your being able to have a quiet heart-to-heart with him.'

She poked her fork into a dish of chicken with ginger and spring onion. He stared at her, thinking, then he asked her, 'Do you have a cellphone? Mine's been cancelled. Cut off. It was the paper's, unfortunately, not my own.'

She fished hers from her bag and handed it to him. He took out a notebook and checked a number, then dialled.

'Jeff? Hi, it's John. Listen, you know that proposal I put to you a little while ago. You haven't spoken to any of your guys about it yet, have you? That's good. It's just . . . would you mind if we put it on hold for a time? For a day or two? It . . . eh, well, it's hard to explain right now – I'm in a restaurant with someone – but it might suit me better. That would be terrific. Look, I'm sorry if this buggers you about. You're sure? Great. I'll call you.'

He rang off and gave the phone back to her. 'Another good story bites the dust.'

'Well, it's not a question of—'

'No, no, you're right. I suppose if I'd known about the Eisener thing first, I mightn't have come up with the idea. I don't know, Annie, I just feel so goddamned frustrated, you know. Trapped, I want to *do* something.' He grabbed air in his hands and clenched his fists.

'That's understandable.'

'So what happens now?' He gave a little laugh. 'Here we go again. I always seem to be asking you that.'

It was a good question. She wished she had a good answer. She thought for a second and said, 'I'm not entirely out of this.'

'Meaning?'

She looked into the night. She could see lights moving slowly, marking the progress of a container vessel as it made its way out of the basin, on towards where the harbour spread itself open and the Atlantic began.

If Taggart wasn't the same person he had been when they had first met, then neither was she. Together, they had been thrown about by the same seismic shifts. Somehow, it was as if they had been through a kind of bonding experience. In spite of the earlier difficulties caused by the *Chronicle* article she felt unconcerned now about confiding in him. It wasn't just because he had been neutralised, with no newspaper to write for, but because she knew that he was painfully aware of having let her down and that he would not do it again.

She told him, 'My boss has given me the okay to keep a watch on the case, unofficially.'

'How's that going to work?'

She told him of her conversation with Gamble. Now it was Taggart's turn to find the flaws in the plan although in her case the word *plan* was stretching it a bit.

'Bit risky, isn't it? You're bound to step on someone's toes if you start wandering around asking questions. Then again, if you don't you won't find out much.'

He was right. Anything she did was going to be highly visible.

She said, 'You know what you'd feel like if you were in the middle of a good story and somebody whipped it away from you, especially if you thought they were going to get it all wrong.'

He nodded. 'Got the T-shirt.'

'Well, I'm just the same. It's assumptions I don't like, in this case the assumption that Gaunt is the man. Sure, he's part of the answer and maybe he did kill Cobb Landry, but why? Now everybody's got hung up on this Eisener thing. I don't know. There's something wrong with all this, something we're missing.'

A waiter came and cleared their plates away and then asked them if they'd like to see the dessert menu. They said yes but when they had viewed it they decided there was nothing either of them wanted.

Taggart turned to the liqueurs page. 'Good God, Irish coffee. Now that might be an experience. Irish coffee in a Chinese restaurant in Canada. What do you say?'

'Fine by me. I'm not driving.'

He ordered two. The waiter in the white tuxedo brought a little trolley to their table. On it was a massive bottle of Jameson whisky, a coffee jug on a heated tray, sugar, and chunky glasses with handles.

'Now what have we here?' Taggart wondered.

They sat back and watched an elaborate ritual unfolding. It involved the whisky being lit, then being poured from a great height into the coffee in the glasses. Not a drop was spilled. It was an impressive performance, like a magic act, Annie thought.

'But where's the cream?' she whispered to Taggart. 'Isn't it supposed to be poured in over a spoon or something?'

Her question was answered as the waiter set their drinks on the table, then lifted something from his trolley. It was a can. He squirted each drink with a fluffy dollop of white foam, before stepping back proudly to wait for their approbation.

'Very nice,' Taggart said.

The second his back was turned they started to laugh, which was a strain since they had to do it silently so as not to offend. When they had recovered enough, they sampled his creation and had to agree that in spite of the unorthodox finishing touch, it was pretty good.

In fact, the drinks were so good that they had two more,

which gave Annie a distinctly dangerous inner warmth. She and Taggart sat and talked and looked at each other across the table, eyes twinkling from the alcohol.

Behind, at a table not far away, two people were getting up to leave. Annie didn't see them until they were passing.

'It *is* you. We thought it was but we couldn't be sure.'

She glanced up and saw a man and a woman in their late forties. It was the woman who had spoken. She was small, with heavy black-framed glasses. The man was taller, with a high forehead and thinning, upswept hair. In recent years Annie had never been able to look at him without thinking that he bore a rather unfortunate resemblance to Slobodan Milosevic.

'Janet . . . and Doug,' she said. 'Good to see you. This is a surprise.'

'Yes indeed. We haven't bumped into each other in ages,' the man called Doug said. 'How's crime?'

'Still paying me.' She looked from them to Taggart. 'Janet and Doug Singlewood, John Taggart.'

Taggart stood and shook hands. 'Pleased to meet you.'

'John's a friend, visiting from the UK.'

'A Brit, eh?' Doug said. 'What part you from?'

'Scotland.'

'What part Scotland?'

'A little place called Portpatrick. On the south-west coast. Wigtownshire. You heard of it?'

'Can't say I have, can't say I have. So what brings you to Nova Scotia?'

'A business trip. Annie and I happen to have mutual friends.'

'You're not a cop yourself, then?'

'No.'

Doug waited for further enlightenment but it wasn't forthcoming.

'How are things?' Janet wondered.

'Fine, fine,' Annie told her. 'Yourselves?'

'Oh, you know. The same as ever. Doug's being his usual winter pain in the butt, hanging around the house, waiting for the weather to change and the golf season to start.'

'We went to Florida over Christmas,' Doug said. 'Got in plenty of golf there. You play?'

'No,' Taggart said. 'I don't. I'm afraid I'm with Mark Twain on that one.'

'How d'you mean?'

'I think he's right. It spoils a good walk.'

'And those lovely boys,' Janet said. 'How are they?'

'Great. They're on a ski trip with their father right now.'

'Ah, that'll be nice for them, the poor things. Do you and Terry see—'

'Come along, dear. Time we were going.'

'Sure you won't join us for a drink first?' Taggart said.

Annie would have flashed him a look if she had been able to do so without it being noticed but Doug said, 'No, thanks, we've called a cab. It's waiting for us.'

'Nice meeting you,' Janet told Taggart. She shook his hand again and so that she could get a good look at him she held it a little longer than was necessary.

'You too,' Taggart said.

'We'll tell all your old friends that we saw you,' Janet said as they wandered off.

Annie nodded and smiled at her. 'I'm sure you will,' she said behind her teeth.

'What's the story with Mr and Mrs Milosevic?' Taggart asked when they had gone.

Annie laughed with delight that he had thought the same thing. 'They used to be neighbours, lived across the street from us. Still live there, I guess. Terry, my husband – *ex*-husband – he and Doug used to play golf. Janet likes to know everyone's business. It'll be all round the old neighbourhood tomorrow that I've got myself a new man.'

She took some more of her drink. It had become cold and unpleasant and she pushed it away.

'Still,' she said, 'it's nice to be reminded every now and then of what you're not missing.'

'And Terry – do you ever miss him?'

A couple of days ago, maybe even a couple of hours ago, she wouldn't have wanted to respond to that. She might even have told him it was not his concern. He seemed to appreciate the point. He said, 'I'm sorry. I shouldn't ask you that. It's none of my business.'

'No, it's okay.' She paused. 'I think . . . I think I miss the way he used to be, the way he was once. I don't miss the Terry I know now. But I guess the old Terry went a long time ago, even before we broke up.'

'And your sons – you're their mother – how come they don't live with you?'

She told him how the divorce had gone and how custody had been awarded to Terry.

'That's outrageous.'

She shrugged. 'I used to think so. Now I'm not so sure. They need somebody who's always there for them. I can't give them that, not on my own, not in this job. But Barbara, Terry's wife – she can. Damn it, I can't even guarantee to be on the end of a phone when they call. They speak to the voicemail more than they speak to me.'

The waiter came back to ask them if they'd like another drink because they were closing up soon. Annie looked around and saw that there was hardly anybody left. She checked her watch. It was twelve thirty.

'Not for me,' she said. 'You?'

Taggart shook his head.

'Just the check,' she said, 'and can you call us a cab?'

The waiter departed. 'We can drop me off first – it's not far – and then you can take it on into Halifax.'

'Whatever suits but, wait, let me pay for this.'

'Absolutely not.'

She gave him a defiant look that said that was the end of the argument. He responded with a smile and a little nod of deference.

'In that case, thank you for a terrific evening. And I'll take care of the cab. I insist on that at least.'

When the taxi arrived, the waiter brought her coat. Taggart didn't have one. She told him he was mad.

'Do you know what the temperature is tonight?'

'I don't feel cold,' he said as they got into the back of the car.

'That's the whisky trying to fool you. That's how hypothermia starts.'

Inside the cab, the heat was like a blanket and as they drove she could feel herself becoming drowsy. But when their hands met on the seat between them she was instantly alert again. For a few moments, it was just a touch but then the taxi swung hard left across the highway at the junction with Hammond's Plains Road and when it straightened up again, she found that she was gripping Taggart's hand.

'This the place?' the driver said.

'Yes, in here.' She took her hand away reluctantly and sat forward, pointing to the parking lot in front of her building.

Taggart got out with her. They stood and looked at each other.

'I'm not asking you in.'

'Of course not. That's okay. I just wanted to say goodnight and thank you.'

'You already did.'

'I don't mean dinner.'

'In that case, you haven't got much to thank me for.'

'Oh yes, I have. Annie, everything that happened today . . . I don't know. No matter who this man – my father – is, I can't help thinking that at least my life isn't a lie now. Except I wish I could tell my mother that. I wish I could tell her that it's okay, that she doesn't have to pretend any more.'

'You will. You will tell her that. There will come a moment when you can, when she's better.'

'Maybe. Maybe you're right.'

He stood looking at the frozen ground, as if uncertain what to do or say next. She leaned forward and kissed him on the cheek. His skin was cold.

'You'll get your death. And we both need to get some sleep.'

They said goodnight. He got back into the cab and she watched it drive away.

Down at the shore, a freight train was moving, a long dark ribbon that seemed to have no end. She listened to its slow, rumbling rhythm as it began a journey that would take it all the way up to Montreal. She let herself into the building and took the lift up to her apartment. Once inside, she undressed and hung her clothes up. She brushed her teeth and slipped into bed and as she turned out the light she could still hear the train going past.

22

Something was going on this morning. Gamble could sense it as soon as he arrived in the building. But for the moment he was more concerned with the fact that his heartburn wasn't any better.

It had begun in the bar last night, then it had woken him at three at his home in Dartmouth and after lying in discomfort for a while he had got up for a glass of water and an indigestion tablet which hadn't done much good. At breakfast his wife said he looked pale and told him he should go to the doctor. To placate her he said he would call the surgery as soon as he got into the office. She drove him down to the ferry terminal after that and then took the kids to school.

At the time he hadn't had any intention of doing what she asked but now he was thinking that maybe it wasn't such a bad idea. He closed his office door so no one could hear and then he looked up the number. Since he was calling early he was lucky. There was a cancellation at four o'clock this afternoon. He said that would be fine. He took another tablet from the box in his desk drawer and began to chew it, tasting the dry chalkiness in his mouth. The unpleasantness began to ease.

The phone rang half an hour later and Gryce asked him if he'd mind popping up. Getting the call didn't give him the stab of anxiety which usually accompanied a summons from above, nor did he feel the need to bound up the stairs at his usual clip. Instead he took them one at a time, noting the way the heartburn had returned and had gathered itself into a knot in the centre of his chest.

He had had this before. One giant burp would probably shift it. Rich food sometimes gave it to him, which is why he normally avoided such things, not that the bland cuisine at home provided many temptations.

He got to the top of the stairs and turned on to the management floor.

'Mark, how's it going?'

Wearing a wide smile and a dark wool jacket, Michael Marriott who ran Fraud was coming down the corridor towards him. He was younger than Gamble by about five years, tall, with long arms and legs, and he had a loose-limbed walk, like an athlete limbering up. Usually he and Gamble never did much more than grunt the time of day so Gamble felt it odd that he seemed so pleased to see him.

'Fine. You?'

'Just great.' Marriott stood with his hands in his pockets and shuffled his feet. 'You going to see Gryce?'

'Yeah.'

Marriott nodded and then looked at the floor, poking at something invisible with his toe. Gamble wondered why he had asked the question. He could have been going to one of several offices on this corridor. Maybe he was being unduly suspicious but the guy had the look of someone who knew something he didn't.

'We should talk later,' Marriott said.

'What about?'

'Oh, you know – stuff.' He started to back away, as if he had said enough or maybe too much. 'I'll give you a call.'

Now just why the hell would you do that? Gamble asked himself.

* * *

Annie woke later than usual, but clear-headed, although her doubts were with her, as they always were first thing.

All she and Taggart had in common was the situation in which they found themselves. Strip that away and what did you have? She was a divorced mother of two, a police officer in a small city at the edge of Canada, while he was a successful and no doubt highly paid London journalist, albeit one not being paid at all at the moment, although she was certain that was a situation which wouldn't last for long. She was fooling herself if she imagined he could be anything more than a passing breeze.

Other things were on her mind too. Thoughts which had been vague yesterday were turning into distinct shapes as she worked out a course of action.

She brewed coffee and while it trickled into the pot she turned on the TV. In the shelter of a heavy parka with a hood, Bill Strong, one of the local CBC reporters, was standing in front of some gates, holding a microphone fitted with a furry cover. It looked like he had broken off some animal's leg.

He was talking to a news anchor in the studio, Judy Kovacs, a woman with blonde hair arranged in stately folds. In the bottom left hand corner of the screen it said: *Live report. Lunenburg, NS.* Annie turned the sound up.

'So will we know tomorrow, Bill, if Mr Carne is definitely going to be extradited?'

Bill's hood blew back suddenly and he pulled it up again before he answered. His voice had an exaggerated baritone boom with heavy emphasis placed on certain words to make sure you were getting the message.

'No, Judy, tomorrow's hearing in Halifax will simply decide whether there *are* grounds for his extradition. As you know, his lawyers have made a submission to the court saying that he should *not* be extradited and tomorrow we'll know how that's been received. But even if the decision is a negative one as far as he's concerned, that's *not* the end of the story. The *final* decision on all of this will be taken by the Attorney General.'

'And what's your own reading, Bill?'

'Well, it's anyone's guess as to how this might go, Judy. What I *do* predict is that we'll be told tomorrow that there *is* reason for extradition. If that's how it goes, then that's virtually the court saying that Mr Carne *has* a case to answer in relation to the Karachi bombing and of course that's something he has denied through his lawyers. But then you've got to add in the fact that the US authorities want him to be extradited to Colorado where there's the death penalty. So whatever happens, this is going to be no easy decision for the Attorney General. Certainly one I wouldn't want to have to take.'

'Of course,' Judy said, 'the authorities must be anxious to get all this out of the way before the visit of Prince William to Nova Scotia next week. Does that figure at all in the fact that the hearing's being held tomorrow?'

'Oh, I'd say without a doubt. This is *not* the sort of atmosphere that the Premier and the Government want at all. The Justice Department and the Attorney General, the RCMP, too, they'll want this whole thing cleared up before then. Security here in Lunenburg will undoubtedly be increased anyway and no one wants all this activity on the fringes. So I think we'll see a fairly quick decision by the Attorney General one way or another. But don't forget if he says yes, extradite, Mr Carne *can* appeal to the Supreme Court.'

'Won't that mean he'll still be there in Lunenburg while that's going on?'

'No, that's not my understanding. He's a private man and

this is all *much* too public for him. And there's the question of his health. It's well known that he has some sort of heart condition and his doctors are saying the stress of this is bad for him. No, I think you'll see the house here being closed up and Mr Carne conducting his appeal from a different location. And let me say that if that happens, then a *lot* of people here in Lunenburg won't be one bit sorry. I've been talking to some of them.'

It was the cue for a video report in which Strong interviewed local public representatives who were concerned about all the media activity and about the number of RCMP personnel hanging around, all of which was making life difficult for people trying to get on with their lives.

After that Judy went to another reporter, a young woman in a hat with flaps over her ears, standing at the end of Duke Street in Halifax with the Law Courts building visible behind her. Annie could see people holding placards although she couldn't read what was written on them.

The reporter's name was Diane something. The tip of her nose was red with cold and her voice was a whine that reminded Annie of a model airplane her brother once had, that he used to fly in the public gardens.

'Ever since it was announced early this morning that the hearing was going to take place tomorrow, protestors have been starting to drift down here.'

'But where do all these people come from, Diane?'

'Well, some of them live here in Nova Scotia, of course, but others will have travelled from different parts of Canada and from the US. From further afield, too. It's been a big headache for the RCMP, Judy. A lot of concern about what happened in Seattle last year, a lot of anxiety that that kind of thing shouldn't happen here. You'll have read reports about a special screening team being set up to watch the airports and the ferry ports for known troublemakers.'

'Of course. There was something of a fuss about it.'

Indeed there was, Annie agreed.

'Quite how successful that operation has been, we don't know,' Diane said.

Not very, Annie would have thought. She had always reckoned there was a finger-in-the-dyke uselessness to it. She wondered if any of the protestors at the court were faces from Steyn's rogues gallery.

The coffee was ready. She poured herself a cup and sipped it while she watched.

'So what are they protesting about?' Judy wanted to know in an incredulous tone, the voice of someone who kept as far away as possible from grubby little people in the streets. The question was the signal to switch to shots which had been gathered earlier. Annie could see now that the Halifax police and uniformed RCMP officers were out in some numbers, keeping the protestors behind taped-off lines and away from the entrance to the court building.

'Well, as you can see,' Diane said, 'part of the problem is that there are different groups here and they don't all agree with each other. So a difficulty the police have is trying to keep them apart and to make sure that they can't obstruct people coming and going in and out of the building, particularly when Mr Carne arrives here tomorrow.'

And indeed, as Bill Strong might have put it, that *was* going to be a problem, Annie saw. On one side, there was a handful of angry Asians, carrying placards written in Arabic which Annie could not understand but she assumed they were not a translation of those being carried by another group standing opposite proclaiming, among other things, 'Colorado Says Kill The Bastard'. A third gathering carried signs with the words 'Canadian Rights for Canadian Citizens', and elsewhere there was the message 'RCMP =

Royal Clinton Messenger Police'. The camera lingered on that.

For the moment, the groups were noisy but orderly. 'But it could be a different story tomorrow,' Diane said.

Well, it will be now, Annie muttered to herself, wondering why some journalists thought that their cherished objectivity meant they didn't need to have any public responsibility. She would try Taggart with that one when she got the chance.

'And where does the new Lieutenant Governor fit into all of this?' Judy asked.

Diane chose her words carefully. 'Well, he's quite simply a friend of Mr Carne's and not implicated in any way in any of the issues which have yet to be resolved.'

'But this must be an embarrassment, surely, especially with the royal visit coming up?'

'Undoubtedly so but the fact remains that the Lieutenant Governor is Her Majesty the Queen's representative here, he's not being accused of any wrongdoing, and he'll be the first person Prince William meets when he touches down on Canadian soil.'

Annie turned the sound down again, wondering if Steyn and Claussen were watching any of this and if they'd got any further with their search for Gaunt. She picked up the phone and called Walter Flagg at the office.

'You two looked like you were getting on well in the bar last night,' he said when she reached him.

'Walter, don't even think it. He asked me to go for a drink. I couldn't refuse. We'd hardly have gone to the Late Watch if there was anything . . . Christ, I don't want to be even talking like this.'

Flagg laughed at her discomfort. 'So what's going on? He's teamed me with Crisp. He says you've got a couple of rest days.'

'Yes, I have. There are things I need to do. I've got to see someone from EAP for a start. That other little matter hasn't gone away, you know. But I don't think the boss is going to let it go much further. He hinted at that last night.'

'Mmm,' Flagg said with a note of uncertainty.

'What? What is it?'

'Rumours.'

'What kind of rumours?'

'Rumours that Wilson might not be back at all.'

How quickly we forget. She had almost erased Staff Sergeant Wilson, the head of CIS, from her consciousness. If Wilson wasn't coming back, then Gryce would have to do something about replacing him.

'So what's the story?'

'Early retirement. Stressed out. Lucky bastard.'

'Where are you getting all this?'

'Oh, here and there.'

She didn't pursue it. Like Bart down in the lock-up, Walter heard things and his sources were usually good. And in her experience it was rare for a rumour, once it was on a roll, to turn out to be untrue.

'So where does that leave the boss?' she asked him.

'Good question.'

She paused for a few moments, trying to work out the possible permutations of what might happen. For instance, if Gamble got a move up into Wilson's job, it would leave a vacancy which Claussen had his eye on. He had recovered from the minor setback over the leak to his friend at the paper and as things stood for him right now, he would get a promotion to sergeant without any trouble. But the way Flagg had introduced the subject puzzled her.

She shook her head. All this stuff would have to wait.

'Listen, Walter, I'm curious about a couple of things. I realise it's not any of our business any more but, well, you know how I don't like loose ends.'

'I'm listening.'

'The Landry murder. Who made the formal identification? A relative?'

'No, the neighbour, Orbach, the guy who found the body and saw our friend Gaunt. Which reminds me – you got a call this morning.'

'Who from?'

'Benjamin, the parole supervisor. He wants to know what's going on. He had a visit from Steyn and his people and they took away some of his files. He's not too happy about it.'

'No, I guess he's not. I'll call him. So, Landry – he doesn't have any living relatives?'

'Oh sure, there's his father, but there was no point in asking him.'

'Why not?'

'The poor old guy's kind of 10-15, if you know what I mean. He lives in a place down at Chester now.'

Annie paused. The term 10-15 was police slang for someone mentally ill. 'What's the problem?'

'Alzheimer's. He's an old man in his eighties, name of Charles Landry. The family used to own a furniture store in Dartmouth. Maybe you remember it?'

She didn't.

'Anyway he sold out years ago. The Orbach couple told me about him. They were friendly with Landry so that's how they knew. The father was the only relative. I went down to Chester to see him. They told me I was wasting my time but I went anyway. He's in a nursing home, has been for the past ten years. I thought I'd inform him of his son's death, maybe ask him a few questions. No dice. He's long gone, doesn't know what day it is, poor guy.'

'You don't know whether Steyn and Claussen might try to talk to him?'

'I don't know but I don't think so. I told Claussen about my visit. I don't figure he'll want to waste his time going to Chester when there isn't any point. Anyway, why the interest?'

'I told you. Curiosity.'

When she'd said goodbye and hung up, she told herself that curiosity wasn't much of an answer. Flagg would be wondering.

She had no intention of contacting anyone from EAP. That was just something to explain her absence from the office. Second, she didn't want anyone, not even Walter, to know what she was doing. It was better that way, there was less chance of anyone else getting to hear and, besides, it might not amount to anything at all.

She thought of Eric Benjamin and decided not to call him yet. Right at this moment, she didn't want to listen to his complaints.

She didn't have a phone book that covered the Chester area so she rang MT&T looking for the numbers of any nursing homes there. There was only the one, called HillCrest, with an address on Haddon Hill Road. She rang it and asked for the matron, only they were called Chief Nursing Assistants these days and could be male or female.

The woman's name was Rosemary Field. Annie told her who she was and asked if Charles Landry was a patient there and was relieved that the woman didn't bother to put up a smokescreen about how they didn't give out information.

'He's a resident here, if that's what you mean, yes.'

'Resident,' Annie said. 'Of course.'

'Someone from the Halifax police department came here at the end of the week. A big man.'

'Officer Flagg.'

'I think that was his name, yes.'

'And no other police officers have been in contact since then? Perhaps the RCMP?'

'No, no one. Are you a colleague of Officer Flagg?'

'Yes.'

'Then I'm sure he'll have told you about Mr Landry's condition.'

'Yes, he has.'

'So can I ask what the purpose of your call is?'

'As a matter of fact,' Annie said. 'I wondered if I might have a talk with you.'

Chester wasn't far away, about forty minutes. A bit hesitantly, Rosemary Field agreed to see her at 11.30. After that, Annie dialled Taggart at the hotel.

23

When she arrived to pick him up, Taggart was sitting waiting for her in the lobby. He was dressed more sensibly than last night, in the warm clothes he'd been wearing on the day when she'd given him her tour of the city, and he looked as if he had slept well. He smiled broadly when he saw her, as if it had been an age rather than only a matter of hours since he had done so.

'Where are we going?'

He jumped up eagerly, like a kid about to be taken on a day trip to the beach, which, in a way, Annie thought, wasn't far from the truth. When she'd called, she hadn't gone into details but had simply asked him if he'd like to help her out.

'Down the coast a little bit. I thought you might enjoy being my assistant for the day.'

'Sounds good.' He put his hand in his pocket. 'Look what I got.'

She half expected it to be a bag of candy but it was his passport.

'How come?'

'Your pal Steyn turned up this morning. Seemed a bit sheepish. He said he thought they might have over-reacted by hanging on to this but that they'd still appreciate it if I didn't leave town for a while. I told them that was no problem, that it would take me some time to get over my shock and I wanted to see how things turned out. All of which happens to be true.'

'He's not still here, is he?'

She looked around. A bell boy was carrying bags in from a car, followed by a couple speaking in French. A heavy-set woman was sitting on a leather armchair reading *Vanity Fair*, her grey hair reflected in the big gilt-framed mirror behind her. From a speaker high on the wall came a track she knew, 'So What' from the *Kind of Blue* album. Miles Davis was hotel lobby music now. What was the world coming to?

'No, he left fifteen minutes ago, just before I started to get ready, otherwise he might have wondered where I was going when he saw me with my coat on. Anyway, I'm glad to have this back.' He put the passport in his pocket again. 'I got the impression it had occurred to them that when I'm no longer unemployed I might want to write something about heavy-handed police tactics.'

'Which right now they could do without.'

They went outside to the car. A uniformed doorman with a Napoleonic greatcoat and a peaked cap saluted and hurried forward to help Annie in but Taggart beat him to it, earning a resentful look in the process. As a result, the doorman didn't try to open the passenger door. Taggart had to do that for himself.

'So what have we here – a mystery tour?' he asked as they drove away.

'Not exactly. We're going down the south shore to a little place called Chester.'

'And why are we going there?'

'There's a nursing home called HillCrest. Cobb Landry's father's there. We're going to see him.'

'You think he might be able to tell you something?'

'Unlikely. He's suffering from Alzheimer's.'

'So what good will seeing him do?'

'I don't know. I just feel the need to go back to basics. I want to talk to the staff about the son. He used to visit a lot. If we find out more about the victim, then we might find out why he was killed, don't you think? Maybe that way we'll be able to establish what the connection is with your father.'

She headed out of town and took Route 103. If circumstances had been different she would have taken the winding road round the coast and shown Taggart picturesque places like Peggy's Cove, with its pepper pot lighthouse perched on the headland. But that would have to wait. There wasn't time for that today.

As they drove, she told him more about her conversation with Gamble last night and how he had tried to persuade her to spill the beans about Claussen's behaviour towards her.

'The guy sounds paranoid,' Taggart said.

'It's because Claussen's after his job.'

She thought about her talk with Flagg this morning and wondered if there had been any developments back at the office. No doubt she would find out soon enough.

It didn't take them long to get to their destination.

Chester sat on the curve of Mahone Bay. It had a population of one thousand one hundred, although it seemed like zero as they drove up a main street that was empty and still, like the place was in hibernation. Frozen snow unmarked by footprints coated the sidewalks. Gift shops and art galleries were boarded and shuttered while curtained restaurant windows teased them with menus left over from last year.

'Where'd everybody go?' Taggart said.

'You should see this place in the summer. The bay out there's crammed full of sailing boats. Half the property round here is owned by people from Halifax and the other half's owned by Americans with big bucks. They come up here from Boston and even New York because to them the property is dirt cheap.'

Only the grocery store showed any sign of life, with lights in its window and open boxes of fruit and vegetables on the front porch. A red-haired man with a pony-tail and a leather flying jacket was loading bags into the back of a grimy Plymouth. Annie pulled up alongside him and asked for directions to Haddon Hill Road.

He straightened up. 'Where exactly you looking for?'

'HillCrest. It's a nursing home. You know it?'

He nodded that he did and then said, 'I'm heading that way myself. Why don't you follow me and I'll show you?'

They set off out of town, passing no other vehicle on the way, and in a couple of minutes she saw a signpost telling them they were on Haddon Hill Road. Their guide sounded his horn and stuck his arm out the window, pointing left towards the beginning of a driveway. There was a sign that said *HillCrest Private Nursing Home*. Annie sounded a note of thanks, then swung across the road.

The driveway was steep and rutted. There was scrawny woodland on one side and a field of dull grass patched with snow on the other. A dilapidated red barn stood in the centre for no good reason that she could ascertain.

At the top, the drive flattened out into a plateau and HillCrest stood in front of them, a rambling mansion in gunmetal blue with turrets and verandahs, carved patterns round the windows and elaborate decorative overhangs. It would have been an enormous private home once, owned no doubt by some Victorian-era businessman with eight or nine children, as was the trend of the day, but the period charm was marred now by the addition of a long, single-storey extension which grew like an arm out of one side.

They pulled into a parking bay and got out, walking towards the main door past garden seats with icicle fringes.

Frozen flower-beds had been dug over and looked like graves.

Annie rang the bell and the door was opened by a well-built young man in a green jacket such as a shop assistant might wear. A badge in his lapel said his name was Dave. She showed him her own identification and said that Rosemary Field was expecting her. She didn't mention who Taggart was and Dave didn't ask. Instead he showed them into a high, panelled entrance hall with a big staircase that divided at the top. On the walls hung portraits of demure women in frills and heavyweight men in winged collars. They looked down with dead-eyed detachment on what had become of their home.

Dave knocked on a heavy door and a woman's voice, subdued by the thickness of the wood, asked them to come in.

Rosemary Field's office window gave out on the open expanse at the front of the house and Annie figured she might have been watching them arrive. The room was finished with soft, elderly chairs. It did not have a desk but a big table made of some ancient dark wood. The Dell PC parked at its edge and a printer on a low stand next to it looked like intruders. Such modern paraphernalia was like the extension to the house: ill-suited but probably necessary.

Rosemary Field herself was another story altogether. Annie found herself shaking hands with a slim woman of about her own age who was possessed of a remarkable beauty. It was in the softness of her skin, in the pale blue of her eyes and in the sheen of her long blonde hair. She wore a dark wool suit cut tight into her waist and a white silk blouse open at the neck. A silver Tiffany heart hung lopsided on a delicate chain.

Annie found herself staring. She couldn't help it. And she knew that Taggart would be staring, too. But it appeared that Rosemary Field was used to this kind of reaction and believed in dealing with it up front.

'Most people expect to meet an old dragon of some kind. They don't know what to make of me or what to say at first.'

She spoke with resignation, as if her beauty was a burden, an accident of birth, like some terrible disfigurement. She gestured to the chairs and then she moved round to sit behind her table.

'Indeed,' Annie said, 'I can understand that. You're . . . well, you're not what I imagined.'

Rosemary looked at her and smiled. 'May I say that the feeling's mutual, Officer Welles.'

Annie nodded to acknowledge what she took to be a compliment. Rosemary's eyes held hers. Annie wondered suddenly if there had been a hint of something in the remark and it occurred to her that she might be gay. She saw no rings on the left hand but of course that didn't mean anything. She didn't wear a ring there herself. Not any more.

Rosemary shifted her attention to Taggart who was as yet unannounced. The look she gave him was not quite as welcoming.

'This is an associate of mine, John Taggart,' Annie explained. 'He's helping me with the investigation.'

Taggart leaned forward and shook Rosemary's hand. He smiled and mumbled a greeting. They had agreed that he wouldn't do any of the talking since his accent was bound to arouse curiosity and perhaps suspicion but equally, Annie realised now, it was going to look odd if he just sat there.

Rosemary seemed to accept the explanation of his presence without further investigation. 'So how can I help?'

'Like I said when I called, I'm not entirely sure,' Annie began. 'I'm really trying to get some background about Mr Landry and his son. For example, how long has Mr Landry been here?'

'Ten years. Longer than I have. I took over this post

eighteen months ago after a spell working in similar residential homes in Montreal and Ottawa.'

'Isn't this a bit out of the way? I'd have thought—'

'What?' Her expression suggested that what Annie might be thinking was something she had heard before.

'Well, Montreal, Ottawa . . .'

'You figure a woman like me would prefer bright lights, big cities? Am I right?'

'As a matter of fact, that's not what I meant. I was thinking more of a career path.'

Rosemary nodded. 'That's fair.' She gestured towards the wall. A couple of framed diplomas written in italic script hung side by side. Annie could see the name *Rosemary Field* written on the dotted line in the centre of each.

'I started off as a nurse and I've worked in several hospitals but my specialist qualifications are in the care of seniors. This is my most senior post so far, no pun intended. I'll be honest – the job here and the experience it gives me will look good on the résumé when I eventually move on but for the moment I like it here.'

Out of the corner of her eye, Annie saw Taggart take his notebook from his pocket and start to write things down. She felt relieved. It would make up for his lack of verbal contribution.

'Do you live here?'

'I have an apartment upstairs but I own a place in Ottawa. It's where I come from.'

'It could be a little . . . uneventful, here.'

Rosemary gave a shrug. 'Socially, maybe, until the summer comes around. But running HillCrest has its demands. I don't have time to get bored.'

'So, tell me, how often did Cobb Landry come to see his father?'

'That poor man. Murdered.' She said it with a slight gasp,

as if she'd just remembered. 'I still can't believe it. He was such a nice guy. As a matter of fact, he came here a lot, compared to some. Other people don't visit their relatives at all. Certainly he came once a week anyhow.'

'Did you talk to him much when he was here?'

'I guess we got to know each other reasonably well, yes. Not as friends, exactly, but I think he felt he could discuss things with me.'

She laced her fingers into her hair and swept it back from her perfect face. Annie could well imagine Cobb Landry being happy to have a heart-to-heart with her. Any man would. She wondered what was going on in Taggart's head.

Rosemary said, 'Mostly we discussed how his father was doing and of course there were administrative matters to attend to.'

'Like?'

'Well, like the fees.'

'Who paid those?'

'He did – Cobb.'

'Must be expensive, private care like this.'

She saw Rosemary look at her quickly to see if there was any kind of a barb hidden in the observation. When she appeared not to find one, she said, 'Since you're probably going to ask anyway, let me explain the Landry situation to you. Charles, Mr Landry senior, is eighty three. Some time ago, before he came to us, before he became ill, he handed over all his assets to Cobb, who is – *was* – his only son. His wife was dead, he'd retired by then, sold up his business, and was living by himself in Dartmouth. He was, well not rich exactly, but comfortably well off and he knew he wasn't going to live forever.'

'And if the son is legally in control of the estate,' Annie said, 'then it stops the Government getting its hands on it when it comes to death taxes.'

'That's the idea. Fortunately, all that was in place before Mr Landry's Alzheimer's began to develop otherwise the situation would be a mess now. As far as I understand it, Cobb tried to look after him for a while, moved him into his own place, but it's impossible for people to be effective carers unless they're around all the time. Cobb had a job. Who was going to keep an eye on his father when he was at work? He tried hiring a nurse but for various reasons that didn't work out so in the end he got him a place here.'

'Why here? Why not a nursing home in Halifax or Dartmouth?'

'I never asked that. I just assumed they liked the setting.'

Never assume. She was stuck with that motto now. She said, 'I can see how they would. I imagine it's very restful here.'

Outside the window a squirrel scampered along a branch of a birch tree and hopped on to the trunk, its russet tail vivid against the grey bark until it scurried upwards and disappeared from view.

Rosemary smiled. 'I can show you around later if you like.'

'That would be good,' Annie said. She looked at Taggart who nodded in agreement before going back to his notes.

'And then, a year or so ago,' Rosemary said, 'Cobb's illness was diagnosed.'

'You knew about that?'

'Yes, he came to talk to me about it as soon as he heard. He'd been ill before and then there was a period of remission but the disease was back. I was shocked. I felt very sorry for him. He was such a caring guy. He didn't deserve this.'

'Nobody does.'

'No, I guess not. He told me everything, said that he hadn't long and that he was making arrangements so that his father would be able to stay here after he was gone. It was a kind of surreal conversation. I don't think either of us could really believe what was going on.'

'These arrangements – can you say what they were?'

'Yes, he formed a trust to be administered by his lawyer for the sole purpose of caring for his father for as long as he lived. Oh, there were insurance policies, investments, you know – I don't claim to understand the technicalities entirely – proceeds from the sale of his house would go into the trust fund, that kind of thing. He'd worked it all out so that he could die knowing that his father was being looked after. Unfortunately, he died sooner than any of us had anticipated.'

Annie asked if she knew who the lawyer was. Rosemary opened a file in front of her. It had the name Charles Landry at its edge under a transparent plastic clip. She leafed through several pages and then wrote something down on a piece of HillCrest headed notepaper.

'There you go. Address and phone number. I'm going to have to talk to him myself within the next couple of days, now that this new phase of Mr Landry's care is about to come into operation.'

Annie looked at the note and recognised the name of a well-established Halifax firm. She thanked her and put the paper in her pocket. It might be another avenue to explore.

Rosemary said, 'Have you any idea why he was killed? Was it a robbery? I saw the drawing in the paper and on TV. The picture of the man you're looking for. Have you found him yet? No, of course you haven't, otherwise you wouldn't be here.'

Annie said, 'In your conversation with Cobb Landry, did the name Aaron Gaunt ever come up?'

Rosemary thought for a second or two, her eyes focussed on the surface of the table, as if there was something in the varnished grain that would tell her, then she looked up again and shook her head.

'No, I don't think so.'

'You're sure?'

'As sure as I can be. Our conversations weren't very wide-ranging, mostly about him and about his father. Who is this person anyway?'

'Someone who might be connected with the Landry family.'

Rosemary's eyes widened. 'Is it him – the man in the picture?'

'Sorry, I can't go into details, I'm afraid. Can I ask you, did Mr Landry have any other visitors?'

'No, none. Cobb was the only one.' She paused. 'I guess there won't be any visitors at all now. Fortunately for him he won't notice.'

'He doesn't know his son's dead. At least he's spared that grief.'

'Never mind that he's dead, the poor man didn't even know who Cobb was half the time. That was so distressing. You know, sometimes Cobb sat in the room while his father talked to him about his son as if Cobb was a complete stranger. I saw him crying over that one day. It must have broken his heart.'

'Alzheimer's is a difficult thing to cope with,' Annie said. 'You feel abandoned by the person you love. They're there in body but not in mind. They may look the same but it's an illusion. The individual you know has gone.'

Rosemary was looking at her with new interest. She could feel Taggart's eyes on her too.

'My father suffered from it.'

'Then you'll know,' Rosemary said, her glance trying to assess whether Annie was being truthful or whether this was some kind of detective's ploy. But it was not. Annie knew that in her face she would see the truth of what she was saying.

'My father's dead now. But my mother looked after him for a long time. It took a lot out of her. It was like she was living with a stranger.'

'Didn't she have help?'

'Couldn't afford it. She was on her own until he became too ill, physically. They took him into hospital then and he died of a chest infection in the end. But before his mind really deteriorated, there were times when he was lucid, you know, when it seemed as if he was totally normal.'

'Yes, sometimes there are these false dawns. It's depressing for everyone when they disappear again.'

'And there was a long time when he couldn't tell you anything about the present but seemed to have an incredible grasp of the past. Is that usual?'

'It can be.'

'Was Mr Landry ever like that?'

'Yes but only with his son. Not with any of the rest of us. Cobb used to be able to trigger things that would start a conversation about events that even he couldn't remember. Sometimes it was just fragments that his father could recall, vague images. I don't know how much is left there now.'

They sat in silence for a moment and then Annie said, 'Can I see him?'

'See him? Mr Landry?'

'Yes.'

'But why? He doesn't know anything. Your friend – what's his name? Flagg – he realised that pretty quickly when he was here.'

'I know. But I'd still like to meet him. Just for a few minutes. To see for myself.'

Rosemary looked at her and debated in her mind. Annie waited. She couldn't push this. If the answer was no, it was no.

'Okay. I'll say yes. That's if he's not resting. Just for a few minutes. No longer.'

'Sure. That's fine.'

Rosemary got up. 'I'll lead the way.'

Taggart gave Annie a wink as if to tell her how well she had manipulated the situation but Annie didn't share his sense of success. Somehow she felt as if she was abusing her father's memory.

They went into the hallway again where Rosemary opened a door that led into the extension, a long airy corridor with glass panels in the ceiling and doors on either side. Somewhere a television was playing very loudly. Most of the doors were open, each of them revealing a little bedroom beyond. Some of the beds were empty but in others people were asleep. Even at a glance Annie could tell that they were all very old. There were ashen faces, open mouths and chins wet with spittle, wispy white hair on pillows.

Halfway along the corridor was a recess where a young woman in nurse's uniform sat behind a curved desk talking to Dave.

'Maybe somebody could turn that down, wherever it is,' Rosemary said.

'It's Mrs Emerson as usual,' the nurse answered. She had an oval face and dark hair tied back. She smiled at Annie and explained, 'Hearing-impaired.'

'You mean she's as deaf as a post,' Rosemary corrected.

Dave disappeared without a word and in a second the sound of the television dipped. A woman called out, 'Hey, I can't hear that.' Her voice was scratched like an old gramophone record. The volume went up again and then a door closed. Behind it, the TV sounded like someone was holding a gag over its mouth.

'Is Mr Landry in the conservatory?' Rosemary asked.

'Yes,' the nurse said. 'We'll be taking him back to his room for lunch soon.'

'Okay, we'll have a minute with him first.'

She swivelled on her heel and led the way along the corridor again, turning left, at which point Annie saw that the building was actually T-shaped, with a long return, something you didn't realise from the front. The conservatory sat at the end of this section, a wide semicircle with enormous windows which looked down the hill at the back of the house and out over the bay. Soft armchairs and settees were arranged so that anyone sitting in them could take advantage of the view while palms in big pots gave the room the appearance of a tropical greenhouse.

In a corner, two white-haired women in glasses and cardigans sat on a settee, leafing through magazines. On either side Zimmer frames stood like sentries at attention. The women looked up and smiled.

'Hello, Miss Field,' one said.

'How are you today, Mrs Annett?'

'I haven't had any breakfast.'

'Oh, really? That's too bad.' She gave Annie a quick look that said *don't believe any of this*. 'Well, don't worry. It'll be time for lunch soon.'

'Good, that's good. Because I haven't had any breakfast.'

She went back to her reading. Rosemary shook her head. 'They forget. It's sad.' She looked around. 'They like it in here, most of them. They've all got TV in their rooms but this is somewhere they can come and just sit in peace together. And there's the view.'

The bay, sheltered and calm under a sky of dense white cloud like a blanket, was dotted with hundreds of small islands, each with a little rocky shoreline and a tuft of woodland.

'No one's ever counted the islands, as far as I know,'

Rosemary said, 'but the local people reckon there's one for every day of the year.'

Annie's interest lay elsewhere. 'I thought Mr Landry was in here.'

'He is.'

Rosemary nodded behind her, Annie turned. At a window, almost hidden behind a sturdy yucca plant, a man sat motionless, his gaze seeming to be fixed on something outside.

'Mr Landry – Charles – there are some people here to see you.'

Charles Landry was dressed in a well-pressed dark suit, a white shirt and a blue tie with a little maple leaf motif. He wore black shoes that were not new but gleamed from constant careful attention. He looked as if he were waiting for a boardroom meeting to start. Or maybe a funeral service.

'He always likes to be well turned out,' Rosemary explained. She tried to get his attention again. 'Charles,' she said, a little louder this time.

The old man turned slowly from the window, his head bowed slightly as if it were too heavy for him. His skin was grey and dry and spotted with age. The slick whites of his eyes glistened.

'Dear me, the poor old soul. Where is he today?' Rosemary pulled a chair up. Annie did the same. Taggart stood out of the way, beside the plant.

'Charles,' Rosemary said, 'this is Miss Welles. She's come to visit you.'

Charles Landry looked at Annie but if he saw her, his eyes didn't acknowledge the fact. On impulse, she reached out and took his hand. It felt like her father's. In an instant she was back in another time, another place. She remembered how, when her father was like this, she would sometimes lead him over to the piano. Then, when he sat down, he would start to play as if nothing had changed, as if he was not ill at all. Except that the music that came to him was always fragile, melancholy.

An echo of Billy Strayhorn's 'Lotus Blossom' traced ghostly patterns in her thoughts. Landry looked away from her again, towards the window, but he did not move his hand from her touch.

'Miss Welles and I were talking about your son, Cobb,' Rosemary said. 'Do you know who I mean? Do you know Cobb?'

He did not answer. In other circumstances it might have been a strange question to ask a father about his son. But not here.

'How are you feeling today, Charles? Did you sleep well?' Rosemary asked.

There was still no answer. Annie looked towards Taggart. He shook his head slightly as if to indicate that there wasn't any point in persisting with this. She had to agree.

She started to take her hand away but suddenly the old man's fingers curled round hers and gripped her tight. He turned his face towards Rosemary.

'Cobb,' he said. 'Cobb's my son.'

His voice sounded like that of a man waking from sleep.

'Yes,' Rosemary answered. 'Cobb.' She smiled in agreement, as if they'd both discovered something.

Annie didn't move. Landry still held her hand. She felt that if she tried to take it away he would disappear back to wherever he had been.

She had a thought. She put her left hand into the right inside pocket of her coat and took out the little wallet which held her police badge and ID card. Fumbling in it, she located two photographs that she kept there. They were of Peter and James and she had taken them herself, at the same time she had taken the picture that hung on her apartment wall. She looked at them. The boys smiled identical smiles. Only the colour of their shirts and the fact that Peter's hair was slightly longer told them apart.

'I have two sons,' she said. She handed old man Landry one of the pictures. 'This is Peter.'

He did nothing for a second but then he let go of her and took the photograph. He stared at it for a full sixty seconds, as if he were trying to memorise every detail, then he turned away to the window. Annie felt they had lost him again.

Dave and the nurse came in. 'Okay, everybody,' he called. 'It's time for lunch.'

'Good,' Mrs Annett said. Dave went over and helped her to her feet and she took up a position behind her Zimmer. She looked at him, 'I didn't have breakfast, you know.'

'I think we better leave this for now,' Rosemary said, 'let the staff get on with it.'

Annie stood and reached for the photograph in the old man's hand. He wasn't holding it tightly and he didn't notice when she took it. She felt sad for him. He reminded her so much of her father.

As they walked towards the door, she slipped the picture back into the wallet. Behind her, she could hear Dave speaking gently to the old man, trying to get him interested in lunch but without much success.

And then she looked and realised that she had only one photograph. The second one wasn't in its place. She turned and saw that she had dropped it on the floor beside Charles Landry's feet.

'My photograph,' she said to Dave, pointing. 'Could you pick it up for me?'

The old man reacted to her voice.

He looked at her, then at the floor and before Dave could do anything, he bent down and lifted the picture himself.

He stared at it.

'Damned boat,' he said. 'Always in that damned boat. He'll fall out and drown himself.'

The nurse and the two old women had reached the corridor, starting their snail race to lunch.

'I hope it's chicken,' Mrs Annett said. 'It's a long time since we had chicken.'

'It's fish,' the nurse informed her. 'You had chicken yesterday.'

Slowly, as if a wrong movement would disturb everything, Annie went back over to Charles Landry and sat down. She took his hand once more.

'Who? Who'll fall out?'

Rosemary motioned to Dave to disappear.

Landry took his hand away and tapped the picture with a fingernail. 'Cobb.' He swung round to Annie abruptly. 'He can't swim, you see.'

She felt a tingle at the back of her neck and down her spine. It was like being at a seance.

'He should learn,' she said.

'I tried to teach him a couple of times.' He shook his head. 'Just no good. He'll fall out. He'll fall out and drown himself.'

He paused. She wanted to move him on but she had to find the right current that would take them out into the stream and she had to do it gently.

'Where's the boat now, Mr Landry?'

'It's at the back of the house. In the water. I tell him to sit in it, leave it tied. I tell him not to go out in it when I'm not there. But I know he doesn't listen.'

Annie looked at Rosemary and Taggart. They were both standing still, aware of the delicacy of the moment. But Annie was beginning to feel more confident. Whatever this was that he was talking about, he was back with it, living it again.

'The house, Mr Landry. Where's the house that you're

talking about? Is it your house? In Dartmouth?'

He didn't answer. Instead, he handed the picture back to her and looked towards the window and the bay.

She tried again. 'Where's the house, Mr Landry? Can you tell me what it's like?'

But he said nothing.

She had lost him. *Damn.* She had pushed too hard. She waited a few moments more, then stood up slowly and put a hand on his shoulder.

'It's time for your lunch, Mr Landry. I'm sorry that I disturbed you.'

'Disturbed,' he muttered suddenly, without looking round. 'Gonna sell the damned thing. My wife doesn't like it. She won't go back there. She says it's not safe, not after what happened to that woman. I tell her . . . I tell her . . .' His voice drifted.

Annie held her breath.

A house. A woman. What *was* this? Was it possible?

'What woman?' She almost whispered the question.

He didn't seem to be listening. But she wanted to keep on asking him. She wanted to hear him say what was there, in his head.

She made a decision. The photograph was in her lap. She thrust it into his hand.

'There's Cobb. Cobb. Your boy. Look at him, Mr Landry. Where's the boat? Where's the house?'

She knew she was beginning to sound agitated.

Rosemary stepped forward. 'Look, I think—'

Annie went for broke. 'Where's the house, Mr Landry? Is it at Heckman's Island?'

'Heckman's Island,' he echoed. 'Heckman's Island.'

He said the words as if he were trying to become familiar with them. It was like listening to a man learning a foreign language.

He looked round at Annie. 'I'm going to sell the damn place.' His eyes were glistening and there was a feeling in them that she could not fathom. 'We're not going back there. None of us.'

His gaze wandered over the room and he noticed Taggart for the first time. He stared at him for a second as if trying to work out who he was, then he pointed.

'That's him. That's the guy from the garage.' He smiled and got to his feet. He buttoned his jacket and stood with a straight-backed dignity. 'Have you brought my car back? Good. I'll be on my way then. I said I'd be home for dinner.'

Rosemary stepped forward and put her arm round him. Immediately she did so, he began to relax into her embrace. She spoke softly but firmly.

'No, Charles, your car's not ready yet but we'll let you know when it is. Don't worry about it. It's time you came along and had some lunch.'

Annie hadn't finished. She needed more from him. 'Mr Landry—' she began.

'No,' Rosemary said. 'I think we've had enough of this.'

24

Back in the office, Rosemary stood in the centre of the room with her arms folded. Around her, the temperature seemed to drop.

'What's going on here?'

'I hope I didn't upset him,' Annie said.

'So do I.'

'It wasn't my intention.'

'Then maybe you'd like to tell me what you were doing. What is this place – Heckman's Island? What was all that about?'

As if she were flashing her badge again, Annie decided to drop in a reminder that this was a murder investigation. It didn't cut any ice. In fact, it seemed to create some.

'Murder investigation or not, this involves one of my residents.' Rosemary's eyes narrowed. 'You didn't come here to talk to me at all, did you? You wanted to question Mr Landry and you thought I'd say no if you asked right out.'

'No, I did come here to see what you could tell me. From talking to my colleague Walter Flagg I had assumed –' that word again ' – that Mr Landry wouldn't be able to help us. It was only when we got here that I decided to ask.'

Rosemary gestured towards Taggart. 'And what's the story with Tonto here – this guy who never says anything?'

Annie thought before deciding it would be best to be

straight with her although maybe a bit economical.

'Mr Taggart's a journalist from England.'

'A journalist? You said he was a cop.'

'No, I said he was an associate of mine.'

'Which means what, exactly?'

'Which means he's been helping us. He's been able to provide us with information about this man we're looking for, Aaron Gaunt.'

It wasn't strictly true. As a matter of fact, it wasn't true at all. But it would do instead of the real explanation. Rosemary looked confused and Annie didn't blame her.

Taggart said, 'Aaron Gaunt is a man who was released from prison not long ago after serving a thirty-year life sentence for murder. He killed a woman by the name of Cassandra Breaux at a place called Heckman's Island. It's on the outskirts of Lunenburg. Have you ever heard of it?'

Rosemary shook her head. She looked as startled by the fact that he had spoken as by anything he had said.

Annie told her, 'You were right about the computer-fit picture – the man who was spotted at the scene of Cobb Landry's murder. We think it could be him. But I – we – are as surprised by what Mr Landry said as you are.'

Rosemary sat down on one of the soft chairs. 'I don't understand any of this.'

Annie said, 'Until we spoke to Mr Landry just now we had no idea what the connection was, why Gaunt might want to kill Cobb. Frankly, I still don't know why. But you heard him, talking about a house at Heckman's Island, about something happening to a woman, that his wife thought the place wasn't safe.'

'You were the one who mentioned Heckman's Island,' Rosemary reminded her. 'He didn't mention it until you did.'

'That's true. But did he ever say anything about a place there? Did Cobb ever mention it?'

'No, never. I never heard it from either of them. I don't know what it might mean.'

From her pocket Annie took a business card with an imprint of the police badge on it. She lifted a pen from Rosemary's table and wrote on the back.

'That's my home number. You'll get me there rather than at the office over the next twenty-four hours or so. If Mr Landry should say anything else about Heckman's Island, I'd appreciate a call.'

Rosemary stood. Annie said, 'I'd also appreciate it if you didn't mention this to anyone else for a while, not until we take care of a few things.'

'It could be his imagination, couldn't it?' Taggart said. 'It could all be some fantasy of his.'

'Yes, it could,' Rosemary agreed, 'or he might be talking about some other place, not this Heckman's Island at all. Who knows?'

Annie looked at them both. 'You're missing the point. There's a way to find out.'

When they got to the bottom of the drive they turned left towards Lunenburg. They had to go there now, she told Taggart. Only in Lunenburg would they know if there was any substance in the things the old man had said.

'That stuff about your father,' he asked. 'Was it true?'

'Every word.'

While they drove she told him more, that when her father's mind had gone, he had imagined her mother was some other woman.

'Mom knew who this woman was but she never explained. It had to have been someone in his past. Whoever she was, she was very real to him and he embodied her in my mother. He started to become very affectionate towards Mom but in reality it was so unbelievably cruel. Because it was the wrong woman, you see? Of course he wasn't aware of what he was doing but I think round about then she began to change towards him. She still took care of him until it was out of her hands but the love went – what was left of it. After he died, she'd had enough of Halifax. She went west to Winnipeg to be with my brother.'

'Leaving you.'

'Leaving me. But of course at that stage I was happily married with a husband and a couple of kids, remember?' She gave him a bitter smile. 'The thing is, when Dad was like that, he was really living in this other time, with this other person, whoever she was. When we spoke to Charles Landry back there, I felt the same thing. That wasn't some dream he was having. That was real.'

They soon reached Lunenburg, crossing over the intersection at Highway 332 and up into what was known as the new town. At the top of Dufferin Street, a couple of RCMP cars were parked and uniformed officers were stopping vehicles at random. One of the officers flagged them down. Annie lowered the window and showed her badge.

'So what's the scene here?' she asked, although she knew.

'Oh, it's this Carne business. We're watching for undesirables. These damn protesters.' He laughed and glanced in. Taggart smiled back at him. 'Where you headed? You guys got business here?'

Annie answered. 'The police station.'

'It's just down the end of this street.' He pointed over his shoulder.

'Thanks. I know.'

'Hope you can get parked okay,' he said as she began to move off. She wondered what he meant.

After a few hundred yards, Dufferin Street sloped down to a crossroads then rose again towards Lincoln Street and the old town. On top of a hill, the vast shape of Lunenburg Academy with its russet roof and pointed towers loomed like the giant's castle at the end of the beanstalk.

The police station sat in to the left. 'Here we are,' Annie said.

Taggart gaped. 'Is this for real?'

'Yep. It used to be the railway station. But I thought you'd been here before.'

The object of their interest was a dainty little wooden building painted red and cream with the word 'POLICE' in blue letters just underneath the window in its eaves. A porch to keep train travellers dry while they waited had been built as a thoughtful gesture. No one waited now. The line to Lunenburg had long since been discontinued.

'Yes but I didn't come into town this way. I went out along the shore.' He gave a laugh. 'It's like something out of a western. You know, like *High Noon*, when they're waiting for the bad guy to arrive. And who runs the place these days? Bruce Willis?'

Annie saw now what the Mountie had meant about getting parked. In front of the police station was a tarmacked lot normally used as a public car park when the old town got busy in the summer and there was limited space along its quaint streets. At this time of the year it should have been empty. Instead, an RCMP fleet, composed of several cars and off-road vehicles and a couple of big vans, stood lined up. One van was providing food. Men in black clothing and flak jackets lingered beside it, eating hot dogs out of greaseproof paper.

Annie drove past the gauntlet of their stares and parked alongside a white cruiser which had 'Lunenburg – Mahone Bay Police' on its flank. As she and Taggart got out, she could smell fried onions and coffee and suspicion in the cold air.

The main door of the police station was at the side, where the platform used to be. A sign said it was open Monday to Friday, no weekends. They walked into what might once have been the waiting room or maybe the stationmaster's office. There was a counter and at the corner of it a couple of baseball caps in blue denim were propped up with 'Lunenburg – Mahone Bay Police' across the front in yellow lettering. A notice said they were twelve dollars apiece and that the proceeds would go to the local Red Cross. On the wall hung black and white photographs of the Lunenburg police force in 1960, seven smiling uniformed men who looked like they had already retired from some other job.

The room had enough space for three desks. A woman with grey hair in tight curls and glasses with lenses like prisms sat by the window, while a big man with fat red cheeks leaned against the wall beside her, sipping coffee from a thick mug decorated with Cartman's angry face. He wore a dark blouson jacket and grey trousers which were under some strain at the belly. His gun and his nightstick were slung on either side of a leather belt which sat low on his hips as if it had been jammed there.

'Can I do something for you?' the woman said although she wasn't interested enough to move. Annie got the feeling that, like Rosemary Field, she had probably watched them arrive.

In the car they had worked out how they would play this.

'My name's Welles. You're not, by any chance, Debbie Randall?'

'Yes, I am,' the woman said and got up now. She didn't look to Annie like a Debbie Randall but that was because she'd somehow got Debbie Reynolds into her head. This Debbie was small, square-shouldered and wide in the hips and looked as if sitting, rather than standing or doing any kind of moving around, was her natural position. But maybe Debbie Reynolds was like that these days, too.

She wore little moccasin things and as she came over to the counter her feet made swishing noises on the floor. Annie produced the badge again. 'I'm with the Halifax Regional Police. We spoke on the phone. You were kind enough to check something for me.'

Debbie considered this for a second. 'Oh yeah. The Gaunt case. The Cassandra Breaux murder.' She turned to the man behind her. 'I told you about the call I got, Gus.'

The big man nodded.

She said, 'This is Constable Gus Peterson.'

He levered himself away from the wall, put his cup down on Debbie's desk and came forward. Close up, Annie saw that the weight he carried made him look older than he actually was. She'd taken him for a man of about Walter Flagg's age but he was younger than that.

He shook her hand. Annie said, 'This is John Taggart, a friend of mine.'

'Pleased to meet you. So what's with this Gaunt fella? I read in the RCMP bulletin that he's disappeared, skipped his parole. Is that why you guys are here? You think he might be in Lunenburg?' He sounded as if he didn't believe it was all that likely.

'Well, as a matter of fact, I've come to see you because of John here. He's a journalist from London, doing some research into the Cassandra Breaux murder. To tell you the truth, this is all kind of unofficial.'

Taggart said, 'Officer Welles – Annie – and I have mutual friends in Halifax. She very kindly volunteered to help me. I'm trying to write some background stuff about Lunenburg before the royal visit next week. I was here a few days ago and I heard about that murder case, then she told me about Gaunt and the fact that he'd disappeared.'

Peterson frowned. 'According to the bulletin, that's not public knowledge as yet.'

'I know,' Annie said. 'But John's not going to write anything before Gaunt turns up again.'

'I wanted to have a look around,' Taggart said. 'Annie's being my guide, opening a few doors for me.'

'On your department's time?' Peterson asked, an eyebrow cocked in doubt. 'That's pretty damn understanding of them.'

She smiled. 'You can wipe that thought. I'm on my own time.' She turned to Taggart. 'And don't you forget it.'

He raised his hands in mock surrender.

Peterson said, 'Normally, I'd tell you we don't get many journalists around here but right now that wouldn't be true.'

'No, I can see that,' Taggart agreed.

'It's a weird experience turning on your TV every morning and seeing Lunenburg right there. Goddamn maps and everything explaining where it is.'

'You're not short of a bit of company of the other kind, either,' Annie said, nodding towards the window.

Peterson looked like he was about to spit. 'They just sailed in here like they owned the place. I'll be glad to see the back of them.'

'So I take it then,' Annie said, 'you're not involved in the Carne business or the royal visit?'

'Nope. That's all RCMP territory. We just do our usual job, looking after the interests of the good people of Lunenburg and Mahone Bay.'

She wasn't able to decipher whether his philanthropic tone was real or tongue-in-cheek. Her glance went to the old photograph.

'The old days, huh?' She counted. 'Seven officers. How many of you are there now?'

'Nine, including the Chief. And we cover Mahone Bay as well. They had Lunenburg only.'

'Is the Chief here today?'

'No, he's on vacation. Debbie here's running the place while he's away.'

Annie smiled at her in a woman-to-woman way to say she knew that Debbie always ran the place.

Debbie asked her, 'So how can we help?'

'We wondered if you might know where Aaron Gaunt's house was. And we wanted to go to Heckman's Island to see where the murder took place. We figured that if we came here, maybe you could give us directions.'

'I can do better than that,' Peterson said, 'I can show you myself. Maybe show you a bit of old Lunenburg at the same time.'

'He's the secretary of the local historical society,' Debbie explained.

'Really? Then we're in luck,' Taggart said.

Peterson looked at a clock on the wall. 'No time like the present.' He buttoned his jacket and grabbed his cap from a hook. 'Have you guys eaten?'

'Not yet,' they said together.

'Then why don't we grab a bite of lunch and have a talk?'

As he opened the door in the counter and came through, he told Debbie, 'You know where we'll be.'

'Nice meeting you,' Annie said to her. She fished in her pocket, found her wallet and took out three tens, then put the money on the counter and took the two caps. 'I've got two sons. I think they might like these.'

'What about change?' Debbie said.

'Keep it for the Red Cross.'

Outside, Peterson announced that they were going to a nearby pub and that they could walk. He led the way past the small clutch of RCMP men as if he couldn't see them.

'These are fantastic buildings,' Taggart said. 'I think I've fallen in love with this place.'

They followed his gaze. On the other side of where the railway tracks had been, stood the Lunenburg Inn, a massive wooden edifice painted lime green with a brown roof. It had a long pillared porch propping up an elegant verandah and Annie reckoned it probably looked as good as the day it was built.

'Every room in the town's taken,' Peterson said. 'The innkeepers are enjoying this excitement, even if nobody else is. Most of us like a quiet life. That's why we live here.'

He pointed. At the corner of Falkland Street, the Bluenose Lodge was a towering gothic thing in blue and grey with a turret like a tall hat.

'That was the first house in the town to have a widow's walk.'

'Which is what exactly?' Taggart asked.

'You mean you've been writing about Lunenburg and you don't know what a widow's walk is? You've got a lot to learn.'

Annie explained. 'Widows' walks are balconies where the women used to watch. When a ship was overdue, they'd pace up and down, looking out to sea, waiting for their men to come home. A lot of the time the men didn't. That's why they're widows' walks, not wives' walks.'

The pub they were heading for was called the Knot and it was almost beside the parking lot. It was dark and smoky with a low ceiling, posters promoting forthcoming Irish nights and signed photographs of obscure personalities who had once passed this way. On a TV above the bar, an ice hockey game was being played loud and fast and in a room at the side men in baseball caps were throwing darts.

Peterson called a greeting to the bartender. He glanced briefly at a woman with early Farrah Fawcett hair who was nursing a beer, then he headed for a booth in the corner.

Once they were installed, he handed Annie and Taggart laminated menus.

'They do a great chowder.'

Annie wanted to eat a snack and get out of here and get on with what they had come for but it was clear that Peterson couldn't be rushed.

'If it's all the same to you,' Taggart said, 'I think I've done the chowder thing.'

Peterson laughed. 'In that case, try the hamburgers.'

When they came, they were enormous, with meat an inch thick, served with chunky potato wedges and a dip. Annie gave up half way through hers, much to Peterson's disappointment, but Taggart persisted and earned a pat on the back for his efforts.

As they ate, they talked. Peterson wanted to know who Taggart worked for so he told him about the *Chronicle* and what he did, omitting the fact that he'd been fired. Annie asked the policeman if he remembered the Gaunt case.

'I was ten at the time. But I guess I know more about it now than I did then.'

'Did you ever hear of a family around here called Landry?'

He thought. 'Can't say it rings a bell. Where do they live?'

'They don't live here now but they might have lived at Heckman's Island once.'

'Have they some connection with what happened there?'

'Maybe. They might have been neighbours.'

Taggart sat back and wiped his lips with a napkin. 'I'm looking for people to talk to who might have been around that night. Landry was a name that came up.'

Peterson dished out the menus once more, then while they declined dessert and just drank coffee, he got to work on a big slab of pudding known as death by chocolate. Annie felt that that might not be far off the mark if he kept on eating this way. Taggart insisted on paying and nobody argued with him. A trough for tips ran like a storm drain along the inside of the bar. Peterson tossed a handful of change into it on the way out.

'We'll go in the cruiser,' he said. 'The Gaunt place isn't far, then we'll come back this way and head for Heckman's Island.'

The police car smelled of pine air-freshener and the occasional dog. They drove up Lincoln Street with Annie in the front and Taggart in the back like a prisoner.

'People here like to see us on patrol. If they don't, they call the Chief's office to complain. They like to feel they're being protected.'

'From what?' Annie asked.

'Who knows? Fear of crime bears no relation to the actual amount of crime we have here. Sure, there are robberies from time to time, private houses, stores. Right now I'm dealing with a break-in at a pharmacy in Mahone Bay last weekend. But most of our problems arise in the summer. We get people drifting through, young people with summer jobs, dead-beats, criminals, sometimes, who know there are tourists to rob. But it's not exactly an easy town to get lost in and sooner or later, most strangers end up in the Knot. It's the only pub in town so it's not difficult for us to keep an eye on who goes in and out. Like that blonde who was in there. That wasn't a face I knew.'

Annie was impressed by his watchfulness. At another time she might have been impressed by the guided tour, too, but it looked like it might take forever. They took a convoluted route around the cracked and worn streets. She tried to show interest rather than impatience when Peterson slowed every now and then to indicate a particular building and to give a summary of its history.

He made a point of showing them houses which had the

elaborately extended dormer windows known as the Lunenburg Bump. There was a big one on a house in Hopson Street. He stopped opposite.

'That's it. That's the old Gaunt place.'

Taggart was first out of the car. He stood and looked at the house. Apart from the bump and some ornate panelling around the porch, it was a simple, solid, wooden building painted a terracotta pink. Old snow lay in a grubby mound on the patch of grass in front and leafless shrubs huddled in the shelter of the banistered steps which led up to the door. From inside a front window a black and white cat watched them with cautious eyes.

'It was built by the Gaunt family around 1880,' Peterson said. 'They were boat-builders and fishermen. Not one of the better-known local families. I mean, you don't get streets and other landmarks named after them, like with some, but I guess the Gaunt name made its impression in Lunenburg in other ways.'

'Who lives here now?' Annie asked.

'A doctor from the hospital over in Bridgewater. I think it's changed hands a couple of times since the murder.'

Taggart crossed the road. He stood in the front path and gazed at the upper windows. Peterson's radio crackled and he reached into the car to answer it. Debbie Randall's voice came through. While he talked to her, Annie went over to Taggart.

'You okay?'

He didn't answer for a second. His face was tense. She lifted her hand and squeezed his forearm gently. As they looked at the stillness of the house together, the cat's narrow eyes blinked slowly.

He told her, 'There's so much stuff going through my mind. So much that I'm trying to imagine. I mean, my mother lived here, for God's sake. I just can't get over that. And I'm just standing here wondering which room.'

'What do you mean?'

'Up there. Which room? Which bedroom was I conceived in?'

She had no answer for him. She couldn't say that it mightn't have been here at all, that it might have been somewhere else. He wouldn't want to think like that. He was looking at the house as if he were willing it to impart some message to him, to tell him what it knew. This was a special place. It was where his parents had lived. It was his family home.

He came out of his thoughts abruptly and turned to her. 'The harbour. I've just remembered. There's a monument down there.'

'A monument?'

'Yes. A memorial. To Lunenburg people lost at sea.'

'I don't get it.'

Peterson had finished on the radio. Taggart went back over to him.

'The monument at the harbour. I was looking at it last week. Do you think we could drive down there?'

'Sure. We can go back that way. Why, what's the interest?'

'I'm not entirely sure. I'll know when I get there.'

When they got to the boatyard, they saw an RCMP car parked at the gates while inside, behind a higher fence than before, alsatians were being walked by men in big coats. They looked like guards in a concentration camp.

'This is all new,' Taggart said. 'Heavy stuff.'

'I don't think you'd get much of a tour today,' Annie told him.

'Yeah, they're getting the *Bluenose* ready in there,' Peterson said. 'Look at them. I don't know what kind of trouble they think they're expecting.'

He swung round towards Taggart suddenly. 'Hey, here's

a story for you. Did you know that Cary Eisener, the guy who's behind the whole *Bluenose* thing, did you know that he was Aaron Gaunt's business partner at the time of the murder?'

'As a matter of fact, I did know that, yes.'

Peterson looked disappointed. 'Oh. I thought I was giving you something new.' He smiled again. 'But it's interesting, don't you think? Not that I'm telling you your job or anything.'

'No, you're right. I might incorporate some of that into my story.'

Annie felt a twinge of guilt. Peterson was a decent guy, a good, straight cop. He was being helpful and she didn't like the fact that they were lying to him.

'Here we are,' he said. They stopped beside a clutch of black marble slabs. Down the pier, a truck was parked beside a big trawler. Boxes of fish were being lowered from the vessel. The shouts of seamen mingled with the screech of herring gulls flapping overhead, trying to seize a moment that never seemed to come.

Taggart got out and headed straight for one of the slabs as if he knew what he was doing. Annie followed. He stared, searching, then crouched down.

'There! I knew I'd seen something.'

She looked at where he was pointing. Halfway down the alphabetical list of those lost at sea before 1925 was the name Henry Gaunt.

Taggart traced his fingers along the letters. 'I wonder who he was. If it was 1925, a great-grandfather maybe.'

'Of who?' Peterson said, joining them. 'Aaron Gaunt?' He bent down and looked at the name and the date. 'Probably a bit closer than that. Could be his grandfather or maybe an uncle. Some relative, anyway, that's for sure. You could always look in the town records.'

He straightened up and checked the sky. 'Now, if you guys don't mind, I think maybe we should head on out to Heckman's Island before the light starts to go.'

They drove down the harbour, which was called Bluenose Drive, onto Linden Avenue, then they passed by the police station again and headed on towards Tannery Road and Mason's Beach Road.

'This is the route I took before, 'Taggart said, 'when I went to look at the Carne place.'

'We go right by it,' Peterson said.

Within minutes they had reached the media stake-out at the front of Carne's gates. Since they were in a police cruiser, none of the RCMP patrols bothered to stop them. Peterson gave a little wave as they went by.

Expectation was in the air. Annie could sense it. It was in the way people were moving around. She watched unwanted equipment being loaded up, litter being stuffed into black plastic bags. The wheels of all the vehicles had churned the ground into a mudslide. Some of them were going to have trouble getting out of there.

'And who's going to clear this up?' Peterson wanted to know, forgetting about Taggart's vocation for the moment. 'Look at them. They're like vultures or something.'

Annie thought the scene looked more like a Roman encampment, a legion folding its tents, preparing to move on to the next conquest.

A mile further on, a wooden sign at the roadside announced that they had reached Heckman's Island, although Annie could see no sign of one. Peterson turned left into a winding woodland road pitted with deep hollows. But then they rumbled over a short bridge that crossed a flowing stream and after that they were on the island itself. Snow lined the edge of the road and the trees were thick on either side. Notices saying 'NO SHOOTING' were nailed to some of them.

Annie couldn't see any houses but every so often their presence was marked by an opening in the trees and a mailbox with a name written on it. One bore the name 'HORNER'. On a tree beside it was a wooden sign with 'hand-carved ornaments for sale' etched in a careful script.

They began to bump down a narrow laneway that wound in among the trees. Rough stones had been scattered to provide a grip otherwise they would have sunk into deep leafy earth. After a few yards, the trees fell away, like servants withdrawing, and Annie saw that they had arrived at the side of a bright blue house built almost at the water's edge. In the snow-covered space between the house and the bank, wooden chairs huddled round a picnic table as if for warmth and a gas barbecue sat waiting for summer, snow sprinkled on its lid like icing on a cake.

The main door to the house was at the side, beneath a porch from which icicles hung like wind chimes, and there was a garage, its door open to reveal the back of a Toyota 4 x 4. A few yards away stood a small shed painted the same blue as the house. Annie wondered if a boat might be kept there.

They got out and Peterson went to the front door. 'I'll see if anyone's in.'

Annie wandered to the edge of the bank, the snow and the grass beneath it soft under her feet. The stream was about twenty yards wide and the far bank was lined with trees where the woodland began again. She stared at the cold blackness of the water, listened to it rippling by. She looked to her right, upstream, but there was a curve and some trees and she could not see beyond.

'Can I help you folks?'

She turned to see a woman coming out of what she had

thought was the boathouse. Its door was open and she could see now that it was a workshop with a big bench in the centre. Sawdust and shavings covered the floor and she could smell the dusty sweetness of fresh wood.

The woman had white hair like a helmet and cut in a straight fringe. She was sturdy, dove-chested, wearing jeans and a denim shirt over a white polo neck. She looked at them and at the police car with curiosity but not concern.

Peterson came back down the porch steps and touched his cap. 'Good afternoon. Mrs Horner?'

'Yes, that's right. I'm Florence Horner.'

'I'm sorry to disturb you, Mrs Horner, I'm Constable Gus Peterson.' He gestured to the others. 'This is Officer Welles of the Halifax police and Mr Taggart who's a journalist from London.'

They all shook hands. 'Pleased to meet you,' Mrs Horner said. She looked at Taggart. 'You're not going to tell me that word of my wonderful hand-carved wooden ornaments has spread across the Atlantic and that you've come here to write about them?'

He smiled. 'I'm afraid not.'

She smiled back. 'No, I didn't think so.'

He told her why they had come, or at least a version of it. A voice started crackling out of Peterson's radio again and he leaned in to deal with it. When she thought he couldn't hear, Annie said, 'I had no idea we were just going to drive up like this. We only wanted to have a peep at the outside of the house. We had no intention of intruding.'

Mrs Horner laughed. 'Nonsense. You're not intruding. I don't get visitors much in the winter so you're very welcome.'

'You know about what happened here?' Taggart asked.

'Sure, I know. We bought the house from the late Cassandra Breaux's relatives. But what are we doing standing around here freezing to death? Come on inside and I'll make some coffee. Then we can talk.'

Peterson got off the radio and announced that he had to go and deal with a problem. There had been a traffic accident near the community centre on Victoria Road.

'It's not that far from here but I really don't know how long I'll be or when I'll be able to get back.'

'Don't worry about it,' Mrs Horner said. 'I've got to drive to Lunenburg later anyway. I need to get some groceries. You go on ahead. I can give your friends a ride when we're through here.'

Annie and Taggart shook Peterson's hand again, thanked him for all his help and said they'd be returning to Halifax after this. Then they watched him drive back up the laneway, little stones squirting out from under the tyres and pinging off the trees.

Mrs Horner brought them into the house through the kitchen door. As they wiped their feet on the mat, an overweight golden retriever with its tail swaying in a greeting waddled slowly towards them.

'This is Honey. Note the way she didn't bark when you drove up. Some guard dog, eh?'

She lit a ring on the cooker and put a kettle on to boil, then started to hunt in the cupboards. 'Now, cookies. Let's see what we've got.'

'Not for me,' Annie said.

'Or me,' Taggart agreed. 'We had a substantial lunch. Coffee by itself will be fine.'

Annie looked around. On a dresser there were examples of Mrs Horner's work: carved birds, a fishing boat, a rabbit. Some of them were in the style of native Inuit art. Annie picked up a piece of round wood that turned out to be a cat asleep, curled in on itself. She ran her fingers along its smooth, polished surface. 'These are very good.'

'That's kind of you to say. I do a lot of cats like that. They're very popular.'

'We saw the sign at the road,' Taggart said. 'Do you get much business that way?'

'Good Lord, no. Not a lot of people pass by here, even in the summer season. It's kind of off the beaten track but that's the attraction of the place. No, there's a gallery in Lunenburg that sells them, as well as a shop in Chester, another one in Bridgewater and a shop in one of the malls in Halifax. It started off as a hobby but it's grown from there. Not that I'm depending on it for a living, thank God. We wouldn't eat well if we had to do that, would we, girl?' She reached down and ruffled Honey's coat. 'Some of the people who call do so out of curiosity because they've heard about the murder. I don't mind. I quite enjoy the notoriety in a way. And they usually leave with a little something of mine – so everybody's happy.'

Annie wondered if this was a hint that they should purchase an object on their way out. If that was the case, it was Taggart's turn. She had bought the baseball caps.

'Do you live here alone?' she asked.

'Yes, since my husband died. That's what I meant about not having to depend on my handiwork for a living. Fortunately, with one thing and another, God bless him, he left me well provided for.'

When the coffee was ready, she put the pot and a jug and three mugs on a tray. 'We'll take this up to the sitting room.'

Taggart volunteered to carry. Mrs Horner led the way out of the kitchen and up the stairs to a big room with high windows which overlooked the stream at the back. The grey light of the sky was on the wane. She turned on table lamps. Honey, who had followed, slumped down in front of a glass-fronted wood fire, while Annie and Taggart sank into a couple of chintzy armchairs.

'This is lovely,' Annie said. 'Very comfortable.'

More carvings sat on shelves where unlit candles flirted with just a hint of scent. Lace-patterned glassware glinted from behind the latticed doors of a dark wooden cabinet. Annie's gaze stopped at a photograph propped up on a little table. It was of Mrs Horner, a bald man and two children, a boy and a girl, all in a row, smiling. She recognised the setting. They were sitting at the picnic table by the stream outside.

Mrs Horner poured and handed the mugs round. She said, 'This is where it happened, you know. Right in this room.'

Annie paused with the cup at her lips. 'But the murder took place in the bedroom. It . . .' Then she realised. 'Oh, I see. This was it?' She looked around again, beginning to see the room in a new light.

'Yes. My husband and I bought this place about eighteen months afterwards. It had been on the market for a long time without any takers. We were from Montreal originally, but we liked to come to Nova Scotia in the summer. We just adored the whole south shore, Chester, Mahone Bay, and we spotted the house when we were on vacation. The price was attractive – indeed, I think the poor woman's relatives just wanted to get rid of it – but Phil, my husband, managed to squeeze them down a little further and we bought it as a vacation home.'

'You didn't feel strange about what had happened?' Taggart asked.

'A bit, at first. There was a kind of eeriness but we knew we could deal with that, that it was mostly our imagination. The place had been neglected and needed a bit of work. That's when we decided to convert this from a bedroom into a sitting room. Once we'd done that, it changed the whole nature of the house. It felt more like ours, not at all like where somebody had been murdered.' She raised her arm and gestured towards the window. 'And you can see how nice it is here.'

'Must be beautiful in the summer,' Annie said. She looked at the photograph. 'When did your husband die?'

'Ten years ago. The children were older and had moved away by that stage so I sold up in Montreal and moved here permanently. This has been my home since then.'

Taggart asked, 'Do you see much of your neighbours?'

'Oh, now and then. We see each other when we want to and we keep to ourselves when we don't. That's the great joy of the island. Everybody seems to abide by the same rules. There's just a few of us, though, who live here all the year round. Most of the people are weekenders and a lot of them bring their friends with them when they come.'

'Do you ever remember hearing of a family called Landry around here?' Annie asked.

'Landry, Landry.' She paused for thought. 'Yes, it does strike a chord.' She sat back and studied the ceiling. 'Landry. I think . . . yes, I know now why it's familiar. When we looked at this house, there was another one for sale at the same time.' She pointed to the window again. 'About half a mile upstream. It was in much better shape than this place. Bigger, too, and more expensive, so we didn't consider it for long. Phil got into negotiations over this house instead. But yes, Landry. I think that was the name. They had it as a summer place. A couple with a small boy about the same age as my own kids because I remember thinking it was a shame they weren't going to be here any more. He would have been someone for them to play with. Anybody for more coffee?'

Neither of them answered but Taggart held his cup forward.

Annie sat and listened to the sound of old man Landry's voice in her head. *Damned boat. Always in that damned boat.*

She spoke at last. 'Did they have a boat, do you know? The Landrys?'

'Well now, I wouldn't remember that. But then most people around here have a boat. We had one for a time, too. Just a little flat-bottomed dinghy. Kept it in the boathouse which is my workshop now. But maybe I could ask a question. What's your interest in these Landry people?'

Taggart gave her the familiar explanation. 'It's all part of my research. I'm trying to track down people who might have lived around here at the time of the murder. I thought I might like to interview them about what it was like.'

'Well, there's the Boudreaus. They're the next house along. They might be able to help you. As far as I know, they lived around here then. I can give you their phone number if you like.'

Taggart said that would be terrific and she said she'd look it up on their way out. They finished their coffee and she said that if there was nothing else, then she really did have to get to Lunenburg. They thanked her and said she'd been very helpful.

'For the life of me, I don't see how,' she said.

'Just seeing the place was very important,' Taggart said. 'And I'll be able to write about the woman who makes these lovely wood carvings.'

'Well, I must say that would be just wonderful. You'll have to send me a copy so that I can put it on my workshop wall.'

They headed back downstairs. Mrs Horner got her coat and hat and wrote down the phone number for Taggart. Annie nudged him and nodded towards the little wooden cat. He frowned, then realised what she was getting at.

'This cat, Mrs Horner. It's really very nice. I wonder if I might be able to buy it.'

And of course the answer was yes, for twenty dollars,

which she assured him was less than the shops charged. She wrapped it carefully in pink tissue paper and sealed it with a little sticker which had her name and address printed on it.

They left the house. The dog came too and climbed into a space at the back of the Toyota. Mrs Horner didn't bother locking up. As she started the engine and began to reverse out of the garage, Annie walked down to the edge of the stream.

She gazed across to the far bank and then she turned and looked back at the house. The living room lights were still on.

She walked up to the Toyota. 'Mrs Horner, who lives in the old Landry house now?'

'A family from Halifax. They use it at weekends and in the summer.'

'On the way, do you think you could show us where it is?'

25

The promulgation, as Gryce liked to call these things, was pinned up on the noticeboards at two-thirty, once he had discussed matters with everyone involved. It did not appear on the computer message board since the system had crashed again, the second time in ten days, which a lot of people reckoned had to be something to do with the building work going on.

Gamble didn't give a shit what it was, nor was he in the office when the promulgation made its appearance, announcing that Wilson was retiring at his own request, with immediate effect, and that Marriott from Fraud was being made acting staff sergeant in charge of CIS until the post was advertised internally and a permanent appointment made.

Although he wasn't there to see the notice when it went up, he knew what was in it. He also knew that there was no point in applying when the time came, although he would probably be expected to. Not getting the job was one thing; not showing an interest was another. They didn't like that on the management floor. Even when they had you on the ground with a boot on your neck, they liked you to try to get up. It showed what you were made of.

There was also the question, beginning to loom threateningly in his mind, of whether he would even be around to apply. Over the course of the morning, his physical discomfort had not improved. He had once broken a couple of ribs during a training exercise and he'd had to have them strapped up. That was the way he felt now, as if a bandage had been wrapped around his chest and drawn so tight that it was giving him trouble breathing.

It was why he had phoned the surgery in Dartmouth again and had his appointment brought forward. He wasn't stupid; he knew what this might be, but he couldn't quite admit it. Then again, maybe he was worrying over nothing. Maybe it really was some kind of a digestive thing, like he'd thought this morning. At any rate, he hadn't wanted to say on the phone exactly how he felt, otherwise they'd have sent the paramedics with the cardiac ambulance and that would have looked great in the current promotional circumstances, wouldn't it?

And so when people were reading the noticeboards and looking around for him, seeing the empty office and wondering where he was, Gamble was negotiating the noisy picket lines near the law courts building and walking into the draughty Metro terminal on Upper Water Street to get the ferry. He counted out a dollar sixty-five in change and dropped it into the box. As usual the attendant didn't blink an eyelid, seeming to know from the sound of the money rattling in whether it was the right amount or not.

Gamble took a seat on a bench beside a young woman with a long wool coat and scarf and a drawstring bag which had 'Dalhousie' and its crest embroidered on it. She was buried in a book and didn't notice him. He couldn't see what the title was. It was a paperback and she had doubled it over.

He never read anything now that wasn't related to work. A glance at the paper maybe. Yet he had been an avid reader once. He was forty-two and it wasn't too late and it was time he got his priorities right. He thought of his wife and the children. He tolerated them but didn't have time for them.

It was as if they were an intrusion to be endured, a domestic obligation that got in the way of work. That was wrong.

He looked out through the grimy terminal window and saw the ferry halfway across, ploughing its way through choppy furrows. He felt warm. He put his hand to his brow. There was a sheen of sweat on it. He opened his coat in the hope that it might help him breathe more easily.

He had been eaten up by the job but now it had spat him out like a tasteless piece of gristle. Maybe Gryce was right and he wasn't up to it. He hadn't said as much in the brief meeting this morning but Gamble knew that's what he believed. Maybe his judgement, his style were at fault. He thought about that. The way he had handled Steyn. His relationship with Claussen. The whole business with Annie Welles.

He put his head in his hands. God, he had allowed himself to get obsessed with that job, with holding on to it, using any and every means possible to keep Claussen and whoever else at bay. If Gryce only knew the half of it, if he had seen him slipping into the Internet cafe on Barrington Street to send an anonymous e-mail to Claussen's friend at the *Chronicle-Herald*. That had been despicable. Nor had it made any difference. Claussen would get something out of this new round of musical chairs, that was for sure.

And this business with Welles, first trying to get her to report Claussen for harassment and now allowing her to tag along behind the investigation. That was pathetic, another act of desperation. What was he thinking of? What sort of a person had he become?

He wondered where Annie was now and what she was doing. He should call her later and put an end to all this nonsense.

He turned to look at the approaching ferry.

* * *

The girl closed the book and popped it into her bag as the boat drew near. For the first time, she noticed the man next to her. His face was grey, as if he'd had a shock. There was perspiration on his forehead and she wondered if he was all right. But then he glanced at her, smiled fleetingly, so she smiled back and said nothing.

The ferry docked. Its side fell forward and became a ramp down which the passengers came in an orderly tide, students with bicycles, Metro employees in uniform, men with heavy overcoats and briefcases, reporting into their cellphones that another successful landing had been accomplished. Through the glass, the girl watched them pass down a separate corridor, then a door opened to allow her and the rest of the new passengers to get on.

She picked up her bag and went aboard, electing not to sit inside but to enjoy what was left of the day from the top deck. The light was fading already and there was a wind. She took a ski hat from her bag and pulled it over her hair, then looped her scarf round her neck and sat down. She heard other feet on the stairs. The man who'd been sitting beside her came up. He still looked ill but he wasn't her business. The crossing would take fifteen minutes and she would probably never see him again.

From her bag she took a Rubik's Cube. Time to see if she could break her own record. But she wouldn't start until the journey did. She set the cube in her lap and blew on her fingers like a safecracker about to get to work on a combination.

'I haven't seen one of those things for years.'

The man had sat down directly opposite. She smiled at him. Below, the engines began to rumble, churning the water, and she could feel the ferry start to pull away from the dock. She checked her watch and began.

Click, click, click. Reds together, then not, then most of

the greens, but problems with the yellows. She glanced up once and saw that he was watching in fascination.

'What's your record?'

Click, click. She would rather he didn't talk to her at all because it ruined the concentration but she didn't want to seem rude.

'Twelve minutes. Real experts can do it in as many seconds.'

He didn't say anything else. She was glad. She didn't look at him again. She had a good feeling about this. She kept going. Click, click, twist. Click, twist.

Done it.

She checked her watch. Fantastic.

'Ten minutes forty,' she said and grinned at him.

He didn't answer. He was slumped sideways in the little bucket seat as if he were asleep.

Taggart sat in the back of the Toyota with the dog. It stared at him with its tongue hanging out and its breath rank. Annie glanced back and grinned at his obvious unease.

'This is the place here,' Mrs Horner said, seeming to spot a space among the trees that Annie couldn't. There was no mailbox to signify that they had reached an entrance but an entrance there was and they turned into it and began to drive down a track with bumps and hollows identical to those in Mrs Horner's own lane.

Annie asked about the absence of a mailbox.

'Some of the weekenders don't bother. They have a box at the Post Office instead.'

They rattled on until they could go no further, reaching a locked gate and a wire fence that wound in among the trees.

'Some people do this,' Mrs Horner said. 'Barricade their property. I don't like it. I like the open forest and the fact that the animals can roam freely in the wild. I don't know why people come here if they're going to do this kind of thing.'

They got out and looked over the gate. Down the path, the house was hard to locate among the trees. Annie could just see a dark corner of it and then the open land which, as with Mrs Horner's house, led to the river bank. This place, she saw, had a small jetty beside which a rowing boat had been hauled up. It lay overturned, like a dead turtle.

They got back into the Toyota and Mrs Horner began to reverse up the track. A couple of times she veered into a soft spot but her wheels refused to sink. They spun and whined and spat out earth and stones and eventually the vehicle made it to the road.

Twenty minutes later they were driving up to the police station parking lot, having heard Mrs Horner's views on the Carne affair, on the activities of the RCMP and the forthcoming visit of Prince William. The last of these was the only one for which she had any enthusiasm.

'I'll be there, waving my little flag,' she said. 'Oh my goodness me, look at this.' The menacing row of RCMP vehicles had come into view. 'What on earth do these people think they're playing at?'

She dropped them off and they thanked her, then she hurried away, a little faster, Annie thought, than the speed limit might allow for. They stood in the parking lot and watched her depart.

'What now?' Taggart said.

'Now we're going back.'

They parked the car at the roadside, rather than risk getting stuck down the unreliable track, then they walked down to the gate. Annie climbed over it.

'Are you sure you know what you're doing? Sorry, are

you sure you know what *we're* doing?' Taggart asked, following her.

'No, I'm not sure at all. I want to try this out, that's all.'

She had explained the plan to him on the way but now that they had got here, he seemed less happy about it.

'If someone spots us, or if Mrs Horner comes back, how do we explain what we're doing?'

'You don't have to worry about that. Remember who you're with. I flash the badge and tell them it's a police matter.'

The old Landry house was dark and shuttered but it wasn't the house they were interested in. They walked towards the upturned boat. Except for the marks of animals, their footprints were the first since the last snowfall.

'Right, let's try to lift this thing,' she said. 'With a bit of luck the oars will be underneath.'

Although the boat was not big, it took more effort than she had anticipated. Months of sub-zero temperatures held it to the ground as if it had been bolted down. But they got it turned at last and saw that she was right. Two oars sat on a boat-shaped patch of albino grass across which centipedes and wood lice scurried in search of new dark places.

Taggart gave the boat a quick examination with his hands. 'I hope there isn't a leak in this damned thing.'

There was a rope tied to a ring on the bow. They slid the boat across the snow and into the water, then looped the rope round the end of the jetty and climbed in. Taggart cast off and immediately they began to drift into the current. The boat was wide enough for them to sit side by side and take an oar each. They began to row.

'Except I can't see where I'm going,' Taggart said.

'You know, I wonder if this is it – the boy's boat. Nah, it couldn't be. Too long ago.'

They got into a rhythm and watched the Landry house

disappear in their wake, listening to the creak of the oars in the rowlocks and the sound of the water that bore them along. The stream was a series of bends. Around each one, Annie hoped to see Mrs Horner's house but it took them ten minutes to reach it. The lights were still on in the upstairs window, seeming brighter now as dusk began to claim the sky.

'Almost there,' she said.

They stopped rowing and let the water take them for a while. Annie used her oar to manoeuvre them towards the far bank. When they were opposite the house, Taggart reached out and grabbed a branch but it broke in his hand and they drifted again. He grabbed another, a stronger limb this time, and held on tight until Annie managed to tie the rope to it. When they were secured, he got out and helped her up onto the bank.

They gazed across at the house, at the outdoor furniture and the barbecue, the detritus of summer living. Mrs Horner wasn't back. The garage stood empty, waiting for the Toyota's return.

'You couldn't see anything from here,' Annie said, disappointment in her voice as she looked towards the upstairs window. 'The angle's wrong.'

'From here, maybe. But you're not a twelve-year-old boy.'

'Which means?'

'You've got two sons of your own. Work it out. If you wanted to get a good look into that room, what would you do?'

She turned to him. 'I'd climb a tree.'

The question was, which one? They walked along the bank, first one way and then the other, ruling out the most unlikely, both in terms of difficulty and potential view. Then Annie saw one that was a possibility. It had a broad branch jutting out about ten or twelve feet up its trunk and stubbly lower branches that could be used as petons. It was also a little back from the edge which meant that other trees could provide cover.

'This is the one,' she said. 'If I was going to spy on the house from a tree, this is the one I'd pick.'

'So let's see if you're right.'

Taggart was not as agile as a twelve-year-old boy but then again twelve feet wasn't far off the ground for him. He took off his coat to make the task easier and hauled himself up. When he got to the big branch he settled into it with his legs around the trunk and looked across the stream.

'What can you see?' Annie said.

He looked down at her. 'Come up and see for yourself. There's space here for two. I'll give you a hand.'

She took her coat off and put it on the ground with his. He reached down and helped her aloft, then moved back on the branch to make room for her. When she was on, he sat in against her with his arms around her waist.

'This is cosy,' he said.

She acted as if she hadn't heard him. She looked across the stream. 'God, you can see right into the house from here.' She sighed. 'But it doesn't prove anything, does it? I can't ask Cobb Landry if he saw what happened, if he sat up here that night and watched it all. So what's the use of this?'

'Would this help?' Taggart said.

He was pointing at the trunk, just above her head.

Something had been carved into the wood. It had been darkened by time and thirty years of changing seasons but she could still make out the letters 'CL'.

26

On the way back towards Halifax they gabbled excitedly about their discovery. Annie was taken aback by her own exuberance. Taggart she could understand, but this was not the detached, objective evaluation her training had taught her. And all the messing around in boats, climbing trees – she felt as if they were two characters in a children's adventure story, uncovering something the grown-ups didn't want them to know about.

So she calmed herself down and then him and they tried to assess how it added up.

There was nothing you could prove but they both felt certain now that Cobb Landry had been in that tree that night and had witnessed the murder of Cassandra Breaux. It would not have been the first time he had watched from that position, either, since it was unlikely that the night of the murder was the night he had carved his initials.

And what then? Then, by the looks of things, he had said nothing for thirty years about what he had seen. Which was what, exactly? Aaron Gaunt murdering the woman? Or was there something else? What was it that had brought Gaunt to George Poyner's office with Cobb Landry's car number? And what was it that led him later that night to Landry's house?

'Whatever it was, did Gaunt kill him because of it?' she asked Taggart.

He was quiet for a moment, then he said, 'At his trial, he claimed he didn't do it.' His words were an echo of the backgrounder in the *Herald-Chronicle*. 'He said someone else had come into the room and knocked him unconscious and then that person had killed her.'

'Nobody believed him. He was caught, shall we say, red-handed?'

'But to plead not guilty in circumstances like that – this isn't a stupid man we're talking about here. You said so yourself. If he'd been guilty, wouldn't he have been better off pleading that way, saying it was a crime of passion, trying to lessen the risk of the kind of sentence he got?'

'Maybe.' She'd thought about that herself when she'd started reading about the case in the newspaper files.

'The truth is,' Taggart said, 'they never looked for anybody else because they didn't believe they had to. They'd found him with the body and the knife and the motive and that was that. And it's happening all over again. Once more he's the only person anyone's looking for. It's tunnel vision. They're obsessed with this Eisener-Prince William business. That's the only thing they care about – getting Aaron Gaunt out of the picture.'

Annie couldn't disagree with him. It was why they were here now. But where next?

She said, 'Even if, for the sake of argument, we were to discover that he didn't kill Cassandra Breaux, that still wouldn't prove that he didn't murder Landry or even Poyner.'

'It might if we found out who the real killer was.'

She looked at him. They were getting carried away again, piling supposition on top of supposition. They needed facts.

She said, 'I need to know more about Landry. I thought I might talk to the Orbachs, his neighbours. They were friendly with him.'

'Your people will already have done that.'

'Yes. But I still want to talk to them myself.'

'Oh, I get you. You want to talk to them now that we know what we know.'

'We don't know anything. We just have theories.'

'Good ones, if you ask me. So what way do you want to play it when we get there?'

'There's no "we". I'm doing this alone. You're not coming on this one.'

'Why not?'

'They live just across the street from the Landry house. There might be police or RCMP still there. I don't want anyone to see you and start asking questions about why you're with me.'

'But they might wonder about you anyway.'

'I'll take that chance, see how the land lies.'

She dropped him off at the Royal Citadel and told him she would call later. He was having dinner at Jeff Cameron's house tonight. Outside the hotel, before she drove off again, she called the office to speak to Flagg.

'There's news,' he told her. 'Marriott from Fraud has been appointed acting officer in charge of CIS. Wilson's gone. I was right about that.'

'You're kidding? They stepped over Gamble? But that's crazy. How's he taking it?'

'Nobody knows. He hasn't been seen since before the announcement went up. Gryce brought Marriott round to meet the troops a little while ago and they both seemed surprised to find that he wasn't here.'

She was shocked. Gamble would have been the obvious person to get the temporary post. It would have recognised his seniority and experience and for him not to be given it was tantamount to telling him he was on the way out. She thought about her forthcoming disciplinary and wondered if she should speak to someone from EAP after all.

She pushed the thought from her mind. She said, 'Those Orbach people. The guy who found Landry – do you have an address for them?'

Flagg gave a chuckle and lowered his voice. 'You're up to something. I knew it. All that stuff this morning about Landry's old man. Why do you want to know?'

She waited a second before answering. She couldn't keep Flagg in the dark forever. He was a good partner. She told him, 'I've been finding out things about Landry.'

'Like what?'

'I can't tell you on the phone.'

'What are you doing – some kind of freelance thing here?'

'That depends on how I get on.' She thought about Gamble and wondered just how much he would be behind her now. 'I want to talk to the Orbachs about him.'

He gave her the address. 'I shouldn't get involved in any of this. And I should tell you the same thing. It'll mean trouble.'

She ignored him. 'Thanks, Walter. You're a pal. I'm on my way.'

'Where are you?'

'Outside the Royal Citadel.'

'Are you sure you know what you're doing?'

'No, and I wish people would stop asking me that.'

The street where the Orbachs lived and where Cobb Landry had lived until recently was still and empty, as if observing a reverential silence because of what had happened there. Few cars stood in the short driveways. It was a dormitory street, couples at work, children at school, a street which didn't see much daytime activity except in summer.

Landry's house wasn't hard to spot. Crime scene tape had been wound all the way round the property and a white

Halifax PD cruiser with one officer in it sat at the kerb. At least it wasn't an RCMP car.

Annie had an idea and pulled in behind it. She didn't know the guy but she produced her badge and he rolled down his window. He had a broad face and heavy black hair with a widow's peak. He blinked his eyes into focus as if he had been asleep.

'I hope you're going to tell me I can go now,' he told her. His voice had a just-awake throatiness. He coughed. She could smell old food and cold coffee from the inside of the car.

'How long have they told you to stay here?'

He shrugged. 'Until I'm relieved or the place is released.'

'Well, I'm afraid that arrangement still stands. Sorry, buddy. I've just come to see if there's anything we missed.'

He looked at her with just a tinge of suspicion. 'A bunch of buffalo heads were here this morning. They took away some cameras and stuff. I kind of figured that would be it.'

Buffalo heads was another term of endearment reserved for the RCMP. It referred to the organisation's emblem. She said, 'It might be. But they sent me to check something out. After that, it shouldn't be long until we're finished.'

She told him she'd be only a few minutes, then she headed up the path, tempted to look back to see if he was watching her, although she was sure he was and not at all certain that she'd been convincing about having legitimate business here.

She went into the house. If you didn't count the fingerprint powder on practically every surface and the outline on the living room floor where Landry's body had lain, there was no sign that anything had happened here. No bloodstains, no broken furniture. Everything neat and in position.

She thought of Aaron Gaunt's house. It was well-kept, too, and bore some resemblance to this place because they were both the houses of men who lived alone. They were comfortable but they lacked what she could only describe as a woman's touch, some sign of intimacy or warmth.

Compared to Gaunt, Landry wasn't much of a reader. But then, compared to Gaunt, nobody was. Landry's library, mostly paperback bestsellers, was all contained in a small bookcase which stood beside the TV and the video player. On the other side, a larger set of shelves held rows of tapes: hockey and football, natural history, lots of modern feature films.

But the main thing that interested her in the room was a group of framed photographs on one wall. At first she thought they might be the usual prints that you saw everywhere. An art shop in Scotia Square Mall sold lots like these, famous Nova Scotia scenes: fishing at Cape Breton, the Evangeline Trail, the three churches at Mahone Bay or the lighthouse at Peggy's Cove in a variety of weathers. These pictures were familiar territory, too, but she didn't think she had seen any of them before. She thought of what the cop outside had said about the RCMP taking cameras away.

She walked back into the hall and there she saw a picture that held her attention immediately. Somehow she had missed it on the way in. It had been taken in the fall and it was a shot of a long winding road. On either side were trees with leaves which looked like polished brass and at the end of the road a blood-red sun was making its descent.

She had been on that road today.

She took the picture off the wall. Instead of a frame, it was held by clips under glass. She undid them and took the photograph out. On the back was written: *Heckman's Island, 1989. Photograph – Cobb Landry.*

There were feet on the wood porch outside.

'So what have you found now?' Walter Flagg asked. He stood in the doorway, his big open overcoat and his bulk blocking out the remains of the daylight.

'What are you doing here?'

He came in and took the photograph out of her hand, studying it while he answered. 'Well, after you called me and asked for the Orbachs' address there was no way I was going to sit in the office with my thumb up my ass, was there? What's this?'

'It's a picture Cobb Landry took. It was hanging on the wall here. It's Heckman's Island.'

He looked at her. 'Meaning?'

Then she told him everything about her day and how it had come about, the visit to see old man Landry at HillCrest and what he had said, the trip to the house where the murder had taken place and then her discovery of the tree and Cobb Landry's initials. But she didn't tell him about Taggart being with her. She didn't want him jumping to conclusions.

She put the picture back together and hung it on the wall again. 'So you see – another piece of the jigsaw.'

'Wait a minute,' Flagg said, 'let me get this straight.'

For the next five minutes they went back and forth over the same arguments she and Taggart had pursued in the car. At the end of it Flagg came to the same conclusion she had.

'Theories. You've got theories.'

'I know.' She tapped the picture. 'But it seems that everywhere I turn now something's trying to lead me in a certain direction.'

'And you tell me Gamble approved of this activity?'

'Kind of. Nothing that would hold up in court.'

'He must be out of his mind. If this gets out, if Steyn and Gryce find out what you're up to, his ass is in a sling and you're long gone, young lady.'

She smiled. 'Since you're here, you want to help me look around? Then maybe we'll go over and see the Orbachs?'

'He'll be at work. I think the wife's there, though.'

'Do I take it that's a yes?'

He grunted. Then he said, 'You're forgetting I've been in this house before. You're forgetting I was on this case at the start. So I can tell you you won't find anything of interest – except the videos, of course.'

He smiled in an odd way. She frowned. 'I saw some videos in the front room. I don't know what you mean.'

He chuckled. 'Oh no, not those. I'm talking about something else.' His face darkened suddenly, 'Unless the Girks have taken them away, the bastards.'

He headed up the stairs, his feet sending earthquake shudders through the house. Annie followed him. He went into a bedroom. The bed was covered in a crisp blue duvet. A couple of freshly ironed shirts sat on a chair. On the bedside table there was a photograph of a Charles Landry who looked younger than the man she had seen today and she wondered if Cobb had taken it too.

Flagg went to a tall cupboard which stood at the foot of the bed. He flung the doors open.

'Great. Still here.'

Inside was another TV set, a videoplayer and several rows of tapes.

'Have a look,' Flagg said. 'Get a load of the deceased's home viewing.'

Annie took one cassette out, then another. They were all porn videos. Four rows of them. She looked at a couple of the boxes. Some of them had titles based on hit films, although she doubted whether any of the content was. There was one called *Sucking Private Ryan*, while another, with elaborate invention, was known as *Indiana Cojones and the Temple of Poon*. The men starring in these epics had names like Randy and, inevitably, Dick. The women sounded like cheap jewellery.

'Here's one for you,' Flagg said.

It was called *Little Anal Annie*. He stuck the cassette into the video player and turned it on. Immediately the screen filled with the sight of a blonde woman and two men engaged in a complex mixture of cunnilingus, fellatio and anal intercourse that must have taken a long time to perfect. The men appeared to have been endowed with organs the size of nightsticks and it occurred to Annie that she had led a sheltered life.

She turned the video off.

'Hey,' Flagg said, 'just when it was getting to the good part.'

'I think I know what happens in the end. They all get the girl.'

She stood looking at the blank screen with its distorted reflection of herself and the bedroom window. Flagg was smiling, perhaps thinking he had embarrassed her, but he hadn't. She was wondering about Cobb Landry, the little boy up a tree watching a woman having sex. How many times had he done that? And how many times had he lain here in bed with these videos?

She closed the cupboard door. 'Let's go see Mrs Orbach.'

Edith Orbach wore a sweater patterned with diamonds and she had round earrings like the shields of miniature centurions. She stood at the front door and from behind her came a smell of fresh baking. Annie introduced herself and Flagg.

'I've spoken to this man before,' Edith said, squinting at him a little, like a woman who needed glasses but wasn't wearing them right now. 'You came to the house after it happened.'

'That's right, Mrs Orbach,' Flagg said. 'My colleague here has a couple of additional questions and I said I'd tag along.'

'My husband spoke to people from the RCMP this

morning. Now you're back again. I really don't see what the point of this is. I didn't see anything that night. I was in here in the kitchen cooking.'

She was wearing black slacks and she had got some flour on them.

Annie said, 'It's not really Mr Landry's death I want to talk about, Mrs Orbach. I want to find out a bit more about him, what sort of a person he was.'

'A very nice man, that's what he was,' Edith said when they were in the living room and she had made coffee and produced the cinnamon-flavoured cookies that were the fruits of her labours in the kitchen.

'These are to die for,' Flagg said through a mouthful of crumbs.

Annie shot him a look that said he could have picked a better phrase.

Edith didn't notice. 'I'm glad you like them.' She turned to Annie. 'We were friendly for quite a while. Cobb was helping my husband build a new deck. Harry's not very good at that sort of thing and Cobb was giving him a hand. To tell the truth, he was really doing the job himself. I think Harry was just passing him the tools, holding the wood while Cobb sawed it.'

She offered the cookies around once more. Annie shook her head but Flagg lifted one from the plate hurriedly in case she changed her mind.

'And then he found out he was ill again – he thought he had it licked, you see – so it was a terrible shock and disappointment to him. For us, too. I was devastated. So the deck job went on hold. While Cobb was having the chemo and everything, it took a lot out of him, you know.' She thought about what she had said. 'Not that the deck was important – I didn't mean that.'

'Of course,' Annie said. 'I understand. You and your husband were obviously very good to him. Did he have many other friends?'

'I think he might have had one or two acquaintances down at the bank.'

'Did you ever see any of them here at his house?'

'No, never. Since we've lived here, I guess you could say that we were about the only people he spent much time with.'

'Was there a girl, anything like that?'

'No, no girl.' She looked at Annie and then at Flagg. 'And I know what you're hinting at. Cobb wasn't gay, if that's what you're trying to say.'

Annie put her cup to her lips and over the rim she flashed Flagg a glance that warned him not to even hint at what they'd been viewing across the street. It would destroy Mrs Orbach if she knew.

'No, I'm sure he wasn't,' she said. She put her cup down. 'The man the police – we – are looking for. You've seen his picture. Had you ever seen him around here before?'

'No, never. Harry doesn't know who he is either. It was a hell of a shock for my husband, you know.'

'Yes, I spoke to him when he came down to the office. He told me. It's a hard thing to get over. It'll take him a little time.' She lifted her cup again. 'I get the impression that Cobb was something of a photographer.'

Edith's face lit up. 'Oh yes. He was real good. We used to tell him he was wasting his time working in a bank.'

'I saw some of his pictures over at the house. They're terrific.'

'Oh sure, they are. But wait until you see these.'

She got up from her chair and left the room for a moment. Annie looked at Flagg, wondering what was coming next.

Edith's voice came from the hall. 'I haven't looked at

this stuff for a while. I wasn't sure I knew where I'd put them.'

She came back into the room. This time she had put her glasses on. 'Here you go.'

She was carrying a photograph album in maroon leather. She perched herself on the arm of Annie's chair and opened it. Flagg came and stood behind them, looking on.

'A couple of years ago, we all went on vacation together to PEI. Cobb took these and then he gave us our own prints.' She turned a page. 'Except that's one that I took myself.'

It was a shot of two men, one of whom she recognised as a slightly slimmer Harry Orbach. The other man was Landry. It was him before his illness had set in, or at least maybe before he was aware of it. She saw a small, thin man in a shirt and baggy shorts, his head slightly to one side, a patient smile on his face as he waited for Edith to get on with it.

'We had no idea he had taken most of these,' Edith said. 'It was such a surprise when he showed them to us.'

Annie leafed through the rest of the pictures. Some were posed, Edith and her husband across the table in restaurants or in front of some scenic spot, but the majority were candid shots of the two of them walking in the street, admiring a view or shopping in a market, clearly unaware that they were being photographed.

'He said he liked pictures like that. He said you get a better impression of people when they don't know you're taking their photograph. Much more natural, he said.'

Annie passed the album behind her to Flagg. 'Mrs Orbach,' she asked, 'did Cobb ever talk much about his childhood at all? His family?'

'Oh sure. He was very fond of his dad. He was an only child. His mother died a long time ago and he was very upset about his father being ill, being in a nursing home and all, but there was nothing he could do about that. We used to tell him it was for the best, that he had done the right thing.'

'But as far as his actual childhood goes, did he ever talk about it, about what he did on summer vacations, for instance?'

'I can't remember us talking much about anything like that, at least not as far as he was concerned. I guess maybe at times we used to talk more about our own kids and our vacations with them.'

'Did you ever hear of a place called Heckman's Island?'

'No, I don't think so.'

'Or a man called Aaron Gaunt?'

'No.' She thought for a second. 'When you showed my husband that photograph – was that him? Is that the man?'

'I can't say for certain, Mrs Orbach. But did Cobb ever mention him or mention Heckman's Island?'

'No, he didn't. Or at least if he did, I don't remember.'

The street lights were on when they came out and the temperature had fallen. Flagg's car was behind hers so they got into it for a while. The cop in the patrol car had gone but the crime scene tape still warned people to keep away.

'You didn't get much out of her,' Flagg said.

'You're wrong there, Walter. I got a lot.'

'Like what? Did I fall asleep and miss something?'

'Like . . . like a whole clear picture of Cobb Landry. When I came here I had only the possibility that Landry saw what happened that night.'

'It's still only a possibility.'

'But don't you think it seems much more likely now, that watching from that tree is the sort of thing he would do? Look at the porn videos we found, the pictures he took of the Orbachs. It's classic voyeur stuff. Damn it, I feel like I'm profiling somebody here.'

'Except you're profiling somebody who's dead.'

She looked at him. 'In order to find out why, Walter. That's the point.'

27

She would just make it downtown to Scotiabank before they went home for the day. The place was closed for normal business but that wasn't what this was.

Flagg said he was leaving her to it, that she was on her own with this merry chase, but he gave her the name of Cobb Landry's supervisor nevertheless, a woman called Ida Stark, and as Annie drove she rang ahead to make sure the woman was still there. She was, just about, but she sounded irritated and said that she would wait fifteen minutes, no longer.

A security man let Annie in through a side door and took her up in the elevator to where Ida Stark worked. She did not have an office as such but worked in a space at the end of a long room which had desks in groups of two. She was separated from the herd by a divider big enough for her to peer over if she wished.

Ida was a sharp-nosed woman with her coat on and an expression which said that Annie's fifteen minutes were up.

'I've already spoken to you people several times. Don't you tell each other what you're doing?'

'I'm sorry. I know it must be tedious for you but I've just been given some responsibilities in this case and I'm trying to catch up.'

'You could ask the man who was here this morning. He could tell you whatever you need to know.'

'Who was that?'

Ida snorted and muttered that this whole thing was ridiculous, then poked through the contents of a wire tray on her desk. She lifted out an HRP business card. Someone had written a phone number on the back.

She read the name on the front. 'Gil Claussen.'

'Gil, yes,' Annie smiled as if pleased to hear this. 'He's been called away on something else. That's why I'm picking up for him.'

Ida stared at her with eyes that held considerable doubt and Annie knew she had made a mistake. If she was 'picking up' for Claussen, as she had put it, then how come she didn't know he'd already been here? Ida's gaze searched her and Annie was glad she hadn't come to ask for a loan. She pressed on as if nothing had happened.

'I needed to see where Cobb Landry worked.'

'Why?'

'Oh, it's just a way of getting a feel for a person. Seeing where they live, where they work, it sometimes helps.'

'What are you – a psychic?'

Annie gave her an exasperated look. 'No, just a cop, trying to do a job, trying to get out of your hair as quickly as possible because it's obvious what a pain in the ass this is for you.'

Ida's thin lips moved in what might have been the first stirring of a smile. 'Go on.'

'This department: as I understand it, what you do here is you oversee the work of outlying bank branches. Is that correct?'

'You could put it like that, yes.'

'So you can check on any particular account in any branch?'

'If we have reason to but normally we wouldn't unless some discrepancy was brought to our attention. We leave individual accounts to the branch managers although they report to us regularly.'

'These reports, what do they involve?'

'All sorts of routine stuff. Details of loans, accounts in trouble perhaps, particulars of new customers.'

'And Cobb Landry would have had access to that information?'

'Yes, he would.' She sat forward. 'Look, Officer Welles, I'll spare you a lot of trouble and save us both time. Your friend this morning wanted to know about a customer called Aaron Gaunt.'

Annie tried not to react.

Ida said, 'I thought he was going to ask me about Mr Gaunt's financial situation and therefore I was going to have to refuse to give him any information but from what I could see, there was nothing I could tell him that he didn't already know. What he did want to find out was whether Cobb would have had access to other personal details, like Mr Gaunt's address and phone number, so I didn't see any harm in telling him that yes, he would. I also told him that this bank has looked after Mr Gaunt's investments and savings accounts for many years but his personal account is a lot more recent, only a few months old.'

'Are you aware of who Mr Gaunt is?'

'As a matter of fact I am. It pays to know about your customers. It's good business, after all. But we keep confidential information to ourselves, as you might expect.'

'But it's possible Mr Landry might have noticed that new account being opened?'

'Yes, he might, especially since it was opened right here at this branch, but we have new accounts being opened all the time. It's unlikely that he'd notice one in particular.'

'Unless the name meant something to him?'

'I suppose that's possible.' She looked at her watch and stood, leaning on the desk with her fingertips. 'Now, that's all your friend wanted to know and that's all I told him so if there's nothing else, I have a home to go to, even if you haven't.'

Outside it was dark and even colder than before, although it had been chilly enough talking to Ida Stark. As Annie walked to her car, she had a mental picture of her picking up the phone and dialling the number Gil Claussen had given her. She was a woman who would check things. That was why she had the job she had.

Annie felt like she was running out of the rope Gamble had given her. Maybe she should tell him where she'd got to. Which was where, exactly?

While driving, she began to lay it all out. Primarily, there was her blossoming suspicion about Cobb Landry, that he'd been a twelve-year-old peeping Tom who had watched Cassandra Breaux in her bedroom and had seen what happened on the night she was killed. Almost everyone she'd talked to today had, unknown to them, steered her towards that conclusion. And talking to Ida Stark at the bank had confirmed that through the opening of the account, Landry might have known that Aaron Gaunt was out of jail.

Might. It wasn't a good word. Not one that Gamble would recognise. He would tell her she was wasting her time chasing fanciful theories.

And just where did these theories lead? Had Gaunt become aware of Landry in some way? He knew his car, which is why he'd gone to George Poyner, but he obviously didn't know the person who owned it. And when he found out, what then?

It all came back to the question of what exactly Landry had seen that night. If he had seen Gaunt kill Cassandra Breaux, was Gaunt likely to kill him over that? Hardly. But if he had seen something else or, rather, not something but someone?

She stopped at a traffic light and waited for it to change. If Landry had seen someone else murder Cassandra, would Gaunt have killed him for not saying anything or would he have wanted Landry to tell the truth and exonerate him?

She moved off again. The first course of action was hardly likely, unless Gaunt had flown into some sort of uncontrollable rage, and according to Eric Benjamin, the parole supervisor, he was just not that sort of person any more, although how could any of us say what we would or wouldn't do if provoked beyond measure?

What had Landry seen? It was hard to get past that question.

Almost without realising it, she found herself pulling into the parking lot at Gottingen Street. She located a space and turned off the engine but she didn't get out of the car straight away. She sat with her thoughts, feeling as if Cobb Landry and Aaron Gaunt and George Poyner were sitting there with her.

Like three ghosts.

She looked up. No, wait a minute, not three – four.

There was a fourth ghost in the car but for that ghost to take on more tangible form you had to believe that Aaron Gaunt hadn't killed anybody.

It was that kind of thinking that had started her down this road in the first place, taking her to Chester and to Lunenburg and to Heckman's Island and Dartmouth and now here.

For the fourth ghost to take shape you had to believe that someone else had stabbed Cassandra Breaux to death and if you could believe that then you could also believe that that person hadn't wanted Cobb Landry to say what he had seen.

And just where did Poyner fit into all this?

Poyner was a brick wall. Brick walls were everywhere. But she had a sense that there were fewer of them than before.

There were things she needed to do but couldn't, things

that she hadn't been able to do before the case was taken away from her, like check Landry's and Gaunt's and Poyner's phone records. Claussen and Steyn would have done all that by now.

Claussen. He had gone to Ida Stark with the same questions she had. Was it possible they were swimming in the same water?

She got out of the car and locked it. She looked at the home-bound traffic on Cogswell Street and then she gazed up at the stars filling the night sky, now that the clouds of the day had gone.

She thought of the sky long ago above the stream at Heckman's Island.

Taggart was right. They had been so certain that Gaunt was the killer – and in the circumstances who could blame them? – that they hadn't bothered to look in any other direction. But who else did Cassandra Breaux know? Who else might have wanted her dead?

She walked towards the building, glancing among the shadows in the parking lot. She couldn't see the fourth ghost yet but she knew he was there.

28

In the lock-up, fresh disinfectant was a sharp, acid tang fighting to obscure the older odours which lingered on the brickwork like a stain. Bart had no guests tonight. Annie walked past the empty and silent cells and round the corner to where he sat at his desk watching monitors on which there was no movement except her own.

'Hey, no customers? Maybe you should lower your rates. Offer weekend breaks or something.'

He looked at her, his face as always registering nothing at all. She waited for his come-back. He said, 'I'm sorry to hear about Gamble.'

It wasn't what she'd expected. But she told him, 'Yeah, well, these things happen. He'll get over it.'

As she went out the door she glanced back at him. He was staring at her as if she had lost her mind.

When she walked into the office, the first thing she felt was the silence. Then she saw that Gryce and the new guy, Marriott, were standing in the middle of the room. Her gaze went quickly from them to Birgit sobbing softly into a Kleenex. Deedes and Neidermayer were there. Flagg was at his desk. Crisp stood with his back to a wall. A few of the others were sitting around. They all looked as if they'd just been told that somebody had died.

And then she realised what Bart had said and why he had stared at her that way. She swung round and looked at

Gamble's office. Someone had shut the door and the light was off. The darkness told its own story.

Flagg saw her and got up. 'I was going to call you at home.'

Gryce and Marriott turned in her direction. Gryce spoke as if she already knew. 'Everybody's devastated. I've been to see his wife. I've just been telling the guys here. Those poor children.'

'What happened?' she asked, although she didn't mean that. She had guessed what. She meant how.

'Heart attack,' Flagg said. 'On the Dartmouth ferry. He was on the way to see his doctor.'

She needed to sit down. Claussen's desk was the nearest. Claussen. He wasn't here. She wondered if he had heard and how he had reacted.

Gryce looked grim. He would be agonising, no doubt, over whether Gamble's death had anything to do with the disappointment of not getting the temporary promotion. No one in this room would rush to console him or to assure him that that wasn't the case. She told Flagg about her brief exchange with Bart downstairs.

'You weren't to know,' he said. He squeezed her shoulder.

'I can't believe it.' She looked at him, wanting him to say that none of it was true. By the very nature of the job, they were all used to sudden death, but this was different.

'I know. None of us can.'

Marriott didn't seem to know what to do with himself, whether to go or stay. He looked too big and ungainly for the room. He stood awkwardly among people who were strangers to him.

'I . . . I just don't know what to say,' he tried.

Annie glanced at him and then at the others. Nobody wanted him to say anything. He wasn't welcome here.

Neidermayer came over, shoving his arms into his coat.

'Some of us are going to the bar. Anybody else want to come?'

'Yeah,' Flagg said. 'That's an idea. What do you say, Annie?'

She shook her head. She was a shock wave or two behind the rest of them. 'No, maybe not. Maybe I'll just sit here for a while.'

Neidermayer moved off. Flagg glanced over his shoulder and lowered his voice. 'So how did you make out at the bank?'

She frowned. 'Come on, Walter. What does it matter?'

He looked at her, then nodded. 'Yeah, you're right, it doesn't. What the hell am I thinking of?' He got his coat. 'You'll be okay?'

'I'll be fine.'

'You know where we'll be. Maybe you'll drop by later?'

'I don't think so. I think I'll go home.'

They all drifted slowly out of the office, passing Gryce and Marriott without a word. No one paused to invite them to the impromptu wake. Deedes had his arm round Birgit who was still sobbing and still didn't know how he felt about her. Maybe tonight would be the night, Annie thought. It was the kind of thing that could happen.

Two officers stayed behind. Their names were Harris and McBrien and they were the current late duty team. It occurred to her that Deedes and Neidermayer were off today and that they must have come in when they heard the news. The two late men sat at the end of the room and talked quietly across their desks. Gryce and Marriott looked abandoned.

Marriott offered her a shy smile. She didn't return it. She said, 'I suppose I should offer you my congratulations.'

As the smile vanished she realised she had made the remark sound like an accusation, which was not really what she'd intended, but then what *had* she intended? Marriott turned to Gryce and said something, then Gryce glanced at her and the two of them left the room.

Great. Why hadn't she just kept her mouth shut? She couldn't afford to alienate anyone else. She had a disciplinary coming up and no Gamble to support her. But the moment she formed the thought she chastised herself for thinking it. A disciplinary wasn't the end of the world. Dying of a heart attack on the Dartmouth ferry was.

She looked at the darkness of Gamble's office and wondered what sort of a relationship she'd had with him and why they were all feeling so bad about someone to whom none of them had been all that close. He had had a wall of reserve around him because he'd thought that was the way you had to be when you were the boss. Now and then he'd let you see over it, although only for a time.

But they liked him and respected him, except that none of them would have bothered to think about it that way until now. He had understood them, that was it. He knew the work they did and knew how tough it was and the penalties you sometimes had to pay. When she'd been going through the separation and the divorce, he hadn't treated her the way most people had, like she had some sort of incurable disease that you didn't talk about. He had tried to face the situation head-on and told her he was sorry and said that if there was anything he could do, she only had to ask. Except that he had been so awkward and embarrassed about the whole thing that *she'd* ended up feeling sorry for *him*.

A sense of guilt began to creep over her. She thought of their drink together in the Late Watch last night. Their first and their last. It had been a strange occasion, hardly relaxing for either of them. She could see now how he had been under enormous pressure, pressure for which she had been partly to blame, first because of the newspaper fiasco with Taggart and then because she hadn't spotted the connection between

Cary Eisener and Aaron Gaunt. He had believed in her and she had given him very little in return.

She thought of the death of Taggart's editor. There was a similarity in their situations, hers and Taggart's. Gamble was dead too and they were both high and dry. You never made it on your own. You were only fooling yourself if you thought that. You always depended on other people's fortunes or the lack of them.

There were two kids. She'd never met Gamble's wife. For a second she tried to put herself in the woman's shoes and wondered what she would do, how the boys would be looked after, if anything ever happened to Terry.

The phone in front of her rang.

She didn't answer it straight away. She was at Claussen's desk and it was his phone, not hers, but on the third ring she picked it up.

'This is Lou Dodgion in ViCLAS,' a voice said. 'I'm looking for Claussen.'

'He's not here right now. Can I help?'

'Yeah, who is this?'

'Annie Welles.'

'Look, are you guys still having trouble with your computers over there?'

'Hold a second.' She called to Harris and McBrien. 'Hey, are we having computer problems?'

Harris nodded. 'Yeah, everything crashed. But we're back up again.'

She said to Dodgion, 'No, we're fine now.'

'Good, because I e-mailed some stuff to Claussen and I just got a message from the system, telling me it couldn't deliver it. It's kind of important so I thought I'd check.'

Annie thought quickly. ViCLAS stood for Violent Crime Linkage Analysis System. Similar to VICAP, the FBI's Violent Crime Apprehension Programme, it was operated by the RCMP and major police forces throughout Canada. Originally designed to identify and track serial violent crimes and criminals, it was now a widely used database, a central repository of information with which to capture, collate and compare violent crimes. Lou Dodgion was the Halifax Regional Police ViCLAS specialist, operating from a technology centre recently created in the police building in Dartmouth.

She made sure Harris and McBrien weren't listening, then she told him, 'Listen, Lou, I'm afraid Claussen left out one important piece of information.'

'Which is what?'

'He's working on a JFO out of Oxford Street right now.'

'Oh, terrific. He didn't tell me that.'

'But, look, I'm working on this thing with him so why don't you send it to him again and copy it to me? That way you'll be sure someone on the team has it.'

'Sure, no problem.'

'First, though, can you give me the headlines on it?'

'Okay – it's this guy Poyner who got whacked last week. In a nutshell, there's nothing at all on the slugs that were taken out of the wall but the two that killed him are sending up fireworks.'

'What kind of fireworks?'

'The gun was used in a hit before.'

She took a breath. 'Tell me more.'

'No. I haven't got the time. That's why we have computers, you know. Read it for yourself.'

Within minutes her PC told her she had incoming and her mailbox registered the e-mail from Dodgion. It was an attachment, with no other message. She clicked on the viewer bar and opened it up, then started to read.

The bullets which killed George Poyner were an identical match to two bullets taken from the body of a man shot dead in Toronto eleven years ago. The victim, a man named Anthony Melnick, had been arrested and questioned about the murders of three young girls aged between eleven and thirteen whose bodies had been dumped at remote parts of the city. They had been strangled and their genitals mutilated. Three weeks after the third victim had been found on a vacant lot, Melnick's body had also been discovered there, shot twice in the head.

Dodgion had included a contact number for an officer called Sal DiGiacomo at the Toronto homicide squad and a postscript saying that the murder was a cold case. No one had ever been arrested for it and the weapon had never been found.

Annie sat back. Learning about what had happened to Gamble had shoved aside all thoughts of Aaron Gaunt and Cobb Landry and George Poyner and everything that might connect them. But they were crowding back in now and she couldn't keep them away.

She looked at the screen. How did it fit into the picture? Instinctively she glanced towards Gamble's office. She couldn't tell him about this. She wouldn't tell him anything ever again.

She rang the Toronto number. Sal DiGiacomo wasn't there but he could be contacted. She left her number and went to get a coffee and ten minutes later he called back. She thanked him for doing so.

'I'll tell you,' he said. 'I knew George Poyner would emerge again one of these days.'

'You knew him?'

'Oh sure.'

'What – you worked with him when he was on the Toronto force?'

'Kind of. I know him more by reputation. Everybody who was around at the time remembers George Poyner.'

'At the time?'

'At the time Anthony Melnick got killed. Oh yeah, we remember George all right. What's he been doing in Halifax?'

'Working as a PI for about the past ten years. I never came across him at all until he got killed last week. So can you tell me anything about him? And this Melnick murder, maybe?'

DiGiacomo gave a little laugh. 'Gee, where do you want to start? First of all, I have to tell you that Melnick was a very nasty piece of work. There were no tears when he got put down although nobody much liked the way it was done. He was the number one suspect in the murders of these young girls, except we just couldn't pin any of it on him. DNA work wasn't the thing it is now, you know. Even though he had alibis, everything, everybody was certain it was him. He had a record of offences against young girls and he'd even been seen talking to a couple of the victims. The guy taunted us, for Christ sake, and you can guess how mad we got about that.'

'I can imagine.'

'And then somebody shot him.'

'I know there were no arrests for that but had you any ideas?'

'There used to be a magazine here in Toronto, a kind of off-the-wall underground thing called *Nemo*, came out once a week. Ever hear of it?'

She hadn't.

'When Melnick got killed, they ran a story claiming that George Poyner was the guy.'

'They what?'

'Oh yeah. Came right out with it. It seems that Melnick himself had gone to them a couple of days before, saying that Poyner and some other guy were conducting a campaign of harassment against him. He said they were following him, making threatening phone calls, leaving dead cats on his doorstep, that kind of thing.'

'But they hadn't run anything about this before his death?'

'No. They were a weekly. He'd been to see them in between editions. Then he got killed.'

'Did I hear you say there was another guy involved?'

'Yeah, but no name was ever mentioned.'

'You sound as if you think this *Nemo* thing was accurate.'

'We did then and I certainly feel that way now. Poyner had been one of the officers who'd questioned Melnick the first time he was arrested. He had to be restrained from beating the shit out of him and then he was taken off the case. After that he used to go around saying somebody should take care of the guy. Made no secret of how he felt. Like I said, when Melnick got killed nobody gave a damn but a lot of us didn't like the idea of cops taking the law into their own hands like that. Once that happened, one or two people kind of helped the *Nemo* thing along.'

'What do you mean?'

'Well, the magazine started getting information about Poyner, about the things he'd said to people on the force, the threats he'd made against Melnick, and then they started printing them. It had to be people on the inside who were doing that. And then Poyner decided to take action himself.'

'What kind of action?'

'He sued the shit out of *Nemo*, that's what. Sued them and won. Took them for about two hundred thousand dollars. Even though the magazine had been a rough and ready kind of thing, it appears it was making money, although not so much that it could stand having to shell out two hundred grand. That just about cleaned them out. Poyner got his dough and took early retirement from the force and a short time after that the magazine folded.'

Annie wondered if DiGiacomo had been one of the people leaking information. She said, 'And now, after all this time, it looks like what Melnick told them was true. But what's with the gun? I wonder how come it turned up again.'

'I guess either Poyner kept it, or the other guy maybe.'

'But why? It would have been safer to get rid of it.'

'You ever meet George Poyner?'

'No.'

'He was a big brash guy who didn't give a damn. He'd just got away with murder and he'd made a fortune out of it and that kind of thing would make him feel invincible. So maybe it's bravado, you know? Off he goes to Nova Scotia with the gun in his pocket as a souvenir. Don't forget we're talking, what – twelve years ago?'

'Eleven.'

'There you go. Our computer systems weren't as highly developed then. Police forces didn't talk to each other the way they do now. ViCLAS didn't exist. Later on, maybe it didn't occur to him that something like the Melnick case, that far back, would be recorded in it. But it was an unsolved murder and all unsolved serious crimes are stored in there.'

'And now there's no *Nemo* to shout about how right they were.'

'Well, as a matter of fact,' DiGiacomo said, 'there is, in a manner of speaking. As it turns out, the guy who ran the magazine and wrote the original story is back in business again, on the Internet this time. You heard of the Drudge Report, Matt Drudge?'

'Sure. The guy who first blew the whistle on Clinton and Lewinski.'

'That's him. Well, this guy – I can't remember his name – he's trying to do the same thing. He has a site that he calls Nemo's Log. Some of the papers here have been writing about it, picking up on some of the political stuff he's been running. I don't know where he operates from but I'd say here in Toronto, at a guess.' He laughed. 'Maybe somebody should let him know that his old friend George is no longer with us.'

They talked for a little while longer and when they'd finished and he'd gone, she got herself another coffee and thought about what they'd discussed. It was all a long way from Aaron Gaunt. The fact that Gaunt had hired Poyner had to be a coincidence; there couldn't be any other connection between them. Yet she didn't believe in coincidences when it came to things like this, especially not when you had two murders back to back.

She turned round to her computer again. She went online and selected Webcrawler as a search engine. She typed in Nemo's Log and found it in between sites for an oceanographic study and some kind of software company.

She clicked and the home page came up. The banner was a nautical figure with a beard, harpooning fierce fish in murky waters, which she supposed was a symbol for what Nemo was trying to achieve. She began to browse through the archive, finding it limited, and finally locating the most up-to-date material. It was about three weeks old and she saw nothing earth-shattering in what it contained, mostly low-grade political gossip about municipal officials in Ontario.

There was a list of links to other sites and it occurred to her that that was what the best investigations were like. One door led to the opening of another. Going down the shore with Taggart today had opened a lot of doors and she simply could not slam them and walk away. She thought of Cassandra Breaux and wondered again who might have wanted her dead.

Nemo had an e-mail address for anyone who wanted to send information. Beside it was an animated graphic of the little man pointing with his harpoon. She debated for a second and then began to type. She wrote a message saying who she was and that she was investigating two murders in Halifax. She said there appeared to be a connection with the Melnick murder in Toronto some years ago and wondered if she and Nemo could talk, 'in our mutual interests,' either by e-mail or on the phone, which she said she would prefer. She left her number.

A voice spoke. 'Where is everybody?' It was Claussen.

She logged off, feeling as if she'd just put the lid back on the cookie jar. She hoped he wouldn't see the guilt which she was certain was on her face.

'They're in the bar,' Harris said. 'I take it you heard?'

'Yeah. I heard. I came over as soon as I could.'

Now that she got a look at him she saw that he was as shocked as everyone else. He went to Gamble's office, opened the door and stood leaning against the frame, looking silently into the darkness. Annie began buttoning her coat to go home. She considered telling him there was an e-mail from ViCLAS but he would find it eventually and when he saw it had been copied to her he would know she had been sticking her nose in. A row would be inevitable. But it could wait.

He turned away and closed the door softly. 'Heart attack. Christ. Bad break.'

She nodded and buttoned her gloves. 'He was one of the good guys. I just wish one of us had told him that.'

29

Snow was falling by the time she got home. It was fine, like powder, and it blanketed the air with a silence. She poured herself a glass of wine and stood at the window of the apartment, watching its soft but determined descent.

She wanted to tell Taggart what had happened but he would be with the Camerons right now and she didn't want to call him there. She felt a deep sadness over Gamble's death but at the same time she had to ask herself if it was out of affection and respect for the man or because she had lost a benefactor, someone who could get her out of a hole. She had dug a deeper one for herself now by getting on the wrong side of Marriott.

Then there was the Poyner business. Who had killed him? Certainly not Gaunt – the blood match on the broken glass didn't have to mean anything – and there was absolutely no way he could be connected with a murder in Toronto eleven years ago. But DiGiacomo had spoken of a possible accomplice in the Melnick killing. Who was out there that she didn't know about, that Claussen and Steyn didn't know about either, for that matter?

Landry. Gaunt. Poyner. Now Melnick. Once again she felt the presence of another figure in all of this, a shadow, a ghost that she couldn't yet make out.

She topped up her wine glass and reminded herself that she hadn't eaten since the burger in Lunenburg. There was some ciabatta bread in the kitchen so she smeared it with a little pesto and toasted it lightly under the grill with sliced tomato and mozzarella. She put on a Dexter Gordon CD, listening to the big tenor saxophone notes, muscular yet tender. Her father used to say he sounded like a good, juicy steak.

Lunenburg. It had all began there thirty years ago with the murder of Cassandra Breaux and somehow she felt that that was where the answers still lay. She had to go further; she couldn't just leave it. For a start, she couldn't do that to Taggart, not after having capsized what was left of his world by telling him who his father was.

The phone rang.

She wondered for a second if it would be him. But it was Walter. She could hear the muted babble of the Late Watch in the background.

'I called to see if you were home yet. How are you feeling?'

'Oh, the same as everyone else, I guess. A bit numb. How's the party?'

'I wouldn't call it that. Most people have gone anyhow. I'll be out of here very soon myself.'

A thought occurred to her. 'Are Birgit and Deedes still there?'

'No, they went about an hour ago.'

She smiled to herself. 'They left together?'

'Well, yes, I think so.' He paused. 'Wait a minute, you're not telling me—'

She chuckled.

'Damn it,' Flagg said. 'Why am I always the last to know?'

'Call yourself a cop?'

'Yeah, well, I was once.'

'And you still are. A good cop, too. Hey, if you're doing

nothing, why don't you come over? I'm sitting here by myself with a sandwich and a drink.'

'By yourself?'

'Yes. So? What's strange about that?'

'Oh, nothing. I just thought you might have invited your reporter friend round.'

Annie felt herself blush. 'What are you talking about?'

He laughed. 'Don't give me that. Maybe I didn't spot Deedes and Birgit but I know you. I could see it in your eyes when we took him off the plane. But it's okay. You're allowed to be interested, you know.'

She waited as she considered what to say to him. 'It's a bit close to home, that's all.'

'Always the careful one. Where is he anyhow?'

'Having dinner with my friend Jeff Cameron. So are you coming over?'

As she said it, she knew she didn't really want him to, not now that he had managed to burrow his way in under her defences. She didn't want to have any more discussions on the Taggart front.

'Nah. But thanks for the thought.'

'Sure. Whatever you think. Maybe I'll turn in early while I have the chance.' She paused. 'Listen, Walter, I've been thinking. You know the way the boss gave me a couple of days.'

'Yeah.'

'Which means I've still got tomorrow. I think I'm going to take it, come back in the day after. I'll be honest with you – I can't shake this Lunenburg thing. I keep thinking about that woman Cassandra Breaux and whatever it was Cobb Landry saw.'

Flagg groaned. 'You mean what you think he saw. Annie, take my advice and drop it. You're crazy, you know that? And Gamble can't back you now.'

'Yes, I've thought of all that. But you know me when I get into something. So I'm going to go back to Lunenburg tomorrow to nose around.'

'Are you taking your friend Taggart with you?'

'I . . . what makes you say that?'

'Because I think he's part of the reason you're so interested. Am I right?'

Walter and his intuition. 'Maybe.'

'Does he know what you're doing?'

She decided to lie. 'No.'

His laugh suggested he might not believe her. 'Fair enough. What the hell – it's up to you. You're on the sheet as off-duty anyway. I'll be with Crisp again. He's an okay guy. By the way, Marriott says he's going to look after the unit himself for a while.'

'I figured that.'

'Until things get sorted out.' He sighed. 'More goddamn musical chairs. You know something – maybe I should retire.'

When her door buzzer rang, she was stretched out on the settee, not far from sleep, while Dexter Gordon was hanging his tears out to dry.

She blinked and checked her watch – almost ten thirty – and then she looked at the wine bottle – about two thirds of it gone. She got up and pressed the intercom button with one hand while with the other she tried to do something with her hair.

'Yes?'

There was nothing.

'Hello, can I help you?'

Still nothing and then a voice said, 'It's . . . it's Barbara.'

'Barbara who?'

She actually meant that; she wasn't being smart. Only

when she'd said it, did she realise.

'Barbara – Barbara Welles. Can I come up?'

Annie pressed the button to open the downstairs door, then she slipped her feet back into her shoes, put the bottle and the glass in the kitchen, ran a brush through her hair and some mouthwash round her teeth, all in the time it took her ex-husband's wife to enter the building, ride up in the elevator and ring the apartment bell.

When she opened the door she thought Barbara looked terrible. She wasn't wearing a coat, just jeans and a loose denim shirt that the snow had soaked and turned a dark blue. Her hair was lank and her eyes were red and moist. Immediately Annie thought the worst.

'What is it? What's happened?'

Barbara seemed suddenly to realise what her unexpected presence looked like.

'It's okay. It's not the boys. They're fine.'

She stuck a hand into her jeans, brought out a Kleenex and blew her nose. As she did so, she swayed slightly, not much, but just enough for Annie to figure that she might be drunk.

'It's . . . I had to come and talk to you.'

'About what?'

'Please. Can I come in?'

Inside the apartment, Barbara gave a sudden shiver as her body adjusted to its warmth. She looked sodden and bedraggled and Annie could smell the booze.

'What the hell have you been doing?'

'Walking around outside, trying to pluck up the courage to ring the doorbell. You've no idea how hard it was for me.'

'How did you get here?'

'The Windstar.'

Terry and Barbara had a minivan. Sometimes they

delivered the boys in it when it was Annie's turn to have them. She frowned.

'I know,' Barbara said. 'I shouldn't be driving. But I had to do this.'

'I've no idea what you're talking about or why you're here and I'm not even sure I want to know. But you're going to get pneumonia if you're in that shirt for much longer.'

She went to her bedroom and came back with a sweater. 'Here, take this. The bathroom's down the hall if you want to change there.'

Barbara caught the garment. She unbuttoned her wet shirt and took it off. Annie glanced almost furtively at her uncovered body. She hadn't realised that Barbara was so slight. When she put the sweater on it seemed to envelope her. Annie took the discarded shirt and hung it on the back of a chair, next to a radiator. Then she said, 'Okay, so maybe you'd better tell me what you're doing here.'

'Please don't be angry.' Barbara sounded near to tears. There was a chair beside her. She didn't so much sit as fold herself into it. She said, 'I know you don't like me.'

'I don't like or dislike you. I have no feelings for you at all.'

It wasn't strictly true but Annie didn't know that until the moment she said it. At first, when all this began, she had hated Barbara with the kind of venom reserved for 'the other woman', the home-wrecker, the husband-stealer, but gradually that anger had been replaced by a controllable contempt and, eventually, a realisation that Barbara wasn't the cause of her misfortune, Terry was. And now? Now she had to admit she had a grudging respect for the woman. She was looking after the boys well. Their affection for her was real, which hurt, admittedly, but their love for their mother hadn't been diminished by it. Barbara had done nothing to try to turn them against her. As she thought about this, Annie remembered how she'd behaved that day at the airport and once again she regretted it.

'If I were you, I'd hate me,' Barbara said.

'Then don't push your luck.'

'I never intended to be the cause of your marriage breaking up.'

Annie started to reply but then she changed her mind, thinking that maybe she should just listen. The woman was trying to tell her something.

Barbara said, 'When we met, Terry and I, he told me you two were all washed up, that things between you had been dead for years. I didn't know, didn't think, that your side of the story might be different.'

Something had happened between Barbara and Terry. That's what this was. She sat back and waited to hear.

'The way he described you – you're not like that.'

'Glad to hear it.' She didn't know what Terry had said but she could guess.

'You're a good woman. The boys shouldn't be with me, they should be with you. You're a good mother. I bet you were a good wife to him.'

Annie looked at her and said nothing but inside she felt the stirrings of a sense of triumph.

Barbara said, 'Do you think I could have a drink?'

Taggart was back at the Royal Citadel just after eleven. Jeff had offered to drive but he had insisted on getting a cab.

Dinner with the Camerons had been a slightly stiff affair with them wanting to know what he was up to, why he had changed his mind about the thing for JournaLink, and Taggart not wanting to say. Annie Welles was on his mind right now every bit as much as Aaron Gaunt but thinking about her was an altogether more pleasant experience. He debated calling her but decided it was too late; he would phone first thing in the morning.

The moment he walked into the hotel, he saw that in his brief absence it had become the centre of the universe. People milled around in a lobby which had been turned into an annex of the bar. Journalists were checking in, greeting old friends, buying each other drinks, and the air was filled with that end-of-the-world abandon that always gripped news people when they were gathered together like this, as if they were never going to meet again.

He decided that he would have a drink. There would be faces he knew, not here in the lobby that he could see, but maybe in the bar. He could feel the excitement around him as he tried to push his way in. These were the invasion forces, the army from which he had been given a dishonourable discharge, thanks to the machinations of Judith Sefton, which is why, when he saw her with her back to the bar, drinking a glass of champagne, he thought for a moment that he was hallucinating.

She was wearing black leather trousers and a red and gold top that he guessed was Versace. There was a second when he could have backed away but then she turned her face and saw him and he knew he couldn't do that now. He also knew there was going to be a scene. It was inevitable. And maybe he wanted one.

'Well, fuck me. If it isn't the great columnist.'

There was a group of people around her. A figure detached itself and Taggart saw Ronnie Boyd. The last time he'd clapped eyes on the man was on the occasion of the fight between him and Ken Shaw in the cloakroom at the Park Lane Hilton. Other faces turned to see who Boyd was talking about. Taggart recognised them all as members of the London newspaper fraternity. They seemed shocked to see him, as if he were an apparition risen from the grave.

'I thought you'd have been back home queuing up at the jobcentre by now,' Boyd said.

Taggart ignored him. Judith Sefton was where his interests lay and she must have seen that on his face. As he moved towards her, she began to look apprehensive, although she tried to mask it.

'This is a surprise,' she said. 'I wondered what had happened to you.'

'But you know what happened to me. You got me fired by faking a story with my name on it.'

'Now, now. Harsh words. Slanderous, even. My friends here will be a witness to that, won't you, boys?'

There were grunts of assent from a couple of members of her entourage, a pair of heavies who passed as reporters for one of the scruffier tabloids. Taggart noticed that other people were moving out of the way slightly, sensing that there was something here that they didn't want to get involved in but at the same time didn't want to miss.

'What are you doing here anyway?' Taggart said. 'A bit far from the Groucho, isn't it?'

Judith began to relax, as if she'd concluded that he wasn't going to get violent. She topped up her glass from a bottle of Bollinger at her elbow.

'I'm here to mastermind the *Chronicle*'s coverage of this momentous royal visit and see what life is like out here among our commonwealth cousins. And may I take this opportunity to introduce you to our new special correspondent?'

She swept an arm in Ronnie Boyd's direction. Taggart turned and looked at him. Boyd had a self-satisfied drunken grin on his face. Taggart started to laugh.

'Oh, he's special all right. You've picked a good one there. What a splendid asset he'll be.'

'Fuck off,' Boyd said.

'Well, I see you haven't lost your masterful use of the language anyway. I'm sure the *Chronicle*'s readers will be terribly impressed.'

He looked at the pair of them and felt suddenly relieved to be out of it. He was no longer in this snake pit. 'What am I doing here?' he said, as much to himself as to them. 'I don't want to waste my time talking to you people. I'll get my lawyer to do that.'

He turned to go.

'Hey, Taggart,' Boyd called. 'Do they have trains in Nova Scotia?'

He wasn't thinking. He made the mistake of answering. 'Of course they do.'

'Then why don't you find one and do us all a favour? Just like your friend Ken Shaw.'

Taggart was still half turned towards the door. Without really looking, he swung his fist and hit Boyd who had chosen that moment to raise his glass to his mouth. It smashed across his face, cutting into his cheek and extending the left side of his top lip by a bloody half inch. Some of the glass sliced into Taggart's fist. Judith Sefton squealed as blood spattered over her and Boyd fell back clutching his face.

It would have been over there and then except that one of the tabloid goons decided to pitch in. He threw a wild punch that hit Taggart hard on the side of the head and made his brain ring like a bell, knocking him across a table, where he scattered drinks in all directions amid the curses of their owners. As he went down, images flashed. He could see the cowboy police station at Lunenburg, Constable Peterson with his low-slung holster. Now here he was in a fight in the saloon.

He got to his knees, holding on to the up-ended table for support. There was a lot of shouting going on. The big guy who'd hit him was looking pleased with himself so Taggart threw himself towards him like a sprinter off the blocks.

Outside in the lobby they were calling the police.

Annie had opened another bottle. The whole thing was ridiculous, sitting here listening to a tale of woe from the woman for whom her husband had left her.

The feelings of victory had come and gone. At first there'd been a certain sadistic pleasure in hearing that Terry's marriage wasn't going well, but that had evaporated.

'Look at me,' Barbara was saying. 'Don't you see it? I'm a younger version of you.'

She could be right. There was a resemblance. They were the same height, same colouring and their hair was similar, now that they both wore it short.

'You see,' Barbara told her, 'I have this theory that he married me to try to recreate something that you two had lost. But it's not me he wants – it's you. It's been you all the time. I'm just some kind of fake version, like a cardboard cut-out.'

'You're being hard on yourself.'

'Am I? Am I? Do you think so? Do you?' She muttered into her glass. 'I don't think so.'

They'd been over most of this ground already. They were beginning to go round in circles, the way these conversations did once there was sufficient lubrication. Annie didn't feel drunk but she knew she was on the edge and that the point of no return was not far off.

Through Barbara's ramblings she had been afforded a glimpse of marital disenchantment. She had learned of Terry's increasing coldness, his dissatisfaction with the way Barbara did things, their disputes over trivial matters like who had left what where. There had been a row on the phone earlier today which had triggered the current distress. All of it, Barbara figured, was because she wasn't Annie. Now, in desperation, she had reached out to her, the one woman who might understand.

'If you asked him to come back to you, I think he'd say yes,' Barbara said.

Annie laughed, 'I hardly think so. He doesn't have any time for me, only when there's something he wants, like getting me to agree to this damn ski trip.'

They would be home in two days. Looking at Barbara's misery, she didn't anticipate much of a reunion and she was beginning to worry about what effect this growing discord was having on the boys.

'And if I asked him back what would you do?'

'I'd bow out. I'd disappear. You wouldn't have to worry about me. I should never have got involved. You two should be together.'

'Not an option,' Annie said and realised with a joyful relief that it was true. Talking like this, she knew that she was finally free of Terry. There were no longer any bonds, however slack, tying her to something that didn't exist.

As if in celebration, she poured more wine into their glasses, thinking that it was probably a good idea if Barbara stayed the night. She'd been going to get her a taxi but it would be best if Barbara had company. That's why she had come here. She could have the boys' room and take the Windstar home in the morning.

She asked her, 'Do you love him?'

'Yes. I do. I do love him,' Barbara said without any hesitation.

'Then don't crumble under this. Don't think of me waiting in the wings to take him from you. That's an easy way out and anyway it's not true. If you love him, work at it. Show him what you're made of.'

She couldn't believe she was saying this, after all the

pain she had been through. But she couldn't get over how liberated she felt. Yet she didn't know whether the advice would do any good. She had certainly not followed it herself. She had not fought to hold on to Terry, not once he'd come home and told her he wanted out.

The phone rang.

She looked at her watch. It was twelve thirty. Her mind went to Taggart, returning to his hotel after dinner at the Camerons, perhaps giving her a call before bed. But then again, in her experience calls at this time of night usually meant trouble.

She picked up the phone. It was Bart, of all people, down at the lock-up.

30

Barbara didn't offer any protest when Annie told her – an order rather than a suggestion – that she was staying the night. She looked exhausted and stressed out and she seemed relieved that she didn't have to go home. Annie did not enlighten her about the content of the phone call, only to say that she had to go down to headquarters to sort something out, but that she wouldn't be long and that they could talk some more in the morning.

She showed her into the boys' room, with its two single beds, bleached pine furniture, storage boxes and the posters and photographs that reflected the enthusiasms of her young sons.

'You can have whichever bed you like.' She pointed to them each in turn. 'That's where James sleeps and that's Peter's.'

Barbara chose the latter. On the wall behind, a poster of Will Smith would watch over her and her head would rest on a pillow adorned with characters from South Park. Annie made coffee, which Barbara declined, then showed her how the bathroom and the kitchen worked. She found a new toothbrush in a cupboard, fresh towels and an outsize Halifax regional police softball team T-shirt for her to sleep in. She called a cab, because she was certainly not going to drive, and by the time it arrived she had freshened up and was feeling more capable of facing what awaited her.

Barbara thanked her for listening. There was a moistness in her eyes.

'Forget about it,' Annie said gruffly, a little fearful that she might become affectionate and want to hug her. 'You better get some rest.'

When the bedroom door was closed, she opened the kitchen drawer where she had left her gun in its holster. Although Barbara would probably sleep soundly and not wake up until the morning, she was depressed, in a fragile emotional state, and there was no point in taking any risks.

Annie took the gun and clipped it on to her belt. You never knew what went through people's minds.

The cab dropped her at the front of the police building. She walked in past the grey zombie gazes of the night staff and made her way through to the lock-up. As soon as she opened the door, voices arguing in Spanish came to her on a wave of booze and body odour. Bart was behind his desk, barricaded from the smell by the defensive aroma of a burger suffocated under fried onions. She looked at the monitors and saw a huddle of shapes in the drunk tank. In another cell a solitary figure sat on the edge of the wooden cot and watched through the bars with the hopeful gaze of a stray dog in a kennel before Christmas.

'I had a word with the uniforms who brought him in,' Bart said through a mouthful of meat and onion. 'The guy your friend hit has been taken to the QEII to get stitched up. There are no charges yet so in the meantime it's okay for you to take him into your custody, like you suggested on the phone. But you're responsible for him.'

'That's fine.'

He nodded to signify that it was a deal, then he put the burger down and came out from behind his counter, something, now she thought of it, that she had rarely seen him do. His belly hung heavy. He walked with a slight roll, like a sailor, and there was a jingle from the ring of keys attached to his belt.

Once the crowd in the drunk tank saw them they got noisier. There were five of them. They had heavy duty moustaches and chins with bristles stiff enough to scrub a floor. In his own cell, Taggart got to his feet. He smiled at Annie but she didn't smile back.

'Who are the guys in the VIP suite?' she asked Bart.

'Off a Venezuelan cargo ship. They went a bit wild in a bar. Broke the place up. Kind of like your friend here.' He unlocked Taggart's cell. 'Let's go, buddy. Mother hen's taking you under her wing.'

Annie looked at Taggart. He had a cut at his right eyebrow. Blood had run in a streak down the side of his face but the bleeding appeared to have stopped. There was more blood on his shirt and on his jacket and it had seeped through a cloth of some kind which was wrapped round his right hand. This was turning into one weird night.

'What kind of idiot are you?'

'Annie, I'm sorry. I was provoked. I was—'

She raised a hand. 'Save it. Save it until we get out of here.'

Bart had his personal belongings, which included his trouser belt, confiscated in case he tried to kill himself with it. Stranger things had happened. Taggart signed for everything and then they were on their way.

As she walked him down the hill to the Royal Citadel, he explained it all through chattering teeth, clutching his jacket round him in a pointless attempt to keep warm. The snowfall was easing but the wind from the harbour blew into their faces.

'When he said that about Ken, my temper snapped and I hit him. The glass – that was unfortunate.'

'You're dead right. You could have blinded the guy.'

'I saw red. I just reacted.'

A bit like your father might have done, she thought. She said, 'We should get that hand seen to.'

In the few minutes it took them to reach the hotel, their hair and eyebrows were coated with snow, like they'd been made up to look elderly for an amateur drama production. They shook themselves and stamped their feet on the mat before they went in. The lobby was alive, resounding to laughter and conversation. Even though it was after one o'clock in the morning, no one seemed to be planning on going to bed any time soon, at least not on their own or with sleep in mind.

Taggart went to the desk and asked for his key. The receptionist was a blonde like a willow sapling. She seemed disconcerted by his request and excused herself in order to dive through a side door. A moment later a slim man with sallow skin and black eyes appeared, announcing that his name was Aldo and that he was the night manager.

'Mr Taggart.'

'That's me.'

'I am afraid, Mr Taggart, that in view of what happened this evening we no longer wish to have you staying here.'

'Excuse me?'

'There has been some damage. Another resident has been injured. We can't have that sort of behaviour at the hotel. We have our guests and our reputation to think about.'

Taggart glared. 'Okay. Then I'll leave in the morning.'

Aldo clasped his hands behind his back and rocked up and down on his heels a couple of times. 'No, I'm sorry, sir. Perhaps you didn't understand. That would not be acceptable. We would like you to leave right away.'

'You mean you're throwing me out in the street.'

Aldo gave a little shrug that said he didn't entirely disagree with that interpretation. 'We would prefer if you found other accommodation.'

'Like where?' Taggart said. 'All the hotels will be full.'

Aldo didn't answer. He handed him a folded sheet of paper. 'I've taken the liberty of making up your bill.'

'I'll take that,' Annie said.

The department were paying – at least that's what Gamble had agreed – but her heart sank when she realised there was no record of that. Marriott, who had a reputation as a cost-cutter, was hardly going to okay this without a quibble.

She said, 'I take it you have no objections if Mr Taggart goes upstairs to pack.'

Aldo smiled. 'Of course, none at all. Perhaps I'll get a member of staff to go with you.'

'I don't think that will be necessary. We're not going to trash the room.'

'I would prefer it.'

She took her badge out and held it under his nose. 'And I would prefer it if you didn't.' She gave him a hostile smile. 'Trust me.'

Upstairs Taggart went into the bathroom and washed the blood off his face. Annie had a look at his hand and picked specks of glass out of the cuts on his knuckles. There was still a bit of bleeding but the worst thing about his injuries was that they were in an awkward position. She got him to hold his hand straight, then she knotted one of the hotel's hand towels round it.

'Keep it like that,' she said. 'Don't bend it for a while. We'll get it cleaned and bandaged properly as soon as we can.'

'Where the hell am I going, Annie? I'll never get a room anywhere.'

She had wondered that herself. She said, 'I'd take you back to my place but I've kind of got a guest and it might be a bit awkward.' She explained about Barbara's unexpected appearance. 'But there are a couple of decent motels out on the Bedford Highway near where I live. We might try there.'

They went back down in the elevator with Taggart's bag. At reception, Aldo was still on hand, as if to see them off the premises. He smiled thinly. Annie slung the room key on to the desk. It slid off and down the other side. She pointed to the towel round Taggart's hand. 'You want to add that to the bill?'

Aldo put his hands up and waved them in a gesture that said that would not be necessary.

As they headed for the front door where the cab rank was, they met two people coming in. One was a slinky dark-haired woman in leather trousers and an expensive black wool coat, the other a man with blood splashed down his front. There were surgical plasters on his cheek and along the edge of his mouth. It didn't take a genius to work out who they were.

Boyd spotted Taggart. He pointed. 'That's the 'ucker.' He sounded like a bad ventriloquist on a bad night. 'I'll see you 'et jail for this.'

He moved forward menacingly but Annie stepped between them.

'Who's this tart?' he said. 'Get out of my 'ucking way.'

He raised his arm to push her aside but Annie grabbed his wrist and held it with a firmness that surprised him.

She told him, 'If you haven't had enough excitement for one night, I could always offer you some more. How would you like me to take you in for assaulting a police officer?'

She let Boyd go and he stepped back as if stung. Judith Sefton said, 'A police officer? Let me guess – you're the woman in the story he wrote. I've forgotten your name.'

'Welles.'

'Yes, that's it.' She looked at Taggart and then back to

Annie. 'What I don't understand is why he's not in jail. The last time I saw him, that's where he was going.'

'I'll be charging him with assault,' Boyd said.

'But since he hasn't been charged with anything yet, he's been released into my custody,' Annie explained.

'Well, isn't that cosy,' Judith said with a smirk.

Boyd wasn't important but in the taxi on the way to Bedford, Annie thought about Judith Sefton. There was only tonight's cursory encounter to go on but she could well believe that she would have rewritten Taggart's story in order to get him fired. She was beautiful and she was dangerous and Annie wondered how brief their relationship had been. Into her mind came a sudden image of Judith and Taggart together and to her surprise she found the thought exciting.

The motel was a row of identical cabins and an office where the 'VACANCY' sign was lit. The night manager was no Aldo. He was a weedy guy of about nineteen, wearing a sweater and jeans, most likely a student trying to earn some extra money. He looked uneasy when he saw Taggart's blood-spattered state but Annie's badge provided enough reassurance for him to give them a key once Taggart had filled in the registration card.

The cabin was warm. There was a bed and an armchair and a closet, plus washing and toilet facilities in a cramped alcove. Taggart scanned his new domain.

'Not the sort of accommodation you're used to, I guess,' Annie said.

'It'll be fine for tonight. I'm just relieved to find a bed.' He sat down on it. 'And thanks for helping me out.'

He had not cleaned the gash on his eyebrow very well. Blood still encrusted it. She unwrapped his hand and looked at the cuts. They would not need stitching but they needed to be bathed properly with antiseptic.

'Wait here,' she said.

She went back to the office where the night guy was reading a biography of Stalin. There was an A4 notepad and a pen beside him.

'Doing history?' Annie said.

'Yeah, second year.'

She pointed to a cupboard on the wall behind him. It had a red cross on the door. 'Do you have first aid stuff in there?'

A couple of minutes later, armed with what she needed, she went back to the cabin. In the heat of the room, Taggart had taken his jacket off. Annie threw her coat on the chair. She was wearing a cotton shirt and chinos.

She got him to sit on the bed again. 'Okay, this may sting a bit,' she said, then she started to clean his hand with cotton wool soaked in antiseptic.

He winced.

'Don't be a baby.'

When she'd finished, she put strong plasters across his knuckles and told him he would live. Next, she dabbed a cloth in water and began to clean his eye, standing in between his legs and holding her hand under his chin to point his face up to her. They were very close. She tried not to look into his eyes.

It didn't do any good. He put his arms behind her back and pulled her towards him. Their lips seemed to fumble at first, trying to find their way, and then there was a warm moistness in the kiss. It seemed to engulf her.

She broke away. 'Wait, we . . .' But her heart was somewhere in her throat and it wouldn't let her say any more, at least not anything that would cause this to stop. Taggart fell back slowly on to the bed, pulling her with him, slipping his arms in under the back of her shirt and finding the catch in her bra, easing his hands forward and cupping her breasts. A shudder went through her as her nipples reacted to his touch. She wondered how Judith Sefton had been with him, how many other women he'd had, but for the moment, with his lips and hands on her, she felt as if she were the only one.

They undressed quickly and got into bed and as he entered her she felt that it was a moment she had been waiting for for a long time. For a second in the midst of it she had a flashback to Terry, to the perfunctory and very occasional love-making of their last days, then the image was gone and she found herself riding the waves of their rhythm until they locked together in a final heart-bursting embrace.

The ripples died away slowly, one by one, and gradually they were replaced by a sense of deep unease.

'You okay?' Taggart said.

'Yes.' She got up and went to the little washroom and when she came back she began to get dressed.

'What are you doing?'

'I'm going. I can't stay here.'

'I don't understand. What's wrong? I thought . . .'

Men always needed reassurance. She looked at him. He was sitting up with the sheet covering his chest modestly, the way women did in bedroom scenes in the movies.

She said, 'Why did it have to be here, like this?'

She knew he couldn't answer that. She thought of all the things that her hunger hadn't allowed her to say. Gamble was dead, her ex-husband's wife was alone in her apartment and here she was fucking a man she hardly knew in a motel room on the Bedford Highway.

'I'm sorry. I have to go.'

There was no phone in his cabin and she hadn't brought her cellphone so she went to the office to call a cab from there. The history student told her there was a taxi company just down the road and that they were usually pretty quick. She wondered if he could see what she had been doing, whether he could sense it from her.

When she'd finished her call, she stood outside in the night air for a minute or two. The snow had stopped and the moon was a wide, white orb. When she went back to the cabin, Taggart had got dressed again.

'I was going to look for you. I thought you weren't coming back.'

'I was calling a cab. It'll be here any moment.'

He came over to her and put his hands on her arms. 'Did we do something wrong?'

She thought. 'No. But I feel as if we did.'

He gestured towards their surroundings. 'I know this isn't exactly ideal. But, Annie, it's not the place – it's the way we feel. And all I know is what happened between us just now.'

She didn't know what to say to him. There was the sound of wheels grinding into the gritty snow outside.

'I have to go,' she said. 'I have to think.'

In the cab, she told herself that she was running away from herself, not from him. It had all happened without any warning. Now she was fleeing, as if from the scene of a crime.

They reached her apartment. As she paid the driver she noted with relief that Barbara's Windstar was still there, parked near her own car. The vehicles sat silent and dark under a glistening thatch of snow. She entered the building and got into the elevator. She was tired and troubled but she doubted if she would sleep.

The elevator slowed and stopped at her floor. The door opened and she heard two sharp bangs. She reached under her coat and drew her Sig.

Experience told her what the sound was. Instinct told her where it had come from. She slipped the safety off.

A door opened in the hallway across from her apartment. Sol Green was a dentist. He stood there in his dressing gown with his hair sticking out like strands of straw.

'Dial 911,' she told him.

He blinked, not comprehending. 'I thought I heard—'

'911 – do it now! Police and ambulance!'

He disappeared back in.

Her apartment door was shut and there was no sound from behind it. She turned her key softly in the lock, flung the door open and stepped back to the side. No shots rained out into the passageway.

She ducked into the darkened hallway, keeping low, the Sig in a two-handed grip in front of her as if it were a torch. A thin tide of light came from what she knew was a bedside lamp in the boys' room and on the polished wooden floor something was glistening.

There was a noise in front of her. For a second she couldn't think what it was and then she realised it sounded like someone with asthma. She swung the gun up.

A door slammed. She recognised the sound as the door from the kitchen out on to the fire escape. She could hear hurried footsteps on metal. As she stepped forward, she heard the gasping sound again and glass crunched under her feet. She stopped and felt for the light switch.

Barbara lay on the floor just beyond the boys' room and near the kitchen. Her breathing was what Annie had heard. Blood soaked the T-shirt and was becoming a widening pool on the floor. The glass was the remains of a broken tumbler. She fought for breath and stared at the ceiling, her eyes wide and anxious and confused.

Sol Green came running in. 'They're on their way. What happened? Oh my God!' He stared at Barbara. In her chest were two dark holes from which the blood was still seeping.

'Stay here,' Annie said.

She ran into the kitchen, although she knew it was too late. She stepped out onto the fire escape but didn't put the kitchen light on, just in case whoever it was was still there and she made herself a target. She looked down. The moon lit the snow like a floodlight but nothing moved in it. At the shore a train was passing and in the distance, like the whooping call of some strange bird, there were the first anxious sounds of emergency sirens.

31

Annie sat along the corridor that led to the QEII's emergency room, guilt and fear struggling for mastery of her. Nearby, a couple of uniformed cops stood keeping an eye. In case of what? In case she tried to run away? In case whoever had shot Barbara came back?

Nursing staff in green overalls hurried past, pushing a groaning figure on a gurney, all wires and IV lines. She knew it wasn't Barbara; they were still operating on her.

She stared at the floor, her mind retracing the steps which the night had taken, and she tried to regain the calmness she had felt immediately after the attack. But shock had set in, she knew that. She held her hand out in front of her and studied the tremor in it.

If she hadn't been in bed with Taggart she might have been there to protect Barbara. But that was nonsense. If she hadn't been with Taggart, then that might be her in there with holes in her chest and surgeons fighting to keep her alive.

Once again she saw Barbara lying on the floor. Once again she heard her struggling for breath. But Barbara hadn't been the target – she had. Of that there was no doubt. The question was, why?

She ruled out robbery. There was no sign of a break-in or anything having been disturbed. Was it a revenge thing, then, someone she had sent to jail in the past maybe? She dismissed that thought quickly. She knew in her bones that it wasn't any of that, that it had to be something to do with Aaron Gaunt and the other killings. If that was the case then what had happened? What was it that she had learned in the past twenty-four hours that had almost got her shot?

The way she saw it, Barbara must have got up for a glass of water and the intruder had seen her in the hall and shot her. Only a few hours earlier Barbara had been making a thing of the fact that there was a resemblance between them. In the dark, the gunman would have believed that's who it was. He might even have recognised her car outside and guessed that she was at home.

It appeared he knew how to get into a locked apartment without making a noise or a mess of the door so that implied some kind of professional knowledge. And was it luck that he'd found the fire escape access or did he know where that was? In other words, was it someone who had been there before?

She shivered at the thought, then looked at her watch. It was after three. She envisaged Terry and the boys packing in a hurry and trying to get flights but airlines were helpful when it came to this sort of thing.

She hadn't called Terry herself; she hadn't felt able to. Someone from the hospital had done that and then Terry had given a number for Barbara's parents who lived in Moncton, New Brunswick. They were on their way now, driving through the dark hours and the snow with their fear and their dread to keep them company.

She didn't know what she would say to Terry when he got back. She didn't know how to tell him how sorry she was and how responsible she felt for what had happened. She would never tell him the things that she and Barbara had discussed although he would want to know what she'd been doing at the apartment. She would say Barbara had called so that they could settle their differences and become friends.

She thought of the red blood darkening to black on the floor. It wasn't a home any more, it was a crime scene, with all that that entailed, the things she'd observed a thousand times before: the forensics people, the sheeting sealing the apartment off, the technical staff with their lights, and the TV vans, inevitably.

Harris and McBrien, the late team, had arrived at the apartment twenty minutes after the 911 call and later Flagg had turned up. He was a bit of an insomniac, she knew, and when he couldn't sleep he sat at home at night and listened to the police waveband on a scanner. That's how he had found out. He had recognised the address and the 'C' code for a serious shooting incident and had driven straight over.

Sol Green's wife had made tea and they'd sat in their apartment while she and Sol had given Harris and McBrien a brief version of what had happened. They would have to give more detailed statements later.

Harris and McBrien had wanted to know where she'd been up until this point and she'd given them a rundown on her eventful evening. When she told them about Taggart she saw them trying to avoid each other's eyes. She knew what they were thinking, that she'd been with him in that motel room. And they were right.

It was awkward being on the receiving end of an investigation. She knew there were things they had to do and that they felt ill at ease about it. She'd shown Harris her Sig so that he would know it hadn't been fired. The bullets taken from Barbara would confirm that anyhow. That and the fact that Sol Green knew she couldn't have been in the apartment and in the corridor at the same time would prevent her from becoming the prime suspect. She'd also given them the number of the cab company whose driver would be able to attest that she'd been dropped off moments before the shooting. As well as that, there would be footprints in the snow on the fire escape.

It was an obvious direction in which to look, though: the vengeful woman trying to kill her ex-husband's new wife. She knew the way Harris and McBrien would have to think. Before they could rule anything in, they had to rule certain things out.

They would want to talk to Taggart too. But she didn't want them to waste time so she told them about the Gaunt case and what she'd been doing. As she did, she could see them mentally backing away from it. Harris and McBrien were people who played things by the book.

'I told her not to get mixed up with any of this,' Flagg said, holding a cup of Mrs Green's tea in a beefy hand.

'So you knew about this . . . investigation?' Harris asked him, as if the word didn't quite apply.

'He knew I was doing something,' Annie said. 'He didn't know the details.' She smiled at Flagg. There was no need for him to get involved.

'Claussen and his pals are going to have to be told,' McBrien said.

'Yes,' she sighed. 'I know.'

Now there were footsteps coming towards her.

She turned her head and saw Claussen, Steyn, Gryce and Marriott striding up the corridor. Like *Reservoir Dogs*, she thought, except they weren't wearing suits. They were all in warm windcheaters of one kind or another and a variety of sweaters and jeans. They looked as if they'd been interrupted while working on their boats. Nina Henry walked slightly ahead of them in a bright yellow parka.

No one said hello to her. No one asked her how she was. Nina said something about having to manage this thing, how they were going to have to keep the media away from her. Steyn wasn't interested. He got straight to the point and asked her what the hell she'd been playing at. Claussen said he'd been speaking to Dodgion at ViCLAS and then to DiGiacomo in Toronto and Ida Stark at the bank had left a message for him. He knew she'd been messing around in this even before McBrien had told him.

They waited, staring down at her. She felt like Oliver Twist in the workhouse after he'd asked for more.

Then a voice said, 'Just a minute – what are all you people doing here?'

A tall, broad-shouldered woman in a nursing uniform was approaching them. She said, 'I'm Kay Gallen. I'm the nursing supervisor in charge of this area tonight. Would you mind telling me what's going on?'

Gryce stepped forward and gave vague introductions. He said, 'We need to have a discussion with Officer Welles here. It's very important.'

'So if you want to have a discussion, then why don't you go to the police headquarters and do it? You're getting in the way here. This is the emergency room.'

'I'm not going anywhere,' Annie said. 'I'm staying until I see how she is.'

They looked at her, as if suddenly reminded of what it was that had brought them to this place.

'That could be a long time,' Kay Gallen said.

'I don't care. I'm staying.' She glared at Gryce. 'If you want to talk, we talk here.'

Looks were exchanged. Kay Gallen said, 'Okay, come with me.'

Like the Pied Piper, she led them through a side doorway and along a short dim corridor, then she opened a big door with glass panels and flicked on the lights. Fluorescent strips blinked into startled life.

They were in the autopsy theatre.

There was a sweet, heavy odour, ether or formaldehyde. It left a taste on the tongue. In the centre of the room were three long stainless steel tables with alleys along the sides. Below them the floor was tiled, with drains at strategic places. There were cabinets and drawers, a couple of wide, deep sinks and two tall refrigerators which held God alone knew what. Annie saw Nina Henry and Gryce trying not to show their uneasiness with these sinister new surroundings.

'This is the best I can do,' Kay said. 'Just make sure you leave the place as you find it.'

'Oh, don't worry,' Gryce said, 'we won't be . . .' And then he realised she was joking.

She left them. There was nowhere to sit, unless you counted the terrace of empty seats which ringed the creepy auditorium. It was from there that the students looked down, watching cadavers being dismembered in the interests of medical science. There were no students tonight but the people who were here wanted to learn something, all the same. They gathered round Annie. She wondered if she should just climb up on one of the tables and let them take her apart.

'I want to know everything you've been doing. From the beginning,' Gryce demanded.

'All right,' she said and then she began.

She told them about the visit to old man Landry and the things he had said and about Lunenburg where Taggart had seen his family home, the house where Aaron Gaunt and his wife once lived. She told them about Heckman's Island and Cobb Landry's initials on the tree that overlooked the room where Cassandra Breaux had died. She told them what she believed: that Cobb Landry had seen what happened that night and that he had died because of it.

While talking she watched their reactions. Steyn was

angry and just about containing it. If a scalpel had been to hand, she would not have been surprised if he had brandished it in her direction. But Claussen was listening, absorbing the information, and she knew he would be trying to see if it fitted with where his own enquiries had taken him. Wherever that was, it did not look like it had produced Aaron Gaunt.

She mentioned the porn videos in Landry's home, the candid photographs he had taken of the Orbachs and her suspicion that Landry was one of nature's watchers. As she talked, she thought of all the people she had come across that day. Was it one of them who'd come to kill her tonight? Was one of them the fourth ghost, as she had come to think of him – or her?

The rest of her story was a wander into territory with which she knew Claussen would be familiar by now: Landry's work at the bank and how it could have told him that Aaron Gaunt was free, then the strange tale of Anthony Melnick in Toronto and the gun that had killed George Poyner.

When she'd finished, Claussen had one piece of information that was new to her.

'We checked Landry's and Gaunt's phone records. There was no contact between them that we can discover other than a thirty-second call which Landry made the night before he died.'

Steyn wanted to know where Taggart was so she told him, recounting most of what had happened during the course of the night: Barbara's visit, Taggart's fight at the hotel and then the horror she had found when she got home. The interlude in the motel she kept to herself.

'Whoever this was at my apartment – I'm convinced they came to kill me. Something I found out today spooked him – or her. I just wish I knew what it was.'

'These enquiries of yours,' Gryce asked. 'What authority did you have?'

She thought of Gamble. There was nothing she could say. The deal had died with him. And anyway, she always knew that if she got into trouble on this she was on her own. If he hadn't died, he would have been here now, widening the circle of inquisitors. She wondered if he would have stood there and let her stew. She would never know.

'I didn't have any authority. I was curious. I was finding it hard to believe that Aaron Gaunt was the man behind all this. I thought the way this enquiry was going was wrong. I had some time off so I used it.'

'Damn it, this is outrageous,' Marriott said. 'You should be suspended. Right now.' He hadn't been involved yet, other than to look suitably bleak. This was his first contribution, an attempt to appear decisive.

'Oh, I don't think so,' Nina Henry said, expressing an opinion that was officially above her station. Annie saw Gryce start to bridle at that and then change his mind.

'I think that for the moment that would be a very bad idea indeed,' Nina went on. 'How would we explain it if it leaked, as it inevitably would?' She looked pointedly at Claussen. The last leak had not been forgotten. He looked offended but he said nothing. 'We can't hide the fact that it was in Officer Welles's home that this woman was shot. How the hell would we explain the fact that she'd been suspended?'

She glared at Marriott who did a brief goldfish impersonation then shut up.

Steyn had had enough. He wasn't subject to Halifax regional police seniority or its internal politics.

'Jesus, what a bunch of fucking amateurs. Who's running this police department of yours? Why am I wasting my time with you people?'

'Now hold on a minute,' Gryce said.

He and Steyn started arguing, both of them talking at once, their voices getting steadily louder, professional contempt battling it out with wounded dignity. Claussen stood apart from it. Not his fight. Marriott looked as if he should do something but didn't know what. Nina Henry was trying to tell them both to cut it out, that they were making fools of themselves, when the door opened and Kay Gallen came back, bringing a look of astonishment and a man in a bloodstained surgeon's gown.

Annie saw them first. 'Shut up, for God's sake!' she said.

Silence followed the echo of her voice.

The surgeon looked at them. Then he said, 'We did everything we could but I'm afraid Mrs Welles died a few minutes ago.'

Annie felt stunned, immobilised by the words.

Mrs Welles. She used to be Mrs Welles. Now Barbara was Mrs Welles. No, Barbara was dead. *Dead?* She frowned at the surgeon as if she didn't believe him.

'I'm sorry,' he said again.

No one spoke, no one moved, then without thinking what she was doing or where she was going, Annie walked out into the corridor.

She stood there, alone, until a door opened next to her.

She looked round and saw a man in a hospital orderly's jacket. He had grey, pitted skin.

He stopped and stared at her. She stared back, puzzled and disorientated for a moment. He didn't say anything, then as the others came out to see where she had gone, Ray McPhee gave her a curt nod of acknowledgement and hurried away.

32

Taggart woke and realised he hadn't locked the cabin door. He knew it because he could sense that he was no longer alone. Someone was there in the darkness. There was a strange sweet smell, something vaguely medicinal, and he remembered that in his sleep just now he had dreamt he heard a car outside.

Slowly, he began to sit up, trying not to make any noise, but as he moved, the bed creaked and the sheets sounded like wind across tall grass. Then he felt the heavy coldness of something metal being pressed against his cheek.

'Steady,' a man's voice murmured.

He froze. For a couple of seconds there was just the sound of two people breathing.

'Who are you? What do you want?' Taggart said, asking the futile questions of the frightened.

'I want you to get dressed.'

Taggart reached towards the bedside lamp. The gun, for he knew beyond doubt that it was a gun, pressed harder against his cheek.

'No. No light.'

He dropped his hand. After a moment, the gun was taken away and he could hear the man step back.

His eyes began to adjust. He could see a shape standing just beyond the bed. His clothes were all piled on a chair, save for his jacket which was hanging in the closet. He got out of bed and began to dress but with difficulty, fumbling when he dropped a sock, feeling along the floor for his shoes. Every now and then he looked towards the shadow but it did not seem to stay in one place long enough for him to get used to its position.

When he'd finished, he said, 'Okay, what now?'

'Walk towards the door and open it. Do not turn around.'

He did as he was told. He wanted to ask where he was going but he didn't think there would be any answers. Outside the cold seized him. At the side of the cabin there was a car.

'It's open,' the man said. 'Get into the passenger seat. Put the safety strap on.'

He got in and clicked the strap into place. He hadn't had a chance to see what kind of a car it was and anyway North American cars were unfamiliar to him. It certainly wasn't new, he could tell that, and it smelled faintly damp.

The passenger door behind him opened. He felt the man lean forward and then something, a cloth, being pressed over his mouth. He struggled as panic took over. There was that smell again, heavier now, cloying. He pushed against the safety strap and reached behind trying to pull the man's hands away, but he wasn't strong enough. The hand held him back. He felt himself weakening and then fading to black.

Annie had nowhere to go except Gottingen Street. Upstairs there were a couple of rooms, used to store things mostly, but there were divan beds there for when the big occasions happened and you couldn't go home. So when Harris and McBrien reported from the motel that Taggart had disappeared, that's where she was, deep in a heavy sleep that was a surprise to her when she woke from it.

After the hospital they'd all come here. Gryce and Marriott had told her she wasn't suspended but that she would not be resuming normal duties until further notice. Nor was she to talk to the media, not that she had any intention of doing so, and Claussen and Steyn would be in again at nine to interview her in more detail.

Barbara's death had calmed them. Before they all left again, Nina Henry asked her what she was going to do since her apartment was not available to her, and she had said she'd thought of moving in with her ex-husband and her sons for a few days.

She wondered how Terry would respond to that idea. They would be back just after two p.m. Someone at the airline had contacted the hospital with the flight details and Annie had volunteered to meet them to break the news.

But for the moment there was the question of where the hell Taggart had gone.

It was five a.m. Flagg had taken it upon himself to wake her. He was still hanging around anxiously, unable to go home, so she asked him to drive her over to the motel to meet Harris and McBrien.

When they arrived the two detectives looked pissed off. They had taken Annie at her word that Taggart hadn't anything to do with this, that it was all connected to the Gaunt thing, so they hadn't been in a rush to come here to talk to him. Now he was gone.

Annie stood in the empty cabin, looking at the rumpled bed, trying not to let her face show what she was thinking. There was no sign of Taggart's bag, nothing hanging in the closet. The only other odd fact was that all the windows were open and the cabin had turned icy cold.

'Did you open those?' she asked the two officers.

'No, the place was like this when we got here,' McBrien said. 'Your pal must like plenty of fresh air.'

'Have you any idea at all where he might have gone?' Harris asked.

She shook her head. 'None. I don't understand this.'

The history student wasn't any help either. There was a room with a cot at the back of the office where he could grab some sleep and after Annie had left, that's where he'd been, him and Stalin. He hadn't been aware that Taggart wasn't there until the two policemen came knocking on the door.

Outside, Harris looked her in the eye. 'Annie – is there anything you're not telling us?'

'Nothing. I swear. Look, it's like I said. John Taggart had nothing to do with what happened to Barbara. The fact that he isn't here is as much a mystery to me as it is to you.'

'We've already notified the airport,' McBrien told her, 'and we're going to have to issue a description to all units. Can you help us with that?'

She nodded her agreement. She also gave them Jeff Cameron's number and said the Royal Citadel might be worth a try although she didn't really think he would have gone back there.

After that, Flagg persuaded her that she should eat. Near the office was a coffee shop that opened early. When they got there, the smell of the place hit her and she realised how hungry she was. She had bacon and eggs and pancakes and a couple of cups of coffee that fuelled her back to full wakefulness. Then they returned to the office where Flagg hooked up with Crisp for the day and left her to freshen up and get ready for the interview with Steyn and Claussen.

The morning passed quickly. Steyn and Claussen were there on the dot of nine and by ten they had finished with her. Largely it was a case of once again going over everything she had told them at the hospital, this time with them making notes. To her surprise, only Steyn approached the task in anything like a hostile manner. Claussen was quiet.

Following that she wrote out a detailed statement for a

very tired Harris and McBrien before they went off to grab a couple of hours' sleep. There was still no word of where Taggart had disappeared to and nothing more they could do until they saw what the technical people might have turned up. There was also the matter of Barbara's autopsy, which they would attend later.

Marriott, who had come in early, trying to appear in charge, allowed her to send a uniformed policewoman in one of the squad cars to get fresh things from her apartment, where the bulk of the crime scene work would be finished by now, and to bring it all back in Annie's own car.

There was no question of her going herself, not when the TV vans were still there and with the news bulletins starting to run stories speculating that a Halifax regional police officer, whom they were not in a position to name so far, may have been the real target. Barbara's name and face had yet to emerge although the fact that this was now a murder case had been confirmed. Her identity would not be released until all the next of kin had been informed.

Barbara's mother and father were sitting with her body at the hospital. In a few hours, out at the airport, Annie would do the rest.

Taggart drifted back to consciousness on a rising wave of nausea.

His stomach heaved and he threw up. But someone was ready for that, holding his forehead with one hand and a plastic basin under his chin with the other.

There was something across his eyes. He tried to move his arms but couldn't. His eyes were filled with tears and his nose ran and then he felt a damp cloth wiping his face carefully. Now he remembered the car and the chloroform or whatever it was and he realised he was blindfolded, sitting on a chair with his hands tied behind his back.

His senses were returning. He heard water running, a toilet flushing. A door opened and closed again. Cold air blew from somewhere and brought with it a tang that gave him a sudden mental image of Portpatrick and the sea. He sniffed. He could detect other odours, kind of antiseptic, like those in a hospital.

Someone moved close to him and then he felt the blindfold being untied. He blinked to clear his vision and saw that he was in a small dim room with painted wooden walls. Heat was being provided by an old black stove. Its door was open and he could see logs blazing.

He looked around. The room was furnished sparsely. There was a table and chairs, to one of which he was tied. There was an old armchair, a chipped dresser with a small TV set on it and a bed. Thin net curtains covered windows through which daylight was seeping but he didn't know whether it was the beginning of the day or the end.

There were two men in the room. A colourless man with bad skin and cold eyes sat at the table with a gun in front of him.

The other man was in the bed. He was older, a thin man with grey hair, but Taggart almost winced when he saw his face. It was bruised and discoloured and peppered with angry red cuts. Only broken glass could have done that and he remembered George Poyner's window.

Across the man's chest and shoulder, bandages had been strapped, covering surgical dressings. A wire coat hanger had been bent out of shape and tied to a length of cord which was suspended from the low ceiling. From it dangled an intravenous fluid pack and a line leading to the back of one hand.

Taggart stared. He did not need anyone to tell him who this was. He watched the blue eyes in the injured face flicker with a mixture of excitement and suspicion.

And then the man spoke.

'Is it true that you're my son?' Aaron Gaunt said.

33

The airport had a private waiting room that they kept for occasions like this. Annie sat in it with a counsellor from the hospital, a woman called Muriel Hall, who had been sent to help her through the ordeal. She couldn't handle it all on her own. At some point Terry would want to go to the hospital. Muriel would take him while Annie stayed at the house with the boys.

Muriel wasn't the only company Annie had. Outside the terminal a white cruiser sat beside her car. Until any possible further threat to her life was removed, a couple of uniformed watchdogs would never be far away.

The plane would be here in twenty minutes. When they got off, Terry and the boys would be given the VIP treatment; there would be no problems with customs or immigration. Annie wondered if that in itself would tell Terry what had happened.

But she had other worries now. She was afraid of what might have happened to Taggart.

Muriel interrupted her thoughts momentarily. 'Why don't I get us a coffee? We could both probably do with one.'

'That would be good. Thanks.'

Muriel left and Annie's anxiety resumed. If, as she suspected, she had almost got herself killed because of something she had found out, then what if the killer had gone after Taggart as well? He had been with her every step of the way yesterday, with the exception of her visit to Cobb Landry's house, her talk with Edith Orbach and her conversation with Ida Stark at the bank.

She stood and looked out of the waiting-room window on to the empty concourse. She couldn't swallow the idea of Taggart just packing up and disappearing of his own free will, yet she couldn't figure out how the killer would have known where he was last night.

Something was niggling at her. Something from yesterday. Something begging to be noticed.

Muriel came back. They sipped their coffee and made subdued small talk for a while and then Annie's cellphone rang.

She didn't want this to be more bad news.

It was Claussen. 'There's been a development. Can you talk?'

The truth was she almost couldn't. She had a vision of Taggart lying somewhere, bleeding to death like Barbara.

She said, 'Yes, go ahead.'

'I'm back in the office again. It's better that way. You miss things otherwise.'

She knew he meant the ViCLAS call she had taken.

He said, 'I'm with Harris and McBrien. I told them I'd call and tell you this. The bullets which killed Barbara are a match for the slugs in the Poyner murder.'

'What? Say that again?' She was finding it hard to absorb this.

'They're from the same gun that killed Poyner.'

She paused as the implications sank in, then she told him, 'I'm grateful.'

'I thought you should know.'

'Things are starting to connect.'

'They always were connected. We just can't figure out why. There's something we're not seeing.'

'That's what I've been telling myself. And I'm worried about John Taggart. Has he turned up yet?'

'No.'

Muriel touched her arm and pointed. Annie turned. Terry and the boys were coming down the concourse. A couple of the airport staff were walking with them like undertakers beside a hearse.

They were at Terry and Barbara's house forty minutes later. Muriel pulled up into the driveway behind them in her own car. The cruiser arrived last and sat across the road as discreetly as its bright livery would allow.

There were letters in the mailbox. Annie thought of all the mundane daily things that would go on as if nothing had happened. There never was an easy way to handle this kind of event, no way you could minimise the distress.

In the waiting-room, she had told Terry her version of why Barbara had been at the apartment and then she had recounted the subsequent events as calmly and as sensitively as possible. When Terry began to weep, she put her arms round him and comforted him like a child.

Her own children looked on, confused and a little frightened. There had been no tears from them, not yet, but that was because none of this seemed real. James had said, 'I never knew anybody who got shot before.' Later they would have to come to terms with it. And later Terry would get angry. She wasn't looking forward to that.

For now he seemed possessed by an urge to keep busy. He unpacked, put soiled clothes into the washing machine, made coffee. He even opened the mail, all except for a letter addressed to Barbara which he set to one side as if she might read it later.

'Are you hungry?' Annie said. 'Can I get you guys something to eat?'

'It's okay,' Terry told her. 'This coffee's fine for me. There was a snack on the plane just before we got in. One of those freezing cold sandwiches they do. You'd think the airlines would try to make the food a bit more appetising so that you get off the plane with positive feelings about them. You know what I mean?'

'Yes, I do.' She responded to him as if this mattered. But none of it did. He was in shock.

'I'm hungry,' Peter said.

'Me too,' James agreed.

Terry wasn't listening. He put his coffee cup down and went into the bedroom, then returned after a few minutes wearing a grey suit, a white shirt and a dark tie. He looked at Muriel. 'I think I'd like to go to the hospital now.'

'If you're sure?'

'No time like the present.'

'Then why don't I take the boys somewhere?' Annie suggested.

'Yes,' Terry said, then he frowned at her. 'Wait a minute, your apartment. It must be . . . you can't stay there.'

'I was going to mention that later. I thought you might put me up here for a few days, that's if you don't feel—'

He nodded. 'Sure, of course. That would be for the best, I think.'

When he and Muriel had gone, James said, 'Are you moving in, Mom?'

'Nothing permanent. Just for a couple of days, darling, that's all.'

'I guess you can sleep in Dad's bed now that Barbara's not—'

She held up her hand like a traffic cop. 'We can sort out the sleeping arrangements later. Now let's go and eat.'

As she drove into Halifax, the cruiser on her tail, she went down the list of options with them. Pizza was out, they said, so was anything else Italian for a while, and they didn't want to hear about Tim Horton's or Subway or any of that stuff. Then she remembered that in the food court at the Spring Garden Place mall there was a new fish and chip counter, a branch of the British franchise, Harry Ramsden's. That idea hit the spot.

The food court was on the lowest level of the mall and it had a fountain where coins glinted at the bottom. A couple of trees which never felt rain stretched towards the light from the glass roof high above. They took a table right in front of the Harry Ramsden's stand. Annie got cod and chips for three plus three cokes. One of the cops came in with them and sat nearby while the other one stayed outside in the car.

'Now,' she said when they were settled, 'I want to hear all about this holiday of yours.'

They told her about the fun they'd had. She tried to listen but as they talked her mind kept dragging her elsewhere. She thought of the bullets that had killed Barbara. She thought of Taggart. She thought of Terry sitting with Barbara's parents in the hospital mortuary. Was he here now, the person who had done this? Could he have followed her? She glanced around, aware of the reassuring presence of her Sig against her hip. People sat at scattered tables. None of them paid any attention to her, except the cop in uniform. He smiled over and sipped a coffee.

When they'd finished eating, the boys wanted to go to the washroom so she said she'd have a coffee and wait for them. As the girl behind the counter poured it, Annie looked at the photographs that decorated the walls. They were old prints in black and white designed to illustrate the traditional nature of the establishment. Edwardian men in aprons and straw hats posed behind baskets piled high with fish. People smiled to the camera from tables in a big dining hall, knives and forks poised, plates of fish and chips waiting in front of them. Two men with moustaches and proud looks stood outside a seaside shack holding an enormous fish that she thought might be a marlin. It was like the sort of picture you always saw of Ernest Hemingway in his heyday.

She stared at it. What was there about it? What did it remind her of?

Suddenly, in her mind, she saw the photograph that hung on the wall in Ray McPhee's front room. She saw him standing outside a cabin not unlike this one, a seaside place where nets had been hung out to dry.

Ray McPhee.

She'd run into him at the hospital last night. For a second, in the midst of her shock over Barbara's death, she hadn't been able to figure out what he was doing there and then it had come back to her and she'd remembered that he was an orderly.

She thought of the day she'd learned about his new, reformed life, the day she'd called at the house. And now she remembered something else, an image that hadn't made sense at the time.

As she'd driven up, a man had been getting into a car. She'd noticed him because both he and the car had looked out of place, the car dark blue and new-looking, the man well dressed, sixty-ish, thin and grey-haired.

Like Aaron Gaunt.

The boys came back. 'What are we doing now, Mom?'

34

Gaunt looked at Ray McPhee. 'He's my closest friend,' he said.

McPhee untied Taggart then sat and watched him with hawk eyes, the gun not far from his hand. But Taggart no longer felt fear. He did not think anything was going to happen to him here, not when he looked at the man in the bed. Even with his injuries, he could see that the face bore a strong resemblance to his own.

He wanted to know what had happened. But Gaunt had questions first. In a tired voice, he asked about Taggart: his mother's first name, her age, background, where they'd been living for the past thirty years. Taggart answered in detail.

Then he said, 'I have a photograph of her in my wallet.'

McPhee searched him for it.

If there had been any doubt left, this dispelled it. Taggart saw Gaunt's eyes becoming moist as he looked at the picture, one that he had taken on a sunny day about five years ago in the verdant setting of Ardwell gardens, a short drive from Portpatrick. Noreen Taggart – or should it be Gaunt? – stood in front of an old wall on which wild roses roamed freely. She smiled towards her son. That made the picture a rarity.

'She's still a lovely woman,' Gaunt whispered.

'Then maybe you should hear the rest.'

As Taggart told him about his mother's thirty-year pretence and her attack on him which had finally broken the barriers holding severe mental illness at bay, Gaunt's lips tightened and his face seemed to grow paler. At the end, he closed his eyes as if in pain.

Taggart watched his discomfort with confused feelings. He had wanted to confront him about the things that had happened to his mother, the things for which he was responsible, but now that he had done so he did not feel it giving him any satisfaction.

This was his father. Not the person he used to invent at school – this was real. He kept telling himself that. But although he understood what the words meant they did nothing for him.

It wasn't as if he'd lost something and had now regained it. He'd never had a father or any kind of paternal presence in his life so he had no idea what that was like. The truth was, he didn't know how to feel, except that he thought Aaron Gaunt looked more like a victim than a killer.

'How did you know about me?' he asked.

'I work at the hospital,' McPhee said. 'I saw that policewoman Welles last night when they brought in a woman who had been shot in her apartment.'

'Hold on a minute – what are you talking about?'

With growing horror, he listened to McPhee tell the story of Barbara's murder.

McPhee said, 'I saw all the top brass coming in. The nursing supervisor put them into the autopsy theatre so that they could talk. There's a gallery upstairs and I decided to listen to what was going on. Welles told them everything she'd been doing, sniffing around Lunenburg with you, Heckman's Island. She told them where you were but I decided to get to you first.' He looked at Gaunt and then back to Taggart. 'I thought you two should meet.'

Taggart felt frightened again but this time it was not for

himself. 'If someone tried to kill Annie and failed, then maybe they'll try again.'

'Possible,' McPhee said, 'but it will be difficult for a while. There'll be people around her.'

He wasn't convinced. He turned to Gaunt. 'So someone else is dead because of you. How many is that? Three? Four?'

'Now, wait a minute,' McPhee said.

Gaunt raised a weak hand. 'Ray, it's okay. I understand why he's angry. If I were in his shoes, I'd feel the same way.' He tried a smile. 'He wouldn't be my son if he didn't get angry.'

'There's a panic on,' Taggart said. 'Everyone's looking for you. They think you killed that man Landry and probably Poyner the private detective as well but they're more concerned that you might want to kill your old friend Eisener and that you might be a threat to Prince William when he launches the new *Bluenose*.'

'What? Why would they think that?' Gaunt said.

'Because you threatened Eisener at your trial and now you've disappeared. It was your parole supervisor who first drew attention to the fact that you were missing. Now there are two murders with you linked to both of them and with Eisener coming back to Lunenburg for the launch, they're not taking any chances.'

'We've been watching the TV news, trying to follow what's going on,' McPhee said. 'We didn't hear any of that.'

'They don't want to start a scare and have the royal visit called off. Things are bad enough here as it is with the Carne extradition business. They want to find you and eliminate you as a threat.'

'You mean kill me?'

'Annie thinks anything's possible. I suppose it would depend on whether you resisted arrest or not.'

Gaunt smiled again, as if the thought was ludicrous. 'And do I look as if I could do that?'

'No, but he does.' Taggart glanced at McPhee and his gun.

'Ray has looked after me since this happened. I'm grateful to him. He wants to keep me free from harm.'

'You can't stay here forever.'

'I know that. But until now there hasn't been an option. Now you're here and you might be able to help.'

'Help? You drug me and kidnap me and now you want me to help?'

Gaunt ignored his indignation. 'You have to talk to your friend Miss Welles. You have to tell her the truth, tell her that I didn't kill anyone.'

'Then why are you hiding out here with an armed bodyguard? What the hell happened to you anyway?'

'I took a slug out of his shoulder.' McPhee said. 'He'd lost a lot of blood by the time I managed to get him here.'

'And where are we exactly?'

'I can't tell you that yet,' McPhee said.

Taggart looked at him. 'You're not a doctor.' It was a statement, not a question.

'No, I'm a hospital orderly studying to be a paramedic. I used to have a different line of work.' He tapped the gun. 'Armed robbery was my thing. That was until my last spell in prison which, incidentally, was thanks to your friend Welles. Then, when I was in jail, I met this man.'

He looked at Gaunt with what Taggart could see was something close to reverence. 'He was an inspiration to me. He encouraged me to focus on myself, to see how pointless it all was. My life changed. He helped me to find a new way, free from crime.'

'Until now,' Taggart said.

'Things happened,' McPhee said. 'It wasn't Aaron's fault.

He had no one else to turn to for help.'

Gaunt coughed. McPhee got up from the table and poured a drink into a cup from a plastic jug. While Gaunt sipped it, he took a thermometer from his shirt pocket and checked the older man's temperature, then he had a look at the IV line to make sure it was still flowing adequately.

'This is ridiculous,' Taggart said. 'That man should be in a hospital.'

'And he will be, with your help.'

Gaunt handed the cup back. 'You need to know everything. From the beginning. That's the only way you'll understand.' He sighed. Taggart could hear a rattle in his breathing. 'I didn't kill her – Cassandra. I was a fool, I was obsessed by her, but I didn't kill her.' He looked at Taggart. 'I don't expect you to believe me but it's the truth.'

Taggart said nothing. He thought of the tree at Heckman's Island and waited to hear the rest.

'It was like I said at the trial. I went to see her that night to end the affair once and for all. But I was weak. She was like a drug. I couldn't resist her. And then when we . . . when . . .' He was having trouble talking about it. 'Someone came into the room or else they were hidden there, I don't know. I got hit on the head, knocked unconscious, and when I came to she was dead. There was blood everywhere, the place was wrecked. There was a knife. I picked it up. And then people came. Neighbours, the police, I—'

'Take it easy, Aaron,' McPhee said. 'Don't torture yourself.'

'No, I have to tell this.' He paused to collect his thoughts and his emotions. 'There had to be somebody else, somebody else Cassandra was seeing, maybe more than one person, for all I knew. I'd suspected that I wasn't the only man in her life and that she wasn't the sort of woman who would put any restriction on the number of partners she had. Those were the days of free love, remember, at least for some people. People didn't have to worry about AIDS then. But the police didn't bother to look for anybody else. As far as they were concerned they had caught their killer. Hell, if you find a body and a man holding the knife, what's the point in looking any further?'

McPhee went over to the stove. He took a couple of logs from a pile in the corner and shoved them in. Taggart looked at him and then towards the curtained windows but he couldn't see what lay beyond, although he was certain they were at the shore somewhere.

Gaunt said, 'I can't expect you to understand what it was like – the prospect of life in prison for a crime you hadn't committed. I blamed everybody. I blamed Chuck – Cary, as he calls himself now. It's true – I shouted out in court, threatened him. But it wasn't his fault. I have no intention of harming him. Christ, what's the point? Anyway, for a while, all those years ago, I thought of an appeal but there were no grounds for one and gradually, as prison life began to kind of wrap itself around me and I faced the fact that it was for the next thirty years, I got myself into a mental state where I convinced myself that I *had* killed Cassandra.'

He looked at Taggart. 'That sounds crazy, I know, and maybe I was a little crazy then. Maybe I still am. I'd been drinking that night. So, what if I'd had a blackout or something and couldn't remember or at least had imagined there was someone else in the room? That was possible, wasn't it? That was the sort of thing I brainwashed myself into thinking. And then there was your mother. I knew I'd done things that were very wrong and I hated myself for it. That's why I'd gone to Heckman's Island that night – to bring the relationship to an end. After the arrest, I saw Noreen just once, when she came to visit me in the jail where I was being held. She told me that it was over between us, that she was going to leave Nova Scotia and I'd never see her again. I didn't know . . . about you. I didn't know that she was pregnant. God, if I had, it would have driven me totally insane.'

He shook his head in disbelief. 'And so I convinced myself that my incarceration was just and that I had to atone for what I had done. The prison at Dorchester became my world. There's a saying: if you can't get out of it, get into it. So that's what I did.'

He told Taggart about how he had studied, the doctorate he'd obtained, the papers on the correctional system he had written.

'After I'd been inside for twenty-two years, I was allowed out on supervised day parole but I found the outside world impossible to handle. There was nothing for me. I had no family, no friends. I had become institutionalised, a victim of the system I'd been studying for so long. Nevertheless, I knew I had to prepare myself to face freedom. And after all that time, that thought frightened me almost as much as being sent to prison had. I would have been eligible for full parole after twenty-five years, but a few days before submitting my application, there was an incident.'

'Incident?' McPhee said. 'It was a damn sight more than that.'

'Someone planted drugs in my cell. But that's the way it goes. I made enemies in prison as well as friends. Someone didn't want me to end my sentence any sooner than I was supposed to. I never found out who. After that, early release was out and I tore the application up. The strange thing was, I was kind of relieved. It was a problem I didn't have to face for a few years. And then I met this guy.'

He looked at McPhee. Taggart could see that if there had been reverence in McPhee's glance, there was at least respect and affection in Gaunt's.

'We found ourselves sharing a cell. There was a big difference in our background and our ages but we seemed to hit it off, didn't we, Ray?'

McPhee smiled. 'Eventually.'

'We were determined to maintain our friendship once we were out. I don't think I'd have survived if it hadn't been for Ray. He left prison before I did. I had parole days and when I was out he helped me with all the practical things, steering me through what was a totally hostile environment to me. Life had changed a lot in thirty years. Ray kept looking around for a suitable house and kept sending me real estate lists. Later he helped me with driving lessons, stuff like that, did my shopping for me, showed me how ATM machines worked, all the details of modern living. I tell you, it was tough going.'

Taggart said, 'And then what happened?' He gestured to Gaunt's bandaged shoulder and injured face. 'How did we get to this?'

'I never stopped thinking about your mother, wondering about her, whether she was alive or dead, where she'd gone. I even looked up the name of a private detective, George Poyner – I just got him out of the phone book – and thought about seeing what someone like that could do to find her. But Ray talked me out of it. He told me I was making a mistake trying to go back, that Noreen could be anywhere in the world, that she'd probably changed her name. He had a point, of course, painful though it was to admit it. I was the one who'd convinced him to put the past behind him, to look to the future. So I decided to make this year zero, start my life from here.'

He paused. 'I need another drink, Ray.' McPhee helped him. 'And then I got a phone call from some guy who'd got hold of my number somehow. I didn't know who he was. He didn't give his name but he said he knew all about me, that he knew I hadn't killed Cassandra and that he knew who had. Of course, that opened everything up again, all the things I'd been trying to put behind me. He could have been a crank – I was aware of that – but I had to be sure and he'd said things on the phone that intrigued me, about the heat that night, about the music Cassandra liked to listen to. It sounded like he knew something about Heckman's Island.

'He asked me if I'd meet him at a coffee shop near the ferry terminal and I said I would. I didn't tell Ray about any of this because I thought I would handle it on my own. If the guy turned out to be some kind of a joker, I'd feel foolish and I didn't want anybody else to know I'd been conned. Then when I went to the coffee shop it occurred to me that maybe I shouldn't go in, maybe I should observe him instead and find out who he was. So I watched from across the street. He wasn't hard to identify because he said he was bald – I didn't know at that time that it was cancer, poor guy – and when he came out I followed him and got the number of his car.'

'And then you went to Poyner with it,' Taggart said.

'Yes. I told Poyner who I was and why the guy had called me. I asked him if he could find out his name and any other information he could pick up. He told me he'd have what I needed by that afternoon. When I went back, I paid him in cash and as far as I was concerned he and I had no further business. On paper, this man Landry turned out to be a straight enough guy. I saw that he worked at the bank so I figured that might be how he knew my telephone number. Anyway, I decided to go to his house when he wasn't expecting me, to see what he knew, if anything.'

'You should have told me. You should have taken me with you,' McPhee said.

'I know that. But it's too late now.'

They'd had this discussion before, Taggart could see.

'I drove to Dartmouth that night and as I was looking for the house I saw a car driving off from it. Of course, I paid no attention to that at the time. I went to the door. The lights were on so I knew there was someone in and I could hear the TV. I rang the doorbell a couple of times but there was no answer. Then I tried the handle and it was open, so I walked in and followed the sound of the TV. Landry was lying on the floor. I knew it was him because I'd seen him in the coffee shop. He looked like his neck was broken. I was kneeling over him, trying to feel for a pulse, when some man walked in and saw me. I saw the shock on his face and it was Heckman's Island all over, like history was repeating itself, and I didn't want to stand around and get arrested again for something I hadn't done. So I panicked and ran. It was wrong, it was a mistake, but that's what I did.'

'And then he came to me,' McPhee said. 'He was pretty freaked out by the whole thing. I tried to calm him down. He was talking about this guy being murdered but I told him he didn't know that for certain. Maybe the guy had died of natural causes and Aaron just happened to find him. So I decided we should drive back and take a look. When we got there, the cops were all over the place. It looked like a crime scene to me and there was no way we were going to walk up the path and say – here you are, guys, here's who you're looking for. While we thought about what to do, Aaron said he was due another insulin shot.'

'I was diagnosed as diabetic a few years ago,' Gaunt explained, 'so we drove over to my house to get what I needed, although I was almost out. As soon as we arrived, I knew someone had been there. The place wasn't ransacked or anything but things had been moved, drawers had been opened and the contents gone through. You develop obsessively tidy habits when you're in prison. Everything has to be perfect and in its place. It was obvious to me, although not necessarily to anyone else, that somebody'd been in the house.'

'You should have gone to the police when you had the chance,' Taggart said.

'Someone with my background,' McPhee told him, 'that's not the first course of action you think of and I didn't like the idea of my friend here being behind bars again while they decided whether they believed his story or not. As a matter of fact, they'd most likely have locked me up, too. A couple of ex-cons, one of them already with a murder rap, you think they're going to believe anything we say? I don't trust the police. Your friend Miss Welles would have hung a stick-up in Dartmouth on me if I hadn't—'

He stopped suddenly. He stood up and went to the window, standing back a little from it and looking out through the net curtain.

'What is it?' Gaunt asked.

'I don't know. I thought I heard something.'

He listened for another few seconds. Taggart did, too, trying to hear anything that would give some clue as to where they were, but the only sound was the hissing of the logs in the stove.

McPhee sat down again. 'Something very strange was going on. I wondered if Poyner had anything to do with it or if there was anything he'd found out about Landry but hadn't mentioned. I figured that talking to him was worth a try and that maybe he'd even come to the police with us, you know, to help bear out at least part of Aaron's story. We looked him up in the phone book. He had a place on Shore Drive in Bedford so we decided to drive over there.'

'And you brought a gun,' Taggart said.

'Yeah. If I hadn't, we might both be dead. We stopped off at my house on the way. I used to have a dog, kept it in a compound at the back. There's a concrete floor with a cracked slab that nobody ever noticed on account of the fact that they didn't dare go near the dog.' He patted the gun. 'I kept this buried underneath, wrapped up in a tin. A remnant of a previous life. I never thought I'd have to use it again.'

'Did you kill Poyner with it?'

'Jesus Christ, I didn't kill anybody.'

'But there was a lot of shooting at that house.'

Gaunt said, 'We called Poyner from a payphone in Bedford so we knew he was at home. It all went crazy when we got to the house. It was in darkness but there were a couple of cars outside. We tried the front door and got no answer so then we went round the side to the deck and saw that the back door was open. We went in and found Poyner's body on the floor and that was when the shooting started. I got hit in the shoulder. I didn't know what was happening. The noise. The gun flashes. A couple of bullets shattered the living-room window. The glass showered over me. I managed to throw myself through it to get away.'

'I got him back here,' McPhee said. 'I got the bullet out and patched him up.'

'Where did you get all this?' Taggart asked, gesturing to the medical equipment.

'I kind of borrowed some stuff from a pharmacy in Mahone Bay without their knowledge, including some insulin. The rest I got from the hospital before I called in sick. I needed to be here to keep an eye on Aaron but if I stayed away from work too long people would get suspicious. That's why I went back last night although I disappeared again before my shift finished. They'll be curious about that.'

'You've backed yourselves into a corner here,' Taggart said.

'Yes,' Gaunt agreed. 'That's why we need your help to get out of it.'

'What makes you think I can do any good? What makes

you think the police will believe any of this?'

McPhee put his hand in his pocket and took out a stubby piece of metal. 'This is the slug I took from Aaron's shoulder. I'll bet it matches the bullets in Poyner's body.'

'That won't prove anything.'

'But there's something else,' Gaunt said. 'In the darkness I saw the man who shot me. I think I'd be able to identify him.'

'Quiet a minute,' McPhee said suddenly.

From somewhere outside there was a rumbling. Taggart stood. McPhee lifted the gun. 'Stay where you are.'

He went to the window and looked out. The sound was getting louder and nearer.

'What can you see?' Gaunt asked.

'Helicopters. Four of them.'

35

In Annie's mind, things were clicking into place at breakneck speed.

Gaunt and McPhee would have been in Dorchester prison at the same time. Had they met there? When she'd been in McPhee's house, he'd spoken about the encouragement he'd received in jail and how his life had been changed. Gaunt had written papers on rehabilitation.

This was how they were connected. She would bet on it.

From a corner of the food court where she wouldn't be overheard, she called Glenda Paige, the human resources officer at the QEII. This time there was no cover story to cloak her real interest.

'I'm checking on one of your orderlies, a man called Ray McPhee. He was on shift last night. I happen to know that because I saw him myself. I want to find out if he's on duty now. If he's not then I want to know when he'll be in again.'

'May I ask why you're interested?'

'You may, although I'm afraid you won't get an answer, not while the matter's still under investigation. But I can tell you that your help will be much appreciated. This is something that's very important.'

There was a pause. 'It will take a minute or two.'

'Thank you. Call me back as soon as you can.'

She gave Glenda her number and rang off, then she sat down at the edge of the fountain. Under the water the coins were a rippling mirage. In it she saw McPhee's face and his startled look in the hospital corridor.

He had come out of a door. Where did it lead? The gallery. Was that it? Had he been up there, listening to everything? Was it possible he was involved in Taggart's disappearance?

She thought of Claussen. She had to tell him about this.

James looked at her. 'Mom, what are you doing? Can we go soon?'

'Just a minute or two, honey.' She put her hand in her pocket and took out some change. 'Why don't you get another drink for yourself and Peter. I won't be long. I've just got a couple of calls to make.'

She always worried about her children having an excessive sugar intake. Sweet fizzy drinks were something she didn't approve of much but she would make an exception if it gave her a few minutes to think.

Her phone rang. It was Glenda Paige calling back.

'Well, I don't know what all this is with Ray McPhee but the supervisor in the ER is keen to talk to him, too. Seems he walked off the job early this morning some time before his shift was due to finish. Disappeared with no explanation. That and the fact that he's just back after a few days when he called in sick doesn't exactly make him a front runner for employee of the month.'

'What days was he sick – what dates?'

Glenda checked and told her. Annie paced up and down as she learned that the morning after the two murders, McPhee hadn't made it into work. Then he'd come in briefly on the Saturday but had gone off sick halfway into the shift and hadn't been back until last night. She thought of their encounter in the corridor. He must have left the hospital soon after that.

She thanked Glenda and rang off. She was about to hit the office number to speak to Claussen but then she thought better of it. This wasn't the sort of thing to talk about on a cellular connection. She wouldn't call; she would drive to Gottingen Street. Anyway, the boys always liked going there. They found it exciting.

There was a sudden squawk from the handset of the cop who was keeping an eye on her. He spoke into it and got to his feet. People were looking at him as he headed towards her.

'We're being pulled off this detail. We're going to have to leave you on your own. All hell's breaking loose down at the Law Courts.'

In spite of every possible security precaution, hundreds of protestors had gathered in the street outside the court building and more were arriving all the time.

The parking lots along Lower Water Street had been taken over by the police, the RCMP and the satellite vans of the media battalions who had advanced on Halifax after the invasion of Lunenburg. They were now augmented by fresh troops: the journalists and camera crews who had arrived specifically for Prince William's impending visit.

Lines of police with flak jackets and riot shields were trying to keep the road clear, holding the various protest groups apart, but every so often someone would break away and run towards the opposing ranks only to be caught and bundled into a police van. The cops looked awkward when this happened. In spite of the way they were kitted out they weren't used to civil disturbance.

The first helicopter Ray McPhee had seen was a Bell 206 with RCMP markings along its flanks. Behind it came three TV news choppers decorated with logos screaming the identity of their individual channels. Normally based at Fredericton, New Brunswick, the Bell had flown down to Lunenburg during the night, landing in the grounds of A.J.

Carne's mansion. Now it was approaching Halifax with Carne, his doctor and two of his lawyers on board. They sat uncomfortably, shoulder to shoulder with special duty RCMP men wearing SWAT uniforms and carrying assault rifles.

Once the helicopters were seen in the air over the city, the uproar around the court building grew in intensity. There was more than just noise now. Missiles were thrown towards the police, just a couple of empty bottles at first, then there were rocks and within seconds, the first petrol bomb. That was the signal for the police to fire tear gas.

As the drama developed below, the Bell banked away from the harbour and up towards its destination, the Citadel. There it hovered and began descending to the ground inside the fortifications. Like acolytes at a mass, the other helicopters circled in attendance, sending pictures of its arrival to mix with the riot shots being screened from the bottom of the street where reporters, talking live to their audiences, were calling this Seattle all over again.

The moment its wheels touched down, the Bell's doors opened and the passengers were bundled out and into an armoured RCMP van with darkened windows for the ride down Duke Street which had been closed to everyone except them.

This was the last part of the journey but it was going to be the hardest.

Annie heard all this on the car radio as she crawled through the traffic on Spring Garden Road, heading away from trouble, going for a long roundabout sweep that would take a little time but would bring her down to Gottingen Street eventually.

She knew that every police officer in town would be hauled into this thing, that the reverberations would go on interminably, but right now she had other things on her mind.

She should have called Claussen from a land line but she hadn't time to pull in now to do so. With one hand on the steering wheel she used her cellphone and got through to Birgit who told her he wasn't there. As she'd guessed, everybody had been pressed into service by the disturbances.

A journey that would normally have taken a few minutes took her nearly an hour and when she got to Gottingen Street, Flagg was the only member of the unit still in the office, along with Birgit and a couple of people from downstairs who were helping with the phones.

'Hey, these boys are getting big,' Flagg said. Peter and James looked tired. They stared up warily as his huge shape bent over them.

'Where's Claussen? Can he be reached?' Annie asked him.

'I wouldn't try. It's bedlam down there. The damn lock-up's full already. And have you heard the latest?'

'What?'

'It just came over the radio. They've abandoned the extradition hearing. Carne apparently got sick on the way to the court so they've taken him to the QEII with a suspected heart attack. Fake, if you ask me, but who's to say.'

Annie felt angry. She thought of Mark Gamble dying alone on the Dartmouth ferry while A.J. Carne, whether feigning illness or not, would receive the best medical care that was available. There was no justice.

Flagg laughed. 'You should have seen them all heading out of here, Marriott and Gryce and everybody, leading from the front, uniforms, teflon vests, the works. It was like the charge of the fucking Light Brigade. Oh, sorry. Excuse the language.' He put his hand to his mouth but the boys were across the room talking to Birgit and hadn't heard him.

Plainclothes officers kept uniforms in their lockers in case the occasion required. But occasions like this didn't arise very often. Annie hadn't worn hers in a long time.

She had never seen Flagg in uniform. 'What about you? Why didn't you go?'

'Somebody has to mind the store. I guess they left me behind on account of my great age.' He smiled and winked at her. 'So what's going on?'

She told him about Ray McPhee and what her theory was. 'It's just guesswork so far but I'd bet my life on it. I'm certain McPhee's involved and that he knows where Gaunt is. That's why I came – to tell Claussen so that he could take it from here.'

'Well, he's otherwise occupied right now. I hope he hasn't forgotten how to use a nightstick. He might have to crack a few skulls down there. So what are you going to do?'

'The only thing I can do in the circumstances, I guess – follow it up myself, which means going to McPhee's house.'

He looked at her with a slight frown, then he said, 'Well, if that's the plan, then you're not going alone. I'm coming with you.'

She smiled. 'I was hoping you'd say that.' She squeezed his shoulder. 'But what about this place?'

'Hell, they can take care of themselves. They know how to find us.'

She made certain that Peter and James were content to stay with Birgit. She told her she didn't know how long they would be and asked her to contact Muriel Hall, the counsellor at the hospital, who would be with Terry.

They drove off in Flagg's car. Terry wouldn't be pleased about this. She felt guilty, as if she were abandoning the boys, but they were happy where they were and wouldn't come to any harm. She reassured herself that she was on a roll now. She had tried to hand this all to Claussen and that hadn't been possible so it was up to her to follow it through. Anything else would be negligent.

When they got to McPhee's street, she saw that its normally derelict appearance had been disguised by the snowfall of the previous night. The neighbourhood looked as white and twinkling as a picture on a Christmas card but the rot and the grime would emerge again, worse then before, once a thaw began.

They parked a couple of doors down. A skinny terrier barked at them from behind a wire fence. A man came out of his house and began telling it to be quiet. When he saw them, his eyes registered that they were cops so he went back inside. The dog kept barking.

There was a car at the side of McPhee's house where the burgundy Buick had been on her previous visit. It was covered with a dust sheet and on top of that a layer of snow had fallen. Annie pulled a corner of the sheet up to reveal a dark blue Dodge underneath. It was Aaron Gaunt's car, hidden away here where no patrol would ever notice it and where winter had helped to conceal its presence.

She showed Flagg what she had found. He nodded, then went round the back of the house.

She rang the front doorbell. There was no response so she rang once more. As she listened she heard the sound of someone moving about inside and when the door opened several seconds later, she was holding her breath and had her Sig at the ready.

'I let myself in,' Flagg said. 'There's nobody here.'

She breathed out and put the gun away. 'You might have told me you were going to do that.'

'Sorry.' He stood back to let her in.

They searched the little house quickly but there was no sign of life, nothing to indicate where McPhee might have gone or whether Gaunt had ever been there. The paramedic study books were where they'd been before but the hospital tunic wasn't on the hook.

'What do you think?' Flagg said.

'Wait a minute.'

She was staring at the photograph on the wall. It was this picture that had started the train of thought that had brought her here. She looked at McPhee standing outside the fishing cabin.

She pointed. 'Where do you think that is?'

Flagg went close, examining it like an art dealer looking for Rembrandt's signature. 'The ground around it looks rocky. There's a bit of sea there in the background. Could be Peggy's Cove or somewhere. Any of those little places along the south shore.'

She thought for a second, then reached for the phone.

'What are you doing?' he asked.

She rang enquiries and asked for the number of the police station at Lunenburg. Debbie Randall answered and seemed surprised by the call. 'What can we do for you today? I thought you'd be kind of busy with everything that's happening in Halifax. I've been sitting here watching it on TV. It's just terrible.'

'Yeah, well, life's got to go on, I guess. No rest for the wicked. Listen, your colleague, Constable Peterson, Gus – he wouldn't be there, would he?'

'Well, no, not right now. But I can reach him for you if it's urgent.'

Annie thought for a moment. She said, 'When we were with him yesterday, he was talking about the kind of crime you sometimes have, like break-ins. I think he mentioned in passing that there'd been a robbery at a pharmacy recently. Am I right? Would you have the report there?'

'Sure. I know what he was talking about. It's the pharmacy at Mahone Bay. I should have it in the current case file.'

Which would be a slim volume, Annie would bet. She waited.

'Yep, here we go. So what's your interest in this?'

'Does it list the things that were stolen?'

'Let's see . . . yes it does.'

'Was any insulin taken? Insulin pens, the kind that diabetics use?'

'Dum-de-dum . . . why, that's right. One box of insulin pens, plus morphine and a load of bandages and antiseptic and stuff. My goodness, how did you know that?'

'Long story,' Annie said. 'Listen, you've been a big help but can you get hold of Gus and ask him to meet me there in about an hour?'

'No problem. Can I tell him why?'

'I want him to help me find a house.'

She rang off and pointed to the photograph again. 'Grab that. We're going to Lunenburg.'

As they drove, she filled Flagg in on the details of her conversation with Debbie.

'So what's the story with the insulin?' he asked.

She turned the radio down. There was still mayhem outside the courts but the reporters reckoned the police were getting on top of it now.

She told him what she and Crisp had found in Gaunt's bathroom. 'According to his doctor, he was due to pick up a new batch. Crisp started ringing round pharmacies and medical supply places but it was a crazy task. He didn't get very far and anyway it would have taken him forever. Then the whole thing got removed from us and I guess he must have dropped it. Incidentally, I don't think Claussen knows about the insulin. We never told him. It went out of my mind until today.'

She looked at the photograph on her lap. 'If there's insulin missing from a pharmacy in Mahone Bay, I figure this cabin is somewhere near there and that's where Gaunt is, injured probably, with our friend McPhee looking after him.'

'Then let's go see,' Flagg said.

When they reached Lunenburg, she saw that the parking lot outside the police station was back to normal, empty except for Gus Peterson's patrol car. He and Debbie were waiting for them. The TV was on in the office, showing the violence outside the law courts, but the reporter said these were earlier scenes and that the trouble was over. Annie introduced Flagg. Peterson shook his hand.

'Well, I gotta say I'm intrigued. Debbie told me about your call. I've been trying to figure out why you're interested in the break-in at Mahone Bay and how the hell you knew insulin was missing.'

'The thing is—'

'The thing is, you weren't being straight with me yesterday, were you, when you were here with that reporter?'

Flagg glanced at her and she remembered she hadn't told him about Taggart being along.

She said, 'No, maybe not.' She looked at Peterson and acknowledged his reproach. 'I'm sorry. I couldn't level with you because I was working on something and it wasn't official.'

'And this is?'

'Yes.'

She told him about the murder of Cobb Landry and George Poyner and the truth about the hunt for Aaron Gaunt. Debbie gasped when she got to the shooting of Barbara in the apartment last night. As she spoke, Peterson's indignation eased and excitement took its place. They had a big-time case on their hands and he was in the middle of it.

'We think Gaunt's hiding out somewhere around here,'

Annie said. She showed him the photograph. 'Does this place look familiar to you?'

'Oh, yeah,' he said without any hesitation. 'I know where that is. That's out at Blue Rocks.'

'Blue Rocks?'

'A little fishing community just a few miles from here. A handful of houses built on a chunk of stone.'

'I'm impressed,' Flagg said.

'You drive around these roads as much as I do, the whole darn place gets imprinted on your brain. Blue Rocks is very small. Not many people live there.'

He told them how to get to it. 'You go out of town the way you came in, then turn right at the main highway and head along the road past the back harbour. You'll see a sign. It won't take more than a few minutes. So you think this guy Gaunt's the killer?'

'No,' Annie said. 'I don't. But I think he knows what happened.'

'What about back-up? We should notify the RCMP. I better come with you.'

She didn't want him getting in the way. This wasn't his kind of gig. 'No, it's best if your car isn't seen. It might be too obvious. We'll try to find the house by ourselves, see if there's any sign of life, then we'll come back and decide what to do, whether we need to involve anyone else.'

He didn't look happy with that but he went along with it. Minutes later they were driving past the stretch of water he had described as the back harbour. It lay to their left, a long thin inlet coated with ice like grey marble. On the far side, houses in bright colours were huddled and wood smoke rose from their chimneys.

Gradually, the road curved away until Annie saw that they were on a rocky peninsula with the open sea on their right. Small wooden dwellings were dotted along the roadside but none of them looked as if anyone was at home. Snow-covered boats lay upturned beside rusting trailers and damp piles of kindling.

'Here we go,' Flagg said and pointed.

In front, a sign told them that they had arrived at Blue Rocks.

It was a finger of land jutting out into the ocean. Somehow, a scattering of houses, even a church, had been built on it, apparently placed at random along its rocky surface. Flagg slowed as they approached. Where the rock dipped, a road had been built, winding round the edge of the shore past boardwalks leading to fishing sheds set on stilts in the water. There were cabins, some of them no more than shacks.

As she looked at the photograph she held in her lap, her phone rang. She fumbled in her coat pocket.

'Leave it,' Flagg said.

'I can't. It might be about the boys.'

But it wasn't. It was Claussen.

Before she could say anything, he told her, 'Don't say my name. Is Flagg with you?'

She hesitated, startled, and then she said, 'Yes.'

'I want you to pretend that this is your husband calling you. Have you got that? Believe me, this is important.'

His words and the firmness of his voice alarmed her. She knew she should not argue. She found herself saying, 'Yes, Terry, I can hear you.'

'I'm going to be quick. I've just spoken to a man called Michael Liebmann. He called you.'

Michael Liebmann? She didn't know anyone of that name. What the hell was he talking about?

'I don't understand.'

'He operates a website known as Nemo's Log.'

The e-mail she'd sent. She'd forgotten all about it.

Claussen told her, 'We spoke about the Melnick murder, about who might have been involved with Poyner. He said Melnick never had a name for the other person, just a nickname. It was Anvil. Have you got that? The nickname was Anvil.'

Anvil.

It took her a second.

Anvil.

She saw the bar of the Late Watch. She saw the TV screen.

She felt weak, dizzy. She thought she might be going to be sick. She looked out of the window but she didn't see the ocean or the shore or the houses of Blue Rocks. Instead, she saw Walter Flagg at one of the high tables, logging on for a game of Trivia.

Anvil. The name he used because his grandfather had been a blacksmith.

Claussen was talking to her. 'Have you registered that? Do you understand what it means?'

She tried to find her voice but her mouth was as dry as sand.

'Can you hear me?' He was becoming more anxious. 'Annie, tell me where you are.'

She managed to speak. She said, 'I'm sorry, Terry. It was urgent. I left the boys with Birgit because I had to drive down to Lunenburg with Walter. There's a constable there called Peterson. I needed to talk to him about something. He was very helpful.'

'Got it,' Claussen said. 'Now for God's sake be careful.'

He rang off and at once she felt helpless and alone.

Flagg glanced at her. 'You okay? You look a bit pale.'

She nodded. 'I'm fine. Trouble with Terry. He didn't like me leaving the boys. I'll have to sort it out when we get back.'

'What was it you didn't understand?'

'What?'

'When you were talking to him you said "I don't understand".'

She could hear the suspicion in his voice but she tried not to react.

She said, 'Birgit tried to get a message to him at the hospital. Apparently, he didn't get it and he called the office to see if anyone knew where we were.'

'He could have tried your cellphone.'

Her heart was beating hard.

'Yeah, he could, couldn't he? But he didn't for some reason.'

She looked away from him. She didn't want to see his face and didn't want him to read what was written on hers.

He had killed Barbara.

He had been in the apartment before and he would have remembered his way around it. He would have been able to get in easily enough. She'd seen him do that kind of thing once or twice, using a couple of lock-picking tools that he always carried in his pocket. And he would have seen her car parked outside. He would have thought she had been in because he had called her that night. Damn it, she had invited him over. He had not been listening on his scanner, either. He had known about the shooting because he was the one who had done it.

But why?

Wait a minute, this was Walter she was talking about. Walter Flagg. Her partner. It couldn't possibly be true.

He had turned the car and was back at the beginning of the road that led along the shore. He stopped. 'We'd better park here and walk so that we're not heard. My guess is that it's somewhere down there.' He pointed.

Had he killed Poyner and Landry? She didn't understand any of this.

'Yeah, I think you're right.'

She was scared. Claussen couldn't be any help to her. He was an hour away. He would call Peterson and find out where they were but it would take too long for anyone to get here. She was on her own, more so than at any time in her life.

They got out of the car. Behind the clouds, the light of day was beginning to fade. She didn't lift McPhee's photograph; she didn't need it. She would know the house when she saw it. And if Gaunt was there, and maybe McPhee and Taggart too, then what? What was going through Walter's mind right now?

They began to walk, past boats pulled up to the edge of little slipways, past creels and lobster pots stacked into piles in the snow. In some places there was a drop of about six feet to the shore. The tide was low. Wading birds strutted among the stones and the shells, pecking at crusty delicacies hidden in the dank weed.

'There's a car down there,' Flagg said.

She looked to where he was pointing. They'd turned a curve where they couldn't be seen from the main road. A reddish Buick sat in front of a cabin. Smoke was rising from a stovepipe chimney and she could smell the sharpness of burning wood. There were no fishing nets hanging out to dry today but she recognised the place just the same.

'That's it,' she said.

'Better take it cautiously from here,' Flagg advised, taking his gun from its holster. He stepped up on to a patch of scrub grass so that his feet wouldn't make any noise on the stones.

As they moved forward, she allowed herself to fall behind him and then she took her own Sig out. When he was directly in front of her she raised it and pointed it at his back.

She said, 'Okay, Walter, stop right there. Hold your hands away from your body slowly and drop the gun.'

He stopped walking but he didn't turn round. He said,

'Annie, what the hell are you playing at? Is this a joke? Because if it is, your timing's way off.'

'Do it, Walter.'

For a second he still didn't respond but then he lifted his arms gradually until they were outstretched. The gun fell from his hand and landed in a pile of snow.

He said, 'That wasn't Terry on the phone, was it?'

'No.' She paused. 'It was Claussen. He told me he was talking to someone in Toronto about the murder of a man called Anthony Melnick. A nickname came up in the conversation – Anvil. It was a give-away, Walter.' A thought occurred to her. 'You read my e-mail, didn't you?'

He nodded. 'Yeah, I read it. I went back to the office last night to see if you were still there but you'd gone. I wanted to know what you'd been doing so I checked the out tray in your PC and found the message. There was nothing I could do about it. One of the things in life that you can't take back is an e-mail.'

For a second she had hoped that all this was a mistake, that when she confronted him he might be as horrified as she was by the whole idea. But he wasn't trying to deny anything. With an increasing sense of shock she saw that it had to be true.

She said, 'You killed Barbara.'

He didn't answer directly. 'I figured that if you got to speak to this Nemo guy, well, that would be that. I went back to the bar and called from there to see if you were at home. You told me you were planning to come back to Lunenburg today to see what you could find out about Cassandra Breaux. I knew that if you did that and got talking to Nemo as well, then it was only a matter of time. You'd know about Poyner and you'd know about Cassandra too.'

'Cassandra? I'm talking about Barbara.'

'Damn it, Annie, don't you get it? Gaunt didn't kill Cassandra. I did.'

She stared at his broad back, trying to grasp what he was saying, trying to work out how this could be.

He said, 'Are you still there? Can I turn around? You know, we should talk about this face to face.'

She didn't say anything. She let him turn. He did so slowly, keeping his arms held out wide. It was an oddly graceful pivot. He smiled shyly at her and looked almost embarrassed.

He said, 'Barbara was in the wrong place at the wrong time. It was dark and I thought it was you. You look alike, you know. Did you realise that? It was nothing personal, Annie. You were getting too close to me so I had to try to put a stop to that. And damn it, I warned you often enough to let the thing drop. After all this time, thirty years, I couldn't just stand back and let everything fall apart.'

She wanted to know about Cassandra Breaux, she wanted to ask him, but at that moment someone put a lamp on in the cabin. It cast a dim light through the lace-curtained window.

They were about fifty yards away. She told Flagg to back towards the front of the house. She walked forward too until they were both in full view of the windows, then she called out. 'McPhee – Ray McPhee. If you're in there, this is Annie Welles.'

The only answer was the light going out again.

'I want you to know that you're not in any danger. If you look out of the window, you'll see me and a man with his hands raised. The man is an officer with the Halifax regional police. His name is Walter Flagg. I've just found out that he's the man responsible for the killings. I'm holding a gun on him so you're safe to come out.'

There was still no response from the cabin. She tried to

put herself into McPhee's mind. He was unlikely to trust her. He might think this was being stage-managed, that it was some kind of an elaborate trap. And he might have a gun. That couldn't be ruled out.

'Ray,' she called again. 'This is the man who's been trying to kill me. He shot the woman in my apartment last night. This is not a trick. I give you my word.'

She waited, listening to the silence from the house, smelling the salty, weedy seashore in the wind. Then the door of the cabin opened slowly and Ray McPhee stood there. He had a gun in his hand. He held it low, uncertainly. Annie's heart was pounding. She kept her own weapon trained on Flagg in what she hoped was a demonstration that she was telling the truth.

'Put the gun down, Ray. We can sort this out. I know you didn't kill anybody – your friend Gaunt either. But you have to get rid of that thing.'

He stared at her. Several seconds of silence passed and then he dropped the gun at his feet.

Annie spoke to him without taking her eyes off Flagg. 'Is John Taggart in there?'

He nodded.

'And Gaunt?'

'Yes.'

She called out, 'John, are you okay.'

A voice came from inside the cabin. 'I'm fine. But there's an injured man in here who should be in a hospital.'

Taggart appeared at the door and stood beside McPhee. He stared at Annie and Flagg and the gun.

'Let's all get inside,' she said.

It would be better if she could handcuff Walter but she didn't have any cuffs of her own. She could use his if he was carrying a set but going near him was a risk and she didn't want anyone else to try searching him. Claussen was a long way away. She wondered if he had alerted Gus Peterson.

Taggart and McPhee went back in, then she motioned for Flagg to do the same. She picked up McPhee's gun. When she entered the cabin herself she knew that Taggart was right. Aaron Gaunt needed proper medical treatment. But she could also see that McPhee had been doing his best to care for him.

She put the gun down on a shelf beside her. There were now five people in the little room. Too many. If Flagg tried anything and she had to open fire, there was a risk that she might hit somebody else. She told him to sit down at the table with his hands on the surface, then she took up a position at the open door. Peterson was bound to get here first. He would see her straight away.

'It was you in Poyner's house,' Gaunt said. 'It was you who shot me.'

'Yes,' Flagg said in a quiet voice. Annie thought he looked very tired.

'And you killed Landry,' she said. She thought of how the man had died. She remembered Flagg in the office giving her a demonstration of how to break a neck.

He nodded. 'He saw what happened that night at Heckman's Island. He was a kid, twelve years old. He saw Gaunt with her that night. And he saw me. I thought no one knew. But all the time he did.'

He shook his head and seemed to be on the verge of tears.

'I want to hear the rest,' Annie said.

He sat silently for a moment and looked at her with moist eyes. He said, 'It's all over for me, isn't it?'

She nodded.

He bowed his head as if in prayer and stared down at his hands. 'I was nineteen at the time. Cassandra was like no other woman I ever met, before or since. I was down from

Newfoundland, working my way round the coast that summer, doing odd jobs, gardening work, that kind of thing. You know, the night I killed Landry, all the time I was talking to him in his house, the poor guy didn't realise who I was.' He looked up at her and smiled sadly. 'I was a lot thinner in those days, a lot better looking then, not so much of this.' He gestured towards his stomach.

'Keep your hands on the table,' Annie said.

'It's okay. You don't have to worry.' He cleared his throat. 'I'd been in a few places but I liked Lunenburg best so I decided to hang around. I put a card in a store window. Cassandra needed an old shed fixed up so she hired me and before you knew it, one thing was leading to another. The trouble about Cassandra was that she got a grip on you. First I was fascinated by her, infatuated, then I was in love with her and then I was obsessed. That's right, isn't it? That's about the way you felt, too?'

He looked at Gaunt as if he were appealing to a fellow sufferer. But there was no answer.

'I knew she had another lover but I wanted her badly that night. I'd been drinking beer and then rum. I walked from Lunenburg all the way out to the house. It was hot. I saw your car. I let myself in the back door. I could hear the two of you upstairs. I got mad so I grabbed a kitchen knife. You were making so much noise you couldn't hear me. I hit you and threw you on the floor. You banged your head on a table or something. Cassandra went crazy. She started throwing things, then she came at me and I stabbed her. I don't know how many times.'

'Twenty-one,' Annie said. She looked at Gaunt. He was staring at Flagg as if hypnotised.

'I was going to kill him too,' Flagg said, 'but then I realised that if there were two bodies, they'd be looking for somebody else. Plus there'd been a lot of noise, screaming and everything, and the neighbours were bound to have heard it. Sound carries on the water. So I decided to get out of there. Gaunt here was unconscious. I wiped my prints off the knife and put it in his hand so that his would be on it, then I dropped it on the floor.' He laughed. 'But it turns out that when he came to he picked the damned thing up anyway.'

'How did you get rid of the blood?' Annie said. 'It must have been all over you.'

'I used my head. I was only wearing shorts and sandals and a T-shirt, you see, because it was such a hot night. I took them off in the bedroom, then I went out of the house and got into the water. I swam away and washed the blood off. There was a house about a mile downstream. Nobody there. I slept in the barn that night and in the morning I went on my way. Nobody ever looked for me, nobody ever wanted to question me. They figured they'd got the killer.'

He looked at Gaunt with fascination. 'Man, I never thought you'd last out the thirty years. I thought you'd die in jail for sure and that I was safe forever.'

'And all that time, there was a kid who saw the whole thing,' Taggart said.

'How did you find out about him?' Annie asked.

He gave her a smile. 'You know, you're out of order here, Annie. We should be doing this in the interview room with you letting me know my rights and giving me the opportunity to contact a lawyer. This isn't proper procedure.'

'Don't worry. That'll come.'

'George Poyner and I go way back. I joined the army after that summer and that's how I met him. We were both in the same outfit. After the army we went into the police, him in Toronto, me in Hamilton. We stayed friends.'

'And Melnick?' Annie asked.

'That guy made us both mad. Child-killers are the worst.

George wanted to give him a hard time, to see if he'd crack. I helped him out with some of the small stuff. I didn't know he was going to kill the bastard. That was nothing to do with me. After the lawsuit, George had money. He came down to Halifax and set up as a PI and then he called me and said that the cops here were expanding their investigative division. So I got a job and moved. For years after that, George and I had an arrangement. I was in a position to provide him with information about people, information he could use in his work. In return, he saw me right financially. He didn't know about Cassandra – I never told anyone that – but then Gaunt came to see him with a licence plate number, told him who he was and that some guy had called to say he knew he hadn't killed her. George didn't know anything about the case so he called me to see if I did. Little did he know.'

'So then you went to Landry's house,' Annie said.

'It was easy to get him to talk. I just showed him my badge and said that Mr Gaunt had taken his licence number and come to us with his story. He sat there and told me everything. Said he didn't know who Cassandra's killer was but that he'd recognised the guy as a young man who'd been doing odd job work round the area. As soon as I heard that, I knew what I had to do. It turned out he never told anyone at the time because he was afraid of his father, afraid of what he would do if he found out his son was a peeping Tom. After a while, keeping the secret got easier. Until he got sick and he found out that Gaunt was out. So he decided to do the right thing before he died. Poor bastard. I guess in a way I did him a favour.'

'Very noble of you,' Taggart said.

Flagg ignored him. 'Then I went to Gaunt's house. Landry had confirmed the address. But Gaunt wasn't there of course, he was two steps behind me. After that I went to find George.

I knew that when he heard about Landry's murder, he'd be kind of curious and I wanted to make sure he didn't open his mouth. But he was drunk, totally twisted. We had an argument and then it turned physical and what does he do but produce a gun. I didn't know it was the one he'd used to kill Melnick. I didn't know he'd kept that. Asshole. I managed to take it away from him and I suppose you could say it went off by accident. Killing George wasn't part of the plan but these things happen. And then Gaunt turns up with his friend here and the whole thing went shit over heels.'

He sighed and sat back but didn't move his hands from the table. 'That's it, the whole story. You know, it's kind of a relief to get that off my chest. Strange, isn't it, Annie? We've heard people say that before. You never think it's going to be yourself.'

She was tired holding the gun. She wanted to get Flagg to the Lunenburg lock-up.

'I'm thirsty,' Gaunt said.

And she needed to send for an ambulance.

McPhee moved towards the bed to get Gaunt a drink and as he did he walked right in front of her. At that moment, Flagg stood suddenly and his hand reached towards his belt.

Too late, Annie remembered that she hadn't frisked him. Too late she remembered there was another gun.

Flagg opened fire. The sound was deafening. The shot hit McPhee in the side. He fell across Annie and knocked her backwards. The Sig went flying from her hand.

As Flagg stepped forward and raised his gun again, Annie scrambled out of the door and hurled herself over the edge of the road. She slid down the slimy bank and through her chinos she felt the stones tearing the skin on her knees. She began to run as fast as she could, keeping her head down, waiting for his next shot to hit her. But for some reason it didn't come.

There was a boat shed, its wood green and rotting. She dived behind it for momentary cover but she knew she couldn't stay there. Somehow she had to get to Flagg's gun, the one she had made him drop. She cursed herself for getting into this position. By confessing like a broken man, he had fooled her. He had pretended to be beaten and she had fallen for it.

She heard his voice.

'Annie? Annie, can you hear me? I'm not going to chase after you. I'm too old for that sort of thing. So why don't you be a good girl and just come back in here?'

Her heart and her mind were racing. She realised now that he couldn't come after her because he had to watch Taggart. Or maybe he would just shoot him and Gaunt and then come looking.

He called to her again. 'You're very quiet, Annie. You're out there thinking I'm going to kill them, right? And I am, that's true. But if you don't come in here, then I'm going to have to do it slowly. Ever seen someone shot in the liver, Annie? What am I talking about – of course you have. That little guy in *Saving Private Ryan*, remember? We talked about that scene, how awful a death that would be. Except those guys gave him a whole bunch of morphine to help him on his way. There won't be any of that here, Annie, just a terrible agony that'll go on for hours. I'll start with Mr Taggart. How does that grab you?'

'Wait,' she shouted. 'Give me a minute. I need to think about this.'

He laughed. 'I'm not consulting you here. I'm telling you what I'm going to do if you don't walk in that door.' He paused. 'Thirty seconds. That's it.'

'Annie – don't do—'

It was Taggart's voice but whatever he was going to say was cut off abruptly and she knew that Flagg had hit him.

The light in the sky was going. She moved away from the shed and, still keeping low, scurried along the shore. Then, when she thought she was far enough away, she climbed up the bank.

She saw the spot where he had dropped the gun. She got it then slipped over the edge of the road again and hurried back. She jammed the gun behind her into her belt.

Flagg called out, 'You've got ten seconds.'

'Okay – I'll do what you say.'

She got up from her cover and began to move towards the cabin. She felt the gun pressing into her back and she hoped it was secure and wouldn't fall out. At any moment now he could shoot her. She was a simple target. Her legs felt weak but she kept on going, waiting with every step for the shot.

But it didn't happen.

She reached the door. McPhee was lying there. His eyes were open and he blinked a few times. He wasn't dead but, from the blood spreading on the ground around him, it might not be long.

Taggart was sitting on the floor against the wall and there was blood in the corner of his mouth. Aaron Gaunt looked frail and frightened.

As she walked through the door, Flagg came from behind it and put his gun to the side of her head. His other hand frisked her quickly and found the Sig in her belt.

He smiled. 'Do you think I'm fucking stupid, Annie?' Then he kissed her on the cheek. 'Still, I guess it was worth a try.'

The touch of his lips felt like a burn. She looked at Taggart. 'You okay?'

'I'll live.'

Flagg laughed. 'No, you won't. That's why I want you all in here. No untidy bodies lying around outside.' He pushed Annie into a chair and put his gun back into its holster, then he sat on Gaunt's bed and looked around. 'You know, it's a cosy little hideaway you have here, Gaunt. Pity we all have to leave it.'

Gaunt said, 'It belongs to Ray. It was a gift from me. I wanted to thank him for everything he'd done. It was the sort of place he'd always wanted.'

'If you're trying to make me feel bad about shooting him, then don't waste your breath.' He studied Gaunt's face. 'The thing is, you see, she told me I was the best fuck she'd ever had. She couldn't get enough of me. I thought you'd like to know that. Want to hear the details, compare a few notes?'

'Some other time maybe,' Gaunt said.

Flagg laughed. 'But that's just it. There isn't going to be another time because right now I'm going to shoot the three of you and get the fuck out of here before the cavalry arrives.'

He looked at Annie. 'This is where you're supposed to tell me I'll never get away with it.'

'You won't.'

He laughed. 'Annie, my love, do you know how many boat-owners there are between here and Yarmouth who'll be happy to take me down to Maine for a fee? I cleaned out my accounts just in case and turned it all into US dollars. It's in the glove compartment of the car.'

'But you don't have to kill anyone else,' Taggart said. 'What's the point?'

'The point is that you've fucked it all up. Leaving you alive is not an option.'

Annie saw that he had set her gun on the shelf where she had left McPhee's. She wondered what the chances were of getting to it.

Flagg noticed her glance. 'Look at you, Annie, still trying to work a move. That means you'll have to go first. You're the dangerous one.'

He got off the bed and walked over to where she was sitting. With his back to the door, he stood in front of her and aimed the gun at her head.

'Second time lucky, I guess.'

Taggart screamed. 'No!'

Annie closed her eyes and turned away from the shot. In her mind she saw the faces of her two beloved boys.

There was a sharp crack, then another one. A window behind her shattered.

A hole opened in Flagg's forehead and the back of his head disintegrated like a smashed egg. For a second there was confusion in his eyes but then the light died in them and he pitched backwards onto the floor.

Men in SWAT uniform began pouring through the door. Behind them came Steyn and Claussen along with Constable Gus Peterson.

Annie stared, bewildered.

'Are you all right?' Claussen asked. He was still in his uniform.

'I don't . . . how did you get here so fast?'

'The helicopter. It was still at the Citadel. The parking lot at the police station is perfect and Constable Peterson had two cars waiting for us. We came round the back of the house. I see we made it just in time.'

She could hear the siren of an approaching ambulance. One of the SWAT team, a paramedic, was kneeling down beside McPhee.

Claussen turned to the man in the bed. 'Now then – Aaron Gaunt, I presume?'

Epilogue

A thaw had begun. Grubby and forlorn, piles of slush stood dwindling by the roadsides, turning to water that trickled along the gutterings and into the drains.

There was a hint of heat in the sun. It shone from a sky without cloud and lit up the polished brass of the *Bluenose III* as it sailed slowly across Lunenburg harbour.

Beside Government Wharf, the forty-five-strong band of the Maritime Forces Atlantic, splendid in full dress uniform, struck up *Heart of Oak*. Its rousing strains echoed across the calm waters and stirred the spirits of even the most apathetic spectator, of whom there were not many. The entire dockside was lined with people. From the old town, to almost as far as Kaulback Head, they cheered and waved flags both Canadian and British. Union Jack and Maple Leaf were united in celebration. And from the deck of the *Bluenose*, the young Prince, tall, blond and handsome, waved back.

Above the crowd, on the verandah outside the Grand Banker restaurant, which had been turned into a VIP enclosure, Taggart and Annie stood with her boys, feeling the excitement in the air and their own sense of relief that the day had come at last and that they were alive to enjoy it.

Like everyone else, the boys flourished their flags and cheered as they watched the graceful progress of the *Bluenose*. Beside Prince William stood the Premier, beside him the Lieutenant Governor, carrying on his duties as if nothing had happened. Mansell the skipper was there, as sturdy as one of the masts, and with him the stocky figure of Cary Eisener, the man who had loomed so large in everything that had happened, yet had played no part in it except to create this proud and beautiful vessel.

Annie hooded her eyes with her hand as she peered at him. Eisener would undoubtedly be aware of the drama that had unfolded. Everybody was. It had dominated the media in the days since it had happened, shoving the Carne controversy onto the sidelines, but as far as she was aware Eisener had made no attempt to visit the hospital in Bridgewater where Aaron Gaunt was being treated.

'Do you think he'll try to see your father?' she asked Taggart.

'I don't know. If he didn't bother with him in the thirty years he was in prison, why would he bother now?'

She had gone with him to see Gaunt this morning, before they'd collected the boys and come here. The man had remarkable vigour. He was determined to recover quickly – hospital was too much like incarceration again – and he was well enough now to walk along the corridor to the intensive care ward where Ray McPhee lay. Flagg's shot had not been fatal. McPhee had lost a lot of blood but his life had been saved. Now he was ill but stable.

'So when you go back to London tomorrow, what's the plan?'

'I'll see my agent –' he smiled '– now that I've got one, and make a decision about which offer to take.'

In the days following the events at Blue Rocks, he had been contacted by a show business agent offering to take him on as a client and he had accepted. Several newspapers were flashing their cheque books around now. There was discussion of a television talk show of his own and a possible book deal.

'It must be nice to be in such demand,' she said.

He looked along the dockside to where the cameramen and reporters were herded into an enclosure like unruly animals.

'Yeah, well, at the moment, I've kind of lost my appetite for it. There are other priorities on my mind – a mother in hospital on one side of the Atlantic and a father in hospital on the other. Whatever I decide, it looks like I'll be notching up the air miles for a while.' He smiled. 'But that's for another day. There's still tonight.'

'Sorry, I'm busy tonight,' Annie said.

His smile vanished. 'What are you talking about?'

'I'm having dinner with someone: a young man I met, a journalist from England. He kind of stumbled into my life a little while ago and got me into all sorts of trouble.'

He smiled again. 'Really?' He took her hand and held it in both of his. 'And how do you feel about that?'

She looked into his eyes, as if searching for something, and then she kissed him gently. 'I'm not sure. Only time will tell.'

Acknowledgements

I owe an enormous debt of gratitude to Judy Pal, who is in charge of public affairs for the Halifax regional police, for all her help during the writing of this book. For the best part of a year she was an invaluable source of information, first when I was in Nova Scotia and then later in response to endless e-mails which she always answered promptly and willingly. However, LUNENBURG is a work of fiction. The police force on these pages is not the one which serves the people of Halifax, Dartmouth and Bedford so well. It is a creation of my own, realistic, I hope, but not real.

I would also like to thank the Chief and the staff of the Lunenburg–Mahone Bay police and Mitch Rumbolt, now of the Royal Newfoundland Constabulary.

My thanks go, too, to my good friends Dick and Paddy Pentland of Bedford and their daughter, Danielle, my god-daughter, for making their home available to me during my research and for reading this manuscript.

And as ever I am grateful to Carole Blake and Bill Massey for their enthusiasm and their judgement.

Inheritance

Keith Baker

When retired RUC officer Bob McCallan is killed in a gas explosion in a caravan in Donegal, his son Jack inherits an unexpected fortune. He also inherits a key to the past.

The violence in Northern Ireland has been over for two decades, but there are still secrets that could shatter the foundations of peace. Secrets that Bob McCallan's untimely death threatens to bring to the surface. Secrets that some people would do anything to keep buried.

'A gripping read' Michael Dobbs

'Breathtaking . . . if you buy no other thriller this year, buy this one' *Irish Times*

'Gripping' *Belfast Telegraph*

0 7472 5235 1

HEADLINE FEATURE

The Locust Farm

Jeremy Dronfield

Carole Perceval lives alone on a remote Yorkshire farm, trying to forget a traumatic past. Her life is one of tranquil routine, until one rain-swept night when a dishevelled figure hammers on her door.

Lost and confused, the man has no memory, no idea who he is. His only certainty is that he is being pursued, that he has to flee at all costs. Exhausted, desperate, the farm is his final refuge.

Both of them dream of escape. Of change. Of redemption. And both are about to step into a nightmare.

'A tense page-turner . . . dodging between serial-killer thriller, psychological suspense and full-on action drama' Val McDermid

0 7472 5947 X

HEADLINE FEATURE